# THE BEAST IN THE JUNGLE
AND OTHER TALES

# THE BEAST IN THE JUNGLE AND OTHER TALES

*Henry James*

*Selected and with a preface by*
Frances Wilson

riverrun

This paperback edition first published in Great Britain in 2025 by riverrun

an imprint of Quercus
Part of John Murray Group

1

Preface copyright © 2025 Frances Wilson

Frances Wilson asserts her moral right in the copyright of the preface

All rights reserved. No part of this publication may be reproduced or
transmitted in any form or by any means, electronic or mechanical,
including photocopy, recording, or any information storage and retrieval
system, without permission in writing from the publisher.

This book is a work of fiction. Names, characters, businesses, organizations, places
and events are either the product of the author's imagination or used fictitiously. Any
resemblance to actual persons, living or dead, events or locales is entirely coincidental.

A CIP catalogue record for this book is available from the British Library

Paperback ISBN 978 1 52943 116 2
eBook ISBN 978 1 52943 117 9

Typeset in Fournier MT Std by Manipal Technologies Limited
Printed and bound in Great Britain by Clays Ltd, Elcograf S.p.A.

Papers used by Quercus are from well-managed forests and other responsible sources.

Quercus
Carmelite House
50 Victoria Embankment
London EC4Y 0DZ

John Murray Group
Part of Hodder & Stoughton Limited
An Hachette UK company

The authorized representative in the EEA is Hachette Ireland, 8 Castlecourt
Centre, Dublin 15, D15 XTP3, Ireland (email: info@hbgi.ie)

# Contents

| | |
|---|---:|
| Preface | vii |
| The Figure in the Carpet (1896) | 3 |
| The Real Right Thing (1899) | 57 |
| The Great Good Place (1900) | 77 |
| Maud-Evelyn (1900) | 114 |
| The Two Faces (1900) | 154 |
| The Beldonald Holbein (1901) | 175 |
| The Story in It (1902) | 205 |
| Flickerbridge (1902) | 230 |
| The Beast in the Jungle (1903) | 260 |
| The Papers (1903) | 325 |
| The Jolly Corner (1908) | 463 |
| A Round of Visits (1910) | 513 |
| A Note on the Texts | 555 |

# Preface

THIS SELECTION OF Henry James's late tales, published between 1896 and 1910, opens with 'The Figure in the Carpet', a warning to those readers bent on uncovering the 'general intention' of his fiction, the 'string' his 'pearls are strung on'. The tale's nameless narrator, who is a critic, writes an 'acute little study' of his favourite novelist Hugh Vereker, which its subject – whom he meets at a house party – dismisses as 'the usual twaddle'. No one, Vereker despairs, has understood the 'particular thing I've written my books *for*', despite 'my little point' being 'shouted' with 'every stroke of my pen' into the reader's 'great blank face'. His 'exquisite scheme', Vereker continues, throwing down the gauntlet, is 'the thing for the critic to look for', the critic being a 'little demon of subtlety'.

There is nothing subtle, however, about the wild goose chase that follows, which is where the tale's comedy lies: years are wasted in the critic's attempt to find the 'mouth of the cave', the 'buried treasure', the elusive idea described by Vereker as 'stuck into every volume as your foot is stuck into your shoe'. What, the poor critic wonders, is he even looking for? 'Is it a kind of esoteric knowledge?' (a suggestion dismissed by Vereker as 'cheap journalese'). 'Is it something in the style or something in the thought?' Is it 'some idea about life'? Is it 'a preference for the letter P'? Is it hidden deep down in the text, or sitting solidly on the surface? Vereker's secret is apparently discovered by a friend of the narrator called George Corvick, who dies before revealing it to the world. Corvick has, however, confided it to his wife, Gwendolen (author of a novel called, ironically, *Deep Down*), who also dies before sharing with us what she knows. The women in James's tales are often the sources, and recipients, of a greater understanding.

'Nowadays,' T. S. Eliot wrote in the preface to *A Choice of Kipling's Verse* (1941), 'we all look for the Figure in the Carpet,' which shows that James's satire on critical vulgarity anticipated English Departments of the future. The tale is the precursor to 'The Turn of the Screw' (1898), published two years later and described by James as an 'amusette' to 'catch those not easily caught ... the jaded, the disillusioned, the fastidious'. 'The Turn of the Screw' accordingly caught every critic in its trap: thousands of pages have been filled with the problem of whether the children were innocent or evil, the ghosts real or made-up, the Governess mad or sane. Why did James not come out and tell us what he meant?

'The Figure in the Carpet' might be read as an ironic commentary on Keats's theory of 'negative capability', by which – as the poet explained the idea in a letter to his brothers

## Preface

– the 'Man of Achievement' is 'capable of being in uncertainties, Mysteries, doubts, without any irritable reaching after fact and reason'. Shakespeare was such a man, while Coleridge, like the narrator of 'The Figure in the Carpet', being ill at ease in 'half knowledge', was not. To know and not know a writer's intention, to understand and not understand his work: this was the lesson of the Master. James's ideal reader would have no desire to 'solve' the tales in this following selection, which were dictated rather than written and therefore present a whole new order of challenge. Ideally, there would be no ink spilled on explaining their 'little tricks' and ambiguities, or decoding their loaded sentences. If the early James, as Rebecca West quipped, is James I, and the James of the middle years is James II, next came the Old Pretender with his 'paragraphs two pages long', so a reviewer of *The Ambassadors* (1903) complained, 'and sentences that wander along and side-track, and back up, and switch out a few cars of words, and then pull out again on the main track, and travel in a leisurely way to the end of the division'. The Old Pretender, who embraced difficulty, made reading so effortful that it might be another of Vereker's challenges. Are we approaching him the 'wrong' way? Are we are missing his little points? Have we, in fact, forgotten quite *how* to read? How can we enjoy the textures of the carpet itself, without looking for the complex figure in its weave?

This is the subject of 'The Story in It', one of James's subtlest, and briefest, tales. 'I know you don't read,' Maud Blessingbourne, a consumer of French romances, tells her hostess Mrs Dyott, 'but why should you? *You* live!' Maud and Mrs Dyott are joined by Colonel Voyt who is Mrs Dyott's secret lover. Maud and the Colonel have a flirtatious argument about the lack of respectable women in the novels she enjoys: it must be possible, Maud argues, to make drama out of a virtuous woman. She herself is such a woman, being in love, as Mrs Dyott realizes, with the Colonel and apparently content to leave that love unexpressed and unexplored. Love of this sort – a form of negative capability – is what Mrs Dyott mockingly calls, in conversation with Voyt, 'small, scared and starved', in contrast to a 'romance like their own, a thing to make the fortune of any author up to the mark'. Only 'a duffer', Mrs Dyott concludes of Maud's 'shy romance', 'would see the shadow of a "story" in it'. And only a duffer, like the artist-narrator of 'The Beldonald Holbein', would see the beauty in a plain old woman. To highlight her own loveliness, Lady Beldonald keeps a 'hideous' companion, and when the latest of these, Mrs Brash, is described by the artist-narrator as a 'Holbein', her ladyship bristles. This reinterpretation of Mrs Brash is likened to the unlocking of meaning from a well-known text:

> The curious thing was that, all the while, the reasons of her having passed for plain – the reasons for Lady Beldonald's fond calculation, which they quite justified – were written large in her face, so large that it was easy to understand them as the only ones she herself had ever read. What was it, then, that actually made the old stale sentence mean something so

different? – into what new combinations, what extraordinary language, unknown but understood at a glance, had time and life translated it?

She had quite missed, Lady Beldonald tells the artist, the 'picture' in Mrs Brash.

Were he to be known primarily as a writer of short stories we would see James in a different light. He explored in his novels the fears and desires of his characters, but threw at the tales the full weight of his own preoccupations, private and professional. His early tales look towards Europe, the Land of Promise for his young protagonists and the soil in which his art will grow. The tales of his middle years develop his concerns about the artist in society, and the late tales examine the fear that in looking for the experiences he distilled into literature, he might – like Maud Blessingbourne – have missed out on 'life'. Literature and life are again pitched against one another in 'Flickerbridge', where Frank Granger, the guest at an English manor house, wants to protect its English charm from the literary imagination of his on/off American fiancée Addie, whose mind is 'engrossed, to the exclusion of all else, with the study of the short story'. The house must remain for Frank Granger the 'real thing', and not be enjoyed for the story in it.

In 'The Private Life' (1892), one of the finest tales of his middle period, James had played with the idea of a famous writer protecting his art by splitting himself in two: while the public figure roars away with the dinner guests downstairs, his private self sits upstairs, working silently at his desk. In 'The Papers', the longest tale in this selection, James explores a celebrity culture in which there is no private self to hide. 'The Papers' is a satire on 'cheap journalese', and in particular the recent birth of the 'at home' interview in which the reader is ostensibly brought 'face to face' with the artist.

Maud Blandy, a young journalist with disdain for her work, does an 'at home' with a mediocre playwright desperate for fame. The form of the practice is, as she knows, false intimacy: describing 'with humour his favourite pug', Maud reveals 'with permission his favourite make of Kodak', and 'extorts' from him 'the shy confession' that he prefers 'after all the novel of adventure to the novel of subtlety'. She and her fellow journalist, Howard Blight, discuss the hunger for celebrity. 'People – as I see them,' says Howard,

> would almost rather be jabbered about unpleasantly than not be jabbered about at all: whenever you try them – whenever, at least, I do – I'm confirmed in that conviction. It isn't only that if one holds out the mere tip of the perch they jump at it like starving fish; it is that they leap straight out of the water themselves, leap in their thousands and come flopping, open-mouthed and goggle-eyed, to one's very door.

The most sought-after man in London is currently the self-publicity machine, Sir A. B. C. Beadel-Muffet, K.C.B., M.P. 'It *is* genius, you know, to get yourself so celebrated for nothing – to carry out your idea in the face of everything. I mean your idea of *being* celebrated.' When Howard is asked by Beadel-Muffet to help him disappear from public life, his disappearance becomes the subject of further publicity.

In contrast to the 'jabbering', 'overflowing', 'rattling' and 'gushing' talk of the talent-free figures they interview, the growing intimacy between Howard and Maud is non-verbal. Their 'understanding' is communicated 'by signs, mannerless and meagre, that would have escaped the notice of witnesses. Maud Blandy had no need to kiss her hand across to him to show she felt what he meant.' The deepest communication, for James, is telepathic.

James's tales can be traps and ruses; they can also be complex self-descriptions in which his own contradictions have full reign. At the same time as fearing invisibility (he needed, after all, a readership), he loathed the culture of the interview, with its promise to reveal the 'inner' man. 'It has, for me, nothing to do with *me*, *my* me, at all,' James said in 1905, in the second of the three newspaper interviews he reluctantly agreed to, 'but only with the other person's equivalent of that mystery, whatever it may be.'

As his tales become more and more 'Jamesian', evolving into a genre of their own, they also become more 'modern' and concerned with the 'monstrous' march of modernity. Maud Blandy, a mannish woman who smokes and drinks beer, is 'fairly a product of the day – so fairly that she might have been born afresh each morning, to serve, after the fashion of certain agitated ephemeral insects, only till the morrow. It was as if a past had been wasted on her and a future were not to be fitted.' James's late tales are time machines in which his protagonists live either in the future or the past, the present tense having become an impossibility. George Dane, the overworked writer in 'The Great Good Place', published in *Scribner's Magazine* in the first month of the twentieth century, is transported one morning to a surreal and dreamlike place the 'very essence' of whose 'bliss' is that 'there was nothing now to time'. The inhabitants of the Great Good Place in which he finds himself have 'escaped' from 'the vague movements of the monster – madness, surrender, collapse'. The purpose served by this place, the narrator explains, is to provide 'the scene of [Dane's] new consciousness', which is itself a duplication because Dane's old consciousness has been adopted by a younger acolyte (another of James's motifs) who 'yearns' to be Dane: to 'live with my life, and think with my brain, and write with my hand, and speak with my voice'. 'What will become of *you*?' the acolyte asks Dane, sitting at his desk and opening his mail as the older man prepares for departure. He will become, Dane says, 'Nobody. That was the fun.' When Dane recounts his strange experience to a 'Brother' at the Great Good Place, it is 'as nobody talking with nobody'.

In 'Maud-Evelyn', Marmaduke is taken up as a young man by a middle-aged couple called the Dedricks, who inhabit a fantasy of their dead daughter. 'You see,' Marmaduke explains to

Lavinia, his former lover, 'they couldn't do much, the old people – and they can do still less now – with the future; so they had to do what they could with the past.' Marmaduke, now no longer young, finds that his own past, 'rolling up year after year', has become too interesting to leave behind, and so once the Dedricks are themselves dead, he wanders the rooms of the mausoleum to their daughter on Westbourne Terrace. 'He's driven over there every day,' says Lavinia; 'he remains there for hours. He keeps it for that.' George Withermore in 'The Real Right Thing', appointed biographer to the deceased writer Ashton Doyne, whose private papers he reads at his subject's former desk, comes 'face to face' with the novelist's ghost: 'he could scarcely have told, for the instant, if their meeting occurred in the narrow passage and tight squeeze of the past, or at the hour and in the place that actually held him. Was it '67, or was it but the other side of the table?'

'Face to face' is another Jamesian motif, and again and again in these tales, consciousness is figured as a place: this might be James's 'exquisite scheme'. Fiction, he said, was a 'house' with 'not one window, but a million'. In biography – a genre he distrusted and feared as much as the interview – the shutters and blinds are closed. The mind of Ashton Doyne, George Withermore discovers in 'The Real Right Thing', is an unlit mansion:

He was learning many things that he had not suspected, drawing many curtains, forcing many doors, reading many riddles, going, in general, as they said, behind almost everything. It was at an occasional sharp turn of some of the duskier of these wanderings 'behind' that he really, of a sudden, most felt himself, in the intimate, sensible way, face to face with his friend.

The house on 'The Jolly Corner', itself a place of closed curtains, shut doors, riddles and wanderings, is where Spencer Brydon comes 'face to face' with his alter ego, wearing evening dress, with a monocle on one eye and two digits missing from his hand: 'the bared identity was too hideous as *his*, and his glare was the passion of his protest.' What Brydon discovers, when he returns to his native New York after thirty years in Europe, is that he has a genius for architecture: 'If he had but stayed at home he would have anticipated the inventor of the sky-scraper.' Returning to the house of his birth, he 'stalks', like 'a beast of the forest', the man he might have been had he not left America.

He found himself at moments – once he had placed his single light on some mantel-shelf or in some recess – stepping back into shelter or shade, effacing himself behind a door or in an embrasure, as he had sought of old the vantage of rock and tree; he found himself holding his breath and living in the joy of the instant, the supreme suspense created by big game alone.

The space itself, rather than the ghost who haunts it, is the subject of James's impressionistic prose-poem. Brydon explores what he calls 'the great vague place' from 'attic to cellar', but it is anything but a house: the Jolly Corner is a jungle, a 'great glass bowl', 'the great gaunt shell', 'the bottom of the sea', a 'mystical other world', an unread book.

> He spoke of the value of all he read into it, into the mere sight of the walls, mere shapes of the rooms, mere sound of the floors, mere feel, in his hand, of the old silver-plated knobs of the several mahogany doors, which suggested the pressure of the palms of the dead; the seventy years of the past in fine that these things represented, the annals of nearly three generations, counting his grandfather's, the one that had ended there, and the impalpable ashes of his long-extinct youth, afloat in the very air like microscopic motes.

'The Jolly Corner' anticipates, by fifty years, Gaston Bachelard's phenomenological inquiry into the stairwells of the mind, *The Poetics of Space* (1958). A house, says Bachelard, is where we house our memories and the unconscious finds a home. It is 'a shell'; 'our corner of the world', the 'dream space' in which we encounter 'the I and the non-I'. Spencer Brydon experiences, in his own corner house, 'the waiting life': 'It was what in these weeks he was living for – since he really felt life to begin.' James was fixated by the expenditure involved in waiting ('She waited, Kate Croy,' begins *The Wings of the Dove*), and the 'waiting life' might describe all these tales. While Brydon's life begins when the clocks are turned back, his friend Alice Staverton

– who has loved him since her youth – invests in their joint future, just as Marmaduke waits to join the dead Maud-Evelyn, and the narrator of 'The Figure in the Carpet' waits in vain for the meaning of Vereker's books.

Beasts lurk through these late tales, horror stories of the self where the jungle is everywhere. James's masterpiece of waiting is 'The Beast in the Jungle', where May Bartram waits a lifetime for John Marcher to recognize her love while Marcher, incapable of being in uncertainty, wastes his own life waiting for the thing which he believes 'lay in wait for him, amid the twists and the turns of the months and the years, like a crouching beast'. The beast in the tale 'The Two Faces', meanwhile, is Mrs Grantham, a vicious society hostess whose prey is the wife of her former lover.

'On or about December 1910,' declared Virginia Woolf (referring to the Post-Impressionist exhibition of that date), 'human character changed.' James's final tale, 'A Round of Visits', was published that same year, six years before his death, but the change in human character, a forward march rather than an overnight alteration, had been documented by him in half a century of stories. The Jamesian protagonist evolves from exploring his relations with other people to exploring his relation to himself: hence the recurrence of alter egos, or what James called in 'The Jolly Corner' the 'duplication of consciousness'. 'The Beast in the Jungle' and 'The Jolly Corner' are the same anxious, guilt-ridden story with two faces: John Marcher looks forward, Spencer Brydon looks back, each failing to see the waiting woman, looking him in the eye, holding the answer to everything. 'The Beast in the Jungle' ends with Marcher's collapse, weeping, on May Bartram's tomb. The meaning of his story, the string upon which the pearls are strung, has at last become apparent, but it is too late.

**Frances Wilson**

*The Beast in the Jungle and Other Tales*

# The Figure in the Carpet

## I

I HAD DONE A few things and earned a few pence – I had perhaps even had time to begin to think I was finer than was perceived by the patronizing; but when I take the little measure of my course (a fidgety habit, for it's none of the longest yet) I count my real start from the evening George Corvick, breathless and worried, came in to ask me a service. He had done more things than I, and earned more pence, though there were chances for cleverness I thought he sometimes missed. I could only however that evening declare to him that he never missed one for kindness. There was almost rapture in hearing it proposed to me to prepare for *The Middle*, the organ of our lucubrations, so called from the position in the week of its day of appearance, an article for which he had made himself responsible and of which, tied up with a stout string, he laid on my table the subject. I pounced upon my opportunity – that is on the first volume of it – and paid scant attention to my friend's explanation of his appeal. What explanation could be more to the point than my obvious fitness for the task? I had written on Hugh Vereker, but never a word in *The Middle*, where my dealings were mainly with the ladies and the minor poets. This was his new novel, an advance copy, and whatever much or little it should do for his reputation I was clear on the spot as to what it should do for mine. Moreover if I always read him as soon as I could get hold of him I had a particular reason for wishing to read him now: I had accepted an invitation to Bridges for the following Sunday, and it had been mentioned in Lady Jane's note that Mr Vereker was to be there. I was young enough to have an emotion about meeting a man of his renown and innocent enough to believe the occasion would demand the display of an acquaintance with his 'last'.

Corvick, who had promised a review of it, had not even had time to read it; he had gone to pieces in consequence of news requiring – as on precipitate reflection he judged – that he should catch the night-mail to Paris. He had had a telegram from Gwendolen Erme in answer to his letter offering to fly to her aid. I knew already about Gwendolen Erme; I had never seen her, but I had my ideas, which were mainly to the effect that Corvick would marry her if her mother would only die. That lady seemed now in a fair way to oblige him; after some dreadful mistake about some climate or some waters she had suddenly collapsed on the return from abroad. Her daughter, unsupported and alarmed, desiring to make a rush for home but hesitating at the risk, had accepted our friend's assistance, and it was my secret belief that at the sight of him Mrs Erme would pull round. His own belief was scarcely to be called secret; it discernibly at any rate differed from mine. He had showed me Gwendolen's photograph with the remark that she wasn't pretty but was awfully interesting; she had published at the age of nineteen a novel in three volumes, *Deep Down*, about which, in *The Middle*, he had been really splendid. He appreciated my present eagerness and undertook that the periodical in question should do no less; then at the last, with his hand on the door, he said to me: 'Of course you'll be all right, you know.' Seeing I was a trifle vague he added: 'I mean you won't be silly.'

'Silly — about Vereker! Why, what do I ever find him but awfully clever?'

'Well, what's that but silly? What on earth does "awfully clever" mean? For God's sake try to get *at* him. Don't let him suffer by our arrangement. Speak of him, you know, if you can, as *I* should have spoken of him.'

I wondered an instant. 'You mean as far and away the biggest of the lot — that sort of thing?'

Corvick almost groaned. 'Oh, you know, I don't put them back to back that way; it's the infancy of art! But he gives me a pleasure so rare; the sense of —' he mused a little — 'something or other.'

I wondered again. 'The sense, pray, of what?'

'My dear man, that's just what I want *you* to say!'

Even before Corvick had banged the door I had begun, book in hand, to prepare myself to say it. I sat up with Vereker half the night; Corvick couldn't have done more than that. He was awfully clever – I stuck to that, but he wasn't a bit the biggest of the lot. I didn't allude to the lot, however; I flattered myself that I emerged on this occasion from the infancy of art. 'It's all right,' they declared vividly at the office; and when the number appeared I felt there was a basis on which I could meet the great man. It gave me confidence for a day or two, and then that confidence dropped. I had fancied him reading it with relish, but if Corvick was not satisfied how could Vereker himself be? I reflected indeed that the heat of the admirer was sometimes grosser even than the appetite of the scribe. Corvick at all events wrote me from Paris a little ill-humouredly. Mrs Erme was pulling round, and I hadn't at all said what Vereker gave him the sense of.

## II

THE EFFECT OF my visit to Bridges was to turn me out for more profundity. Hugh Vereker, as I saw him there, was of a contact so void of angles that I blushed for the poverty of imagination involved in my small precautions. If he was in spirits it was not because he had read my review; in fact on the Sunday morning I felt sure he hadn't read it, though *The Middle* had been out three days and bloomed, I assured myself, in the stiff garden of periodicals which gave one of the ormolu tables the air of a stand at a station. The impression he made on me personally was such that I wished him to read it, and I corrected to this end with a surreptitious hand what might be wanting in the careless conspicuity of the sheet. I am afraid I even watched the result of my manoeuvre, but up to luncheon I watched in vain.

When afterwards, in the course of our gregarious walk, I found myself for half an hour, not perhaps without another manoeuvre, at the great man's side, the result of his affability was a still livelier desire that he should not remain in ignorance of the peculiar justice I had done him. It was not that he seemed to thirst for justice; on the contrary I had not yet caught in his talk the faintest grunt of a grudge – a note for which my young experience had already given me an ear. Of late he had had more recognition, and it was pleasant, as we used to say in *The Middle*, to see that it drew him out. He wasn't of course popular, but I judged one of the sources of his good-humour to be precisely that his success was independent of that. He had none the less become in a manner the fashion; the critics at least had put on a spurt and caught up with him. We had found out at last how clever he was, and he had had to make the best of the loss of his mystery. I was strongly tempted, as I walked beside him, to let him know how much of that unveiling was my act; and there was a moment when I probably should have done so had not one of the ladies of our party, snatching a place at his other elbow, just then appealed to him in a spirit comparatively selfish. It was very discouraging: I almost felt the liberty had been taken with myself.

I had had on my tongue's end, for my own part, a phrase or two about the right word at the right time; but later on I was glad not to have spoken, for when on our return we clustered at tea I perceived Lady Jane, who had not been out with us, brandishing *The Middle* with her longest arm. She had taken it up at her leisure; she was delighted with what she had found, and I saw that, as a mistake in a man may often be a felicity in a woman, she would practically do for me what I hadn't been able to do for myself. 'Some sweet little truths that needed to be spoken,' I heard her declare, thrusting the paper at rather a bewildered couple by the fireplace. She grabbed it away from them again on the reappearance of Hugh Vereker, who after our walk had been upstairs to change something. 'I know you don't in general look at this kind of thing, but it's an occasion really for doing so. You *haven't* seen it? Then you must. The man has actually got *at* you, at what *I* always feel, you know.' Lady Jane threw into her eyes a look evidently intended to give an idea of what she always felt; but she added that she couldn't have expressed it. The man in the paper expressed it in a striking manner. 'Just see there, and there, where I've dashed it, how he brings it out.' She had literally marked for him the brightest patches of my prose, and if I was a little amused Vereker himself may well have been. He showed how much he was when before us all Lady Jane wanted to read something aloud. I liked at any rate the way he defeated her purpose by jerking the paper affectionately out of her clutch. He would take it upstairs with him, would look at it on going to dress. He did this half an hour later – I saw it in his hand when he repaired to his room. That was the moment at which, thinking to give her pleasure, I mentioned to Lady Jane that I was the author of the review. I did give her pleasure, I judged, but perhaps not quite so much as I had expected. If the author was 'only me' the thing didn't seem quite so remarkable. Hadn't I had the effect rather of diminishing the lustre of the article than of adding to my own? Her ladyship was subject to the most extraordinary drops. It didn't matter; the only effect I cared about was the one it would have on Vereker up there by his bedroom fire.

At dinner I watched for the signs of this impression, tried to fancy there was some happier light in his eyes; but to my disappointment Lady Jane gave me no chance to make sure. I had hoped she would call triumphantly down the table, publicly demand if she hadn't been right. The party was large – there were people from outside as well, but I had never seen a table long enough to deprive Lady Jane of a triumph. I was just reflecting in truth that this interminable board would deprive *me* of one when the guest next me, dear woman – she was Miss Poyle, the vicar's sister, a robust, unmodulated person – had the happy inspiration and the unusual courage to address herself across it to Vereker, who was opposite, but not directly, so that when he replied they were both leaning forward. She inquired, artless body, what he thought of Lady Jane's 'panegyric', which she had read – not connecting it however with her right-hand neighbour; and while I strained my ear for his reply I heard him, to my stupefaction, call back gaily, with his mouth full of bread: 'Oh, it's all right – it's the usual twaddle!'

I had caught Vereker's glance as he spoke, but Miss Poyle's surprise was a fortunate cover for my own. 'You mean he doesn't do you justice?' said the excellent woman.

Vereker laughed out, and I was happy to be able to do the same. 'It's a charming article,' he tossed us.

Miss Poyle thrust her chin half across the cloth. 'Oh you're so deep!' she drove home.

'As deep as the ocean! All I pretend is, the author doesn't see—'

A dish was at this point passed over his shoulder, and we had to wait while he helped himself.

'Doesn't see what?' my neighbour continued.

'Doesn't see anything.'

'Dear me – how very stupid!'

'Not a bit,' Vereker laughed again. 'Nobody does.'

The lady on his further side appealed to him, and Miss Poyle sank back to me. 'Nobody sees anything!' she cheerfully announced; to which I replied that I had often thought so too, but had somehow taken the thought for a proof on my own part of a tremendous eye. I didn't tell her the article was mine; and I observed that Lady Jane, occupied at the end of the table, had not caught Vereker's words.

I rather avoided him after dinner, for I confess he struck me as cruelly conceited, and the revelation was a pain. 'The usual twaddle' – my acute little study! That one's admiration should have had a reserve or two could gall him to that point? I had thought him placid, and he was placid enough; such a surface was the hard, polished glass that encased the bauble of his vanity. I was really ruffled, and the only comfort was that if nobody saw anything George Corvick was quite as much out of it as I. This comfort however was not sufficient, after the ladies had dispersed, to carry me in the proper manner – I mean in a spotted jacket and humming an air – into the smoking-room. I took my way in some dejection to bed; but in the passage I encountered Mr Vereker, who had been up once more to change, coming out of his room. *He* was humming an air and had on a spotted jacket, and as soon as he saw me his gaiety gave a start.

'My dear young man,' he exclaimed, 'I'm so glad to lay hands on you! I'm afraid I most unwittingly wounded you by those words of mine at dinner to Miss Poyle. I learned but half an hour ago from Lady Jane that you wrote the little notice in *The Middle*.'

I protested that no bones were broken; but he moved with me to my own door, his hand on my shoulder, kindly feeling for a fracture; and on hearing that I had come up to bed he asked leave to cross my threshold and just tell me in three words what his qualification of my remarks had represented. It was plain he really feared I was hurt, and the sense of his solicitude suddenly made all the difference to me. My cheap review fluttered off into space, and the best things I had said in it became flat enough beside the brilliancy of his being there. I can see him there still, on my rug, in the firelight and his spotted jacket, his fine, clear face all bright with the desire to be tender to my youth. I don't know what he had at first meant to say, but I think the sight of my relief touched him, excited him, brought up words to his lips from far within. It was so these words presently conveyed to me something that, as I afterwards knew, he had never uttered to anyone. I have always done justice to the generous impulse that made him speak; it was simply compunction for a snub unconsciously administered to a man of letters in a position inferior to his own, a man of letters moreover in the very act of praising him. To make the thing right he talked to me exactly as an equal and on the ground of what we both loved best. The hour, the place, the unexpectedness deepened the impression: he couldn't have done anything more exquisitely successful.

## III

'I DON'T QUITE know how to explain it to you,' he said, 'but it was the very fact that your notice of my book had a spice of intelligence, it was just your exceptional sharpness that produced the feeling – a very old story with me, I beg you to believe – under the momentary influence of which I used in speaking to that good lady the words you so naturally resent. I don't read the things in the newspapers unless they're thrust upon me as that one was – it's always one's best friend that does it! But I used to read them sometimes – ten years ago. I daresay they were in general rather stupider then; at any rate it always seemed to me that they missed my little point with a perfection exactly as admirable when they patted me on the back as when they kicked me in the shins. Whenever since I've happened to have a glimpse of them they were still blazing away – still missing it, I mean, deliciously. *You* miss it, my dear fellow, with inimitable assurance; the fact of your being awfully clever and your article's being awfully nice doesn't make a hair's breadth of difference. It's quite with you rising young men,' Vereker laughed, 'that I feel most what a failure I am!'

I listened with intense interest; it grew intenser as he talked. '*You* a failure – heavens! What then may your "little point" happen to be?'

'Have I got to *tell* you, after all these years and labours?' There was something in the friendly reproach of this – jocosely exaggerated – that made me, as an ardent young seeker for truth, blush to the roots of my hair. I'm as much in the dark as ever, though I've grown used in a sense to my obtuseness; at that moment, however, Vereker's happy accent made me appear to myself, and probably to him, a rare donkey. I was on the point of exclaiming 'Ah, yes, don't tell me: for my honour, for that of the craft, don't!' when he went on in a manner that showed he had read my thought and had his own idea of the probability of our some day redeeming ourselves. 'By my little point I mean – what shall I call it? – the particular thing I've written my books most *for*. Isn't there for every writer a particular thing of that sort, the thing that most makes him apply himself, the thing without the effort to achieve which he wouldn't write at all, the very passion of his passion, the part of the business in which, for him, the flame of art burns most intensely? Well, it's *that*!'

I considered a moment. I was fascinated – easily, you'll say; but I wasn't going after all to be put off my guard. 'Your description's certainly beautiful, but it doesn't make what you describe very distinct.'

'I promise you it would be distinct if it should dawn on you at all.' I saw that the charm of our topic overflowed for my companion into an emotion as lively as my own. 'At any rate,' he went on, 'I can speak for myself: there's an idea in my work without which I wouldn't have given a straw for the whole job. It's the finest, fullest intention of the lot, and the application of it has been, I think, a triumph of patience, of ingenuity. I ought to leave that to somebody else to say; but that nobody does say it is precisely what we're talking about. It stretches, this little trick of mine, from book to book, and everything else, comparatively, plays over the surface of it. The order, the form, the texture of my books will perhaps some day constitute for the initiated a complete representation of it. So it's naturally the thing for the critic to look for. It strikes me,' my visitor added, smiling, 'even as the thing for the critic to find.'

This seemed a responsibility indeed. 'You call it a little trick?'

'That's only my little modesty. It's really an exquisite scheme.'

'And you hold that you've carried the scheme out?'

'The way I've carried it out is the thing in life I think a bit well of myself for.'

I was silent a moment. 'Don't you think you ought – just a trifle – to assist the critic?'

'Assist him? What else have I done with every stroke of my pen? I've shouted my intention in his great blank face!' At this, laughing out again, Vereker laid his hand on my shoulder to show that the allusion was not to my personal appearance.

'But you talk about the initiated. There must therefore, you see, be initiation.'

'What else in heaven's name is criticism supposed to be?' I'm afraid I coloured at this too; but I took refuge in repeating that his account of his silver lining was poor in something or other that a plain man knows things by. 'That's only because you've never had a glimpse of it,' he replied. 'If you had had one, the element in question would soon have become practically all you'd see. To me it's exactly as palpable as the marble of this chimney. Besides, the critic just *isn't* a plain man: if he were, pray, what would he be doing in his neighbour's garden? You're anything but a plain man yourself, and the very *raison d'être* of you all is that you're little demons of subtlety. If my great affair's a secret, that's only because it's a secret in spite of itself – the amazing event has made it one. I not only never took the smallest precaution to do so, but never dreamed of any such accident. If I had I shouldn't in advance have had the heart to go on. As it was I only became aware little by little, and meanwhile I had done my work.'

'And now you quite like it?' I risked.

'My work?'

'Your secret. It's the same thing.'

'Your guessing that,' Vereker replied, 'is a proof that you're as clever as I say!' I was encouraged by this to remark that he would clearly be pained to part with it, and he confessed that it was indeed with him now the great amusement of life. 'I live almost to see if it will ever be detected.' He looked at me for a jesting challenge; something at the back of his eyes seemed to peep out. 'But I needn't worry – it won't!'

'You fire me as I've never been fired,' I returned; 'you make me determined to do or die.' Then I asked: 'Is it a kind of esoteric message?'

His countenance fell at this – he put out his hand as if to bid me good-night. 'Ah, my dear fellow, it can't be described in cheap journalese!'

I knew of course he would be awfully fastidious, but our talk had made me feel how much his nerves were exposed. I was unsatisfied – I kept hold of his hand. 'I won't make use of the expression then,' I said, 'in the article in which I shall eventually announce my discovery, though I daresay I shall have hard work to do without it. But meanwhile, just to hasten that difficult birth, can't you give a fellow a clue?' I felt much more at my ease.

'My whole lucid effort gives him the clue – every page and line and letter. The thing's as concrete there as a bird in a cage, a bait on a hook, a piece of cheese in a mouse-trap. It's stuck into every volume as your foot is stuck into your shoe. It governs every line, it chooses every word, it dots every *i*, it places every comma.'

I scratched my head. 'Is it something in the style or something in the thought? An element of form or an element of feeling?'

He indulgently shook my hand again, and I felt my questions to be crude and my distinctions pitiful. 'Good-night, my dear boy – don't bother about it. After all, you do like a fellow.'

'And a little intelligence might spoil it?' I still detained him.

He hesitated. 'Well, you've got a heart in your body. Is that an element of form or an element of feeling? What I contend that nobody has ever mentioned in my work is the organ of life.'

'I see – it's some idea about life, some sort of philosophy. Unless it be,' I added with the eagerness of a thought perhaps still happier, 'some kind of game you're up to with your style, something you're after in the language. Perhaps it's a preference for the letter P!' I ventured profanely to break out. 'Papa, potatoes, prunes – that sort of thing?' He was suitably indulgent: he only said I hadn't got the right letter. But his amusement was over; I could see he was bored. There was nevertheless something else I had absolutely to learn. 'Should you be able, pen in hand, to state it clearly yourself – to name it, phrase it, formulate it?'

'Oh,' he almost passionately sighed, 'if I were only, pen in hand, one of *you* chaps!'

'That would be a great chance for you of course. But why

should you despise us chaps for not doing what you can't do yourself?'

'Can't do?' He opened his eyes. 'Haven't I done it in twenty volumes? I do it in my way,' he continued. 'You don't do it in yours.'

'Ours is so devilish difficult,' I weakly observed.

'So is mine. We each choose our own. There's no compulsion. You won't come down and smoke?'

'No. I want to think this thing out.'

'You'll tell me then in the morning that you've laid me bare?'

'I'll see what I can do; I'll sleep on it. But just one word more,' I added. We had left the room — I walked again with him a few steps along the passage. 'This extraordinary "general intention", as you call it — for that's the most vivid description I can induce you to make of it — is then generally a sort of buried treasure?'

His face lighted. 'Yes, call it that, though it's perhaps not for me to do so.'

'Nonsense!' I laughed. 'You know you're hugely proud of it.'

'Well, I didn't propose to tell you so; but it *is* the joy of my soul!'

'You mean it's a beauty so rare, so great?'

He hesitated a moment. 'The loveliest thing in the world!' We had stopped, and on these words he left me; but at the end of the corridor, while I looked after him rather yearningly, he turned and caught sight of my puzzled face. It made him earnestly, indeed I thought quite anxiously, shake his head and wave his finger. 'Give it up — give it up!'

This wasn't a challenge – it was fatherly advice. If I had had one of his books at hand I would have repeated my recent act of faith – I would have spent half the night with him. At three o'clock in the morning, not sleeping, remembering moreover how indispensable he was to Lady Jane, I stole down to the library with a candle. There wasn't, so far as I could discover, a line of his writing in the house.

# IV

RETURNING TO town I feverishly collected them all; I picked out each in its order and held it up to the light. This gave me a maddening month, in the course of which several things took place. One of these, the last, I may as well immediately mention, was that I acted on Vereker's advice: I renounced my ridiculous attempt. I could really make nothing of the business; it proved a dead loss. After all, before, as he had himself observed, I liked him; and what now occurred was simply that my new intelligence and vain preoccupation damaged my liking. I not only failed to find his general intention – I found myself missing the subordinate intentions I had formerly found. His books didn't even remain the charming things they had been for me; the exasperation of my search put me out of conceit of them. Instead of being a pleasure the more, they became a resource the less; for from the moment I was unable to follow up the author's hint

I of course felt it a point of honour not to make use professionally of my knowledge of them. I *had* no knowledge – nobody had any. It was humiliating, but I could bear it – they only annoyed me now. At last they even bored me, and I accounted for my confusion – perversely, I confess – by the idea that Vereker had made a fool of me. The buried treasure was a bad joke, the general intention a monstrous *pose*.

The great incident of the time however was that I told George Corvick all about the matter and that my information had an immense effect upon him. He had at last come back, but so, unfortunately, had Mrs Erme, and there was as yet, I could see, no question of his nuptials. He was immensely stirred up by the anecdote I had brought from Bridges; it fell in so completely with the sense he had had from the first that there was more in Vereker than met the eye. When I remarked that the eye seemed what the printed page had been expressly invented to meet he immediately accused me of being spiteful because I had been foiled. Our commerce had always that pleasant latitude. The thing Vereker had mentioned to me was exactly the thing he, Corvick, had wanted me to speak of in my review. On my suggesting at last that with the assistance I had now given him he would doubtless be prepared to speak of it himself he admitted freely that before doing this there was more he must understand. What he would have said, had he reviewed the new book, was that there was evidently in the writer's inmost art something to *be* understood. I hadn't so much as hinted at that: no wonder the writer hadn't been flattered! I asked Corvick what he really considered he meant by his own supersubtlety, and, unmistakably kindled, he replied: 'It isn't for the vulgar – it isn't for the vulgar!' He had hold of the tail of something; he would pull hard, pull it right out. He pumped me dry on Vereker's strange confidence and, pronouncing me the luckiest of mortals, mentioned half a dozen questions he wished to goodness I had had the gumption to put. Yet on the other hand he didn't want to be told too much – it would spoil the fun of seeing what would come. The failure of my fun was at the moment of our meeting not complete, but I saw it ahead, and Corvick saw that I saw it. I, on my side, saw likewise that one of the first things he would do would be to rush off with my story to Gwendolen.

On the very day after my talk with him I was surprised by the receipt of a note from Hugh Vereker, to whom our encounter at Bridges had been recalled, as he mentioned, by his falling, in a magazine, on some article to which my signature was appended. 'I read it with great pleasure,' he wrote, 'and remembered under its influence our lively conversation by your bedroom fire. The consequence of this has been that I begin to measure the temerity of my having saddled you with a knowledge that you may find something of a burden. Now that the fit's over I can't imagine how I came to be moved so much beyond my wont. I had never before related, no matter in what expansion, the history of my little secret, and I shall never speak of the business again. I was accidentally so much more explicit with you than it had ever entered into my game to be, that I find this game – I mean the pleasure of playing it – suffers considerably. In short, if you can understand it, I've spoiled a part of my fun. I really don't want to give anybody what I believe you clever young men call the tip. That's of course a selfish solicitude, and I name it to you for what it may be worth to you. If you're disposed to humour me don't repeat my revelation. Think me demented – it's your right; but don't tell anybody why.'

The sequel to this communication was that as early on the morrow as I dared I drove straight to Mr Vereker's door. He occupied in those years one of the honest old houses in Kensington Square. He received me immediately, and as soon as I came in I saw I had not lost my power to minister to his mirth. He laughed out at the sight of my face, which doubtless expressed my perturbation. I had been indiscreet – my compunction was great. 'I *have* told somebody,' I panted, 'and I'm sure that person will by this time have told somebody else! It's a woman, into the bargain.'

'The person you've told?'

'No, the other person. I'm quite sure he must have told her.'

'For all the good it will do her – or do *me*! A woman will never find out.'

'No, but she'll talk all over the place: she'll do just what you don't want.'

Vereker thought a moment, but he was not so disconcerted as I had feared: he felt that if the harm was done it only served him right. 'It doesn't matter – don't worry.'

'I'll do my best, I promise you, that your talk with me shall go no further.'

'Very good; do what you can.'

'In the meantime,' I pursued, 'George Corvick's possession of the tip may, on his part, really lead to something.'

'That will be a brave day.'

I told him about Corvick's cleverness, his admiration, the intensity of his interest in my anecdote; and without making too much of the divergence of our respective estimates mentioned that my friend was already of opinion that he saw much further into a certain affair than most people. He was quite as fired as I had been at Bridges. He was moreover in love with the young lady: perhaps the two together would puzzle something out.

Vereker seemed struck with this. 'Do you mean they're to be married?'

'I daresay that's what it will come to.'

'That may help them,' he conceded, 'but we must give them time!'

I spoke of my own renewed assault and confessed my difficulties; whereupon he repeated his former advice: 'Give it up, give it up!' He evidently didn't think me intellectually equipped for the adventure. I stayed half an hour, and he was most good-natured, but I couldn't help pronouncing him a man of shifting moods. He had been free with me in a mood, he had repented in a mood, and now in a mood he had turned indifferent. This general levity helped me to believe that, so far as the subject of the tip went, there wasn't much in it. I contrived however to make him answer a few more questions about it, though he did so with visible impatience. For himself, beyond doubt, the thing we were all so blank about was vividly there. It was something, I guessed, in the primal plan, something like a complex figure in a Persian carpet. He highly approved of this image when I used it, and he used another himself. 'It's the very string,' he said, 'that my pearls are strung on!' The reason of his note to me had been that he really didn't want to give us a grain of succour – our density was a thing too perfect in its way to touch. He had formed the habit of depending upon it, and if the spell was to break it must break by some force of its own. He comes back to me from that last occasion – for I was never to speak to him again – as a man with some safe secret for enjoyment. I wondered as I walked away where he had got *his* tip.

# V

WHEN I SPOKE to George Corvick of the caution I had received he made me feel that any doubt of his delicacy would be almost an insult. He had instantly told Gwendolen, but Gwendolen's ardent response was in itself a pledge of discretion. The question would now absorb them, and they would enjoy their fun too much to wish to share it with the crowd. They appeared to have caught instinctively Vereker's peculiar notion of fun. Their intellectual pride, however, was not such as to make them indifferent to any further light I might throw on the affair they had in hand. They were indeed of the 'artistic temperament', and I was freshly struck with my colleague's power to excite himself over a question of art. He called it letters, he called it life – it was all one thing. In what he said I now seemed to understand that he spoke equally for Gwendolen, to whom, as soon as Mrs Erme was sufficiently better to allow her a little leisure, he made a point of introducing me. I remember our calling together one Sunday in August at a huddled house in Chelsea, and my renewed envy of Corvick's possession of a friend who had some light to mingle with his own. He could say things to her that I could never say to him. She had indeed no sense of humour and, with her pretty way of holding her head on one side, was one of those persons whom you want, as the phrase is, to shake, but who have learned Hungarian by themselves. She conversed perhaps in Hungarian with Corvick; she had remarkably little English for his friend. Corvick afterwards told me that I had chilled her by my apparent indisposition to oblige her with the detail of what Vereker had said to me. I admitted that I felt I had given thought enough to this exposure: hadn't I even made up my mind that it was hollow, wouldn't stand the test? The importance they attached to it was irritating – it rather envenomed my dissent.

That statement looks unamiable, and what probably happened was that I felt humiliated at seeing other persons derive a daily joy from an experiment which had brought me only chagrin. I was out in the cold while, by the evening fire, under the lamp, they followed the chase for which I myself had sounded the horn. They did as I had done, only more deliberately and sociably – they went over their author from the beginning. There was no hurry, Corvick said – the future was before them and the fascination could only grow; they would take him page by page, as they would take one of the classics, inhale him in slow draughts and let him sink deep in. I doubt whether they would have got so wound up if they had not been in love: poor Vereker's secret gave them endless occasion to put their young heads together. None the less it represented the kind of problem for which Corvick had a special aptitude, drew out the particular pointed patience of which, had he lived, he would have given more striking and, it is to be hoped, more fruitful examples. He at least was, in Vereker's words, a little demon of subtlety. We had begun by disputing, but I soon saw that without my stirring a finger his infatuation would have its bad hours. He would bound off on false scents as I had done – he would clap his hands over new lights and see them blown out by the wind of the turned page. He was like nothing, I told him, but the maniacs who embrace some bedlamitical theory of the cryptic character of Shakespeare. To this he replied that if we had had Shakespeare's own word for his being cryptic he would immediately have accepted it. The case there was altogether different – we had nothing but the word of Mr Snooks. I rejoined that I was stupefied to see him attach such importance even to the word of Mr Vereker. He inquired thereupon whether I treated Mr Vereker's word as a lie. I wasn't perhaps prepared, in my unhappy rebound, to go as far as that, but I insisted that till the contrary was proved I should view it as too fond an imagination. I didn't, I confess, say – I didn't at that time quite know – all I felt. Deep down, as Miss Erme would have said, I was uneasy, I was expectant. At the core of my personal confusion – for my curiosity lived in its ashes – was the sharpness of a sense that Corvick would at last probably come out somewhere. He made, in defence of his credulity, a great point of the fact that from of old, in his study of this genius, he had caught whiffs and hints of he didn't know what, faint wandering notes of a hidden music. That was just the rarity, that was the charm: it fitted so perfectly into what I reported.

If I returned on several occasions to the little house in Chelsea I daresay it was as much for news of Vereker as for news of Miss Erme's mamma. The hours spent there by Corvick were present to my fancy as those of a chessplayer bent with a silent scowl, all the lamp-lit winter, over his board and his moves. As my imagination filled it out the picture held me fast. On the other side of the table was a ghostlier form, the faint figure of an antagonist good-humouredly but a little wearily secure – an antagonist who leaned back in his chair with his hands in his pockets and a smile on his fine clear face. Close to Corvick, behind him, was a girl who had begun to strike me as pale and wasted and even, on more familiar view, as rather handsome, and who rested on his shoulder and hung upon his moves. He would take up a chessman and hold it poised a while over one of the little squares, and then he would put it back in its place with a long sigh of disappointment. The young lady, at this, would slightly but uneasily shift her position and look across, very hard, very long, very strangely, at their dim participant. I had asked them at an early stage of the business if it mightn't contribute to their success to have some closer communication with him. The special circumstances would surely be held to have given me a right to introduce them. Corvick immediately replied that he had no wish to approach the altar before he had prepared the sacrifice. He quite agreed with our friend both as to the sport and as to the honour – he would bring down the animal with his own rifle. When I asked him if Miss Erme were as keen a shot he said after a hesitation: 'No; I'm ashamed to say she wants to set a trap. She'd give anything to see him; she says she requires another tip. She's really quite morbid about it. But she must play fair – she *shan't* see him!' he emphatically added. I had a suspicion that they had even quarrelled a little on the subject – a suspicion not corrected by the way he more than once exclaimed to me: 'She's quite incredibly literary, you know – quite fantastically!' I remember his saying of her that she felt in italics and thought in capitals. 'Oh, when I've run him to earth,' he also said, 'then, you know, I shall knock at his door. Rather – I beg you to believe. I'll have it from his own lips: "Right you are, my boy; you've done it this time!" He shall crown me victor – with the critical laurel.'

Meanwhile he really avoided the chances London life might have given him of meeting the distinguished novelist; a danger however that disappeared with Vereker's leaving England for an indefinite absence, as the newspapers announced – going to the south for motives connected with the health of his wife, which had long kept her in retirement. A year – more than a year – had elapsed since the incident at Bridges, but I had not encountered him again. I think at bottom I was rather ashamed – I hated to remind him that though I had irremediably missed his point a reputation for acuteness was rapidly overtaking me. This scruple led me a dance; kept me out of Lady Jane's house, made me even decline, when in spite of my bad manners she was a second time so good as to make me a sign, an invitation to her beautiful seat. I once saw her with Vereker at a concert and was sure I was seen by them, but I slipped out without being caught. I felt, as on that occasion I splashed along in the rain, that I couldn't have done anything else; and yet I remember saying to myself that it was hard, was even cruel. Not only had I lost the books, but I had lost the man himself: they and their author had been alike spoiled for me. I knew too which was the loss I most regretted. I had liked the man still better than I had liked the books.

# VI

SIX MONTHS after Vereker had left England George Corvick, who made his living by his pen, contracted for a piece of work which imposed on him an absence of some length and a journey of some difficulty, and his undertaking of which was much of a surprise to me. His brother-in-law had become editor of a great provincial paper, and the great provincial paper, in a fine flight of fancy, had conceived the idea of sending a 'special commissioner' to India. Special commissioners had begun, in the 'metropolitan press', to be the fashion, and the journal in question felt that it had passed too long for a mere country cousin. Corvick had no hand, I knew, for the big brush of the correspondent, but that was his brother-in-law's affair, and the fact that a particular task was not in his line was apt to be with himself exactly a reason for accepting it. He was prepared to out-Herod the metropolitan press; he took solemn precautions against priggishness, he exquisitely outraged taste. Nobody ever knew it – the taste was all his own. In addition to his expenses he was to be conveniently paid, and I found myself able to help him, for the usual fat book, to a plausible arrangement with the usual fat publisher. I naturally inferred that his obvious desire to make a little money was not unconnected with the prospect of a union with Gwendolen Erme. I was aware that her mother's opposition was largely addressed to his want of means and of lucrative abilities, but it so happened that, on my saying the last time I saw him something that bore on the question of his separation from our young lady, he exclaimed with an emphasis that startled me: 'Ah, I'm not a bit engaged to her, you know!'

'Not overtly,' I answered, 'because her mother doesn't like you. But I've always taken for granted a private understanding.'

'Well, there *was* one. But there isn't now.' That was all he said, except something about Mrs Erme's having got on her feet again in the most extraordinary way – a remark from which I gathered he wished me to think he meant that private understandings were of little use when the doctor didn't share them. What I took the liberty of really thinking was that the girl might in some way have estranged him. Well, if he had taken the turn of jealousy for instance it could scarcely be jealousy of me. In that case (besides the absurdity of it) he wouldn't have gone away to leave us together. For some time before his departure we had indulged in no allusion to the buried treasure, and from his silence, of which mine was the consequence, I had drawn a sharp conclusion. His courage had dropped, his ardour had gone the way of mine – this inference at least he left me to enjoy. More than that he couldn't do; he couldn't face the triumph with which I might have greeted an explicit admission. He needn't have been afraid, poor dear, for I had by this time lost all need to triumph. In fact I considered that I showed magnanimity in not reproaching him with his collapse, for the sense of his having thrown up the game made me feel more than ever how much I at last depended on him. If Corvick had broken down I should never know; no one would be of any use if *he* wasn't. It wasn't a bit true that I had ceased to care for knowledge; little by little my curiosity had not only begun to ache again, but had become the familiar torment of my consciousness. There are doubtless people to whom torments of such an order appear hardly more natural than the contortions of disease; but I don't know after all why I should in this connection so much as mention them. For the few persons, at any rate, abnormal or not, with whom my anecdote is concerned, literature was a game of skill, and skill meant courage, and courage meant honour, and honour meant passion, meant life. The stake on the table was of a different substance, and our roulette was the revolving mind, but we sat round the green board as intently as the grim gamblers at Monte Carlo. Gwendolen Erme, for that matter, with her white face and her fixed eyes, was of the very type of the lean ladies one had met in the temples of chance. I recognized in Corvick's absence that she made this analogy vivid. It was extravagant, I admit, the way she lived for the art of the pen. Her passion visibly preyed upon her, and in her presence I felt almost tepid. I got hold of *Deep Down* again: it was a desert in which she had lost herself, but in which too she had dug a wonderful hole in the sand – a cavity out of which Corvick had still more remarkably pulled her.

Early in March I had a telegram from her, in consequence of which I repaired immediately to Chelsea, where the first thing she said to me was: 'He has got it, he has got it!'

She was moved, as I could see, to such depths that she must mean the great thing. 'Vereker's idea?'

'His general intention. George has cabled from Bombay.'

She had the missive open there; it was emphatic, but it was brief. 'Eureka. Immense.' That was all – he had saved the money of the signature. I shared her emotion, but I was disappointed. 'He doesn't say what it is.'

'How could he – in a telegram? He'll write it.'

'But how does he know?'

'Know it's the real thing? Oh, I'm sure when you see it you do know. *Vera incessu patuit dea!*'

'It's you, Miss Erme, who are a dear for bringing me such

news!' – I went all lengths in my high spirits. 'But fancy finding our goddess in the temple of Vishnu! How strange of George to have been able to go into the thing again in the midst of such different and such powerful solicitations!'

'He hasn't gone into it, I know; it's the thing itself, let severely alone for six months, that has simply sprung out at him like a tigress out of the jungle. He didn't take a book with him – on purpose; indeed he wouldn't have needed to – he knows every page, as I do, by heart. They all worked in him together, and some day somewhere, when he wasn't thinking, they fell, in all their superb intricacy, into the one right combination. The figure in the carpet came out. That's the way he knew it would come and the real reason – you didn't in the least understand, but I suppose I may tell you now – why he went and why I consented to his going. We knew the change would do it, the difference of thought, of scene, would give the needed touch, the magic shake. We had perfectly, we had admirably calculated. The elements were all in his mind, and in the *secousse* of a new and intense experience they just struck light.' She positively struck light herself – she was literally, facially luminous. I stammered something about unconscious cerebration, and she continued: 'He'll come right home – this will bring him.'

'To see Vereker, you mean?'

'To see Vereker – and to see *me*. Think what he'll have to tell me!'

I hesitated. 'About India?'

'About fiddlesticks! About Vereker – about the figure in the carpet.'

'But, as you say, we shall surely have that in a letter.'

She thought like one inspired, and I remembered how Corvick had told me long before that her face was interesting. 'Perhaps it won't go in a letter if it's "immense".'

'Perhaps not if it's immense bosh. If he has got something that won't go in a letter he hasn't got *the* thing. Vereker's own statement to me was exactly that the "figure" *would* go in a letter.'

'Well, I cabled to George an hour ago – two words,' said Gwendolen.

'Is it indiscreet of me to inquire what they were?'

She hung fire, but at last she brought them out. '"Angel, write."'

'Good!' I exclaimed. 'I'll make it sure – I'll send him the same.'

# VII

MY WORDS however were not absolutely the same – I put something instead of 'angel'; and in the sequel my epithet seemed the more apt, for when eventually we heard from Corvick it was merely, it was thoroughly to be tantalized. He was magnificent in his triumph, he described his discovery as stupendous; but his ecstasy only obscured it – there were to be no particulars till he should have submitted his conception to the supreme authority. He had thrown up his commission, he had thrown up his book, he had thrown up everything but the instant need to hurry to Rapallo, on the Genoese shore, where Vereker was making a stay. I wrote him a letter which was to await him at Aden – I besought him to relieve my suspense. That he found my letter was indicated by a telegram which, reaching me after weary days and without my having received an answer to my laconic dispatch at Bombay, was evidently intended as a reply to both communications. Those few words were in familiar French, the French of the day, which Corvick often made use of to show he wasn't a prig. It had for some persons the opposite effect, but his message may fairly be paraphrased. 'Have patience; I want to see, as it breaks on you, the face you'll make!' '*Tellement envie de voir ta tête!*' – that was what I had to sit down with. I can certainly not be said to have sat down, for I seem to remember myself at this time as rushing constantly between the little house in Chelsea and my own. Our impatience, Gwendolen's and mine, was equal, but I kept hoping her light would be greater. We all spent during this episode, for people of our means, a great deal of money in telegrams, and I counted on the receipt of news from Rapallo immediately after the junction of the discoverer with the discovered. The interval seemed an age, but late one day I heard a hansom rattle up to my door with the crash engendered by a hint of liberality. I lived with my heart in my mouth and I bounded to the window – a movement which gave me a view of a young lady erect on the footboard of the vehicle and eagerly looking up at my house. At sight of me she flourished a paper with a movement that brought me straight down, the movement with which, in melodramas, handkerchiefs and reprieves are flourished at the foot of the scaffold.

'Just seen Vereker — not a note wrong. Pressed me to bosom — keeps me a month.' So much I read on her paper while the cabby dropped a grin from his perch. In my excitement I paid him profusely and in hers she suffered it; then as he drove away we started to walk about and talk. We had talked, heaven knows, enough before, but this was a wondrous lift. We pictured the whole scene at Rapallo, where he would have written, mentioning my name, for permission to call; that is *I* pictured it, having more material than my companion, whom I felt hang on my lips as we stopped on purpose before shop-windows we didn't look into. About one thing we were clear: if he was staying on for fuller communication we should at least have a letter from him that would help us through the dregs of delay. We understood his staying on, and yet each of us saw, I think, that the other hated it. The letter we were clear about arrived; it was for Gwendolen, and I called upon her in time to save her the trouble of bringing it to me. She didn't read it out, as was natural enough; but she repeated to me what it chiefly embodied. This consisted of the remarkable statement that he would tell her when they were married exactly what she wanted to know.

'Only when we're married — not before,' she explained. 'It's tantamount to saying — isn't it? — that I must marry him straight off!' She smiled at me while I flushed with disappointment, a vision of fresh delay that made me at first unconscious of my surprise. It seemed more than a hint that on me as well he would impose some tiresome condition. Suddenly, while she reported several more things from his letter, I remembered what he had told me before going away. He found Mr Vereker deliriously interesting and his own possession of the secret a kind of intoxication. The buried treasure was all gold and gems. Now that it was there it seemed to grow and grow before him; it was in all time, in all tongues, one of the most wonderful flowers of art. Nothing, above all, when once one was face to face with it, had been more consummately done. When once it came out it came out, was there with a splendour that made you ashamed; and there had not been, save in the bottomless vulgarity of the age, with everyone tasteless and tainted, every sense stopped, the smallest reason why it should have been overlooked. It was immense, but it was simple – it was simple, but it was immense, and the final knowledge of it was an experience quite apart. He intimated that the charm of such an experience, the desire to drain it, in its freshness, to the last drop, was what kept him there close to the source. Gwendolen, frankly radiant as she tossed me these fragments, showed the elation of a prospect more assured than my own. That brought me back to the question of her marriage, prompted me to ask her if what she meant by what she had just surprised me with was that she was under an engagement.

'Of course I am!' she answered. 'Didn't you know it?' She

appeared astonished; but I was still more so, for Corvick had told me the exact contrary. I didn't mention this, however; I only reminded her that I had not been to that degree in her confidence, or even in Corvick's, and that moreover I was not in ignorance of her mother's interdict. At bottom I was troubled by the disparity of the two assertions; but after a moment I felt that Corvick's was the one I least doubted. This simply reduced me to asking myself if the girl had on the spot improvised an engagement – vamped up an old one or dashed off a new – in order to arrive at the satisfaction she desired. I reflected that she had resources of which I was destitute; but she made her case slightly more intelligible by rejoining presently: 'What the state of things has been is that we felt of course bound to do nothing in mamma's lifetime.'

'But now you think you'll just dispense with your mother's consent?'

'Ah, it may not come to that!' I wondered what it might come to, and she went on: 'Poor dear, she may swallow the dose. In fact, you know,' she added with a laugh, 'she really *must*!' – a proposition of which, on behalf of everyone concerned, I fully acknowledged the force.

# VIII

NOTHING MORE annoying had ever happened to me than to become aware before Corvick's arrival in England that I should not be there to put him through. I found myself abruptly called to Germany by the alarming illness of my younger brother, who, against my advice, had gone to Munich to study, at the feet indeed of a great master, the art of portraiture in oils. The near relative who made him an allowance had threatened to withdraw it if he should, under specious pretexts, turn for superior truth to Paris – Paris being somehow, for a Cheltenham aunt, the school of evil, the abyss. I deplored this prejudice at the time, and the deep injury of it was now visible – first in the fact that it had not saved the poor boy, who was clever, frail and foolish, from congestion of the lungs, and second in the greater remoteness from London to which the event condemned me. I am afraid that what was uppermost in my mind during several anxious weeks was the sense that if we had only been in Paris I might have run over to see Corvick. This was actually out of the question from every point of view: my brother, whose recovery gave us both plenty to do, was ill for three months, during which I never left him and at the end of which we had to face the absolute prohibition of a return to England. The consideration of climate imposed itself, and he was in no state to meet it alone. I took him to Meran and there spent the summer with him, trying to show him by example how to get back to work and nursing a rage of another sort that I tried not to show him.

The whole business proved the first of a series of phenomena so strangely combined that, taken together (which was how I had to take them) they form as good an illustration as I can recall of the manner in which, for the good of his soul doubtless, fate sometimes deals with a man's avidity. These incidents certainly had larger bearings than the comparatively meagre consequence we are here concerned with – though I feel that consequence also to be a thing to speak of with some respect. It's mainly in such a light, I confess, at any rate, that at this hour the ugly fruit of my exile is present to me. Even at first indeed the spirit in which my avidity, as I have called it, made me regard this term owed no element of ease to the fact that before coming back from Rapallo George Corvick addressed me in a way I didn't like. His letter had none of the sedative action that I must today profess myself sure he had wished to give it, and the march of occurrences was not so ordered as to make up for what it lacked. He had begun on the spot, for one of the quarterlies, a great last word on Vereker's writings, and this exhaustive study, the only one that would have counted, have existed, was to turn on the new light, to utter – oh, so quietly! – the unimagined truth. It was in other words to trace the figure in the carpet through every convolution, to reproduce it in every tint. The result, said Corvick, was to be the greatest literary portrait ever painted, and what he asked of me was just to be so good as not to trouble him with questions till he should hang up his masterpiece before me. He did me the honour to declare that, putting aside the great sitter himself, all aloft in his indifference, I was individually the connoisseur he was most working for. I was therefore to be a good boy and not try to peep under the curtain before the show was ready: I should enjoy it all the more if I sat very still.

I did my best to sit very still, but I couldn't help giving a jump on seeing in *The Times*, after I had been a week or two in Munich and before, as I knew, Corvick had reached London, the announcement of the sudden death of poor Mrs Erme. I instantly wrote to Gwendolen for particulars, and she replied that her mother had succumbed to long-threatened failure of the heart. She didn't say, but I took the liberty of reading into her words, that from the point of view of her marriage and also of her eagerness, which was quite a match for mine, this was a solution more prompt than could have been expected and more radical than waiting for the old lady to swallow the dose. I candidly admit indeed that at the time – for I heard from her repeatedly – I read some singular things into Gwendolen's words and some still more extraordinary ones into her silences. Pen in hand, this way, I live the time over, and it brings back the oddest sense of my having been for months and in spite of myself a kind of coerced spectator. All my life had taken refuge in my eyes, which the procession of events appeared to have committed itself to keep astare. There were days when I thought of writing to Hugh Vereker and simply throwing myself on his charity. But I felt more deeply that I hadn't fallen quite so low, besides which, quite properly, he would send me about my business. Mrs Erme's death brought Corvick straight home, and within the month he was united 'very quietly' – as quietly I suppose as he meant in his article to bring out his *trouvaille* – to the young lady he had loved and quitted. I use this last term, I may parenthetically say, because I subsequently grew sure that at the time he went to India, at the time of his great news from Bombay, there was no engagement whatever. There was none at the moment she affirmed the opposite. On the other hand he certainly became engaged the day he returned. The happy pair went down to Torquay for their honeymoon, and there, in a reckless hour, it occurred to poor Corvick to take his young bride a drive. He had no command of that business: this had been brought home to me of old in a little tour we had once made together in a dog-cart. In a dog-cart he perched his companion for a rattle over Devonshire hills, on one of the likeliest of which he brought his horse, who, it was true, had bolted, down with such violence that the occupants of the cart were hurled forward and that he fell horribly on his head. He was killed on the spot; Gwendolen escaped unhurt.

I pass rapidly over the question of this unmitigated tragedy, of what the loss of my best friend meant for me, and I complete my little history of my patience and my pain by the frank statement of my having, in a postscript to my very first letter to her after the receipt of the hideous news, asked Mrs Corvick whether her husband had not at least finished the great article on Vereker. Her answer was as prompt as my inquiry: the article, which had been barely begun, was a mere heart-breaking scrap. She explained that Corvick had just settled down to it when he was interrupted by her mother's death; then, on his return, he had been kept from work by the engrossments into which that calamity plunged them. The opening pages were all that existed; they were striking, they were promising, but they didn't unveil the idol. That great intellectual feat was obviously to have formed his climax. She said nothing more, nothing to enlighten me as to the state of her own knowledge – the knowledge for the acquisition of which I had conceived her doing prodigious things. This was above all what I wanted to know: had *she* seen the idol unveiled? Had there been a private ceremony for a palpitating audience of one? For what else but that ceremony had the previous ceremony been enacted? I didn't like as yet to press her, though when I thought of what had passed between us on the subject in Corvick's absence her reticence surprised me. It was therefore not till much later, from Meran, that I risked another appeal, risked it in some trepidation, for she continued to tell me nothing. 'Did you hear in those few days of your blighted bliss,' I wrote, 'what we desired so to hear?' I said 'we' as a little hint; and she showed me she could take a little hint. 'I heard everything,' she replied, 'and I mean to keep it to myself!'

## IX

IT WAS IMPOSSIBLE not to be moved with the strongest sympathy for her, and on my return to England I showed her every kindness in my power. Her mother's death had made her means sufficient, and she had gone to live in a more convenient quarter. But her loss had been great and her visitation cruel; it never would have occurred to me moreover to suppose she could come to regard the enjoyment of a technical tip, of a piece of literary experience, as a counterpoise to her grief. Strange to say, none the less, I couldn't help fancying after I had seen her a few times that I caught a glimpse of some such oddity. I hasten to add that there had been other things I couldn't help fancying; and as I never felt I was really clear about these, so, as to the point I here touch on, I give her memory the benefit of every doubt. Stricken and solitary, highly accomplished and now, in her deep mourning, her maturer grace and her uncomplaining sorrow incontestably handsome, she presented herself as leading a life of singular dignity and beauty. I had at first found a way to believe that I should soon get the better of the reserve formulated the week after the catastrophe in her reply to an appeal as to which I was not unconscious that it might strike her as mistimed. Certainly that reserve was something of a shock to me – certainly it puzzled me the more I thought of it, though I tried to explain it, with moments of success, by the supposition of exalted sentiments, of superstitious scruples, of a refinement of loyalty. Certainly it added at the same time hugely to the price of Vereker's secret, precious as that mystery already appeared. I may as well confess abjectly that Mrs Corvick's unexpected attitude was the final tap on the nail that was to fix, as they say, my luckless idea, convert it into the obsession of which I am for ever conscious.

But this only helped me the more to be artful, to be adroit, to allow time to elapse before renewing my suit. There were plenty of speculations for the interval, and one of them was deeply absorbing. Corvick had kept his information from his young friend till after the removal of the last barriers to their intimacy; then he had let the cat out of the bag. Was it Gwendolen's idea, taking a hint from him, to liberate this animal only on the basis of the renewal of such a relation? Was the figure in the carpet traceable or describable only for husbands and wives — for lovers supremely united? It came back to me in a mystifying manner that in Kensington Square, when I told him that Corvick would have told the girl he loved, some word had dropped from Vereker that gave colour to this possibility. There might be little in it, but there was enough to make me wonder if I should have to marry Mrs Corvick to get what I wanted. Was I prepared to offer her this price for the blessing of her knowledge? Ah! that way madness lay — so I said to myself at least in bewildered hours. I could see meanwhile the torch she refused to pass on flame away in her chamber of memory — pour through her eyes a light that made a glow in her lonely house. At the end of six months I was fully sure of what this warm presence made up to her for. We had talked again and again of the man who had brought us together, of his talent, his character, his personal charm, his certain career, his dreadful doom, and even of his clear purpose in that great study which was to have been a supreme literary portrait, a kind of critical Van Dyck or Velázquez. She had conveyed to me in abundance that she was tongue-tied by her perversity, by her piety, that she would never break the silence it had not been given to the 'right person', as she said, to break. The hour however finally arrived. One evening when I had been sitting with her longer than usual I laid my hand firmly on her arm.

'Now, at last, what *is* it?'

She had been expecting me; she was ready. She gave a long, slow, soundless head-shake, merciful only in being inarticulate. This mercy didn't prevent its hurling at me the largest, finest, coldest 'Never!' I had yet, in the course of a life that had known denials, had to take full in the face. I took it and was aware that with the hard blow the tears had come into my eyes. So for a while we sat and looked at each other; after which I slowly rose. I was wondering if some day she would accept me; but this was not what I brought out. I said as I smoothed down my hat: 'I know what to think then; it's nothing!'

A remote, disdainful pity for me shone out of her dim smile; then she exclaimed in a voice that I hear at this moment: 'It's my *life*!' As I stood at the door she added: 'You've insulted him!'

'Do you mean Vereker?'

'I mean – the Dead!'

I recognized when I reached the street the justice of her charge. Yes, it was her life – I recognized that too; but her life none the less made room with the lapse of time for another interest. A year and a half after Corvick's death she published in a single volume her second novel, *Overmastered*, which I pounced on in the hope of finding in it some tell-tale echo or some peeping face. All I found was a much better book than her younger performance, showing I thought the better company she had kept. As a tissue tolerably intricate it was a carpet with a figure of its own; but the figure was not the figure I was looking for. On sending a review of it to *The Middle* I was surprised to learn from the office that a notice was already in type. When the paper came out I had no hesitation in attributing this article, which I thought rather vulgarly overdone, to Drayton Deane, who in the old days had been something of a friend of Corvick's, yet had only within a few weeks made the acquaintance of his widow. I had had an early copy of the book, but Deane had evidently had an earlier. He lacked all the same the light hand with which Corvick had gilded the gingerbread – he laid on the tinsel in splotches.

# X

SIX MONTHS LATER appeared *The Right of Way*, the last chance, though we didn't know it, that we were to have to redeem ourselves. Written wholly during Vereker's absence, the book had been heralded, in a hundred paragraphs, by the usual ineptitudes. I carried it, as early a copy as any, I this time flattered myself, straightway to Mrs Corvick. This was the only use I had for it; I left the inevitable tribute of *The Middle* to some more ingenious mind and some less irritated temper. 'But I already have it,' Gwendolen said. 'Drayton Deane was so good as to bring it to me yesterday, and I've just finished it.'

'Yesterday? How did he get it so soon?'

'He gets everything soon. He's to review it in *The Middle*.'

'He – Drayton Deane – review Vereker?' I couldn't believe my ears.

'Why not? One fine ignorance is as good as another.'

I winced, but I presently said: 'You ought to review him yourself!'

'I don't "review",' she laughed. 'I'm reviewed!'

Just then the door was thrown open. 'Ah yes, here's your reviewer!' Drayton Deane was there with his long legs and his tall forehead: he had come to see what she thought of *The Right of Way*, and to bring news which was singularly relevant. The evening papers were just out with a telegram on the author of that work, who, in Rome, had been ill for some days with an attack of malarial fever. It had at first not been thought grave, but had taken in consequence of complications a turn that might give rise to anxiety. Anxiety had indeed at the latest hour begun to be felt.

I was struck in the presence of these tidings with the

fundamental detachment that Mrs Corvick's public regret quite failed to conceal: it gave me the measure of her consummate independence. That independence rested on her knowledge, the knowledge which nothing now could destroy and which nothing could make different. The figure in the carpet might take on another twist or two, but the sentence had virtually been written. The writer might go down to his grave: she was the person in the world to whom – as if she had been his favoured heir – his continued existence was least of a need. This reminded me how I had observed at a particular moment – after Corvick's death – the drop of her desire to see him face to face. She had got what she wanted without that. I had been sure that if she hadn't got it she wouldn't have been restrained from the endeavour to sound him personally by those superior reflections, more conceivable on a man's part than on a woman's, which in my case had served as a deterrent. It wasn't however, I hasten to add, that my case, in spite of this invidious comparison, wasn't ambiguous enough. At the thought that Vereker was perhaps at that moment dying there rolled over me a wave of anguish – a poignant sense of how inconsistently I still depended on him. A delicacy that it was my one compensation to suffer to rule me had left the Alps and the Apennines between us, but the vision of the waning opportunity made me feel as if I might in my despair at last have gone to him. Of course I would really have done nothing of the sort. I remained five minutes, while my companions talked of the new book, and when Drayton Deane appealed to me for my opinion of it I replied, getting up, that I detested Hugh Vereker

— simply couldn't read him. I went away with the moral certainty that as the door closed behind me Deane would remark that I was awfully superficial. His hostess wouldn't contradict him.

I continue to trace with a briefer touch our intensely odd concatenation. Three weeks after this came Vereker's death, and before the year was out the death of his wife. That poor lady I had never seen, but I had had a futile theory that, should she survive him long enough to be decorously accessible, I might approach her with the feeble flicker of my petition. Did she know and if she knew would she speak? It was much to be presumed that for more reasons than one she would have nothing to say; but when she passed out of all reach I felt that renouncement was indeed my appointed lot. I was shut up in my obsession for ever — my gaolers had gone off with the key. I find myself quite as vague as a captive in a dungeon about the time that further elapsed before Mrs Corvick became the wife of Drayton Deane. I had foreseen, through my bars, this end of the business, though there was no indecent haste and our friendship had rather fallen off. They were both so 'awfully intellectual' that it struck people as a suitable match, but I knew better than anyone the wealth of understanding the bride would contribute to the partnership. Never, for a marriage in literary circles — so the newspapers described the alliance — had a bride been so handsomely dowered. I began with due promptness to look for the fruit of their union — that fruit, I mean, of which the premonitory symptoms would be peculiarly visible in the husband. Taking for granted the splendour of the lady's nuptial gift, I expected to see him make a show commensurate with his increase of means. I knew what his means had been – his article on *The Right of Way* had distinctly given one the figure. As he was now exactly in the position in which still more exactly I was not I watched from month to month, in the likely periodicals, for the heavy message poor Corvick had been unable to deliver and the responsibility of which would have fallen on his successor. The widow and wife would have broken by the rekindled hearth the silence that only a widow and wife might break, and Deane would be as aflame with the knowledge as Corvick in his own hour, as Gwendolen in hers had been. Well, he was aflame doubtless, but the fire was apparently not to become a public blaze. I scanned the periodicals in vain: Drayton Deane filled them with exuberant pages, but he withheld the page I most feverishly sought. He wrote on a thousand subjects, but never on the subject of Vereker. His special line was to tell truths that other people either 'funked', as he said, or overlooked, but he never told the only truth that seemed to me in these days to signify. I met the couple in those literary circles referred to in the papers: I have sufficiently intimated that it was only in such circles we were all constructed to revolve. Gwendolen was more than ever committed to them by the publication of her third novel, and I myself definitely classed by holding the opinion that this work was inferior to its immediate predecessor. Was it worse because she had been keeping worse company? If her secret was, as she had told me, her life – a fact discernible in her increasing bloom, an air of conscious privilege that, cleverly corrected by pretty charities, gave distinction to her appearance – it had yet not a direct influence on her work. That only made – everything only made – one yearn the more for it, rounded it off with a mystery finer and subtler.

## XI

IT WAS THEREFORE from her husband I could never remove my eyes: I hovered about him in a manner that might have made him uneasy. I went even so far as to engage him in conversation. *Didn't* he know, hadn't he come into it as a matter of course? – that question hummed in my brain. Of course he knew; otherwise he wouldn't return my stare so queerly. His wife had told him what I wanted, and he was amiably amused at my impotence. He didn't laugh – he was not a laugher: his system was to present to my irritation, so that I should crudely expose myself, a conversational blank as vast as his big bare brow. It always happened that I turned away with a settled conviction from these unpeopled expanses, which seemed to complete each other geographically and to symbolize together Drayton Deane's want of voice, want of form. He simply hadn't the art to use what he knew; he literally was incompetent to take up the duty where Corvick had left it. I went still further – it was the only glimpse of happiness I had. I made up my mind that the duty didn't appeal to him. He wasn't interested, he didn't care. Yes, it quite comforted me to believe him too stupid to have joy of the thing I lacked. He was as stupid after as before, and that deepened for me the golden glory in which the mystery was wrapped. I had of course however to recollect that his wife might have imposed her conditions and exactions. I had above all to recollect that with Vereker's death the major incentive dropped. He was still there to be honoured by what might be done – he was no longer there to give it his sanction. Who, alas, but he had the authority?

Two children were born to the pair, but the second cost the mother her life. After this calamity I seemed to see another ghost of a chance. I jumped at it in thought, but I waited a certain time for manners, and at last my opportunity arrived in a remunerative way. His wife had been dead a year when I met Drayton Deane in the smoking-room of a small club of which we both were members, but where for months – perhaps because I rarely entered it – I had not seen him. The room was empty and the occasion propitious. I deliberately offered him, to have done with the matter for ever, that advantage for which I felt he had long been looking.

'As an older acquaintance of your late wife's than even you were,' I began, 'you must let me say to you something I have on my mind. I shall be glad to make any terms with you that you see fit to name for the information she had from George Corvick – the information, you know, that he, poor fellow, in one of the happiest hours of his life, had straight from Hugh Vereker.'

He looked at me like a dim phrenological bust. 'The information——?'

'Vereker's secret, my dear man – the general intention of his books: the string the pearls were strung on, the buried treasure, the figure in the carpet.'

He began to flush – the numbers on his bumps to come out. 'Vereker's books had a general intention?'

I stared in my turn. 'You don't mean to say you don't know it?' I thought for a moment he was playing with me. 'Mrs Deane knew it; she had it, as I say, straight from Corvick, who had, after infinite search and to Vereker's own delight, found the very mouth of the cave. Where *is* the mouth? He told after their marriage – and told alone – the person who, when the circumstances were reproduced, must have told you. Have I been wrong in taking for granted that she admitted you, as one of the highest privileges of the relation in which you stood to her, to the knowledge of which she was after Corvick's death the sole depositary? All *I* know is that that knowledge is infinitely precious, and what I want you to understand is that if you will in your turn admit *me* to it you will do me a kindness for which I shall be everlastingly grateful.'

He had turned at last very red; I daresay he had begun by thinking I had lost my wits. Little by little he followed me; on my own side I stared with a livelier surprise. 'I don't know what you're talking about,' he said.

He wasn't acting – it was the absurd truth. 'She *didn't* tell you—?'

'Nothing about Hugh Vereker.'

I was stupefied; the room went round. It had been too good even for that! 'Upon your honour?'

'Upon my honour. What the devil's the matter with you?' he demanded.

I'm astounded – I'm disappointed. I wanted to get it out of you.'

'It isn't *in* me! he awkwardly laughed. 'And even if it were—'

'If it were you'd let me have it – oh yes, in common humanity. But I believe you. I see – I see!' I went on, conscious, with the full turn of the wheel, of my great delusion, my false view of the poor man's attitude. What I saw, though I couldn't say it, was that his wife hadn't thought him worth enlightening. This struck me as strange for a woman who had thought him worth marrying. At last I explained it by the reflection that she couldn't possibly have married him for his understanding. She had married him for something else. He was to some extent enlightened now, but he was even more astonished, more disconcerted: he took a moment to compare my story with his quickened memories. The result of his meditation was his presently saying with a good deal of rather feeble form:

'This is the first I hear of what you allude to. I think you must be mistaken as to Mrs Drayton Deane's having had any unmentioned, and still less any unmentionable, knowledge about Hugh Vereker. She would certainly have wished it – if it bore on his literary character – to be used.'

'It *was* used. She used it herself. She told me with her own lips that she "lived" on it.'

I had no sooner spoken than I repented of my words; he grew so pale that I felt as if I had struck him. 'Ah, "lived"—!' he murmured, turning short away from me.

My compunction was real; I laid my hand on his shoulder. 'I beg you to forgive me – I've made a mistake. You *don't* know what I thought you knew. You could, if I had been right, have rendered me a service; and I had my reasons for assuming that you would be in a position to meet me.'

'Your reasons?' he asked. 'What were your reasons?'

I looked at him well; I hesitated; I considered. 'Come and sit down with me here, and I'll tell you.' I drew him to a sofa, I lighted another cigarette and, beginning with the anecdote of Vereker's one descent from the clouds, I gave him an account of the extraordinary chain of accidents that had in spite of it kept me till that hour in the dark. I told him in a word just what I've written out here. He listened with deepening attention, and I became aware, to my surprise, by his ejaculations, by his questions, that he would have been after all not unworthy to have been trusted by his wife. So abrupt an experience of her want of trust had an agitating effect on him, but I saw that immediate shock throb away little by little and then gather again into waves of wonder and curiosity – waves that promised, I could perfectly judge, to break in the end with the fury of my own highest tides. I may say that today as victims of unappeased desire there isn't a pin to choose between us. The poor man's state is almost my consolation; there are indeed moments when I feel it to be almost my revenge.

# *The Real Right Thing*

## I

WHEN, AFTER THE death of Ashton Doyne – but three months after – George Withermore was approached, as the phrase is, on the subject of a 'volume', the communication came straight from his publishers, who had been, and indeed much more, Doyne's own; but he was not surprised to learn, on the occurrence of the interview they next suggested, that a certain pressure as to the early issue of a Life had been brought to bear upon them by their late client's widow. Doyne's relations with his wife had been, to Withermore's knowledge, a very special chapter – which would present itself, by the way, as a delicate one for the biographer; but a sense of what she had lost, and even of what she had lacked, had betrayed itself, on the poor woman's part, from the first days of her bereavement, sufficiently to prepare an observer at all initiated for some attitude of reparation, some espousal even exaggerated of the interests of a distinguished name. George Withermore was, as he felt, initiated; yet what he had not expected was to hear that she had mentioned him as the person in whose hands she would most promptly place the materials for a book.

These materials – diaries, letters, memoranda, notes, documents of many sorts – were her property, and wholly in her control, no conditions at all attaching to any portion of her heritage; so that she was free at present to do as she liked – free, in particular, to do nothing. What Doyne would have arranged had he had time to arrange could be but supposition and guess. Death had taken him too soon and too suddenly, and there was all the pity that the only wishes he was known to have expressed were wishes that put it positively out of account. He had broken short off – that was the way of it; and the end was ragged and needed trimming. Withermore was conscious, abundantly, how close he had stood to him, but he was not less aware of his comparative obscurity. He was young, a journalist, a critic, a hand-to-mouth character, with little, as yet, as was vulgarly said, to show. His writings were few and small, his relations scant and vague. Doyne, on the other hand, had lived long enough – above all had had talent enough – to become great, and among his many friends gilded also with greatness were several to whom his wife would have struck those who knew her as much more likely to appeal.

The preference she had, at all events, uttered – and uttered in a roundabout, considerate way that left him a measure of freedom – made our young man feel that he must at least see her and that there would be in any case a good deal to talk about. He immediately wrote to her, she as promptly named an hour, and they had it out. But he came away with his particular idea immensely strengthened. She was a strange woman, and he had never thought her an agreeable one; only there was something that touched him now in her bustling, blundering impatience. She wanted the book to make up, and the individual whom, of her husband's set, she probably believed she might most manipulate was in every way to help it to make up. She had not taken Doyne seriously enough in life, but the biography should be a solid reply to every imputation on herself. She had scantly known how such books were constructed, but she had been looking and had learned something. It alarmed Withermore a little from the first to see that she would wish to go in for quantity. She talked of 'volumes' – but he had his notion of that.

'My thought went straight to *you*, as his own would have done,' she had said almost as soon as she rose before him there in her large array of mourning – with her big black eyes, her big black wig, her big black fan and gloves, her general gaunt, ugly, tragic, but striking and, as might have been thought from a certain point of view, 'elegant' presence. 'You're the one he liked most; oh, *much*!' – and it had been quite enough to turn Withermore's head. It little mattered that he could afterward wonder if she had known Doyne enough, when it came to that, to be sure. He would have said for himself indeed that her testimony on such a point would scarcely have counted. Still, there was no smoke without fire; she knew at least what she meant, and he was not a person she could have an interest in flattering. They went up together, without delay, to the great man's vacant study, which was at the back of the house and looked over the large green garden – a beautiful and inspiring scene, to poor Withermore's view – common to the expensive row.

'You can perfectly work here, you know,' said Mrs Doyne: 'you shall have the place quite to yourself – I'll give it all up to you; so that in the evenings, in particular, don't you see? for quiet and privacy, it will be perfection.'

Perfection indeed, the young man felt as he looked about – having explained that, as his actual occupation was an evening paper and his earlier hours, for a long time yet, regularly taken up, he would have to come always at night. The place was full of their lost friend; everything in it had belonged to him; everything they touched had been part of his life. It was for the moment too much for Withermore – too great an honour and even too great a care; memories still recent came back to him, and, while his heart beat faster and his eyes filled with tears, the pressure of his loyalty seemed almost more than he could carry. At the sight of his tears Mrs Doyne's own rose to her lids, and the two, for a minute, only looked at each other. He half expected her to break out: 'Oh, help me to feel as I know you know I want to feel!' And after a little one of them said, with the other's deep assent – it didn't matter which: 'It's here that we're *with* him.' But it was definitely the young man who put it, before they left the room, that it was there he was with *them*.

The young man began to come as soon as he could arrange it,

and then it was, on the spot, in the charmed stillness, between the lamp and the fire and with the curtains drawn, that a certain intenser consciousness crept over him. He turned in out of the black London November; he passed through the large, hushed house and up the red-carpeted staircase where he only found in his path the whisk of a soundless, trained maid, or the reach, out of a doorway, of Mrs Doyne's queenly weeds and approving tragic face; and then, by a mere touch of the well-made door that gave so sharp and pleasant a click, shut himself in for three or four warm hours with the spirit – as he had always distinctly declared it – of his master. He was not a little frightened when, even the first night, it came over him that he had really been most affected, in the whole matter, by the prospect, the privilege and the luxury, of this sensation. He had not, he could now reflect, definitely considered the question of the book – as to which there was here, even already, much to consider: he had simply let his affection and admiration – to say nothing of his gratified pride – meet, to the full, the temptation Mrs Doyne had offered them.

How did he know, without more thought, he might begin to ask himself, that the book was, on the whole, to be desired? What warrant had he ever received from Ashton Doyne himself for so direct and, as it were, so familiar an approach? Great was the art of biography, but there were lives and lives, there were subjects and subjects. He confusedly recalled, so far as that went, old words dropped by Doyne over contemporary compilations, suggestions of how he himself discriminated as to other heroes and other panoramas. He even remembered how his friend, at moments, would have seemed to show himself as holding that the 'literary' career might – save in the case of a Johnson and a Scott, with a Boswell and a Lockhart to help – best content itself to be represented. The artist was what he *did* – he was nothing else. Yet how, on the other hand, was not *he*, George Withermore, poor devil, to have jumped at the chance of spending his winter in an intimacy so rich? It had been simply dazzling – that was the fact. It hadn't been the 'terms', from the publishers – though these were, as they said at the office, all right; it had been Doyne himself, his company and contact and presence – it had been just what it was turning out, the possibility of an intercourse closer than that of life. Strange that death, of the two things, should have the fewer mysteries and secrets! The first night our young man was alone in the room it seemed to him that his master and he were really for the first time together.

## II

MRS DOYNE had for the most part let him expressively alone, but she had on two or three occasions looked in to see if his needs had been met, and he had had the opportunity of thanking her on the spot for the judgement and zeal with which she had smoothed his way. She had to some extent herself been looking things over and had been able already to muster several groups of letters; all the keys of drawers and cabinets she had, moreover, from the first placed in his hands, with helpful information as to the apparent whereabouts of different matters. She had put him, in a word, in the fullest possible possession, and whether or no her husband had trusted her, she at least, it was clear, trusted her husband's friend. There grew upon Withermore, nevertheless, the impression that, in spite of all these offices, she was not yet at peace, and that a certain unappeasable anxiety continued even to keep step with her confidence. Though she was full of consideration, she was at the same time perceptibly *there*: he felt her, through a supersubtle sixth sense that the whole connection had already brought into play, hover, in the still hours, at the top of landings and on the other side of doors, gathered from the soundless brush of her skirts the hint of her watchings and waitings. One evening when, at his friend's table, he had lost himself in the depths of correspondence, he was made to start and turn by the suggestion that someone was behind him. Mrs Doyne had come in without his hearing the door, and she gave a strained smile as he sprang to his feet. 'I hope,' she said, 'I haven't frightened you.'

'Just a little – I was so absorbed. It was as if, for the instant,' the young man explained, 'it had been himself.'

The oddity of her face increased in her wonder. 'Ashton?'

'He does seem so near,' said Withermore.

'To you too?'

This naturally struck him. 'He does then to you?'

She hesitated, not moving from the spot where she had first stood, but looking round the room as if to penetrate its duskier angles. She had a way of raising to the level of her nose the big black fan which she apparently never laid aside and with which she thus covered the lower half of her face, her rather hard eyes, above it, becoming the more ambiguous. 'Sometimes.'

'Here,' Withermore went on, 'it's as if he might at any moment come in. That's why I jumped just now. The time is so short since he really used to – it only *was* yesterday. I sit in his chair, I turn his books, I use his pens, I stir his fire, exactly as if, learning he would presently be back from a walk, I had come up here contentedly to wait. It's delightful – but it's strange.'

Mrs Doyne, still with her fan up, listened with interest. 'Does it worry you?'

'No – I like it.'

She hesitated again. 'Do you ever feel as if he were – a – quite – a – personally in the room?'

'Well, as I said just now,' her companion laughed, 'on hearing you behind me I seemed to take it so. What do we want, after all,' he asked, 'but that he shall be with us?'

'Yes, as you said he would be – that first time.' She stared in full assent. 'He *is* with us.'

She was rather portentous, but Withermore took it smiling. 'Then we must keep him. We must do only what he would like.'

'Oh, only that, of course – only. But if he *is* here—?' And her sombre eyes seemed to throw it out, in vague distress, over her fan.

'It shows that he's pleased and wants only to help? Yes, surely; it must show that.'

She gave a light gasp and looked again round the room. 'Well,' she said as she took leave of him, 'remember that I too want only to help.' On which, when she had gone, he felt sufficiently – that she had come in simply to see he was all right.

He was all right more and more, it struck him after this, for as he began to get into his work he moved, as it appeared to him, but the closer to the idea of Doyne's personal presence. When once this fancy had begun to hang about him he welcomed it, persuaded it, encouraged it, quite cherished it, looking forward all day to feeling it renew itself in the evening, and waiting for the evening very much as one of a pair of lovers might wait for the hour of their appointment. The smallest accidents humoured and confirmed it, and by the end of three or four weeks he had come quite to regard it as the consecration of his enterprise. Wasn't it what settled the question of what Doyne would have thought of what they were doing? What they were doing was what he wanted done, and they could go on, from step to step, without scruple or doubt. Withermore rejoiced indeed at moments to feel this certitude: there were times of dipping deep into some of Doyne's secrets when it was particularly pleasant to be able to hold that Doyne desired him, as it were, to know them. He was learning many things that he had not suspected, drawing many curtains, forcing many doors, reading many riddles, going, in general, as they said, behind almost everything. It was at an occasional sharp turn of some of the duskier of these wanderings 'behind' that he really, of a sudden, most felt himself, in the intimate, sensible way, face to face with his friend; so that he could scarcely have told, for the instant, if their meeting occurred in the narrow passage and tight squeeze of the past, or at the hour and in the place that actually held him. Was it '67, or was it but the other side of the table?

Happily, at any rate, even in the vulgarest light publicity could ever shed, there would be the great fact of the way Doyne was 'coming out'. He was coming out too beautifully – better yet than such a partisan as Withermore could have supposed. Yet, all the while, as well, how would this partisan have represented to anyone else the special state of his own consciousness? It wasn't a thing to talk about – it was only a thing to feel. There were moments, for instance, when, as he bent over his papers, the light breath of his dead host was as distinctly in his hair as his own elbows were on the table before him. There were moments when, had he been able to look up, the other side of the table would have shown him this companion as vividly as the shaded lamplight showed him his page. That he couldn't at such a juncture look up was his own affair, for the situation was ruled – that was but natural – by deep delicacies and fine timidities, the dread of too sudden or too rude an advance. What was intensely in the air was that if Doyne *was* there it was not nearly so much for himself as for the young priest of his altar. He hovered and lingered, he came and went, he might almost have been, among the books and the papers, a hushed, discreet librarian, doing the particular things, rendering the quiet aid, liked by men of letters.

Withermore himself, meanwhile, came and went, changed his place, wandered on quests either definite or vague; and more than once, when, taking a book down from a shelf and finding in it marks of Doyne's pencil, he got drawn on and lost, he had heard documents on the table behind him gently shifted and stirred, had literally, on his return, found some letter he had mislaid pushed again into view, some wilderness cleared by the opening of an old journal at the very date he wanted. How should he have gone so, on occasion, to the special box or drawer, out of fifty receptacles, that would help him, had not his mystic assistant happened, in fine prevision, to tilt its lid, or to pull it half open, in just the manner that would catch his eye? – in spite, after all, of the fact of lapses and intervals in which, *could* one have really looked, one would have seen somebody standing before the fire a trifle detached and over-erect – somebody fixing one the least bit harder than in life.

## III

THAT THIS auspicious relation had in fact existed, had continued, for two or three weeks, was sufficiently proved by the dawn of the distress with which our young man found himself aware that he had, for some reason, from a certain evening, begun to miss it. The sign of that was an abrupt, surprised sense – on the occasion of his mislaying a marvellous unpublished page which, hunt where he would, remained stupidly, irrecoverably lost – that his protected state was, after all, exposed to some confusion and even to some depression. If, for the joy of the business, Doyne and he had, from the start, been together, the situation had, within a few days of his first new suspicion of it, suffered the odd change of their ceasing to be so. That was what was the matter, he said to himself, from the moment an impression of mere mass and quantity struck him as taking, in his happy outlook at his material, the place of his pleasant assumption of a clear course and a lively pace. For five nights he struggled; then, never at his table, wandering about the room, taking up his references only to lay them down, looking out of the window, poking the fire, thinking strange thoughts and listening for signs and sounds not as he suspected or imagined, but as he vainly desired and invoked them, he made up his mind that he was, for the time at least, forsaken.

The extraordinary thing thus became that it made him not only sad not to feel Doyne's presence, but in a high degree uneasy. It was stranger, somehow, that he shouldn't be there than it had ever been that he *was* – so strange indeed at last that Withermore's nerves found themselves quite inconsequently affected. They had taken kindly enough to what was of an order impossible to explain, perversely reserving their sharpest state for the return to the normal, the supersession of the false. They were remarkably beyond control when, finally, one night, after resisting an hour or two, he simply edged out of the room. It had only now, for the first time, become impossible to him to remain there. Without design, but panting a little and positively as a man scared, he passed along his usual corridor and reached the top of the staircase. From this point he saw Mrs Doyne looking up at him from the bottom quite as if she had known he would come; and the most singular thing of all was that, though he had been conscious of no notion to resort to her, had only been prompted to relieve himself by escape, the sight of her position made him recognize it as just, quickly feel it as a part of some monstrous oppression that was closing over both of them. It was wonderful how, in the mere modern London hall, between the Tottenham Court Road rugs and the electric light, it came up to him from the tall black lady, and went again from him down to her, that he knew what she meant by looking as if he would know. He descended straight, she turned into her own little lower room, and there, the next thing, with the door shut, they were, still in silence and with queer faces, confronted over confessions that had taken sudden life from these two or three movements. Withermore gasped as it came to him why he had lost his friend. 'He has been with *you*?'

With this it was all out – out so far that neither had to explain and that, when 'What do you suppose is the matter?' quickly passed between them, one appeared to have said it as much as the other. Withermore looked about at the small, bright room in which, night after night, she had been living her life as he had been living his own upstairs. It was pretty, cosy, rosy; but she had by turns felt in it what he had felt and heard in it what he had heard. Her effect there – fantastic black, plumed and extravagant, upon deep pink – was that of some 'decadent' coloured print, some poster of the newest school. 'You understood he had left me?' he asked.

She markedly wished to make it clear. 'This evening – yes. I've made things out.'

'You knew – before – that he was with me?'

She hesitated again. 'I felt he wasn't with *me*. But on the stairs—'

'Yes?'

'Well – he passed, more than once. He was in the house. And at your door—'

'Well?' he went on as she once more faltered.

'If I stopped I could sometimes tell. And from your face,' she added, 'tonight, at any rate, I knew your state.'

'And that was why you came out?'

'I thought you'd come to me.'

He put out to her, on this, his hand, and they thus, for a minute, in silence, held each other clasped. There was no peculiar presence for either, now – nothing more peculiar than that of each for the other. But the place had suddenly become as if consecrated, and Withermore turned over it again his anxiety. 'What *is* then the matter?'

'I only want to do the real right thing,' she replied after a moment.

'And are we not doing it?'

'I wonder. Are *you* not?'

He wondered too. 'To the best of my belief. But we must think.'

'We must think,' she echoed. And they did think — thought, with intensity, the rest of that evening together, and thought, independently — Withermore at least could answer for himself — during many days that followed. He intermitted for a little his visits and his work, trying, in meditation, to catch himself in the act of some mistake that might have accounted for their disturbance. Had he taken, on some important point — or looked as if he might take — some wrong line or wrong view? had he somewhere benightedly falsified or inadequately insisted? He went back at last with the idea of having guessed two or three questions he might have been on the way to muddle; after which he had, above stairs, another period of agitation, presently followed by another interview, below, with Mrs Doyne, who was still troubled and flushed.

'He's there?'

'He's there.'

'I knew it!' she returned in an odd gloom of triumph. Then as to make it clear: 'He has not been again with *me*.'

'Nor with me again to help,' said Withermore.

She considered. 'Not to help?'

'I can't make it out — I'm at sea. Do what I will, I feel I'm wrong.'

She covered him a moment with her pompous pain. 'How do you feel it?'

'Why, by things that happen. The strangest things. I can't describe them – and you wouldn't believe them.'

'Oh yes, I would!' Mrs Doyne murmured.

'Well, he intervenes.' Withermore tried to explain. 'However I turn, I find him.'

She earnestly followed. '"Find" him?'

'I meet him. He seems to rise there before me.'

Mrs Doyne, staring, waited a little. 'Do you mean you see him?'

'I feel as if at any moment I may. I'm baffled. I'm checked.' Then he added: 'I'm afraid.'

'Of *him*?' asked Mrs Doyne.

He thought. 'Well – of what I'm doing.'

'Then what, that's so awful, *are* you doing?'

'What you proposed to me. Going into his life.'

She showed, in her gravity, now, a new alarm. 'And don't you *like* that?'

'Doesn't *he*? That's the question. We lay him bare. We serve him up. What is it called? We give him to the world.'

Poor Mrs Doyne, as if on a menace to her hard atonement, glared at this for an instant in deeper gloom. 'And why shouldn't we?'

'Because we don't know. There are natures, there are lives, that shrink. He mayn't wish it,' said Withermore. 'We never asked him.'

'How *could* we?'

He was silent a little. 'Well, we ask him now. That's, after all, what our start has, so far, represented. We've put it to him.'

'Then – if he has been with us – we've had his answer.'

Withermore spoke now as if he knew what to believe. 'He hasn't been "with" us – he has been against us.'

'Then why did you think—'

'What I *did* think, at first – that what he wishes to make us feel is his sympathy? Because, in my original simplicity, I was mistaken. I was – I don't know what to call it – so excited and charmed that I didn't understand. But I understand at last. He only wanted to communicate. He strains forward out of his darkness; he reaches toward us out of his mystery; he makes us dim signs out of his horror.'

'"Horror"?' Mrs Doyne gasped with her fan up to her mouth.

'At what we're doing.' He could by this time piece it all together. 'I see now that at first—'

'Well, what?'

'One had simply to feel he was there, and therefore not indifferent. And the beauty of that misled me. But he's there to be a protest.'

'Against *my* Life?' Mrs Doyne wailed.

'Against *any* Life. He's there to *save* his Life. He's there to be let alone.'

'So you give up?' she almost shrieked.

He could only meet her. 'He's there as a warning.'

For a moment, on this, they looked at each other deep. 'You *are* afraid!' she at last brought out.

It affected him, but he insisted. 'He's there as a curse!'

With that they parted, but only for two or three days; her last word to him continuing to sound so in his ears that, between his need really to satisfy her and another need presently to be noted, he felt that he might not yet take up his stake. He finally went back at his usual hour and found her in her usual place. 'Yes, I *am* afraid,' he announced as if he had turned that well over and knew now all it meant. 'But I gather that you're not.'

She faltered, reserving her word. 'What is it you fear?'

'Well, that if I go on I *shall* see him.'

'And then—?'

'Oh, then,' said George Withermore, 'I *should* give up!'

She weighed it with her lofty but earnest air. 'I think, you know, we must have a clear sign.'

'You wish me to try again?'

She hesitated. 'You see what it means – for me – to give up.'

'Ah, but *you* needn't,' Withermore said.

She seemed to wonder, but in a moment she went on. 'It would mean that he won't take from me—' But she dropped for despair.

'Well, what?'

'Anything,' said poor Mrs Doyne.

He faced her a moment more. 'I've thought myself of the clear sign. I'll try again.'

As he was leaving her, however, she remembered. 'I'm only afraid that tonight there's nothing ready – no lamp and no fire.'

'Never mind,' he said from the foot of the stairs; 'I'll find things.'

## The Real Right Thing

To which she answered that the door of the room would probably, at any rate, be open; and retired again as if to wait for him. She had not long to wait; though, with her own door wide and her attention fixed, she may not have taken the time quite as it appeared to her visitor. She heard him, after an interval, on the stair, and he presently stood at her entrance, where, if he had not been precipitate, but rather, as to step and sound, backward and vague, he showed at least as livid and blank.

'I give up.'

'Then you've seen him?'

'On the threshold – guarding it.'

'Guarding it?' She glowed over her fan. 'Distinct?'

'Immense. But dim. Dark. Dreadful,' said poor George Withermore.

She continued to wonder. 'You didn't go in?'

The young man turned away. 'He forbids!'

'You say *I* needn't,' she went on after a moment. 'Well then, need I?'

'See him?' George Withermore asked.

She waited an instant. 'Give up.'

'You must decide.' For himself he could at last but drop upon the sofa with his bent face in his hands. He was not quite to know afterwards how long he had sat so; it was enough that what he did next know was that he was alone among her favourite objects. Just as he gained his feet, however, with this sense and that of the door standing open to the hall, he found himself afresh confronted, in the light, the warmth, the rosy space, with her big black perfumed presence. He saw at a glance, as she offered him a huger, bleaker stare over the mask of her fan, that she had been above; and so it was that, for the last time, they faced together their strange question. 'You've seen him?' Withermore asked.

He was to infer later on from the extraordinary way she closed her eyes and, as if to steady herself, held them tight and long, in silence, that beside the unutterable vision of Ashton Doyne's wife his own might rank as an escape. He knew before she spoke that all was over. 'I give up.'

# *The Great Good Place*

## I

GEORGE DANE HAD waked up to a bright new day, the face of nature well washed by last night's downpour and shining as with high spirits, good resolutions, lively intentions – the great glare of recommencement, in short, fixed in his patch of sky. He had sat up late to finish work – arrears overwhelming; then at last had gone to bed with the pile but little reduced. He was now to return to it after the pause of the night; but he could only look at it, for the time, over the bristling hedge of letters planted by the early postman an hour before and already, on the customary table by the chimney-piece, formally rounded and squared by his systematic servant. It was something too merciless, the domestic perfection of Brown. There were newspapers on another table, ranged with the same rigour of custom, newspapers too many – what could any creature want of so much news? – and each with its hand on the neck of the other, so that the row of their bodiless heads was like a series of decapitations. Other journals, other periodicals of every sort, folded and in wrappers, made a huddled mound that had been growing for several days and of which he had been wearily, helplessly aware. There were new books, also in wrappers as well as disenveloped and dropped again – books from publishers, books from authors, books from friends, books from enemies, books from his own bookseller, who took, it sometimes struck him, inconceivable things for granted. He touched nothing, approached nothing, only turned a heavy eye over the work, as it were, of the night – the fact, in his high, wide-windowed room, where the hard light of duty could penetrate every corner, of the unashamed admonition of the day. It was the old rising tide, and it rose and rose even under a minute's watching. It had been up to his shoulders last night – it was up to his chin now.

Nothing had passed while he slept – everything had stayed; nothing, that he could yet feel, had died – many things had been born. To let them alone, these things, the new things, let them utterly alone and see if that, by chance, wouldn't somehow prove the best way to deal with them: this fancy brushed his face for a moment as a possible solution, just giving it, as many a time before, a cool wave of air. Then he knew again as well as ever that leaving was difficult, leaving impossible – that the only remedy, the true, soft, effacing sponge, would be to *be* left, to be forgotten. There was no footing on which a man who had ever liked life – liked it, at any rate, as *he* had – could now escape from it. He must reap as he had sown. It was a thing of meshes;

he had simply gone to sleep under the net and had simply waked up there. The net was too fine; the cords crossed each other at spots so near together, making at each a little tight, hard knot that tired fingers, this morning, were too limp and too tender to touch. Our poor friend's touched nothing – only stole significantly into his pockets as he wandered over to the window and faintly gasped at the energy of nature. What was most overwhelming was that she herself was so ready. She had soothed him rather, the night before, in the small hours by the lamp. From behind the drawn curtain of his study the rain had been audible and in a manner merciful; washing the window in a steady flood, it had seemed the right thing, the retarding, interrupting thing, the thing that, if it would only last, might clear the ground by floating out to a boundless sea the innumerable objects among which his feet stumbled and strayed. He had positively laid down his pen as on a sense of friendly pressure from it. The kind, full swash had been on the glass when he turned out his lamp; he had left his phrase unfinished and his papers lying quite as if for the flood to bear them away on its bosom. But there still, on the table, were the bare bones of the sentence – and not all of those; the single thing borne away and that he could never recover was the missing half that might have paired with it and begotten a figure.

Yet he could at last only turn back from the window; the world was everywhere, without and within, and, with the great staring egotism of its health and strength, was not to be trusted for tact or delicacy. He faced about precisely to meet his servant and the absurd solemnity of two telegrams on a tray. Brown ought to have kicked them into the room – then he himself might have kicked them out.

'And you told me to remind you, sir—'

George Dane was at last angry. 'Remind me of nothing!'

'But you insisted, sir, that I was to insist!'

He turned away in despair, speaking with a pathetic quaver at absurd variance with his words: 'If you insist, Brown, I'll kill you!' He found himself anew at the window, whence, looking down from his fourth floor, he could see the vast neighbourhood, under the trumpet-blare of the sky, beginning to rush about. There was a silence, but he knew Brown had not left him – knew exactly how straight and serious and stupid and faithful he stood there. After a minute he heard him again.

'It's only because, sir, you know, sir, you can't remember—'

At this Dane did flash round; it was more than at such a moment he could bear. 'Can't remember, Brown? I can't forget. That's what's the matter with me.'

Brown looked at him with the advantage of eighteen years of consistency. 'I'm afraid you're not well, sir.'

Brown's master thought. 'It's a shocking thing to say, but I wish to heaven I weren't! It would be perhaps an excuse.'

Brown's blankness spread like the desert. 'To put them off?'

'Ah!' The sound was a groan; the plural pronoun, *any* pronoun, so mistimed. 'Who is it?'

'Those ladies you spoke of – to lunch.'

'Oh!' The poor man dropped into the nearest chair and stared a while at the carpet. It was very complicated.

'How many will there be, sir?' Brown asked.

'Fifty!'

'Fifty, sir?'

Our friend, from his chair, looked vaguely about; under his hand were the telegrams, still unopened, one of which he now tore asunder. '"Do hope you sweetly won't mind, today, 1.30, my bringing poor dear Lady Mullet, who is so awfully bent,"' he read to his companion.

His companion weighed it. 'How many does *she* make, sir?'

'Poor dear Lady Mullet? I haven't the least idea.'

'Is she – a – deformed, sir?' Brown inquired, as if in this case she might make more.

His master wondered, then saw he figured some personal curvature. 'No; she's only bent on coming!' Dane opened the other telegram and again read out: '"So sorry it's at eleventh hour impossible, and count on you here, as very greatest favour, at two sharp instead."'

'How many does *that* make?' Brown imperturbably continued.

Dane crumpled up the two missives and walked with them to the waste-paper basket, into which he thoughtfully dropped them. 'I can't say. You must do it all yourself. I shan't be there.'

It was only on this that Brown showed an expression. 'You'll go instead—'

'I'll go instead!' Dane raved.

Brown, however, had had occasion to show before that *he* would never desert their post. 'Isn't that rather sacrificing the three?' Between respect and reproach he paused.

'*Are* there three?'

'I lay for four in all.'

His master had, at any rate, caught his thought. 'Sacrificing the three to the one, you mean? Oh, I'm not going to *her*!'

Brown's famous 'thoroughness' – his great virtue – had never been so dreadful. 'Then where *are* you going?'

Dane sat down to his table and stared at his ragged phrase. '"There is a happy land – far, far away!"' He chanted it like a sick child and knew that for a minute Brown never moved. During this minute he felt between his shoulders the gimlet of criticism.

'Are you quite sure you're all right?'

'It's my certainty that overwhelms me, Brown. Look about you and judge. Could anything be more "right", in the view of the envious world, than everything that surrounds us here; that immense array of letters, notes, circulars; that pile of printers' proofs, magazines and books; these perpetual telegrams, these impending guests; this retarded, unfinished and interminable work? What could a man want more?'

'Do you mean there's too much, sir?' – Brown had sometimes these flashes.

'There's too much. There's too much. But *you* can't help it, Brown.'

'No, sir,' Brown assented. 'Can't *you*?'

'I'm thinking – I must see. There are hours—!' Yes, there were hours, and this was one of them: he jerked himself up for another turn in his labyrinth, but still not touching, not even again meeting, his interlocutor's eye. If he was a genius for anyone he was a genius for Brown; but it was terrible what that meant, being a genius for Brown. There had been times when he had done full justice to the way it kept him up; now, however, it was almost the worst of the avalanche. 'Don't trouble about me,' he went on insincerely and looking askance through his window again at the bright and beautiful world. 'Perhaps it will rain – that *may* not be over. I do love the rain,' he weakly pursued. 'Perhaps, better still, it will snow.'

Brown now had indeed a perceptible expression, and the expression was fear. 'Snow, sir – the end of May?' Without pressing this point he looked at his watch. 'You'll feel better when you've had breakfast.'

'I daresay,' said Dane, whom breakfast struck in fact as a pleasant alternative to opening letters. 'I'll come in immediately.'

'But without waiting—?'

'Waiting for what?'

Brown had at last, under his apprehension, his first lapse from logic, which he betrayed by hesitating in the evident hope that his companion would, by a flash of remembrance, relieve him of an invidious duty. But the only flashes now were the good man's own. 'You say you can't forget, sir; but you do forget—'

'Is it anything very horrible?' Dane broke in.

Brown hung fire. 'Only the gentleman you told me you had asked—'

Dane again took him up; horrible or not, it came back – indeed its mere coming back classed it. 'To breakfast today? It *was* today; I see.' It came back, yes, came back; the appointment with the young man – he supposed him young – and whose letter, the letter about – what was it? – had struck him. 'Yes, yes; wait, wait.'

'Perhaps he'll do you good, sir,' Brown suggested.

'Sure to – sure to. All right!' Whatever he might do, he would at least prevent some other doing: that was present to our friend as, on the vibration of the electric bell at the door of the flat, Brown moved away. Two things, in the short interval that followed, were present to Dane: his having utterly forgotten the connection, the whence, whither and why of his guest; and his continued disposition not to touch – no, not with the finger. Ah, if he might *never* again touch! All the unbroken seals and neglected appeals lay there while, for a pause that he couldn't measure, he stood before the chimney-piece with his hands still in his pockets. He heard a brief exchange of words in the hall, but never afterward recovered the time taken by Brown to reappear, to precede and announce another person – a person whose name, somehow, failed to reach Dane's ear. Brown went off again to serve breakfast, leaving host and guest confronted. The duration of this first stage also, later on, defied measurement; but that little mattered, for in the train of what happened came promptly the second, the third, the fourth, the rich succession of the others. Yet what happened was but that Dane took his hand from his pocket, held it straight out and felt it taken. Thus indeed, if he had wanted never again to touch, it was already done.

## II

HE MIGHT HAVE been a week in the place – the scene of his new consciousness – before he spoke at all. The occasion of it then was that one of the quiet figures he had been idly watching drew at last nearer and showed him a face that was the highest expression – to his pleased but as yet slightly confused perception – of the general charm. What *was* the general charm? He couldn't, for that matter, easily have phrased it; it was such an abyss of negatives, such an absence of everything. The oddity was that, after a minute, he was struck as by the reflection of his own very image in this first interlocutor seated with him, on the easy bench, under the high, clear portico and above the wide, far-reaching garden, where the things that most showed in the greenness were the surface of still water and the white note of old statues. The absence of everything was, in the aspect of the Brother who had thus informally joined him – a man of his own age, tired, distinguished, modest, kind – really, as he could soon see, but the absence of what he didn't want. He didn't want, for the time, anything but just to *be* there, to stay in the bath. He was in the bath yet, the broad, deep bath of stillness. They sat in it together now, with the water up to their chins. He had not had to talk, he had not had to think, he had scarce even had to feel. He had been sunk that way before, sunk – when and where? – in another flood; only a flood of rushing waters, in which bumping and gasping were all. This was a current so slow and so tepid that one floated practically without motion and without chill. The break of silence was not immediate, though Dane seemed indeed to feel it begin before a sound passed. It could pass quite sufficiently without words that he and his mate were Brothers, and what that meant.

Dane wondered, but with no want of ease – for want of ease was impossible – if his friend found in *him* the same likeness, the proof of peace, the gauge of what the place could do. The long afternoon crept to its end; the shadows fell further and the sky glowed deeper; but nothing changed – nothing *could* change – in the element itself. It was a conscious security. It was wonderful! Dane had lived into it, but he was still immensely aware. He would have been sorry to lose that, for just this fact, as yet, the blessed fact of consciousness, seemed the greatest thing of all. Its only fault was that, being in itself such an occupation, so fine an unrest in the heart of gratitude, the life of the day all went to it. But what even then was the harm? He had come only to come, to take what he found. This was the part where the great cloister, enclosed externally on three sides and probably the largest, lightest, fairest effect, to his charmed sense, that human hands could ever have expressed in dimensions of length and breadth, opened to the south its splendid fourth quarter, turned to the great view an outer gallery that combined with the rest of the portico to form a high, dry loggia, such as he a little pretended to himself he had, in Italy, in old days, seen in old cities, old convents, old villas. This recall of the disposition of some great abode of an Order, some mild Monte Cassino, some Grande Chartreuse more accessible, was his main term of comparison; but he knew he had really never anywhere beheld anything at once so calculated and so generous.

Three impressions in particular had been with him all the week, and he could only recognize in silence their happy effect on his nerves. How it was all managed he couldn't have told – he had been content moreover till now with his ignorance of cause and pretext; but whenever he chose to listen with a certain intentness he made out, as from a distance, the sound of slow, sweet bells. How could they be so far and yet so audible? How could they be so near and yet so faint? How, above all, could they, in such an arrest of life, be, to *time* things, so frequent? The very essence of the bliss of Dane's whole change had been precisely that there was nothing now to time. It was the same with the slow footsteps that always, within earshot, to the vague attention, marked the space and the leisure, seemed, in long, cool arcades, lightly to fall and perpetually to recede. This was the second impression, and it melted into the third, as, for that matter, every form of softness, in the great good place, was but a further turn, without jerk or gap, of the endless roll of serenity. The quiet footsteps were quiet figures; the quiet figures that, to the eye, kept the picture human and brought its perfection within reach. This perfection, he felt on the bench by his friend, was now more in reach that ever. His friend at last turned to him a look different from the looks of friends in London clubs.

'The thing was to find it out!'

It was extraordinary how this remark fitted into his thought. 'Ah, wasn't it? And when I think,' said Dane, 'of all the people who haven't and who never will!' He sighed over these unfortunates with a tenderness that, in its degree, was practically new to him, feeling, too, how well his companion would know the people he meant. He only meant some, but they were all who would want it; though of these, no doubt – well, for reasons, for things that, in the world, he had observed – there would never be too many. Not all perhaps who wanted would really find; but none at least would find who didn't really want. And then what the need would have to have been first! What it at first had to be for himself! He felt afresh, in the light of his companion's face, what it might still be even when deeply satisfied, as well as what communication was established by the mere mutual knowledge of it.

'Every man must arrive by himself and on his own feet – isn't that so? We're brothers here for the time, as in a great monastery, and we immediately think of each other and recognize each other as such; but we must have first got here as we can, and we meet after long journeys by complicated ways. Moreover we meet – don't we? – with closed eyes.'

'Ah, don't speak as if we were dead!' Dane laughed.

'I shan't mind death if it's like this,' his friend replied.

It was too obvious, as Dane gazed before him, that one wouldn't but after a moment he asked, with the first articulation, as yet, of his most elementary wonder: 'Where is it?'

'I shouldn't be surprised if it were much nearer than one ever suspected.'

'Nearer town, do you mean?'

'Nearer everything – nearer everyone.'

George Dane thought. 'Somewhere, for instance, down in Surrey?'

His Brother met him on this with a shade of reluctance. 'Why should we call it names? It must have a climate, you see.'

'Yes,' Dane happily mused; 'without that—!' All it so securely did have overwhelmed him again, and he couldn't help breaking out: '*What* is it?'

'Oh, it's positively a part of our ease and our rest and our change, I think, that we don't at all know and that we may really call it, for that matter, anything in the world we like – the thing, for instance, we love it most for being.'

'I know what *I* call it,' said Dane after a moment. Then as his friend listened with interest: 'Just simply "The Great Good Place".'

'I see – what can you say more? I've put it to myself perhaps a little differently.' They sat there as innocently as small boys confiding to each other the names of toy animals. 'The Great Want Met.'

'Ah, yes, that's it!'

'Isn't it enough for us that it's a place carried on, for our benefit, so admirably that we strain our ears in vain for a creak of the machinery? Isn't it enough for us that it's simply a thorough hit?'

'Ah, a hit!' Dane benignantly murmured.

'It does for us what it pretends to do,' his companion went on; 'the mystery isn't deeper than that. The thing is probably simple enough in fact, and on a thoroughly practical basis; only it has had its origin in a splendid thought, in a real stroke of genius.'

'Yes,' Dane exclaimed, 'in a sense – on somebody or other's part – so exquisitely personal!'

'Precisely – it rests, like all good things, on experience. The "great want" comes home – that's the great thing it does! On the day it came home to the right mind this dear place was constituted. It always, moreover, in the long run, *has* been met – it always must be. How can it not require to be, more and more, as pressure of every sort grows?'

Dane, with his hands folded in his lap, took in these words of wisdom. 'Pressure of every sort *is* growing!' he placidly observed.

'I see well enough what that fact has done to *you*,' his Brother returned.

Dane smiled. 'I couldn't have borne it longer. I don't know what would have become of me.'

'I know what would have become of *me*.'

'Well, it's the same thing.'

# The Great Good Place

'Yes,' said Dane's companion, 'it's doubtless the same thing.' On which they sat in silence a little, seeming pleasantly to follow, in the view of the green garden, the vague movements of the monster – madness, surrender, collapse – they had escaped. Their bench was like a box at the opera. 'And I may perfectly, you know,' the Brother pursued, 'have seen you before. I may even have known you well. We don't know.'

They looked at each other again serenely enough, and at last Dane said: 'No, we don't know.'

'That's what I meant by our coming with our eyes closed. Yes – there's something out. There's a gap – a link missing, the great hiatus!' the Brother laughed. 'It's as simple a story as the old, old rupture – the break that lucky Catholics have always been able to make, that they are still, with their innumerable religious houses, able to make, by going into "retreat". I don't speak of the pious exercises; I speak only of the material simplification. I don't speak of the putting off of one's self; I speak only – if one has a self worth sixpence – of the getting it back. The place, the time, the way were, for those of the old persuasion, always there – are indeed practically there for them as much as ever. They can always get off – the blessed houses receive. So it was high time that we – we of the great Protestant peoples, still more, if possible, in the sensitive individual case, overscored and overwhelmed, still more congested with mere quantity and prostituted, through our "enterprise", to mere profanity – should learn how to get off, should find somewhere *our* retreat and remedy. There was such a huge chance for it!'

Dane laid his hand on his companion's arm. 'It's charming, how, when we speak for ourselves, we speak for each other. That was exactly what I said!' He had fallen to recalling from over the gulf the last occasion.

The Brother, as if it would do them both good, only desired to draw him out. 'What you said—?'

'To *him* – that morning.' Dane caught a far bell again and heard a slow footstep. A quiet figure passed somewhere – neither of them turned to look. What was, little by little, more present to him was the perfect taste. It was supreme – it was everywhere. 'I just dropped my burden – and he received it.'

'And was it very great?'

'Oh, such a load!' Dane laughed.

'Trouble, sorrow, doubt?'

'Oh, no; worse than that!'

'Worse?'

'"Success" – the vulgarest kind!' And Dane laughed again.

'Ah, I know that, too! No one in future, as things are going, will be able to face success.'

'Without something of this sort – never. The better it is the worse – the greater the deadlier. But my one pain here,' Dane continued, 'is in thinking of my poor friend.'

'The person to whom you've already alluded?'

'My substitute in the world. Such an unutterable benefactor. He turned up that morning when everything had somehow got on my nerves, when the whole great globe indeed, nerves, or no nerves, seemed to have squeezed itself into my study. It wasn't a question of nerves, it was a mere question of the displacement of everything – of submersion by our eternal too much. I didn't know *où donner de la tête* – I couldn't have gone a step further.'

The intelligence with which the Brother listened kept them as children feeding from the same bowl. 'And then you got the tip?'

'I got the tip!' Dane happily sighed.

'Well, we all get it. But I daresay differently.'

'Then how did *you*——?'

The Brother hesitated, smiling. 'You tell me first.'

## III

'WELL,' said George Dane, 'it was a young man I had never seen – a man, at any rate, much younger than myself – who had written to me and sent me some article, some book. I read the stuff, was much struck with it, told him so and thanked him – on which, of course, I heard from him again. He asked me things – his questions were interesting; but to save time and writing I said to him: "Come to see me – we can talk a little; but all I can give you is half an hour at breakfast." He turned up at the hour on a day when, more than ever in my life before, I seemed, as it happened, in the endless press and stress, to have lost possession of my soul and to be surrounded only with the affairs of other people and the irrelevant, destructive, brutalizing sides of life. It made me literally ill – made me feel as I had never felt that if I should once really, for an hour, lose hold of the thing itself, the thing I was trying for, I should never recover it again. The wild waters would close over me, and I should drop straight to the bottom where the vanquished dead lie.'

'I follow you every step of your way,' said the friendly Brother. 'The wild waters, you mean, of our horrible time.'

'Of our horrible time – precisely. Not, of course – as we sometimes dream – of any other.'

'Yes, any other is only a dream. We really know none but our own.'

'No, thank God – that's enough,' Dane said. 'Well, my young man turned up, and I hadn't been a minute in his presence before making out that practically it would be in him somehow or other to help me. He came to me with envy, envy extravagant – really passionate. I was, heaven save us, the great "success" for him; he himself was broken and beaten. How can I say what passed between us? – it was so strange, so swift, so much a matter, from one to the other, of instant perception and agreement. He was so clever and haggard and hungry!'

'Hungry?' the Brother asked.

'I don't mean for bread, though he had none too much, I think, even of that. I mean for – well, what *I* had and what I was a monument of to him as I stood there up to my neck in preposterous evidence. He, poor chap, had been for ten years serenading closed windows and had never yet caused a shutter to show that it stirred. My dim blind was the first to be raised an inch; my reading of his book, my impression of it, my note and my invitation, formed literally the only response ever dropped into his dark street. He saw in my littered room, my shattered day, my bored face and spoiled temper – it's embarrassing, but I must tell you – the very blaze of my glory. And he saw in the blaze of my glory – deluded innocent! – what he had yearned for in vain.'

'What he had yearned for was to *be* you,' said the Brother. Then he added: 'I see where you're coming out.'

'At my saying to him by the end of five minutes: "My dear fellow, I wish you'd just try it – wish you'd, for a while, just *be* me!" You go straight to the mark, and that was exactly what occurred – extraordinary though it was that we should both have understood. I saw what he could give, and he did too. He saw moreover what I could take; in fact what he saw was wonderful.'

'He must be very remarkable!' the Brother laughed.

'There's no doubt of it whatever – far more remarkable than I. That's just the reason why what I put to him in joke – with a fantastic, desperate irony – became, on his hands, with his vision of his chance, the blessed guarantee of my sitting on this spot in your company. "Oh, if I could just shift it all – make it straight over for an hour to other shoulders! If there only *were* a pair!" – that's the way I put it to him. And then at something in his face, "Would *you*, by a miracle, undertake it?" I asked. I let him know all it meant – how it meant that he should at that very moment step in. It meant that he should finish my work and open my letters and keep my engagements and be subject, for better or worse, to my contacts and complications. It meant that he should live with my life, and think with my brain, and write with my hand, and speak with my voice. It meant, above all, that I should get off. He accepted with magnificence – rose to it like a hero. Only he said: "What will become of *you*?"'

'There was the hitch!' the Brother admitted.

'Ah, but only for a minute. He came to my help again,' Dane pursued, 'when he saw I couldn't quite meet that, could at least only say that I wanted to think, wanted to cease, wanted to do the thing itself – the thing I was trying for, miserable me, and that thing only – and therefore wanted first of all really to *see* it again, planted out, crowded out, frozen out as it now so long had been. "I know what you want," he after a moment quietly remarked to me. "Ah, what I want doesn't exist!" "I know what you want," he repeated. At that I began to believe him.'

'Had you any idea yourself?' the Brother asked.

'Oh, yes,' said Dane, 'and it was just my idea that made me despair. There it was as sharp as possible in my imagination and my longing – there it was so utterly *not* in fact. We were sitting together on my sofa as we waited for breakfast. He presently laid his hand on my knee – showed me a face that the sudden great light in it had made, for me, indescribably beautiful. "It exists – it exists," he at last said. And so, I remember, we sat a while and looked at each other, with the final effect of my finding that I absolutely believed him. I remember we weren't at all solemn – we smiled with the joy of discoverers. He was as glad as I – he was tremendously glad. That came out in the whole manner of his reply to the appeal that broke from me: "Where is it, then, in God's name? Tell me without delay where it is!"'

The Brother had attended with a sympathy! 'He gave you the address?'

'He was thinking it out – feeling for it, catching it. He has a wonderful head of his own and must be making of the whole thing, while we sit here gossiping, something much better than ever *I* did. The mere sight of his face, the sense of his hand on my knee, made me, after a little, feel that he not only knew what I wanted, but was getting nearer to it than I could have got in ten years. He suddenly sprang up and went over to my study-table – sat straight down there as if to write me my passport. Then it was – at the mere sight of his back, which was turned to me – that I felt the spell work. I simply sat and watched him with the queerest, deepest, sweetest sense in the world – the sense of an ache that had stopped. All life was lifted; I myself at least was somehow off the ground. He was already where I had been.'

'And where were you?' the Brother amusedly inquired.

'Just on the sofa always, leaning back on the cushion and feeling a delicious ease. He was already me.'

'And who were you?' the Brother continued.

'Nobody. That was the fun.'

'That *is* the fun,' said the Brother, with a sigh like soft music.

Dane echoed the sigh, and, as nobody talking with nobody, they sat there together still and watched the sweet wide picture darken into tepid night.

## IV

AT THE END of three weeks – so far as time was distinct – Dane began to feel there was something he had recovered. It was the thing they never named – partly for want of the need and partly for lack of the word; for what indeed was the description that would cover it all? The only real need was to know it, to see it, in silence. Dane had a private, practical sign for it, which, however, he had appropriated by theft – 'the vision and the faculty divine'. That, doubtless, was a flattering phrase for his idea of his genius; the genius, at all events, was what he had been in danger of losing and had at last held by a thread that might at any moment have broken. The change was that, little by little, his hold had grown firmer, so that he drew in the line – more and more each day – with a pull that he was delighted to find it would bear. The mere dream-sweetness of the place was superseded; it was more and more a world of reason and order, of sensible, visible arrangement. It ceased to be strange – it was high, triumphant clearness. He cultivated, however, but vaguely, the question of where he was, finding it near enough the mark to be almost sure that if he was not in Kent he was probably in Hampshire. He paid for everything but that – that wasn't one of the items. Payment, he had soon learned, was definite; it consisted of sovereigns and shillings – just like those of the world he had left, only parted with more ecstatically – that he put, in his room, in a designated place and that were taken away in his absence by one of the unobtrusive, effaced agents – shadows projected on the hours like the noiseless march of the sun-dial – that were always at work. The institution had sides that had their recalls, and a pleased, resigned perception of these things was at once the effect and the cause of its grace.

Dane picked out of his dim past a dozen halting similes. The sacred, silent convent was one; another was the bright country-house. He did the place no outrage to liken it to an hotel; he permitted himself on occasion to trace its resemblance to a club. Such images, however, but flickered and went out – they lasted only long enough to light up the difference. An hotel without noise, a club without newspapers – when he turned his face to what it was 'without' the view opened wide. The only approach to a real analogy was in himself and his companions. They were brothers, guests, members; they were even, if one liked – and they didn't in the least mind what they were called – 'regular boarders'. It was not they who made the conditions, it was the conditions that made them. These conditions found themselves accepted, clearly, with an appreciation, with a rapture, it was rather to be called, that had to do – as the very air that pervaded them and the force that sustained – with their quiet and noble assurance. They combined to form the large, simple idea of a general refuge – an image of embracing arms, of liberal accommodation. What was the effect, really, but the poetization by perfect taste of a type common enough? There was no daily miracle; the perfect taste, with the aid of space, did the trick. What underlay and overhung it all, better yet, Dane mused, was some original inspiration, but confirmed, unquenched, some happy thought of an individual breast. It had been born somehow and somewhere – it had had to insist on being – the blessed conception. The author might remain in the obscure, for that was part of the perfection: personal service so hushed and regulated that you scarce caught it in the act and only knew it by its results. Yet the wise mind was everywhere – the whole thing, infallibly, centred, at the core, in a consciousness. And what a consciousness it had been, Dane thought, a consciousness how like his own! The wise mind had felt, the wise mind had suffered: then, for all the worried company of minds, the wise mind had seen a chance. Of the creation thus arrived at you could none the less never have said if it were the last echo of the old or the sharpest note of the modern.

Dane again and again, among the far bells and the soft footfalls, in cool cloister and warm garden, found himself wanting not to know more and yet liking not to know less. It was part of the general beauty that there was no personal publicity, much less any personal success. Those things were in the world – in what he had left; there was no vulgarity here of credit or claim or fame. The real exquisite was to be without the complication of an identity, and the greatest boon of all, doubtless, the solid security, the clear confidence one could feel in the keeping of the contract. That was what had been most in the wise mind – the importance of the absolute sense, on the part of its beneficiaries, that what was offered was guaranteed. They had no concern but to pay – the wise mind knew what they paid for. It was present to Dane each hour that he could never be overcharged. Oh, the deep, deep bath, the soft, cool plash in the stillness! – this, time after time, as if under regular treatment, a sublimated German 'cure', was the vivid name for his luxury. The inner life woke up again, and it was the inner life, for people of his generation, victims of the modern madness, mere maniacal extension and motion, that was returning health. He had talked of independence and written of it, but what a cold, flat word it had been! This was the wordless fact itself – the uncontested possession of the long, sweet, stupid day. The fragrance of flowers just wandered through the void, and the quiet recurrence of delicate, plain fare in a high, clean refectory where the soundless, simple service was the triumph of art. That, as he analysed, remained the constant explanation: all the sweetness and serenity were created, calculated things. He analysed, however, but in a desultory way and with a positive delight in the residuum of mystery that made for the great artist in the background the innermost shrine of the idol of a temple; there were odd moments for it, mild meditations when, in the broad cloister of peace or some garden-nook where the air was light, a special glimpse of beauty or reminder of felicity seemed, in passing, to hover and linger. In the mere ecstasy of change that had at first possessed him he had not discriminated – had only let himself sink, as I have mentioned, down to hushed depths. Then had come the slow, soft stages of intelligence and notation, more marked and more fruitful perhaps after that long talk with his mild mate in the twilight, and seeming to wind up the process by putting the key into his hand. This key, pure gold, was simply the cancelled list. Slowly and blissfully he read into the general wealth of his comfort all the particular absences of which it was composed. One by one he touched, as it were, all the things it was such rapture to be without.

It was the paradise of his own room that was most indebted to them – a great square, fair chamber, all beautified with omissions, from which, high up, he looked over a long valley to a far horizon, and in which he was vaguely and pleasantly reminded of some old Italian picture, some Carpaccio or some early Tuscan, the representation of a world without newspapers and letters, without telegrams and photographs, without the dreadful, fatal too much. There, for a blessing, he *could* read and write; there, above all, he could do nothing – he could live. And there were all sorts of freedoms – always, for the occasion, the particular right one. He could bring a book from the library – he could bring two, he could bring three. An effect produced by the charming place was that, for some reason, he never wanted to bring more. The library was a benediction – high and clear and plain, like everything else, but with something, in all its arched amplitude, unconfused and brave and gay. He should never forget, he knew, the throb of immediate perception with which he first stood there, a single glance round sufficing so to show him that it would give him what for years he had desired. He had not had detachment, but there was detachment here – the sense of a great silver bowl from which he could ladle up the melted hours. He strolled about from wall to wall, too pleasantly in tune on that occasion to sit down punctually or to choose; only recognizing from shelf to shelf every dear old book that he had to take for lost and unheard. He came back, of course, soon, came back every day; enjoyed there, of all the rare, strange moments, those that were at once most quickened and most caught – moments in which every apprehension counted double and every act of the mind was a lover's embrace. It was the quarter he perhaps, as the days went on, liked best; though indeed it only shared with the rest of the place, with every aspect to which his face happened to be turned, the power to remind him of the masterly general control.

There were times when he looked up from his book to lose himself in the mere tone of the picture that never failed at any moment or at any angle. The picture was always there, yet was made up of things common enough. It was in the way an open window in a broad recess let in the pleasant morning; in the way the dry air pricked into faint freshness the gilt of old bindings; in the way an empty chair beside a table unlittered showed a volume just laid down; in the way a happy Brother – as detached as oneself and with his innocent back presented – lingered before a shelf with the slow sound of turned pages. It was a part of the whole impression that, by some extraordinary law, one's vision seemed less from the facts than the facts from one's vision; that the elements were determined at the moment by the moment's need or the moment's sympathy. What most prompted this reflection was the degree in which, after a while, Dane had a consciousness of company. After that talk with the good Brother on the bench there were other good Brothers in other places – always in cloister or garden some figure that stopped if he himself stopped and with which a greeting became, in the easiest way in the world, a sign of the diffused amenity. Always, always, however, in all contacts, was the balm of a happy ignorance. What he had felt the first time recurred: the friend was always new and yet at the same time – it was amusing, not disturbing – suggested the possibility that he might be but an old one altered. That was only delightful – as positively delightful in the particular, the actual conditions as it might have been the reverse in the conditions abolished. These others, the abolished, came back to Dane at last so easily that he could exactly measure each difference, but with what he had finally been hustled on to hate in them robbed of its terror in consequence of something that had happened. What had happened was that in tranquil walks and talks the deep spell had worked and he had got his soul again. He had drawn in by this time, with his lightened hand, the whole of the long line, and that fact just dangled at the end. He could put his other hand on it, he could unhook it, he was once more in possession. This, as it befell, was exactly what he supposed he must have said to a comrade beside whom, one afternoon in the cloister, he found himself measuring steps.

'Oh, it comes – comes of itself, doesn't it, thank goodness? – just by the simple fact of finding room and time!'

The comrade was possibly a novice or in a different stage from his own; there was at any rate a vague envy in the recognition that shone out of the fatigued, yet freshened face. 'It has come to *you* then? – you've got what you wanted?' That was the gossip and interchange that could pass to and fro. Dane, years before, had gone in for three months of hydropathy, and there was a droll echo, in this scene, of the old questions of the water-cure, the questions asked in the periodical pursuit of the 'reaction' – the ailment, the progress of each, the action of the skin and the state of the appetite. Such memories worked in now – all familiar reference, all easy play of mind; and among them our friends, round and round, fraternized ever so softly, until, suddenly stopping short, Dane, with a hand on his companion's arm, broke into the happiest laugh he had yet sounded.

## V

'WHY, it's raining!' And he stood and looked at the splash of the shower and the shine of the wet leaves. It was one of the summer sprinkles that bring out sweet smells.

'Yes – but why not?' his mate demanded.

'Well – because it's so charming. It's so exactly right.'

'But everything *is*. Isn't that just why we're here?'

'Just exactly,' Dane said; 'only I've been living in the beguiled supposition that we've somehow or other a climate.'

'So have I; so, I daresay, has everyone. Isn't that the blessed moral? – that we live in beguiled suppositions. They come so easily here, and nothing contradicts them.' The good Brother looked placidly forth – Dane could identify his phase. 'A climate doesn't consist in its never raining, does it?'

'No, I daresay not. But somehow the good I've got has been half the great, easy absence of all that friction of which the question of weather mostly forms a part – has been indeed largely the great, easy, perpetual air-bath.'

'Ah, yes – that's not a delusion; but perhaps the sense comes a little from our breathing an emptier medium. There are fewer things *in* it! Leave people alone, at all events, and the air is what they take to. Into the closed and the stuffy they have to be driven. I've had, too – I think we must all have – a fond sense of the south.'

'But imagine it,' said Dane, laughing, 'in the beloved British islands and so near as we are to Bradford!'

His friend was ready enough to imagine. 'To Bradford?' he asked, quite unperturbed. 'How near?'

Dane's gaiety grew. 'Oh, it doesn't matter!'

His friend, quite unmystified, accepted it. 'There are things to puzzle out – otherwise it would be dull. It seems to me one can puzzle them.'

'It's because we're so well disposed,' Dane said.

'Precisely – we find good in everything.'

'In everything,' Dane went on. 'The conditions settle that – they determine us.'

They resumed their stroll, which evidently represented on the good Brother's part infinite agreement. 'Aren't they probably in fact very simple?' he presently inquired. 'Isn't simplification the secret?'

'Yes, but applied with a tact!'

'There it is. The thing's so perfect that it's open to as many interpretations as any other great work – a poem of Goethe, a dialogue of Plato, a symphony of Beethoven.'

'It simply stands quiet, you mean,' said Dane, 'and lets us call it names?'

'Yes, but all such loving ones. We're "staying" with someone – some delicious host or hostess who never shows.'

'It's liberty-hall – absolutely,' Dane assented.

'Yes – or a convalescent home.'

To this, however, Dane demurred. 'Ah, that, it seems to me, scarcely puts it. You weren't *ill* – were you? I'm very sure *I* really wasn't. I was only, as the world goes, too "beastly well"!'

The good Brother wondered. 'But if we couldn't keep it up—?'

'We couldn't keep it *down* – that was all the matter!'

'I see – I see.' The good Brother sighed contentedly; after which he brought out again with kindly humour: 'It's a sort of kindergarten!'

'The next thing you'll be saying that we're babes at the breast!'

'Of some great mild, invisible mother who stretches away into space and whose lap is the whole valley—?'

'And her bosom –' Dane completed the figure – 'the noble eminence of our hill? That will do; anything will do that covers the essential fact.'

'And what do you call the essential fact?'

'Why, that – as in old days on Swiss lake-sides – we're *en pension*.'

The good Brother took this gently up. 'I remember – I remember: seven francs a day without wine! But, alas, it's more than seven francs here.'

'Yes, it's considerably more,' Dane had to confess. 'Perhaps it isn't particularly cheap.'

'Yet should you call it particularly dear?' his friend after a moment inquired.

George Dane had to think. 'How do I know, after all? What practice has one ever had in estimating the inestimable? Particular cheapness certainly isn't the note that we feel struck all round; but don't we fall naturally into the view that there *must* be a price to anything so awfully sane?'

The good Brother in his turn reflected. 'We fall into the view that it must pay – that it does pay.'

'Oh, yes; it does pay!' Dane eagerly echoed. 'If it didn't it wouldn't last. It has *got* to last, of course!' he declared.

'So that we can come back?'

'Yes – think of knowing that we shall be able to!'

They pulled up again at this and, facing each other, thought of it, or at any rate pretended to; for what was really in their eyes was the dread of a loss of the clue. 'Oh, when we want it again we shall find it,' said the good Brother. 'If the place really pays, it will keep on.'

'Yes, that's the beauty; that it isn't, thank heaven, carried on only for love.'

'No doubt, no doubt; and yet, thank heaven, there's love in it too.' They had lingered as if, in the mild, moist air, they were charmed with the patter of the rain and the way the garden drank it. After a little, however, it did look rather as if they were trying to talk each other out of a faint, small fear. They saw the increasing rage of life and the recurrent need, and they wondered proportionately whether to return to the front when their hour should sharply strike would be the end of the dream. Was this a threshold perhaps, after all, that could only be crossed one way? They must return to the front sooner or later – that was certain: for each his hour would strike. The flower would have been gathered and the trick played – the sands, in short, would have run.

There, in its place, *was* life – with all its rage; the vague unrest of the need for action knew it again, the stir of the faculty that had been refreshed and reconsecrated. They seemed each, thus confronted, to close their eyes a moment for dizziness; then they were again at peace, and the Brother's confidence rang out. 'Oh, we shall meet!'

'Here, do you mean?'

'Yes – and I daresay in the world too.'

'But we shan't recognize or know,' said Dane.

'In the world, do you mean?'

'Neither in the world nor here.'

'Not a bit – not the least little bit, you think?'

Dane turned it over. 'Well, so it is that it seems to me all best to hang together. But we shall see.'

His friend happily concurred. 'We shall see.' And at this, for farewell, the Brother held out his hand.

'You're going?' Dane asked.

'No, but I thought *you* were.'

It was odd, but at this Dane's hour seemed to strike – his consciousness to crystallize. 'Well, I am. I've got it. You stay?' he went on.

'A little longer.'

Dane hesitated. 'You haven't yet got it?'

'Not altogether – but I think it's coming.'

'Good!' Dane kept his hand, giving it a final shake, and at that moment the sun glimmered again through the shower, but with the rain still falling on the hither side of it and seeming to patter even more in the brightness. 'Hallo – how charming!'

The Brother looked a moment from under the high arch – then again turned his face to our friend. He gave this time his longest, happiest sigh. 'Oh, it's all right!'

But why was it, Dane after a moment found himself wondering, that in the act of separation his own hand was so long retained? Why but through a queer phenomenon of change, on the spot, in his companion's face – change that gave it another, but an increasing and above all a much more familiar identity, an identity not beautiful, but more and more distinct, an identity with that of his servant, with the most conspicuous, the physiognomic seat of the public propriety of Brown? To this anomaly his eyes slowly opened; it was not his good

Brother, it was verily Brown who possessed his hand. If his eyes had to open, it was because they had been closed and because Brown appeared to think he had better wake up. So much as this Dane took in, but the effect of his taking it was a relapse into darkness, a recontraction of the lids just prolonged enough to give Brown time, on a second thought, to withdraw his touch and move softly away. Dane's next consciousness was that of the desire to make sure he *was* away, and this desire had somehow the result of dissipating the obscurity. The obscurity was completely gone by the time he had made out that the back of a person writing at his study-table was presented to him. He recognized a portion of a figure that he had somewhere described to somebody – the intent shoulders of the unsuccessful young man who had come that bad morning to breakfast. It was strange, he at last reflected, but the young man was still there. How long had he stayed – days, weeks, months? He was exactly in the position in which Dane had last seen him. Everything – stranger still – was exactly in that position; everything, at least, but the light of the window, which came in from another quarter and showed a different hour. It wasn't after breakfast now; it was after – well, what? He suppressed a gasp – it was after everything. And yet – quite literally – there were but two other differences. One of these was that if he was still on the sofa he was now lying down; the other was the patter on the glass that showed him how the rain – the great rain of the night – had come back. It was the rain of the night, yet when had he last heard it? But two minutes before? Then how many were there before the young man at the table, who seemed intensely occupied, found a moment to look round at him and, on meeting his open eyes, get up and draw near?

'You've slept all day,' said the young man.

'All day?'

The young man looked at his watch. 'From ten to six. You were extraordinarily tired. I just, after a bit, let you alone, and you were soon off.' Yes, that was it; he had been 'off' – off, off, off. He began to fit it together; while he had been off the young man had been on. But there were still some few confusions; Dane lay looking up. 'Everything's done,' the young man continued.

'Everything?'

'Everything.'

Dane tried to take it all in, but was embarrassed and could only say weakly and quite apart from the matter: 'I've been so happy!'

'So have I,' said the young man. He positively looked so; seeing which George Dane wondered afresh, and then, in his wonder, read it indeed quite as another face, quite, in a puzzling way, as another person's. Everyone was a little someone else. While he asked himself who else then the young man was, this benefactor, struck by his appealing stare, broke again into perfect cheer. 'It's all right!' That answered Dane's question; the face was the face turned to him by the good Brother there in the portico while they listened together to the rustle of the shower. It was all queer, but all pleasant and all distinct, so distinct that the last words in his ear – the same from both quarters – appeared the effect of a single voice. Dane rose and looked about his room, which seemed disencumbered, different, twice as large. It *was* all right.

# Maud-Evelyn

ON SOME ALLUSION to a lady who, though unknown to myself, was known to two or three of the company, it was asked by one of these if we had heard the odd circumstance of what she had just 'come in for' – the piece of luck suddenly overtaking, in the grey afternoon of her career, so obscure and lonely a personage. We were at first, in our ignorance, mainly reduced to crude envy; but old Lady Emma, who for a while had said nothing, scarcely even appearing to listen and letting the chatter, which was indeed plainly beside the mark, subside of itself, came back from a mental absence to observe that if what had happened to Lavinia was wonderful, certainly, what had for years gone before it, led up to it, had likewise not been without some singular features. From this we perceived that Lady Emma had a story – a story moreover out of the ken even of those of her listeners acquainted with the quiet person who was the subject of it. Almost the oddest thing – as came out afterwards – was that such a situation should, for the world, have remained so in the background of this person's life. By 'afterwards' I mean simply before we separated; for what came out came on the spot, under encouragement and pressure, our common, eager solicitation. Lady Emma, who always reminded me of a fine old instrument that has first to be tuned, agreed, after a few of our scrapings and fingerings, that, having said so much, she couldn't, without wantonly tormenting us, forbear to say all. She had known Lavinia, whom she mentioned throughout only by that name, from far away, and she had also known— But what she had known I must give as nearly as possible as she herself gave it. She talked to us from her corner of the sofa, and the flicker of the firelight in her face was like the glow of memory, the play of fancy, from within.

# I

'THEN WHY on earth don't you take him?' I asked. I think that was the way that, one day when she was about twenty – before some of you perhaps were born – the affair, for me, must have begun. I put the question because I knew she had had a chance, though I didn't know how great a mistake her failure to embrace it was to prove. I took an interest because I liked them both – you see how I like young people still – and because, as they had originally met at my house, I had in a manner to answer to each for the other. I'm afraid I'm thrown baldly back on the fact that if the girl was the daughter of my earliest, almost my only governess, to whom I had remained much attached and who, after leaving me, had married – for a governess – 'well', Marmaduke (it isn't *his* real name!) was the son of one of the clever men who had – I was charming then, I assure you I was – wanted, years before, and this one as a widower, to marry me. I hadn't cared, somehow, for widowers, but even after I had taken somebody else I was conscious of a pleasant link with the boy whose stepmother it had been open to me to become and to whom it was perhaps a little a matter of vanity with me to show that I should have been for him one of the kindest. This was what the woman his father eventually did marry was not, and that threw him upon me the more.

Lavinia was one of nine, and her brothers and sisters, who have never done anything for her, help, actually, in different countries and on something, I believe, of that same scale, to people the globe. There were mixed in her then, in a puzzling way, two qualities that mostly exclude each other – an extreme timidity and, as the smallest fault that could qualify a harmless creature for a world of wickedness, a self-complacency hard in tiny, unexpected spots, for which I used sometimes to take her up, but which, I subsequently saw, would have done something for the flatness of her life had they not evaporated with everything else. She was at any rate one of those persons as to whom you don't know whether they might have been attractive if they had been happy, or might have been happy if they had been attractive. If I was a trifle vexed at her not jumping at Marmaduke, it was probably rather less because I expected wonders of him than because I thought she took her own prospect too much for granted. She had made a mistake and, before long, admitted it; yet I remember that when she expressed to me a conviction that he would ask her again, I also thought this highly probable, for in the meantime I had spoken to him. 'She does care for you,' I declared; and I can see at this moment, long ago though it be, his handsome empty young face look, on the words, as if, in spite of itself for a little, it really thought. I didn't press the matter, for he had, after all, no great things to offer; yet my conscience was easier, later on, for having not said less. He had three hundred and fifty a year from his mother, and one of his uncles had promised him something – I don't mean an allowance, but a place, if I recollect, in a business. He assured me that he loved as a man loves – a man of twenty-two! – but once. He said it, at all events, as a man says it but once.

'Well, then,' I replied, 'your course is clear.'

'To speak to her again, you mean?'

'Yes – try it.'

He seemed to try it a moment in imagination; after which, a little to my surprise, he asked: 'Would it be very awful if she should speak to *me*?'

I stared. 'Do you mean pursue you – overtake you? Ah, if you're running away—'

'I'm not running away!' – he was positive as to that. 'But when a fellow has gone so far—'

'He can't go any further? Perhaps,' I replied dryly. 'But in that case he shouldn't talk of "caring".'

'Oh, but I do, I do.'

I shook my head. 'Not if you're too proud!' On which I turned away, looking round at him again, however, after he had surprised me by a silence that seemed to accept my judgement. Then I saw he had not accepted it; I perceived it indeed to be essentially absurd. He expressed more, on this, than I had yet seen him do – had the queerest, frankest, and, for a young man of his conditions, saddest smile.

'I'm *not* proud. It isn't *in* me, If you're not, you're not, you know. I don't think I'm proud enough.'

It came over me that this was, after all, probable; yet somehow I didn't at the moment like him the less for it, though I spoke with some sharpness. 'Then what's the matter with you?'

He took a turn or two about the room, as if what he had just said had made him a little happier. 'Well, how can a man say more?' Then, just as I was on the point of assuring him that I didn't know what he had said, he went on: 'I swore to her that I would never marry. Oughtn't that to be enough?'

'To make her come after you?'

'No – I suppose scarcely that; but to make her feel sure of me – to make her wait.'

'Wait for what?'

'Well, till I come back.'

'Back from where?'

'From Switzerland – haven't I told you? I go there next month with my aunt and my cousin.'

He was quite right about not being proud – this was an alternative distinctly humble.

## II

AND YET SEE what it brought forth – the beginning of which was something that, early in the autumn, I learned from poor Lavinia. He had written to her, they were still such friends; and thus it was that she knew his aunt and his cousin to have come back without him. He had stayed on – stayed much longer and travelled much further: he had been to the Italian lakes and to Venice; he was now in Paris. At this I vaguely wondered, knowing that he was always short of funds and that he must, by his uncle's beneficence, have started on the journey on a basis of expenses paid. 'Then whom has he picked up?' I asked; but feeling sorry, as soon as I had spoken, to have made Lavinia blush. It was almost as if he had picked up some improper lady, though in this case he wouldn't have told her, and it wouldn't have saved him money.

'Oh, he makes acquaintance so quickly, knows people in two minutes,' the girl said. 'And everyone always wants to be nice to him.'

This was perfectly true, and I saw what she saw in it. 'Ah, my dear, he will have an immense circle ready for you!'

'Well,' she replied, 'if they do run after us I'm not likely to suppose it will ever be for me. It will be for *him*, and they may do to me what they like. My pleasure will be – but you'll see.' I already saw – saw at least what she supposed she herself saw: her drawing-room crowded with female fashion and her attitude angelic. 'Do you know what he said to me again before he went?' she continued.

I wondered; he *had* then spoken to her. 'That he will never, never marry—'

'Anyone but *me*!' She ingenuously took me up. 'Then you knew?'

It might be. 'I guessed.'

'And don't you believe it?'

Again I hesitated. 'Yes.' Yet all this didn't tell me why she had changed colour. 'Is it a secret – whom he's with?'

'Oh no, they seem so nice. I was only struck with the way you know him – your seeing immediately that it must be a new friendship that has kept him over. It's the devotion of the Dedricks,' Lavinia said. 'He's travelling with them.'

Once more I wondered. 'Do you mean they're taking him about?'

'Yes – they've invited him.'

No, indeed, I reflected – he wasn't proud. But what I said was: 'Who in the world are the Dedricks?'

'Kind, good people whom, last month, he accidentally met. He was walking some Swiss pass – a long, rather stupid one, I believe, without his aunt and his cousin, who had gone round some other way and were to meet him somewhere. It came on to rain in torrents, and while he was huddling under a shelter he was overtaken by some people in a carriage, who kindly made him get in. They drove him, I gather, for several hours; it began an intimacy, and they've continued to be charming to him.'

I thought a moment. 'Are they ladies?'

Her own imagination meanwhile had also strayed a little. 'I think about forty.'

'Forty ladies?'

She quickly came back. 'Oh no; I mean Mrs Dedrick is.'

'About forty? Then Miss Dedrick—'

'There isn't any Miss Dedrick.'

'No daughter?'

'Not with them, at any rate. No one but the husband.'

I thought again. 'And how old is *he*?'

Lavinia followed my example. 'Well, about forty, too.'

'About forty-two?' We laughed, but 'That's all right!' I said; and so, for the time, it seemed.

He continued absent, none the less, and I saw Lavinia repeatedly, and we always talked of him, though this represented a greater concern with his affairs than I had really supposed myself committed to. I had never sought the acquaintance of his father's people, nor seen either his aunt or his cousin, so that the account given by these relatives of the circumstances of their separation reached me at last only through the girl, to whom, also – for she knew them as little – it had circuitously come. They considered, it appeared, the poor ladies he had started with, that he had treated them ill and thrown them over, sacrificing them selfishly to company picked upon the road – a reproach deeply resented by Lavinia, though about the company too I could see she was not much more at her ease. 'How can he help it if he's so taking?' she asked; and to be properly indignant in one quarter she had to pretend to be delighted in the other. Marmaduke *was* 'taking'; yet it also came out between us at last that the Dedricks must certainly be extraordinary. We had scant added evidence, for his letters stopped, and that naturally was one of our signs. I had meanwhile leisure to reflect – it was a sort of study of the human scene I always I liked – on what to be taking consisted of. The upshot of my meditations, which experience has only confirmed, was that it consisted simply of itself. It was a quality implying no others. Marmaduke *had* no others. What indeed was his need of any?

# III

HE AT LAST, however, turned up; but then it happened that if, on his coming to see me, his immediate picture of his charming new friends quickened even more than I had expected my sense of the variety of the human species, my curiosity about them failed to make me respond when he suggested I should go to see them. It's a difficult thing to explain, and I don't pretend to put it successfully, but doesn't it often happen that one may think well enough of a person without being inflamed with the desire to meet – on the ground of any such sentiment – other persons who think still better? Somehow – little harm as there was in Marmaduke – it was but half a recommendation of the Dedricks that they were crazy about him. I didn't say this – I was careful to say little; which didn't prevent his presently asking if he mightn't then bring them to *me*. 'If not, why not?' he laughed. He laughed about everything.

'Why not? Because it strikes me that your surrender doesn't require any backing. Since you've done it you must take care of yourself.'

'Oh, but they're as safe,' he returned, 'as the Bank of England. They're wonderful – for respectability and goodness.'

'Those are precisely qualities to which my poor intercourse can contribute nothing.' He hadn't, I observed, gone so far as to tell me they would be 'fun', and he *had*, on the other hand, promptly mentioned that they lived in Westbourne Terrace. They were not forty – they were forty-five; but Mr Dedrick had already, on considerable gains, retired from some primitive profession. They were the simplest, kindest, yet most original and unusual people, and nothing could exceed, frankly, the fancy they had taken to him. Marmaduke spoke of it with a placidity of resignation that was almost irritating. I suppose I should have despised him if, after benefits accepted, he had said they bored him; yet their not boring him vexed me even more than it puzzled. 'Whom do they know?'

'No one but me. There are people in London like that.'

'Who know no one but you?'

'No – I mean no one at all. There are extraordinary people in London, and awfully nice. You haven't an idea. You people don't know everyone. They lead their lives – they go their way. One finds – what do you call it? – refinement, books, cleverness, don't you know, and music, and pictures, and religion, and an excellent table – all sorts of pleasant things. You only come across them by chance; but it's all perpetually going on.'

I assented to this: the world was very wonderful, and one must certainly see what one could. In my own quarter too I found wonders enough. 'But are you,' I asked, 'as fond of them—'

'As they are of *me*?' He took me up promptly, and his eyes were quite unclouded. 'I'm quite sure I shall become so.'

'Then are you taking Lavinia—?'

'Not to see them – no.' I saw, myself, the next minute, of course, that I had made a mistake. 'On what footing *can* I?'

I bethought myself. 'I keep forgetting you're not engaged.'

'Well,' he said after a moment, 'I shall never marry another.'

It somehow, repeated again, gave on my nerves. 'Ah, but what good will that do her, or me either, if you don't marry *her*?'

He made no answer to this – only turned away to look at something in the room; after which, when he next faced me, he had a heightened colour. 'She ought to have taken me that day,' he said gravely and gently; fixing me also as if he wished to say more.

I remember that his very mildness irritated me; some show of resentment would have been a promise that the case might still be righted. But I dropped it, the silly case, without letting him say more, and, coming back to Mr and Mrs Dedrick, asked him how in the world, without either occupation or society, they passed so much of their time. My question appeared for a moment to leave him at a loss, but he presently found light; which, at the same time, I saw on my side, really suited him better than further talk about Lavinia. 'Oh, they live for Maud-Evelyn.'

'And who's Maud-Evelyn?'

'Why, their daughter.'

'Their daughter?' I had supposed them childless.

He partly explained. 'Unfortunately they've lost her.'

'Lost her?' I required more.

He hesitated again. 'I mean that a great many people would take it that way. But *they* don't – they won't.'

I speculated. 'Do you mean other people would have given her up?'

'Yes – perhaps even tried to forget her. But the Dedricks can't.'

I wondered what she had done: had it been anything very bad? However, it was none of my business, and I only said: 'They communicate with her?'

'Oh, all the while.'

'Then why isn't she with them?'

Marmaduke thought. 'She *is* – now.'

'"Now"? Since when?'

'Well, this last year.'

'Then why do you say they've lost her?'

'Ah,' he said, smiling sadly, '*I* should call it that. I, at any rate,' he went on, 'don't see her.'

Still more I wondered. 'They keep her apart?'

He thought again. 'No, it's not that. As I say, they live for her.'

'But they don't want *you* to — is that it?'

At this he looked at me for the first time, as I thought, a little strangely. 'How *can* I?'

He put it to me as if it were bad of him, somehow, that he shouldn't; but I made, to the best of my ability, a quick end of that. 'You can't. Why in the world *should* you? Live for *my* girl. Live for Lavinia.'

# IV

I HAD unfortunately run the risk of boring him again with that idea, and, though he had not repudiated it at the time, I felt in my having returned to it the reason why he never reappeared for weeks. I saw 'my girl', as I had called her, in the interval, but we avoided with much intensity the subject of Marmaduke. It was just this that gave me my perspective for finding her constantly full of him. It determined me, in all the circumstances, not to rectify her mistake about the childlessness of the Dedricks. But whatever I left unsaid, her naming the young man was only a question of time, for at the end of a month she told me he had been twice to her mother's and that she had seen him on each of these occasions.

'Well then?'

'Well then, he's very happy.'

'And still taken up—'

'As much as ever, yes, with those people. He didn't tell me so, but I could see it.'

I could too, and her own view of it. 'What, in that case, did he tell you?'

'Nothing — but I think there's something he wants to. Only not what *you* think,' she added.

I wondered then if it were what I had had from him the last time. 'Well, what prevents him?' I asked.

'From bringing it out? I don't know.'

It was in the tone of this that she struck, to my ear, the first note of an acceptance so deep and a patience so strange that they gave me, at the end, even more food for wonderment than the rest of the business. 'If he can't speak, why does he come?'

She almost smiled. 'Well, I think I *shall* know.'

I looked at her; I remember that I kissed her. 'You're admirable; but it's very ugly.'

'Ah,' she replied, 'he only wants to be kind!'

'To *them*? Then he should let others alone. But what I call ugly is his being content to be so "beholden"—'

'To Mr and Mrs Dedrick?' She considered as if there might be many sides to it. 'But mayn't he do them some good?'

The idea failed to appeal to me. 'What good can Marmaduke do? There's one thing,' I went on, 'in case he should want you to know them. Will you promise me to refuse?'

She only looked helpless and blank. 'Making their acquaintance?'

'Seeing them, going near them – ever, ever.'

Again she brooded. 'Do you mean *you* won't?'

'Never, never.'

'Well, then, I don't think I want to.'

'Ah, but that's not a promise.' I kept her up to it. 'I want your word.'

She demurred a little. 'But why?'

'So that at least he shan't make use of you,' I said with energy.

My energy overbore her, though I saw how she would really have given herself. 'I promise, but it's only because it's something I know he will never ask.'

I differed from her at the time, believing the proposal in question to have been exactly the subject she had supposed him to be wishing to broach; but on our very next meeting I heard from her of quite another matter, upon which, as soon as she came in, I saw her to be much excited.

'You know then about the daughter without having told me? He called again yesterday,' she explained as she met my stare at her unconnected plunge, 'and now I know that he *has* wanted to speak to me. He at last brought it out.'

I continued to stare. 'Brought what?'

'Why, everything.' She looked surprised at my face. 'Didn't he tell you about Maud-Evelyn?'

I perfectly recollected, but I momentarily wondered. 'He spoke of there being a daughter, but only to say that there's something the matter with her. What is it?'

The girl echoed my words. 'What "is" it? – you dear, strange thing! The matter with her is simply that she's dead.'

'Dead?' I was naturally mystified. 'When then did she die?'

'Why, years and years ago – fifteen, I believe. As a little girl. Didn't you understand it so?'

'How *should* I? – when he spoke of her as "with" them and said that they lived for her!'

'Well,' my young friend explained, 'that's just what he meant – they live for her memory. She *is* with them in the sense that they think of nothing else.'

I found matter for surprise in this correction, but also, at first, matter for relief. At the same time it left, as I turned it over, a fresh ambiguity. 'If they think of nothing else, how can they think so much of Marmaduke?'

The difficulty struck her, though she gave me even then a dim impression of being already, as it were, rather on Marmaduke's side, or, at any rate – almost as against herself – in sympathy with the Dedricks. But her answer was prompt: 'Why, that's just their reason—that they can talk to him so much about her.'

'I see.' Yet still I wondered. 'But what's *his* interest—?'

'In being drawn into it?' Again Lavinia met her difficulty. 'Well, that she was so interesting! It appears she was lovely.'

I doubtless fairly gaped. 'A little girl in a pinafore?'

'She was out of pinafores; she was, I believe, when she died, about fourteen. Unless it was sixteen! She was at all events wonderful for beauty.'

'That's the rule. But what good does it do him if he has never seen her?'

She thought a moment, but this time she had no answer. 'Well, you must ask him!'

I determined without delay to do so; but I had before me meanwhile other contradictions. 'Hadn't I better ask him on the same occasion what he means by their "communicating"?'

Oh, this was simple. 'They go in for "mediums", don't you know, and raps, and sittings. They began a year or two ago.'

'Ah, the idiots!' I remember, at this, narrow-mindedly exclaiming. 'Do they want to drag *him* in—?'

'Not in the least; they don't desire it, and he has nothing to do with it.'

'Then where does his fun come in?'

Lavinia turned away; again she seemed at a loss. At last she brought out: 'Make him show you her little photograph.'

But I remained unenlightened. 'Is her little photograph his fun?'

Once more she coloured for him. 'Well, it represents a young loveliness!'

'That he goes about showing?'

She hesitated. 'I think he has only shown it to *me*.'

'Ah, you're just the last one!' I permitted myself to observe.

'Why so, if I'm also struck?'

There was something about her that began to escape me, and I must have looked at her hard. 'It's very good of you to be struck!'

'I don't only mean by the beauty of the face,' she went on; 'I mean by the whole thing – by that also of the attitude of the parents, their extraordinary fidelity and the way that, as he says, they have made of her memory a real religion. That was what, above all, he came to tell me about.'

I turned away from her now, and she soon afterwards left me; but I couldn't help its dropping from me before we parted that I had never supposed him to be *that* sort of fool.

## V

IF I WERE really the perfect cynic you probably think me I should frankly say that the main interest of the rest of this matter lay for me in fixing the sort of fool I *did* suppose him. But I'm afraid, after all, that my anecdote amounts mainly to a presentation of my own folly. I shouldn't be so in possession of the whole spectacle had I not ended by accepting it, and I shouldn't have accepted it had it not, for my imagination, been saved somehow from grotesqueness. Let me say at once, however, that grotesqueness, and even indeed something worse, did at first appear to me strongly to season it. After that talk with Lavinia I immediately addressed to our friend a request that he would come to see me; when I took the liberty of challenging him outright on everything she had told me. There was one point in particular that I desired to clear up and that seemed to me much more important even than the colour of Maud-Evelyn's hair or the length of her pinafores: the question, I of course mean, of my young man's good faith. Was he altogether silly or was he only altogether mercenary? I felt my choice restricted for the moment to these alternatives.

After he had said to me, 'It's as ridiculous as you please, but they've simply adopted me,' I had it out with him, on the spot, on the issue of common honesty, the question of what he was conscious, so that his self-respect should be saved, of being able to give such benefactors in return for such bounty. I'm obliged to say that to a person so inclined at the start to quarrel with him his amiability could yet prove persuasive. His contention was that the equivalent he represented was something for his friends alone to measure. He didn't for a moment pretend to sound deeper than the fancy they had taken to him. He had not, from the first, made up to them in any way: it was all their own doing, their own insistence, their own eccentricity, no doubt, and even, if I liked, their own insanity. Wasn't it enough that he was ready to declare to me, looking me straight in the eye, that he was 'really and truly' fond of them and that they didn't bore him a mite? I had evidently – didn't I see? – an ideal for him that he wasn't at all, if I didn't mind, the fellow to live up to. It was he himself who put it so, and it drew from me the pronouncement that there *was* something irresistible in the refinement of his impudence. 'I don't go near Mrs Jex,' he said – Mrs Jex was their favourite medium: 'I do find *her* ugly and vulgar and tiresome, and I hate that part of the business. Besides,' he added in words that I afterwards remembered, 'I don't require it: I do beautifully without it. But my friends themselves,' he pursued, 'though they're of a type you've never come within miles of, are not ugly, are not vulgar, are not in any degree whatever any sort of a "dose". They're, on the contrary, in their own unconventional way, the very best company. They're endlessly amusing. They're delightfully queer and quaint and kind – they're like people in some old story or of some old time. It's at any rate our own affair – mine and theirs – and I beg you to believe that I should make short work of a remonstrance on the subject from anyone but you.'

I remember saying to him three months later: 'You've never yet told me what they really want of you'; but I'm afraid this was a form of criticism that occurred to me precisely because I had already begun to guess. By that time indeed I had had great initiations, and poor Lavinia had had them as well – hers in fact throughout went further than mine – and we had shared them together, and I had settled down to a tolerably exact sense of what I was to see. It was what Lavinia added to it that really made the picture. The portrait of the little dead girl had evoked something attractive, though one had not lived so long in the world without hearing of plenty of little dead girls; and the day came when I felt as if I had actually sat with Marmaduke in each of the rooms converted by her parents – with the aid not only of the few small, cherished relics, but that of the fondest figments and fictions, ingenious imaginary mementoes and tokens; the unexposed make-believes of the sorrow that broods and the passion that clings – into a temple of grief and worship. The child, incontestably beautiful, had evidently been passionately loved, and in the absence from their lives – I suppose originally a mere accident – of such other elements, either new pleasures or new pains, as abound for most people, their feeling had drawn to itself their whole consciousness: it had become mildly maniacal. The idea was fixed, and it kept others out. The world, for the most part, allows no leisure for such a ritual, but the world had consistently neglected this plain, shy couple, who were sensitive to the wrong things and whose sincerity and fidelity, as well as their tameness and twaddle, were of a rigid, antique pattern.

I must not represent that either of these objects of interest, or my care for their concerns, took up all my leisure; for I had many claims to meet and many complications to handle, a hundred preoccupations and much deeper anxieties. My young woman, on her side, had other contacts and contingencies – other troubles too, poor girl; and there were stretches of time in which I neither saw Marmaduke nor heard a word of the Dedricks. Once, only once, abroad, in Germany at a railway-station, I met him in their company. They were colourless, commonplace, elderly Britons, of the kind you identify by the livery of their footman or the labels of their luggage, and the mere sight of them justified me to my conscience in having avoided, from the first, the stiff problem of conversation with them. Marmaduke saw me on the spot and came over to me. There was no doubt whatever of *his* vivid bloom. He had grown fat – or almost, but not with grossness – and might perfectly have passed for the handsome, happy, full-blown son of doting parents who couldn't let him out of view and to whom he was a model of respect and solicitude. They followed him with placid, pleased eyes when he joined me, but asking nothing at all for themselves and quite fitting into his own manner of saying nothing about them. It had its charm, I confess, the way he could be natural and easy, and yet intensely conscious too, on such a basis. What he was conscious of was that there were things I by this time knew; just as, while we stood there and good-humouredly sounded each other's faces – for, having accepted everything at last, I was only a little curious – I knew that he measured my insight. When he returned again to his doting parents I had to admit that, doting as they were, I felt him not to have been spoiled. It was incongruous in such a career, but he was rather more of a man. There came back to me with a shade of regret after I had got on this occasion into my train, which was not theirs, a memory of some words that, a couple of years before, I had uttered to poor Lavinia. She had said to me, speaking in reference to what was then our frequent topic and on some fresh evidence that I have forgotten: 'He feels now, you know, about Maud-Evelyn quite as the old people themselves do.'

'Well,' I had replied, 'it's only a pity he's paid for it!'

'Paid?' She had looked very blank.

'By all the luxuries and conveniences,' I had explained, 'that he comes in for through living with them. For that's what he practically does.'

At present I saw how wrong I had been. He was paid, but paid differently, and the mastered wonder of that was really what had been between us in the waiting-room of the station. Step by step, after this, I followed.

# VI

I CAN SEE Lavinia for instance in her ugly new mourning immediately after her mother's death. There had been long anxieties connected with this event, and she was already faded, already almost old. But Marmaduke, on her bereavement, had been to her, and she came straightway to me.

'Do you know what he thinks now?' she soon began. 'He thinks he knew her.'

'Knew the child?' It came to me as if I had half expected it.

'He speaks of her now as if she hadn't been a child.' My visitor gave me the strangest fixed smile. 'It appears that she wasn't so young – it appears she had grown up.'

I stared. 'How can it "appear"? They *know*, at least! There were the facts.'

'Yes,' said Lavinia, 'but they seem to have come to take a different view of them. He talked to me a long time, and all about *her*. He told me things.'

'What kind of things? Not trumpery stuff, I hope, about "communicating" – about his seeing or hearing her?'

'Oh no, he doesn't go in for that; he leaves it to the old couple, who, I believe, cling to their mediums, keep up their sittings and their rappings and find in it all a comfort, an amusement, that he doesn't grudge them and that he regards as harmless. I mean anecdotes – memories of his own. I mean things she said to him and that they did together – places they went to. His mind is full of them.'

I turned it over. 'Do you think he's decidedly mad?'

She shook her head with her bleached patience. 'Oh no, it's too beautiful!'

'Then are *you* taking it up? I mean the preposterous theory—'

'It *is* a theory,' she broke in, 'but it isn't necessarily preposterous. Any theory has to suppose something,' she sagely pursued, 'and it depends at any rate on what it's a theory *of*. It's wonderful to see this one work.'

'Wonderful always to see the growth of a legend!' I laughed. 'This is a rare chance to watch one in formation. They're all three in good faith building it up. Isn't that what you made out from him?'

Her tired face fairly lighted. 'Yes – you understand it; and you put it better than I. It's the gradual effect of brooding over the past; the past, that way, grows and grows. They make it and make it. They've persuaded each other – the parents – of so many things that they've at last also persuaded *him*. It has been contagious.'

'It's you who put it well,' I returned. 'It's the oddest thing I ever heard of, but it is, in its way, a reality. Only we mustn't speak of it to others.'

She quite accepted that precaution. 'No – to nobody. *He* doesn't. He keeps it only for me.'

'Conferring on you thus,' I again laughed, 'such a precious privilege!'

She was silent a moment, looking away from me. 'Well, he has kept his vow.'

'You mean of not marrying? Are you very sure?' I asked. 'Didn't he perhaps—?' But I faltered at the boldness of my joke.

The next moment I saw I needn't. 'He *was* in love with her,' Lavinia brought out.

I broke now into a peal which, however provoked, struck even my own ear at the moment as rude almost to profanity. 'He literally tells you outright that he's making believe?'

She met me effectively enough. 'I don't think he *knows* he is. He's just completely in the current.'

'The current of the old people's twaddle?'

Again my companion hesitated; but she knew what she thought. 'Well, whatever we call it, I like it. It isn't so common, as the world goes, for anyone – let alone for two or three – to feel and to care for the dead as much as that. It's self-deception, no doubt, but it comes from something that – well,' she faltered again, 'is beautiful when one does hear of it. They make her out older, so as to imagine they had her longer; and they make out that certain things really happened to her, so that she shall have had more life. They've invented a whole experience for her, and Marmaduke has become a part of it. There's one thing, above all, they want her to have had.' My young friend's face, as she analysed the mystery, fairly grew bright with her vision. It came to me with a faint dawn of awe that the attitude of the Dedricks *was* contagious. 'And she did have it!' Lavinia declared.

I positively admired her, and if I could yet perfectly be rational without being ridiculous, it was really, more than anything else, to draw from her the whole image. 'She had the bliss of knowing Marmaduke? Let us agree to it, then, since she's not here to contradict us. But what I don't get over is the scant material for *him*!' It may easily be conceived how little, for the moment, I could get over it. It was the last time my impatience was to be too much for me, but I remember how it broke out. 'A man who might have had *you*!'

For an instant I feared I had upset her – thought I saw in her face the tremor of a wild wail. But poor Lavinia was magnificent. 'It wasn't that he might have had "me" – that's nothing: it was, at the most, that I might have had *him*. Well, isn't that just what has happened? He's mine from the moment no one else has him. I give up the past, but don't you see what it does for the rest of life? I'm surer than ever that he won't marry.'

'Of course, he won't – to quarrel, with those people!'

For a minute she answered nothing; then, 'Well, for whatever reason!' she simply said. Now, however, I had gouged out of her a couple of still tears, and I pushed away the whole obscure comedy.

## VII

I MIGHT PUSH it away, but I couldn't really get rid of it; nor, on the whole, doubtless, did I want to, for to have in one's life, year after year, a particular question or two that one couldn't comfortably and imposingly make up one's mind about was just the sort of thing to keep one from turning stupid. There had been little need of my enjoining reserve upon Lavinia: she obeyed, in respect to impenetrable silence save with myself, an instinct, an interest of her own. We never therefore gave poor Marmaduke, as you call it, 'away'; we were much too tender, let alone that she was also too proud; and, for himself, evidently, there was not, to the end, in London, another person in his confidence. No echo of the queer part he played ever came back to us; and I can't tell you how this fact, just by itself, brought home to me little by little a sense of the charm he was under. I met him 'out' at long intervals – met him usually at dinner. He had grown like a person with a position and a history. Rosy and rich-looking, fat, moreover, distinctly fat at last, there was almost in him something of the bland – yet not too bland – young head of an hereditary business. If the Dedricks had been

## Maud-Evelyn

bankers he might have constituted the future of the house. There was none the less a long middle stretch during which, though we were all so much in London, he dropped out of my talks with Lavinia. We were conscious, she and I, of his absence from them; but we clearly felt in each quarter that there are things after all unspeakable, and the fact, in any case, had nothing to do with her seeing or not seeing our friend. I was sure, as it happened, that she did see him. But there were moments that for myself still stand out.

One of these was a certain Sunday afternoon when it was so dismally wet that, taking for granted I should have no visitors, I had drawn up to the fire with a book – a successful novel of the day – that I promised myself comfortably to finish. Suddenly, in my absorption, I heard a firm rat-tat-tat; on which I remember giving a groan of inhospitality. But my visitor proved in due course Marmaduke, and Marmaduke proved – in a manner even less, at the point we had reached, to have been counted on – still more attaching than my novel. I think it was only an accident that he became so; it would have been the turn of a hair either way. He hadn't come to speak – he had only come to talk, to show once more that we could continue good old friends without his speaking. But somehow there were the circumstances: the insidious fireside, the things in the room, with their reminders of his younger time; perhaps even too the open face of my book, looking at him from where I had laid it down for him and giving him a chance to feel that he could supersede Wilkie Collins. There was at all events a promise of intimacy, of opportunity for him in the cold lash of the windows by the storm. We should be alone; it was cosy; it was safe.

The action of these impressions was the more marked that what was touched by them, I afterwards saw, was not at all a desire for an effect – was just simply a spirit of happiness that needed to overflow. It had finally become too much for him. His past, rolling up year after year, had grown too interesting. But he was, all the same, directly stupefying. I forget what turn of our preliminary gossip brought it out, but it came, in explanation of something or other, as it had not yet come: 'When a man has had for a few months what *I* had, you know!' The moral appeared to be that nothing in the way of human experience of the exquisite could again particularly matter. He saw, however, that I failed immediately to fit his reflection to a definite case, and he went on with the frankest smile: 'You look as bewildered as if you suspected me of alluding to some sort of thing that isn't usually spoken of; but I assure you I mean nothing more reprehensible than our blessed engagement itself.'

'Your blessed engagement?' I couldn't help the tone in which I took him up; but the way he disposed of that was something of which I feel to this hour the influence. It was only a look, but it put an end to my tone for ever. It made me, on my side, after an instant, look at the fire – look hard and even turn a little red. During this moment I saw my alternatives and I chose; so that when I met his eyes again I was fairly ready. 'You still feel,' I asked with sympathy, 'how much it did for you?'

I had no sooner spoken than I saw that that would be from

that moment the right way. It instantly made all the difference. The main question would be whether I could keep it up. I remember that only a few minutes later, for instance, this question gave a flare. His reply had been abundant and imperturbable – had included some glance at the way death brings into relief even the faintest things that have preceded it; on which I felt myself suddenly as restless as if I had grown afraid of him. I got up to ring for tea; he went on talking – talking about Maud-Evelyn and what she had been for him; and when the servant had come up I prolonged, nervously, on purpose, the order I had wished to give. It made time, and I could speak to the footman sufficiently without thinking: what I thought of really was the risk of turning right round with a little outbreak. The temptation was strong; the same influences that had worked for my companion just worked, in their way, during that minute or two, for me. *Should* I, taking him unaware, flash at him a plain 'I say, just settle it for me once for all. *Are* you the boldest and basest of fortune-hunters, or have you only, more innocently and perhaps more pleasantly, suffered your brain slightly to soften?' But I missed the chance – which I didn't in fact afterwards regret. My servant went out, and I faced again to my visitor, who continued to converse. I met his eyes once more, and their effect was repeated. If anything had happened to his brain this effect was perhaps the domination of the madman's stare. Well, he was the easiest and gentlest of madmen. By the time the footman came back with tea I was in for it; I was in for everything. By 'everything' I mean my whole subsequent treatment of the case. It *was*

– the case was – really beautiful. So, like all the rest, the hour comes back to me: the sound of the wind and the rain; the look of the empty, ugly, cabless square and of the stormy spring light; the way that, uninterrupted and absorbed, we had tea together by my fire. So it was that he found me receptive and that I found myself able to look merely grave and kind when he said, for example: 'Her father and mother, you know, really, that first day – the day they picked me up on the Splügen – recognized me as the proper one.'

'The proper one?'

'To make their son-in-law. They wanted her so,' he went on, 'to have had, don't you know, just everything.'

'Well, if she did have it ' I tried to be cheerful – 'isn't the whole thing then all right?'

'Oh, it's all right *now*,' he replied – 'now that we've got it all there before us. You see, they couldn't like me so much –' he wished me thoroughly to understand – 'without wanting me to have been the man.'

'I see – that was natural.'

'Well,' said Marmaduke, 'it prevented the possibility of anyone else.'

'Ah, that would never have done!' I laughed.

His own pleasure at it was impenetrable, splendid. 'You see, they couldn't do much, the old people – and they can do still less now – with the future; so they had to do what they could with the past.'

'And they seem to have done,' I concurred, 'remarkably much.'

'Everything, simply. Everything,' he repeated. Then he had an idea, though without insistence or importunity – I noticed it just flicker in his face. 'If you *were* to come to Westbourne Terrace—'

'Oh, don't speak of that!' I broke in. 'It wouldn't be decent now. I should have come, if at all, ten years ago.'

But he saw, with his good-humour, further than this. 'I see what you mean. But there's much more in the place now than then.'

'I daresay. People get new things. All the same—!' I was at bottom but resisting my curiosity.

Marmaduke didn't press me, but he wanted me to know. 'There are our rooms – the whole set; and I don't believe you ever saw anything more charming, for *her* taste was extraordinary. I'm afraid too that I myself have had much to say to them.' Then as he made out that I was again a little at sea, 'I'm talking,' he went on, 'of the suite prepared for her marriage.' He 'talked' like a crown prince. 'They were ready, to the last touch – there was nothing more to be done. And they're just as they were – not an object moved, not an arrangement altered, not a person but ourselves coming in: they're only exquisitely kept. All our presents are there – I should have liked you to see them.'

It had become a torment by this time – I saw that I had made a mistake. But I carried it off. 'Oh, I couldn't have borne it!'

'They're not sad,' he smiled – 'they're too lovely to be sad. They're happy. And the things—!' He seemed, in the excitement of our talk, to have them before him.

'They're so very wonderful?'

'Oh, selected with a patience that makes them almost priceless. It's really a museum. There was nothing they thought too good for her.'

I had lost the museum, but I reflected that it could contain no object so rare as my visitor. 'Well, you've helped them – you could do *that*.'

He quite eagerly assented. 'I could do that, thank God – I could do that! I felt it from the first, and it's what I *have* done.' Then as if the connection were direct: 'All *my* things are there.'

I thought a moment. 'Your presents?'

'Those I made her. She loved each one, and I remember about each the particular thing she said. Though I do say it,' he continued, 'none of the others, as a matter of fact, come near mine. I look at them every day, and I assure you I'm not ashamed.' Evidently, in short, he had spared nothing, and he talked on and on. He really quite swaggered.

# VIII

IN RELATION to times and intervals I can only recall that if this visit of his to me had been in the early spring it was one day in the late autumn – a day, which couldn't have been in the same year, with the difference of hazy, drowsy sunshine and brown and yellow leaves – that, taking a short cut across Kensington

Gardens, I came, among the untrodden ways, upon a couple occupying chairs under a tree, who immediately rose at the sight of me. I had been behind them at recognition, the fact that Marmaduke was in deep mourning having perhaps, so far as I had observed it, misled me. In my desire both not to look flustered at meeting them and to spare their own confusion I bade them again be seated and asked leave, as a third chair was at hand, to share a little their rest. Thus it befell that after a minute Lavinia and I had sat down, while our friend, who had looked at his watch, stood before us among the fallen foliage and remarked that he was sorry to have to leave us. Lavinia said nothing, but I expressed regret; I couldn't, however, as it struck me, without a false or a vulgar note speak as if I had interrupted a tender passage or separated a pair of lovers. But I could look him up and down, take in his deep mourning. He had not made, for going off, any other pretext than that his time was up and that he was due at home. 'Home', with him now, had but one meaning: I knew him to be completely quartered in Westbourne Terrace. 'I hope nothing has happened,' I said – 'that you've lost no one whom *I* know.'

Marmaduke looked at my companion, and she looked at Marmaduke. 'He has lost his wife,' she then observed.

Oh, this time, I fear, I had a small quaver of brutality; but it was at him I directed it. 'Your wife? I didn't know you had *had* a wife!'

'Well,' he replied, positively gay in his black suit, his black gloves, his high hatband, 'the more we live in the past, the more things we find in it. That's a literal fact. You would see the truth of it if your life had taken such a turn.'

'*I* live in the past,' Lavinia put in gently and as if to help us both.

'But with the result, my dear,' I returned, 'of not making, I hope, such extraordinary discoveries!' It seemed absurd to be afraid to be light.

'May none of her discoveries be more fatal than mine!' Marmaduke wasn't uproarious, but this treatment of the matter had the good taste of simplicity. 'They've wanted it so for her,' he continued to me wonderfully, 'that we've at last seen our way to it — I mean to what Lavinia has mentioned.' He hesitated but three seconds — he brought it brightly out. 'Maud-Evelyn had *all* her young happiness.'

I stared, but Lavinia was, in her peculiar manner, as brilliant. 'The marriage *did* take place,' she quietly, stupendously explained to me.

Well, I was determined not to be left. 'So you're a widower,' I gravely asked, 'and these are the signs?'

'Yes; I shall wear them always now.'

'But isn't it late to have begun?'

My question had been stupid, I felt the next instant; but it didn't matter — he was quite equal to the occasion. 'Oh, I had to wait, you know, till all the facts about my marriage had given me the right.' And he looked at his watch again. 'Excuse me — I *am* due. Good-bye, good-bye.' He shook hands with each of us, and as we sat there together watching him walk away I was struck with his admirable manner of looking the character. I felt indeed as our eyes followed him that we were at one on this, and I said nothing till he was out of sight. Then by the same impulse we turned to each other.

'I thought he was never to marry!' I exclaimed to my friend.

Her fine wasted face met me gravely. 'He isn't – ever. He'll be still more faithful.'

'Faithful this time to whom?'

'Why, to Maud-Evelyn.' I said nothing – I only checked an ejaculation; but I put out a hand and took one of hers, and for a minute we kept silence. 'Of course it's only an idea,' she began again at last, 'but it seems to me a beautiful one.' Then she continued resignedly and remarkably: 'And now *they* can die.'

'Mr and Mrs Dedrick?' I pricked up my ears. 'Are they dying?'

'Not quite, but the old lady, it appears, is failing, steadily weakening; less, as I understand it, from any definite ailment than because she just feels her work done and her little sum of passion, as Marmaduke calls it, spent. Fancy, with her convictions, all her reasons for wanting to die! And if she goes, he says, Mr Dedrick won't long linger. It will be quite "John Anderson my jo".'

'Keeping her company down the hill, to lie beside her at the foot?'

'Yes, having settled all things.'

I turned these things over as we walked away, and how they had settled them – for Maud-Evelyn's dignity and Marmaduke's high advantage; and before we parted that afternoon – we had taken a cab in the Bayswater Road and she had come home with me – I remember saying to her: 'Well then, when they die won't he be free?'

She seemed scarce to understand. 'Free?'

'To do what he likes.'

She wondered. 'But he does what he likes now.'

'Well then, what *you* like!'

'Oh, you know what *I* like—!'

Ah, I closed her mouth! 'You like to tell horrid fibs – yes, I know it!'

What she had then put before me, however, came in time to pass: I heard in the course of the next year of Mrs Dedrick's extinction, and some months later, without, during the interval, having seen a sign of Marmaduke, wholly taken up with his bereaved patron, learned that her husband had touchingly followed her. I was out of England at the time; we had had to put into practice great economies and let our little place; so that, spending three winters successively in Italy, I devoted the periods between, at home, altogether to visits among people, mainly relatives, to whom these friends of mine were not known. Lavinia of course wrote to me – wrote, among many things, that Marmaduke was ill and had not seemed at all himself since the loss of his 'family', and this in spite of the circumstance, which she had already promptly communicated, that they had left him, by will, 'almost everything'. I knew before I came back to remain that she now saw him often and, to the extent of the change that had overtaken his strength and his spirits, greatly ministered to him. As soon as we at last met I asked for news of him; to which she replied: 'He's gradually going.' Then on my surprise: 'He has had his life.'

'You mean that, as he said of Mrs Dedrick, his sum of passion is spent?'

At this she turned away. 'You've never understood.'

I *had*, I conceived; and when I went subsequently to see him I was moreover sure. But I only said to Lavinia on this first occasion that I would immediately go; which was precisely what brought out the climax, as I feel it to be, of my story. 'He's not now, you know,' she turned round to admonish me, 'in Westbourne Terrace. He has taken a little old house in Kensington.'

'Then he hasn't kept the things?'

'He has kept everything.' She looked at me still more as if I had never understood.

'You mean he has moved them?'

She was patient with me. 'He has moved nothing. Everything is as it was, and kept with the same perfection.'

I wondered. 'But if he doesn't live there?'

'It's just what he does.'

'Then how can he be in Kensington?'

She hesitated, but she had still more than her old grasp of it. 'He's in Kensington – without living.'

'You mean that at the other place——?'

'Yes, he spends most of his time. He's driven over there every day – he remains there for hours. He keeps it for that.'

'I see – it's still the museum.'

'It's still the temple!' Lavinia replied with positive austerity.

'Then why did he move?'

'Because, you see, there –' she faltered again – 'I could come to him. And he wants me,' she said with admirable simplicity.

Little by little I took it in. 'After the death of the parents, even, you never went?'

'Never.'

'So you haven't seen anything?'

'Anything of hers? Nothing.'

I understood, oh perfectly; but I won't deny that I was disappointed: I had hoped for an account of his wonders and I immediately felt that it wouldn't be for me to take a step that she had declined. When, a short time later, I saw them together in Kensington Square – there were certain hours of the day that she regularly spent with him – I observed that everything about him was new, handsome and simple. They were, in their strange, final union – if union it could be called – very natural and very touching; but he was visibly stricken – he had his ailment in his eyes. She moved about him like a sister of charity – at all events like a sister. He was neither robust nor rosy now, nor was his attention visibly very present, and I privately and fancifully asked myself where it wandered and waited. But poor Marmaduke was a gentleman to the end – he wasted away with an excellent manner. He died twelve days ago; the will was opened; and last week, having meanwhile heard from her of its contents, I saw Lavinia. He leaves her everything that he himself had inherited. But she spoke of it all in a way that caused me to say in surprise: 'You haven't yet been to the house?'

'Not yet. I've only seen the solicitors, who tell me there will be no complications.'

There was something in her tone that made me ask more. 'Then you're not curious to see what's there?'

She looked at me with a troubled – almost a pleading – sense, which I understood; and presently she said: 'Will you go with me?'

'Some day, with pleasure – but not the first time. You must go alone then. The "relics" that you'll find there,' I added – for I had read her look – 'you must think of now not as hers—'

'But as his?'

'Isn't that what his death – with his so close relation to them – has made them for you?'

Her face lighted – I saw it was a view she could thank me for putting into words. 'I see – I see. They *are* his. I'll go.'

She went, and three days ago she came to me. They're really marvels, it appears, treasures extraordinary, and she has them all. Next week I go with her – I shall see them at last. Tell *you* about them, you say? My dear man, everything.

# The Two Faces

## I

THE SERVANT, WHO, in spite of his sealed, stamped look, appeared to have his reasons, stood there for instruction, in a manner not quite usual, after announcing the name. Mrs Grantham, however, took it up – 'Lord Gwyther?' – with a quick surprise that for an instant justified him even to the small scintilla in the glance she gave her companion, which might have had exactly the sense of the butler's hesitation. This companion, a shortish, fairish, youngish man, clean-shaven and keen-eyed, had, with a promptitude that would have struck an observer – which the butler indeed was – sprung to his feet and moved to the chimney-piece, though his hostess herself, meanwhile, managed not otherwise to stir. 'Well?' she said, as for the visitor to advance; which she immediately followed with a sharper 'He's not there?'

'Shall I show him up, ma'am?'

'But of course!' The point of his doubt made her at last rise for impatience, and Bates, before leaving the room, might still have caught the achieved irony of her appeal to the gentleman into whose communion with her he had broken. 'Why in the world not——? What a way——!' she exclaimed, as Sutton felt beside his cheek the passage of her eyes to the glass behind him.

'He wasn't sure you'd see anyone.'

'I don't see "anyone", but I see individuals.'

'That's just it; and sometimes you don't see them.'

'Do you mean ever because of *you*?' she asked as she touched into place a tendril of hair. 'That's just his impertinence, as to which I shall speak to him.'

'Don't,' said Shirley Sutton. 'Never notice anything.'

'That's nice advice from you,' she laughed, 'who notice everything!'

'Ah, but I speak of nothing.'

She looked at him a moment. 'You're still more impertinent than Bates. You'll please not budge,' she went on.

'Really? I must sit him out?' he continued as, after a minute, she had not again spoken – only glancing about, while she changed her place, partly for another look at the glass and partly to see if she could improve her seat. What she felt was rather more than, clever and charming though she was, she could hide. 'If you're wondering how you seem, I can tell you. Awfully cool and easy.'

She gave him another stare. She was beautiful and conscious. 'And if you're wondering how *you* seem——'

'Oh, I'm not!' he laughed from before the fire; 'I always perfectly know.'

'How you seem,' she retorted, 'is as if you didn't!'

Once more for a little he watched her. 'You're looking lovely for him – extraordinarily lovely, within the marked limits of your range. But that's enough. Don't be clever.'

'Then who *will* be?'

'There you are!' he sighed with amusement.

'Do you know him?' she asked as, through the door left open by Bates, they heard steps on the landing.

Sutton had to think an instant, and produced a 'No' just as Lord Gwyther was again announced, which gave an unexpectedness to the greeting offered him a moment later by this personage – a young man, stout and smooth and fresh, but not at all shy, who, after the happiest rapid passage with Mrs Grantham, put out a hand with a frank, pleasant 'How d'ye do?'

'Mr Shirley Sutton,' Mrs Grantham explained.

'Oh yes,' said her second visitor, quite as if he knew; which, as he couldn't have known, had for her first the interest of confirming a perception that his lordship would be – no, not at all, in general, embarrassed, only was now exceptionally and especially agitated. As it is, for that matter, with Sutton's total impression that we are particularly and almost exclusively concerned, it may be further mentioned that he was not less clear as to the really handsome way in which the young man kept himself together and little by little – though with all proper aid indeed – finally found his feet. All sorts of things, for the twenty minutes, occurred to

Sutton, though one of them was certainly not that it would, after all, be better he should go. One of them was that their hostess was doing it in perfection – simply, easily, kindly, yet with something the least bit queer in her wonderful eyes; another was that if he had been recognized without the least ground it was through a tension of nerves on the part of his fellow-guest that produced inconsequent motions; still another was that, even had departure been indicated, he would positively have felt dissuasion in the rare promise of the scene. This was in especial after Lord Gwyther not only had announced that he was now married, but had mentioned that he wished to bring his wife to Mrs Grantham for the benefit so certain to be derived. It was the passage immediately produced by that speech that provoked in Sutton the intensity, as it were, of his arrest. He already knew of the marriage as well as Mrs Grantham herself, and as well also as he knew of some other things; and this gave him, doubtless, the better measure of what took place before him and the keener consciousness of the quick look that, at a marked moment – though it was not absolutely meant for him any more than for his companion – Mrs Grantham let him catch.

She smiled, but it had a gravity. 'I think, you know, you ought to have told me before.'

'Do you mean when I first got engaged? Well, it all took place so far away, and we really told, at home, so few people.'

Oh, there might have been reasons; but it had not been quite right. 'You were married at Stuttgart? That wasn't too far for *my* interest, at least, to reach.'

'Awfully kind of you – and of course one knew you *would* be kind. But it wasn't at Stuttgart; it was over there, but quite in the country. We should have managed it in England but that her mother naturally wished to be present, yet was not in health to come. So it was really, you see, a sort of little hole-and-corner German affair.'

This didn't in the least check Mrs Grantham's claim, but it started a slight anxiety. 'Will she be – a, then, German?'

Sutton knew her to know perfectly what Lady Gwyther would 'be', but he had by this time, while their friend explained, his independent interest. 'Oh dear, no! My father-in-law has never parted with the proud birthright of a Briton. But his wife, you see, holds an estate in Würtemberg from *her* mother, Countess Kremnitz, on which, with the awful condition of his English property, you know, they've found it for years a tremendous saving to live. So that though Valda was luckily born at home she has practically spent her life over there.'

'Oh, I see.' Then, after a slight pause, 'Is Valda her pretty name?' Mrs Grantham asked.

'Well,' said the young man, only wishing, in his candour, it was clear, to be drawn out – 'well, she has, in the manner of her mother's people, about thirteen; but that's the one we generally use.'

Mrs Grantham hesitated but an instant. 'Then may *I* generally use it?'

'It would be too charming of you; and nothing would give her – as, I assure you, nothing would give *me*, greater pleasure.' Lord Gwyther quite glowed with the thought.

'Then I think that instead of coming alone you might have brought her to see me.'

'It's exactly what,' he instantly replied, 'I came to ask your leave to do.' He explained that for the moment Lady Gwyther was not in town, having as soon as she arrived gone down to Torquay to put in a few days with one of her aunts, also her godmother, to whom she was an object of great interest. She had seen no one yet, and no one – not that *that* mattered – had seen her; she knew nothing whatever of London and was awfully frightened at facing it and at what – however little – might be expected of her. 'She wants someone,' he said, 'someone who knows the whole thing, don't you see? and who's thoroughly kind and clever, as you would be, if I may say so, to take her by the hand.' It was at this point and on these words that the eyes of Lord Gwyther's two auditors inevitably and wonderfully met. But there was nothing in the way he kept it up to show that he caught the encounter. 'She wants, if I may tell you so, for the great labyrinth, a real friend; and asking myself what I could do to make things ready for her, and who would be absolutely the best woman in London—'

'You thought, naturally, of *me*?' Mrs Grantham had listened with no sign but the faint flash just noted; now, however, she gave him the full light of her expressive face – which immediately brought Shirley Sutton, looking at his watch, once more to his feet.

'She *is* the best woman in London!' He addressed himself

with a laugh to the other visitor, but offered his hand in farewell to their hostess.

'You're going?'

'I must,' he said without scruple.

'Then we do meet at dinner?'

'I hope so.' On which, to take leave, he returned with interest to Lord Gwyther the friendly clutch he had a short time before received.

## II

THEY DID MEET at dinner, and if they were not, as it happened, side by side, they made that up afterwards in the happiest angle of a drawing-room that offered both shine and shadow and that was positively much appreciated, in the circle in which they moved, for the favourable 'corners' created by its shrewd mistress. Her face, charged with something produced in it by Lord Gwyther's visit, had been with him so constantly for the previous hours that, when she instantly challenged him on his 'treatment' of her in the afternoon, he was on the point of naming it as his reason for not having remained with her. Something new had quickly come into her beauty; he couldn't as yet have said what, nor whether on the whole to its advantage or its loss. Till he could make up his mind about that, at any rate, he would say nothing; so that, with sufficient presence of mind, he found a better excuse. If in short he had in defiance of her particular request left her alone with Lord Gwyther, it was simply because the situation had suddenly turned so exciting that he had fairly feared the contagion of it – the temptation of its making him, most improperly, put in his word.

They could now talk of these things at their ease. Other couples, ensconced and scattered, enjoyed the same privilege, and Sutton had more and more the profit, such as it was, of feeling that his interest in Mrs Grantham had become – what was the luxury of so high a social code – an acknowledged and protected relation. He knew his London well enough to know that he was on the way to be regarded as her main source of consolation for the trick that, several months before, Lord Gwyther had publicly played her. Many persons had not held that, by the high social code in question, his lordship could have 'reserved the right' to turn up in that way, from one day to another, engaged. For himself London took, with its short cuts and its cheap psychology, an immense deal for granted. To his own sense he was never – could in the nature of things never be – any man's 'successor'. Just what had constituted the predecessorship of other men was apparently that they had been able to make up their mind. He, worse luck, was at the mercy of her face, and more than ever at the mercy of it now, which meant, moreover, not that it made a slave of him, but that it made, disconcertingly, a sceptic. It was the absolute perfection of the handsome; but things had a way of coming into it. 'I felt,' he said, 'that you were there together at a point at which you had a right to the ease that the absence of a listener would give. I reflected that when you made me promise to stay you hadn't guessed—'

'That he could possibly have come to me on such an extraordinary errand? No, of course I hadn't guessed. Who *would*? But didn't you see how little I was upset by it?'

Sutton demurred. Then with a smile, 'I think *he* saw how little.'

'You yourself didn't, then?'

He again held back, but not, after all, to answer. 'He was wonderful, wasn't he?'

'I think he was,' she replied after a moment. To which she added: 'Why did he pretend that way he knew you?'

'He didn't pretend. He felt on the spot as if we were friends.' Sutton had found this afterwards, and found truth in it. 'It was an effusion of cheer and hope. He was so glad to see me there, and to find you happy.'

'Happy?'

'Happy. Aren't you?'

'Because of *you*?'

'Well – according to the impression he received as he came in.'

'That was sudden then,' she asked, 'and unexpected?'

Her companion thought. 'Prepared in some degree, but confirmed by the sight of us, there together, so awfully jolly and sociable over your fire.'

Mrs Grantham turned this round. 'If he knew I was "happy"

then – which, by the way, is none of his business, nor of yours either – why in the world did he come?'

'Well, for good manners, and for his idea,' said Sutton.

She took it in, appearing to have no hardness of rancour that could bar discussion. 'Do you mean by his idea his proposal that I should grandmother his wife? And, if you do, is the proposal your reason for calling him wonderful?'

Sutton laughed. 'Pray, what's yours?' As this was a question, however, that she took her time to answer or not to answer – only appearing interested for a moment in a combination that had formed itself on the other side of the room – he presently went on. 'What's *his*? – that would seem to be the point. His, I mean, for having decided on the extraordinary step of throwing his little wife, bound hands and feet, into your arms. Intelligent as you are, and with these three or four hours to have thought it over, I yet don't see how that can fail still to mystify you.'

She continued to watch their opposite neighbours. '"Little", you call her. Is she so very small?'

'Tiny, tiny – she *must* be; as different as possible in every way – of necessity – from you. They always *are* the opposite pole, you know,' said Shirley Sutton.

She glanced at him now. 'You strike me as of an impudence—!'

'No, no. I only like to make it out with you.'

She looked away again and, after a little, went on. 'I'm sure she's charming, and only hope one isn't to gather that he's already tired of her.'

'Not a bit! He's tremendously in love, and he'll remain so.'

'So much the better. And if it's a question,' said Mrs Grantham, 'of one's doing what one can for her, he has only, as I told him when you had gone, to give me the chance.'

'Good! So he *is* to commit her to you?'

'You use extraordinary expressions, but it's settled that he brings her.'

'And you'll really and truly help her?'

'Really and truly?' said Mrs Grantham, with her eyes again upon him. 'Why not? For what do you take me?'

'Ah, isn't that just what I still have the discomfort, every day I live, of asking myself?'

She had made, as she spoke, a movement to rise, which, as if she was tired of his tone, his last words appeared to determine. But, also getting up, he held her, when they were on their feet, long enough to hear the rest of what he had to say. 'If you do help her, you know, you'll show him that you've understood.'

'Understood what?'

'Why, his idea – the deep, acute train of reasoning that has led him to take, as one may say, the bull by the horns; to reflect that as you might, as you probably *would*, in any case, get at her, he plays the wise game, as well as the bold one, by assuming your generosity and placing himself publicly under an obligation to you.'

Mrs Grantham showed not only that she had listened, but that she had for an instant considered. 'What is it you elegantly describe as my getting "at" her?'

'He takes his risk, but puts you, you see, on your honour.'

She thought a moment more. 'What profundities indeed then over the simplest of matters! And if your idea is,' she went on, 'that if I do help her I shall show him I've understood them, so it will be that if I don't—'

'You'll show him —' Sutton took her up — 'that you haven't? Precisely. But in spite of not wanting to appear to have understood *too* much—'

'I may still be depended on to do what I can? Quite certainly. You'll see what I may still be depended on to do.' And she moved away.

## III

IT WAS NOT, doubtless, that there had been anything in their rather sharp separation at that moment to sustain or prolong the interruption; yet it definitely befell that, circumstances aiding, they practically failed to meet again before the great party at Burbeck. This occasion was to gather in some thirty persons from a certain Friday to the following Monday, and it was on the Friday that Sutton went down. He had known in advance that Mrs Grantham was to be there, and this perhaps, during the interval of hindrance, had helped him a little to be patient. He had before him the certitude of a real full cup — two days brimming over with the sight of her. He found, however, on his arrival that she was not yet in the field, and presently learned that her place would be in a small contingent that was to join the party on the morrow. This knowledge he extracted from Miss Banker, who was always the first to present herself at any gathering that was to enjoy her, and whom, moreover – partly on that very account – the wary not less than the speculative were apt to hold themselves well-advised to engage with at as early as possible a stage of the business. She was stout, red, rich, mature, universal – a massive, much-fingered volume, alphabetical, wonderful, indexed, that opened of itself at the right place. She opened for Sutton instinctively at G——, which happened to be remarkably convenient. 'What she's really waiting over for is to bring down Lady Gwyther.'

'Ah, the Gwythers are coming?'

'Yes; caught, through Mrs Grantham, just in time. *She'll* be the feature – everyone wants to see her.'

Speculation and wariness met and combined at this moment in Shirley Sutton. 'Do you mean – a – Mrs Grantham?'

'Dear no! Poor little Lady Gwyther, who, but just arrived in England, appears now literally for the first time in her life in any society whatever, and whom (don't you know the extraordinary story? you ought to – *you*!) she, of all people, has so wonderfully taken up. It will be quite – here – as if she were "presenting" her.'

Sutton, of course, took in more things than even appeared. 'I never know what I ought to know; I only know, inveterately, what I oughtn't. So what *is* the extraordinary story?'

'You really haven't heard——?'

'Really!' he replied without winking.

'It happened, indeed, but the other day,' said Miss Banker, 'yet everyone is already wondering. Gwyther has thrown his wife on her mercy – but I won't believe you if you pretend to me you don't know why he shouldn't.'

Sutton asked himself then what he *could* pretend. 'Do you mean because she's merciless?'

She hesitated. 'If you don't know, perhaps I oughtn't to tell you.'

He liked Miss Banker, and found just the right tone to plead. '*Do* tell me.'

'Well,' she sighed, 'it will be your own fault——! They had been such friends that there could have been but one name for the crudity of his original *procédé*. When I was a girl we used to call it throwing over. They call it in French to *lâcher*. But I refer not so much to the act itself as to the manner of it, though you may say indeed, of course, that there is in such cases, after all, only one manner. Least said, soonest mended.'

Sutton seemed to wonder. 'Oh, he said too much?'

'He said nothing. That was it.'

Sutton kept it up. 'But was *what*?'

'Why, what she must, like any woman in her shoes, have felt to be his perfidy. He simply went and *did* it – took to himself this child, that is, without the preliminary of a scandal or a rupture – before she could turn round.'

'I follow you. But it would appear from what you say that she *has* turned round now.'

'Well,' Miss Banker laughed, 'we shall see for ourselves how far. It will be what everyone will try to see.'

'Oh, then we've work cut out!' And Sutton certainly felt that he himself had – an impression that lost nothing from a further talk with Miss Banker in the course of a short stroll in the grounds with her the next day. He spoke as one who had now considered many things.

'Did I understand from you yesterday that Lady Gwyther's a "child"?'

'Nobody knows. It's prodigious the way she has managed.'

'The way Lady Gwyther has——?'

'No; the way May Grantham has kept her till this hour in her pocket.'

He was quick at his watch. 'Do you mean by "this hour" that they're due now?'

'Not till tea. All the others arrive together in time for that.' Miss Banker had clearly, since the previous day, filled in gaps and become, as it were, revised and enlarged. 'She'll have kept a cat from seeing her, so as to produce her entirely herself.'

'Well,' Sutton mused, 'that will have been a very noble sort of return—'

'For Gwyther's behaviour? Very. Yet I feel creepy.'

'Creepy?'

'Because so much depends for the girl – in the way of the right start or the wrong start – on the signs and omens of this first appearance. It's a great house and a great occasion, and we're assembled here, it strikes me, very much as the Roman mob at the circus used to be to see the next Christian maiden brought out to the tigers.'

'Oh, if she *is* a Christian maiden——!' Sutton murmured. But he stopped at what his imagination called up.

It perhaps fed that faculty a little that Miss Banker had the effect of making out that Mrs Grantham might individually be, in any case, something of a Roman matron. 'She has kept her in the dark so that we may only take her from her hand. She will have formed her for us.'

'In so few days?'

'Well, she will have prepared her – decked her for the sacrifice with ribbons and flowers.'

'Ah, if you only mean that she will have taken her to her dressmaker——!' And it came to Sutton, at once as a new light and as a check, almost, to anxiety, that this was all poor Gwyther, mistrustful probably of a taste formed by Stuttgart, might have desired of their friend.

There were usually at Burbeck many things taking place at once; so that wherever else, on such occasions, tea might be served, it went forward with matchless pomp, weather permitting, on a shaded stretch of one of the terraces and in presence of one of the prospects. Shirley Sutton, moving, as the afternoon waned, more restlessly about and mingling in dispersed groups only to find they had nothing to keep him quiet, came upon it as he turned a corner of the house – saw it seated there in all its state. It might be said that at Burbeck it was, like everything else, made the most of. It constituted immediately, with multiplied tables and glittering plate, with rugs and cushions and ices and fruit and wonderful porcelain and beautiful women, a scene of splendour, almost an incident of grand opera. One of the beautiful women might quite have been expected to rise with a gold cup and a celebrated song.

One of them did rise, as it happened, while Sutton drew near, and he found himself a moment later seeing nothing and nobody but Mrs Grantham. They met on the terrace, just away from the others, and the movement in which he had the effect of arresting her might have been that of withdrawal. He quickly saw, however, that if she had been about to pass into the house it was only on some errand — to get something or to call someone — that would immediately have restored her to the public. It somehow struck him on the spot — and more than ever yet, though the impression was not wholly new to him — that she felt herself a figure for the forefront of the stage and indeed would have been recognized by anyone at a glance as the *prima donna assoluta*. She caused, in fact, during the few minutes he stood talking to her, an extraordinary series of waves to roll extraordinarily fast over his sense, not the least mark of the matter being that the appearance with which it ended was again the one with which it had begun. 'The face — the face,' as he kept dumbly repeating; that was at last, as at first, all he could clearly see. She had a perfection resplendent, but what in the world had it done, this perfection, to her beauty? It was her beauty, doubtless, that looked out at him, but it was into something else that, as their eyes met, he strangely found himself looking.

It was as if something had happened in consequence of which she had changed, and there was that in this swift perception that made him glance eagerly about for Lady Gwyther. But as he took in the recruited group – identities of the hour added to those of the previous twenty-four – he saw, among his recognitions, one of which was the husband of the person missing, that Lady Gwyther was not there. Nothing in the whole business was more singular than his consciousness that, as he came back to his interlocutress after the nods and smiles and hand-waves he had launched, she knew what had been his thought. She knew for whom he had looked without success; but why should this knowledge visibly have hardened and sharpened her, and precisely at a moment when she was unprecedentedly magnificent? The indefinable apprehension that had somewhat sunk after his second talk with Miss Banker and then had perversely risen again – this nameless anxiety now produced on him, with a sudden sharper pinch, the effect of a great suspense. The action of that, in turn, was to show him that he had not yet fully known how much he had at stake on a final view. It was revealed to him for the first time that he 'really cared' whether Mrs Grantham were a safe nature. It was too ridiculous by what a thread it hung, but something was certainly in the air that would definitely tell him.

What was in the air descended the next moment to earth. He turned round as he caught the expression with which her eyes attached themselves to something that approached. A little person, very young and very much dressed, had come out of the house, and the expression in Mrs Grantham's eyes was that of the artist confronted with her work and interested, even to impatience, in the judgement of others. The little person drew nearer, and though Sutton's companion, without looking at him now, gave it a name and met it, he had jumped for himself at certitude. He saw many things – too many, and they appeared to be feathers, frills, excrescences of silk and lace – massed together and conflicting, and after a moment also saw struggling out of them a small face that struck him as either scared or sick. Then, with his eyes again returning to Mrs Grantham, he saw another.

He had no more talk with Miss Banker till late that evening – an evening during which he had felt himself too noticeably silent; but something had passed between this pair, across dinner-table and drawing-room, without speech, and when they at last found words it was in the needed ease of a quiet end of the long, lighted gallery, where she opened again at the very paragraph.

'You were right – that *was* it. She did the only thing that, at such short notice, she *could* do. She took her to her dressmaker.'

Sutton, with his back to the reach of the gallery, had, as if to banish a vision, buried his eyes for a minute in his hands. 'And oh, the face – the face!'

'Which?' Miss Banker asked.

'Whichever one looks at.'

'But May Grantham's glorious. She has turned herself out—'

'With a splendour of taste and a sense of effect, eh? Yes.' Sutton showed he saw far.

'She *has* the sense of effect. The sense of effect as exhibited in Lady Gwyther's clothes—!' was something Miss Banker failed of words to express. 'Everybody's overwhelmed. Here, you know, that sort of thing's grave. The poor creature's lost.'

'Lost?'

'Since on the first impression, as we said, so much depends. The first impression's made – oh, made! I defy her now ever to unmake it. Her husband, who's proud, won't like her the better for it. And I don't see,' Miss Banker went on, 'that her prettiness *was* enough – a mere little feverish, frightened freshness; what *did* he see in her? – to be so blasted. It has been done with an atrocity of art—'

'That supposes the dressmaker then also a devil?'

'Oh, your London women and their dressmakers!' Miss Banker laughed.

'But the face – the face!' Sutton woefully repeated.

'May's?'

'The little girl's. It's exquisite.'

'Exquisite?'

'For unimaginable pathos.'

'Oh!' Miss Banker dropped.

'She has at last begun to see.' Sutton showed again how far *he* saw. 'It glimmers upon her innocence, she makes it dimly out – what has been done with her. She's even worse this evening – the way, my eye, she looked at dinner! – than when she came.

Yes –' he was confident – 'it has dawned (how couldn't it, out of all of you?) and she knows.'

'She ought to have known before!' Miss Banker intelligently sighed.

'No; she wouldn't in that case have been so beautiful.'

'Beautiful?' cried Miss Banker; 'overloaded like a monkey in a show!'

'The face, yes; which goes to the heart. It's that that makes it,' said Shirley Sutton. 'And it's that –' he thought it out – 'that makes the other.'

'I see. Conscious?'

'Horrible!'

'You take it hard,' said Miss Banker.

Lord Gwyther, just before she spoke, had come in sight and now was near them. Sutton on this, appearing to wish to avoid him, reached, before answering his companion's observation, a door that opened close at hand. 'So hard,' he replied from that point, 'that I shall be off tomorrow morning.'

'And not see the rest?' she called after him.

But he had already gone, and Lord Gwyther, arriving, amiably took up her question. 'The rest of what?'

Miss Banker looked him well in the eyes. 'Of Mrs Grantham's clothes.'

# *The Beldonald Holbein*

## I

Mrs Munden had not yet been to my studio on so good a pretext as when she first put it to me that it would be quite open to me – should I only care, as she called it, to throw the handkerchief – to paint her beautiful sister-in-law. I needn't go here, more than is essential, into the question of Mrs Munden, who would really, by the way, be a story in herself. She has a manner of her own of putting things, and some of those she has put to me—! Her implication was that Lady Beldonald had not only seen and admired certain examples of my work, but had literally been prepossessed in favour of the painter's 'personality'. Had I been struck with this sketch I might easily have imagined that Lady Beldonald was throwing *me* the handkerchief. 'She hasn't done,' my visitor said, 'what she ought.'

'Do you mean she has done what she oughtn't?'

'Nothing horrid – oh dear, no.' And something in Mrs

Munden's tone, with the way she appeared to muse a moment, even suggested to me that what she 'oughtn't' was perhaps what Lady Beldonald had too much neglected. 'She hasn't got on.'

'What's the matter with her?'

'Well, to begin with, she's American.'

'But I thought that was the way of ways to get on.'

'It's one of them. But it's one of the ways of being awfully out of it too. There are so many!'

'So many Americans?' I asked.

'Yes, plenty of *them*,' Mrs Munden sighed. 'So many ways, I mean, of being one.'

'But if your sister-in-law's way is to be beautiful—?'

'Oh, there are different ways of that too.'

'And she hasn't taken the right way?'

'Well,' my friend returned, as if it were rather difficult to express, 'she hasn't done with it—'

'I see,' I laughed; 'what she oughtn't!'

Mrs Munden in a manner corrected me, but it *was* difficult to express. 'My brother, at all events, was certainly selfish. Till he died she was almost never in London; they wintered, year after year, for what he supposed to be his health – which it didn't help, since he was so much too soon to meet his end – in the south of France and in the dullest holes he could pick out, and when they came back to England he always kept her in the country. I must say for her that she always behaved beautifully. Since his death she has been more in London, but on a stupidly unsuccessful footing. I don't think she quite understands. She hasn't what *I* should call a life. It may be, of course, that she doesn't want one. That's just what I can't exactly find out. I can't make out how much she knows.'

'I can easily make out,' I returned with hilarity, 'how much *you* do!'

'Well, you're very horrid. Perhaps she's too old.'

'Too old for what?' I persisted.

'For anything. Of course she's no longer even a little young; only preserved – oh, but preserved, like bottled fruit, in syrup! I want to help her, if only because she gets on my nerves, and I really think the way of it would be just the right thing of yours at the Academy and on the line.'

'But suppose,' I threw out, 'she should give on *my* nerves?'

'Oh, she will. But isn't that all in the day's work, and don't great beauties always——?'

'*You* don't,' I interrupted; but I at any rate saw Lady Beldonald later on – the day came when her kinswoman brought her, and then I understood that her life had its centre in her own idea of her appearance. Nothing else about her mattered – one knew her all when one knew that. She is indeed in one particular, I think, sole of her kind – a person whom vanity has had the odd effect of keeping positively safe and sound. This passion is supposed surely, for the most part, to be a principle of perversion and injury, leading astray those who listen to it and landing them, sooner or later, in this or that complication; but it has landed her ladyship nowhere whatever – it has kept her from the first moment of full consciousness, one feels, exactly in the same place. It has protected her from every danger, has made her absolutely proper and prim. If she is 'preserved', as Mrs Munden originally described her to me, it is her vanity that has beautifully done it – putting her years ago in a plate-glass case and closing up the receptacle against every breath of air. How shouldn't she be preserved, when you might smash your knuckles on this transparency before you could crack it? And she *is* – oh, amazingly! Preservation is scarce the word for the rare condition of her surface. She looks *naturally* new, as if she took out every night her large, lovely, varnished eyes and put them in water. The thing was to paint her, I perceived, *in* the glass case – a most tempting, attaching feat; render to the full the shining, interposing plate and the general show-window effect.

It was agreed, though it was not quite arranged, that she should sit to me. If it was not quite arranged, this was because, as I was made to understand from an early stage, the conditions for our start must be such as should exclude all elements of disturbance, such, in a word, as she herself should judge absolutely favourable. And it seemed that these conditions were easily imperilled. Suddenly, for instance, at a moment when I was expecting her to meet an appointment – the first – that I had proposed, I received a hurried visit from Mrs Munden, who came on her behalf to let me know that the season happened just not to be propitious and that our friend couldn't be quite sure, to the hour, when it would again become so. Nothing, she felt, would make it so but a total absence of worry.

# The Beldonald Holbein

'Oh, a "total absence",' I said, 'is a large order! We live in a worrying world.'

'Yes; and she feels exactly that – more than you'd think. It's in fact just why she mustn't have, as she has now, a particular distress on at the very moment. She wants to look, of course, her best, and such things tell on her appearance.'

I shook my head. 'Nothing tells on her appearance. Nothing reaches it in any way; nothing gets *at* it. However, I can understand her anxiety. But what's her particular distress?'

'Why, the illness of Miss Dadd.'

'And who in the world's Miss Dadd?'

'Her most intimate friend and constant companion – the lady who was with us here that first day.'

'Oh, the little round, black woman who gurgled with admiration?'

'None other. But she was taken ill last week, and it may very well be that she'll gurgle no more. She was very bad yesterday and is no better today, and Nina is much upset. If anything happens to Miss Dadd she'll have to get another, and, though she has had two or three before, that won't be so easy.'

'Two or three Miss Dadds? Is it possible? And still wanting another!' I recalled the poor lady completely now. 'No; I shouldn't indeed think it would be easy to get another. But why is a succession of them necessary to Lady Beldonald's existence?'

'Can't you guess?' Mrs Munden looked deep, yet impatient. 'They help.'

'Help what? Help whom?'

'Why, everyone. You and me for instance. To do what? Why, to think Nina beautiful. She has them for that purpose; they serve as foils, as accents serve on syllables, as terms of comparison. They make her "stand out". It's an effect of contrast that must be familiar to you artists; it's what a woman does when she puts a band of black velvet under a pearl ornament that may require, as she thinks, a little showing off.'

I wondered. 'Do you mean she always has them black?'

'Dear no; I've seen them blue, green, yellow. They may be what they like, so long as they're always one other thing.'

'Hideous?'

Mrs Munden hesitated. 'Hideous is too much to say; she doesn't really require them as bad as that. But consistently, cheerfully, loyally plain. It's really a most happy relation. She loves them for it.'

'And for what do they love *her*?'

'Why, just for the amiability that they produce in her. Then, also, for their "home". It's a career for them.'

'I see. But if that's the case,' I asked, 'why are they so difficult to find?'

'Oh, they must be safe; it's all in that: her being able to depend on them to keep to the terms of the bargain and never have moments of rising – as even the ugliest woman will now and then (say when she's in love) – superior to themselves.'

I turned it over. 'Then if they can't inspire passions the poor things mayn't even at least feel them?'

'She distinctly deprecates it. That's why such a man as you may be, after all, a complication.'

I continued to muse. 'You're very sure Miss Dadd's ailment isn't an affection that, being smothered, has struck in?' My joke, however, was not well timed, for I afterwards learned that the unfortunate lady's state had been, even while I spoke, such as to forbid all hope. The worst symptoms had appeared; she was not destined to recover; and a week later I heard from Mrs Munden that she would in fact 'gurgle' no more.

## II

ALL THIS, for Lady Beldonald, had been an agitation so great that access to her apartment was denied for a time even to her sister-in-law. It was much more out of the question, of course, that she should unveil her face to a person of my special business with it; so that the question of the portrait was, by common consent, postponed to that of the installation of a successor to her late companion. Such a successor, I gathered from Mrs Munden, widowed, childless, and lonely, as well as inapt for the minor offices, she had absolutely to have; a more or less humble *alter ego* to deal with the servants, keep the accounts, make the tea and arrange the light. Nothing seemed more natural than that she should marry again, and obviously that might come; yet the predecessors of Miss Dadd had been contemporaneous with a first husband, and others formed in her image might be contemporaneous with a second. I was much occupied in those months, at any rate, so that these questions and their ramifications lost themselves for a while to my view, and I was only brought back to them by Mrs Munden's coming to me one day with the news that we were all right again – her sister-in-law was once more 'suited'. A certain Mrs Brash, an American relative whom she had not seen for years, but with whom she had continued to communicate, was to come out to her immediately; and this person, it appeared, could be quite trusted to meet the conditions. She was ugly – ugly enough, without abuse of it, and she was unlimitedly good. The position offered her by Lady Beldonald was, moreover, exactly what she needed; widowed also, after many troubles and reverses, with her fortune of the smallest and her various children either buried or placed about, she had never had time or means to come to England, and would really be grateful in her declining years for the new experience and the pleasant light work involved in her cousin's hospitality. They had been much together early in life, and Lady Beldonald was immensely fond of her – would have in fact tried to get hold of her before had not Mrs Brash been always in bondage to family duties, to the variety of her tribulations. I daresay I laughed at my friend's use of the term 'position' – the position, one might call it, of a candlestick or a signpost, and I daresay I must have asked if the special service the poor lady was to render had been made clear to her. Mrs Munden left me, at all events, with the rather droll image of her faring forth, across the sea, quite consciously and resignedly to perform it.

The point of the communication had, however, been that my sitter was again looking up and would doubtless, on the arrival and due initiation of Mrs Brash, be in form really to wait on me. The situation must, further, to my knowledge, have developed happily, for I arranged with Mrs Munden that our friend, now all ready to begin, but wanting first just to see the things I had most recently done, should come once more, as a final preliminary, to my studio. A good foreign friend of mine, a French painter, Paul Outreau, was at the moment in London, and I had proposed, as he was much interested in types, to get together for his amusement a small afternoon party. Everyone came, my big room was full, there was music and a modest spread; and I have not forgotten the light of admiration in Outreau's expressive face as, at the end of half an hour, he came up to me in his enthusiasm.

'*Bonté divine, mon cher – que cette vieille est donc belle!*'

I had tried to collect all the beauty I could, and also all the youth, so that for a moment I was at a loss. I had talked to many people and provided for the music, and there were figures in the crowd that were still lost to me. 'What old woman do you mean?'

'I don't know her name – she was over by the door a moment ago. I asked somebody and was told, I think, that she's American.'

I looked about and saw one of my guests attach a pair of fine eyes to Outreau very much as if she knew he must be talking of her. 'Oh, Lady Beldonald! Yes, she's handsome; but the great point about her is that she has been "put up", to keep, and that she wouldn't be flattered if she knew you spoke of her as old. A box of sardines is only "old" after it has been opened. Lady Beldonald never has yet been – but I'm going to do it.' I joked, but I was somehow disappointed. It was a type that, with his unerring sense for the *banal*, I shouldn't have expected Outreau to pick out.

'You're going to paint her? But, my dear man, she *is* painted – and as neither you nor I can do it. *Où est-elle donc?*' He had lost her, and I saw I had made a mistake. 'She's the greatest of all the great Holbeins.'

I was relieved. 'Ah, then, not Lady Beldonald! But do I possess a Holbein, of *any* price, unawares?'

'There she is – there she is! Dear, dear, dear, what a head!' And I saw whom he meant – and what: a small old lady in a black dress and a black bonnet, both relieved with a little white, who had evidently just changed her place to reach a corner from which more of the room and of the scene was presented to her. She appeared unnoticed and unknown, and I immediately recognized that some other guest must have brought her and, for want of opportunity, had as yet to call my attention to her. But two things, simultaneously with this and with each other, struck me with force; one of them the truth of Outreau's description of her, the other the fact that the person bringing her could only have been Lady Beldonald. She *was* a Holbein – of the first water; yet she was also Mrs Brash, the imported 'foil', the indispensable 'accent', the successor to the dreary Miss Dadd! By the time I had put these things together — Outreau's 'American' having helped me — I was in just such full possession of her face as I had found myself, on the other first occasion, of that of her patroness. Only with so different a consequence. I couldn't look at her enough, and I started and stared till I became aware she might have fancied me challenging her as a person unpresented. 'All the same,' Outreau went on, equally held, '*c'est une tête à faire*. If I were only staying long enough for a crack at her! But I tell you what —' and he seized my arm — 'bring her over!'

'Over?'

'To Paris. She'd have a *succès fou*.'

'Ah, thanks, my dear fellow,' I was now quite in a position to say; 'she's the handsomest thing in London, and —' for what I might do with her was already before me with intensity — 'I propose to keep her to myself.' It was before me with intensity, in the light of Mrs Brash's distant perfection of a little white old face, in which every wrinkle was the touch of a master; but something else, I suddenly felt, was not less so, for Lady Beldonald, in the other quarter, and though she couldn't have made out the subject of our notice, continued to fix us, and her eyes had the challenge of those of the woman of consequence who has missed something. A moment later I was close to her, apologizing first for not having been more on the spot at her arrival, but saying in the next breath uncontrollably, 'Why, my dear lady, it's a Holbein!'

'A Holbein? What?'

'Why, the wonderful sharp old face – so extraordinarily, consummately drawn – in the frame of black velvet. That of Mrs Brash, I mean – isn't it her name? – your companion.'

This was the beginning of a most odd matter – the essence of my anecdote; and I think the very first note of the oddity must have sounded for me in the tone in which her ladyship spoke after giving me a silent look. It seemed to come to me out of a distance immeasurably removed from Holbein, 'Mrs Brash is not my "companion" in the sense you appear to mean. She's my rather near relation and a very dear old friend. I *love* her – and you must know her.'

'Know her? Rather! Why, to see her is to want, on the spot, to "go" for her. She also must sit for me.'

'*She?* Louisa Brash?' If Lady Beldonald had the theory that her beauty directly showed it when things were not well with her, this impression, which the fixed sweetness of her serenity had hitherto struck me by no means as justifying, gave me now my first glimpse of its grounds. It was as if I had never before seen her face invaded by anything I should have called an expression. This expression, moreover, was of the faintest – was like the effect produced on a surface by an agitation both deep within and as yet much confused. 'Have you told her so?' she then quickly asked, as if to soften the sound of her surprise.

'Dear no, I've but just noticed her – Outreau a moment ago put me on her. But we're both so taken, and he also wants—'

'To *paint* her?' Lady Beldonald uncontrollably murmured.

'Don't be afraid we shall fight for her,' I returned with a laugh for this tone. Mrs Brash was still where I could see her without appearing to stare, and she mightn't have seen I was looking at her, though her protectress, I am afraid, could scarce have failed of this perception. 'We must each take our turn, and at any rate she's a wonderful thing, so that, if you'll take her to Paris, Outreau promises her there—'

'*There?*' my companion gasped.

'A career bigger still than among *us*, as he considers that we haven't half their eye. He guarantees her a *succès fou*.'

She couldn't get over it. 'Louisa Brash? In Paris?'

'They do see,' I exclaimed, 'more than we; and they live extraordinarily, don't you know, *in* that. But she'll do something here too.'

'And what will she do?'

If, frankly, now, I couldn't help giving Mrs Brash a longer look, so after it I could as little resist sounding my interlocutress. 'You'll see. Only give her time.'

She said nothing during the moment in which she met my eyes; but then: 'Time, it seems to me, is exactly what you and your friend want. If you haven't talked with her—'

'We haven't seen her? Oh, we see bang off – with a click like a steel spring. It's our trade; it's our life; and we should be donkeys if we made mistakes. That's the way I saw you yourself, my lady, if I may say so; that's the way, with a long pin straight through your body, I've got you. And just so I've got *her*.'

All this, for reasons, had brought my guest to her feet; but her eyes, while we talked, had never once followed the direction of mine. 'You call her a Holbein?'

'Outreau did, and I of course immediately recognized it Don't *you*? She brings the old boy to life! It's just as I should call you a Titian. You bring *him* to life.'

She couldn't be said to relax, because she couldn't be said to have hardened; but something at any rate on this took place in her – something indeed quite disconnected from what I would have called her. 'Don't you understand that she has always been supposed—?' It had the ring of impatience; nevertheless, on a scruple, it stopped short.

I knew what it was, however, well enough to say it for her if she preferred. 'To be nothing whatever to look at? To be unfortunately plain – or even if you like repulsively ugly? Oh yes, I understand it perfectly, just as I understand – I have to as a part of my trade – many other forms of stupidity. It's nothing new to one that ninety-nine people out of a hundred have no eyes, no sense, no taste. There are whole communities impenetrably sealed. I don't say your friend is a person to make the men turn round in Regent Street. But it adds to the joy of the few who do see that they have it so much to themselves. Where in the world can she have lived? You must tell me all about that – or rather, if she'll be so good, *she* must.'

'You mean then to speak to her—?'

I wondered as she pulled up again. 'Of her beauty?'

'Her beauty!' cried Lady Beldonald so loud that two or three persons looked round.

'Ah, with every precaution of respect!' I declared in a much lower tone. But her back was by this time turned to me, and in the movement, as it were, one of the strangest little dramas I have ever known was well launched.

## III

IT WAS A drama of small, smothered intensely private things, and I knew of but one other person in the secret; yet that person and I found it exquisitely susceptible of notation, followed it with an interest the mutual communication of which did much for our enjoyment, and were present with emotion at its touching catastrophe. The small case – for so small a case – had made a great stride even before my little party separated, and in fact within the next ten minutes.

In that space of time two things had happened; one of which was that I made the acquaintance of Mrs Brash, and the other that Mrs Munden reached me, cleaving the crowd, with one of her usual pieces of news. What she had to impart was that, on her having just before asked Nina if the conditions of our sitting had been arranged with me, Nina had replied, with something like perversity, that she didn't propose to arrange them, that the whole affair was 'off' again, and that she preferred not to be, for the present, further pressed. The question for Mrs Munden was naturally what had happened and whether I understood. Oh, I understood perfectly, and what I at first most understood was that even when I had brought in the name of Mrs Brash intelligence was not yet in Mrs Munden. She was quite as surprised as Lady Beldonald had been on hearing of the esteem in which I held Mrs Brash's appearance. She was stupefied at learning that I had just in my ardour proposed to the possessor of it to sit to me. Only she came round promptly – which Lady Beldonald really never did. Mrs Munden was in fact wonderful; for when I had given her quickly 'Why, she's a Holbein, you know,' she took it up, after a first fine vacancy, with an immediate abysmal 'Oh, *is* she?' that, as a piece of social gymnastics, did her the greatest honour; and she was in fact the first in London to spread the tidings. For a face-about it was magnificent. But she was also the first, I must add, to see what would really happen – though this she put before me only a week or two later.

'It will kill her, my dear – that's what it will do!'

She meant neither more nor less than that it would kill Lady Beldonald if I were to paint Mrs Brash; for at this lurid light had we arrived in so short a space of time. It was for me to decide whether my aesthetic need of giving life to my idea was such as to justify me in destroying it in a woman after all, in most eyes, so beautiful. The situation was, after all, sufficiently queer; for it remained to be seen what I should positively gain by giving up Mrs Brash. I appeared to have in any case lost Lady Beldonald, now too 'upset' – it was always Mrs Munden's word about her and, as I inferred, her own about herself – to meet me again on our previous footing. The only thing, I of course soon saw, was to temporize – to drop the whole question for the present and yet so far as possible keep each of the pair in view. I may as well say at once that this plan and this process gave their principal interest to the next several months. Mrs Brash had turned up, if I remember, early in the new year, and her little wonderful career was in our particular circle one of the features of the following season. It was at all events for myself the most attaching; it is not my fault if I am so put together as often to find more life in situations obscure and subject to interpretation than in the gross rattle of the foreground. And there were all sorts of things, things touching, amusing, mystifying – and above all such an instance as I had never yet met – in this funny little fortune of the useful American cousin. Mrs Munden was promptly at one with me as to the rarity and, to a near and human view, the beauty and interest of the position. We had neither of us ever before seen that degree and that special sort of personal success come to a woman for the first time so late in life. I found it an example of poetic, of absolutely retributive, justice; so that my desire grew great to work it, as we say, on those lines. I had seen it all from the original moment at my studio; the poor lady had never known an hour's appreciation – which, moreover, in perfect good faith, she had never missed; The very first thing I did after producing so unintentionally the resentful retreat of her protectress had been to go straight over to her and say almost without preliminaries that I should hold myself immeasurably obliged if she would give me a few sittings. What I thus came face to face with was, on the instant, her whole unenlightened past, and the full, if foreshortened, revelation of what among us all was now unfailingly in store for her. To turn the handle and start that tune came to me on the spot as a temptation. Here was a poor lady who had waited for the approach of old age to find out what she was worth. Here was a benighted being to whom it was to be disclosed in her fifty-seventh year (I was to make that out) that she had something that might pass for a face. She looked much more than her age, and was fairly frightened – as if I had been trying on her some possibly heartless London trick – when she had taken in my appeal. That showed me in what an air she had lived and – as I should have been tempted to put it had I spoken out – among what children of darkness. Later on I did them more justice, saw more that her wonderful points must have been points largely the fruit of time, and even that possibly she might never in all her life have looked so well as at this particular moment. It might have been that if her hour had struck I just happened to be present at the striking. What had occurred, all the same, was at the worst a sufficient comedy.

The famous 'irony of fate' takes many forms, but I had never yet seen it take quite this one. She had been 'had over' on an understanding, and she was not playing fair. She had broken the law of her ugliness and had turned beautiful on the hands of her employer. More interesting even perhaps than a view of the conscious triumph that this might prepare for her, and of which, had I doubted of my own judgement, I could still take Outreau's fine start as the full guarantee – more interesting was the question of the process by which such a history could get itself enacted. The curious thing was that, all the while, the reasons of her having passed for plain – the reasons for Lady Beldonald's fond calculation, which they quite justified – were written large in her face, so large that it was easy to understand them as the only ones she herself had ever read. What was it, then, that actually made the old stale sentence mean something so different? – into what new combinations, what extraordinary language, unknown but understood at a glance, had time and life translated it? The only thing to be said was that time and life were artists who beat us all, working with recipes and secrets that we could never find out. I really ought to have, like a lecturer or a showman, a chart or a blackboard to present properly the relation, in the wonderful old tender, battered, blanched face, between the original elements and the exquisite final 'style'. I could do it with chalks, but I can scarcely do it thus. However, the thing was, for any artist who respected himself, to *feel* it – which I abundantly did; and then not to conceal from *her* that I felt it – which I neglected as little. But she was really, to do her complete justice, the last to understand; and I am not sure that, to the end – for there was an end – she quite made it all out or knew where she was. When you have been brought up for fifty years on black, it must be hard to adjust your organism, at a day's notice, to gold-colour. Her whole nature had been pitched in the key of her supposed plainness. She had known how to be ugly – it was the only thing she had learned save, if possible, how not to mind it. Being beautiful, at any rate, took a new set of muscles. It was on the prior theory, literally, that she had developed her admirable dress, instinctively felicitous, always either black or white, and a matter of rather severe squareness and studied line. She was magnificently neat; everything she showed had a way of looking both old and fresh; and there was on every occasion the same picture in her draped head – draped in low-falling black – and the fine white plaits (of a painter's white, somehow) disposed on her chest. What had happened was that these arrangements, determined by certain considerations, lent themselves in effect much better to certain others. Adopted as a kind of refuge, they had really only deepened her accent. It was singular, moreover, that, so constituted, there was nothing in her aspect of the ascetic or the nun. She was a good, hard, sixteenth-century figure, not withered with innocence, bleached rather by life in the open. She was, in short, just what we had made of her, a Holbein for a great museum; and our position, Mrs Munden's and mine, rapidly became that of persons having such a treasure to dispose of. The world – I speak of course mainly of the art-world – flocked to see it.

# IV

'BUT HAS SHE any idea herself, poor thing?' was the way I had put it to Mrs Munden on our next meeting after the incident at my studio; with the effect, however, only of leaving my friend at

## The Beldonald Holbein

first to take me as alluding to Mrs Brash's possible prevision of the chatter she might create. I had my own sense of that – this prevision had been *nil*; the question was of her consciousness of the office for which Lady Beldonald had counted on her and for which we were so promptly proceeding to spoil her altogether.

'Oh, I think she arrived with a goodish notion,' Mrs Munden had replied when I had explained; 'for she's clever too, you know, as well as good-looking, and I don't see how, if she ever really *knew* Nina, she could have supposed for a moment that she was not wanted for whatever she might have left to give up. Hasn't she moreover always been made to feel that she's ugly enough for anything?' It was even at this point already wonderful how my friend had mastered the case, and what lights, alike for its past and its future, she was prepared to throw on it. 'If she has seen herself as ugly enough for anything, she has seen herself – and that was the only way – as ugly enough for Nina; and she has had her own manner of showing that she understands without making Nina commit herself to anything vulgar. Women are never without ways for doing such things – both for communicating and receiving knowledge – that I can't explain to you, and that you wouldn't understand if I could, as you must *be* a woman even to do that. I daresay they've expressed it all to each other simply in the language of kisses. But doesn't it, at any rate, make something rather beautiful of the relation between them as affected by our discovery?'

I had a laugh for her plural possessive. 'The point is, of course, that if there was a conscious bargain, and our action on

Mrs Brash is to deprive her of the sense of keeping her side of it, various things may happen that won't be good either for her or for ourselves. She may conscientiously throw up the position.'

'Yes,' my companion mused – 'for she *is* conscientious. Or Nina, without waiting for that, may cast her forth.'

I faced it all. 'Then *we* should have to keep her.'

'As a regular model?' Mrs Munden was ready for anything. 'Oh, that would be lovely!'

But I further worked it out. 'The difficulty is that she's *not* a model, hang it – that she's too good for one, that she's the very thing herself. When Outreau and I have each had our go, that will be all; there'll be nothing left for anyone else. Therefore it behoves us quite to understand that our attitude's a responsibility. If we can't do for her positively more than Nina does—'

'We must let her alone?' My companion continued to muse. 'I see!'

'Yet don't,' I returned, 'see too much. We *can* do more.'

'Than Nina?' She was again on the spot. 'It wouldn't, after all, be difficult. We only want the directly opposite thing – and which is the only one the poor dear can give. Unless, indeed,' she suggested, 'we simply retract – we back out.'

I turned it over. 'It's too late for that. Whether Mrs Brash's peace is gone, I can't say. But Nina's is.'

'Yes, and there's no way to bring it back that won't sacrifice her friend. We can't turn round and say Mrs Brash *is* ugly, can we? But fancy Nina's not having *seen*!' Mrs Munden exclaimed.

'She doesn't see now,' I answered. 'She can't, I'm certain, make out what we mean. The woman, for *her* still, is just what she always was. But she has, nevertheless, had her stroke, and her blindness, while she wavers and gropes in the dark, only adds to her discomfort. Her blow was to see the attention of the world deviate.'

'All the same, I don't think, you know,' my interlocutress said, 'that Nina will have made her a scene, or that, whatever we do, she'll ever make her one. That isn't the way it will happen, for she's exactly as conscientious as Mrs Brash.'

'Then what *is* the way?' I asked.

'It will just happen in silence.'

'And what will "it", as you call it, be?'

'Isn't that what we want really to see?'

'Well,' I replied after a turn or two about, 'whether we want it or not, it's exactly what we *shall* see; which is a reason the more for fancying, between the pair there – in the quiet, exquisite house, and full of superiorities and suppressions as they both are – the extraordinary situation. If I said just now that it's too late to do anything but accept, it's because I've taken the full measure of what happened at my studio. It took but a few moments – but she tasted of the tree.'

My companion wondered. 'Nina?'

'Mrs Brash.' And to have to put it so ministered, while I took yet another turn, to a sort of agitation. Our attitude *was* a responsibility.

But I had suggested something else to my friend, who

appeared for a moment detached. 'Should you say she'll hate her worse if she *doesn't* see?'

'Lady Beldonald? Doesn't see what *we* see, you mean, than if she does? Ah, I give *that* up!' I laughed. 'But what I can tell you is why I hold that, as I said just now, we can do most. We can do this: we can give to a harmless and sensitive creature hitherto practically disinherited – and give with an unexpectedness that will immensely add to its price – the pure joy of a deep draught of the very pride of life, of an acclaimed personal triumph in our superior, sophisticated world.'

Mrs Munden had a glow of response for my sudden eloquence. 'Oh, it will be beautiful!'

# V

WELL, THAT IS what, on the whole, and in spite of everything, it really was. It has dropped into my memory a rich little gallery of pictures, a regular panorama of those occasions that were the proof of the privilege that had made me for a moment – in the words I have just recorded – lyrical. I see Mrs Brash on each of these occasions practically enthroned and surrounded and more or less mobbed; see the hurrying and the nudging and the pressing and the staring; see the people 'making up' and introduced, and catch the word when they have had their turn; hear it above all, the great one – 'Ah yes, the famous Holbein!' – passed about with that perfection of promptitude that makes the motions of the London mind so happy a mixture of those of the parrot and the sheep. Nothing would be easier, of course, than to tell the whole little tale with an eye only for that silly side of it. Great was the silliness, but great also as to this case of poor Mrs Brash, I will say for it, the good-nature. Of course, furthermore, it took in particular 'our set', with its positive child-terror of the *banal*, to be either so foolish or so wise; though indeed I've never quite known where our set begins and ends, and have had to content myself on this score with the indication once given me by a lady next whom I was placed at dinner: 'Oh, it's bounded on the north by Ibsen and on the south by Sargent!' Mrs Brash never sat to me; she absolutely declined; and when she declared that it was quite enough for her that I had with that fine precipitation invited her, I quite took this as she meant it, for before we had gone very far our understanding, hers and mine, was complete. Her attitude was as happy as her success was prodigious. The sacrifice of the portrait was a sacrifice to the true inwardness of Lady Beldonald, and did much, for the time, I divined, toward muffling their domestic tension. All that was thus in her power to say – and I heard of a few cases of her having said it – was that she was sure I would have painted her beautifully if she hadn't prevented me. She couldn't even tell the truth, which was that I certainly would have done so if Lady Beldonald hadn't; and she never could mention the subject at all before that personage. I can only describe the affair, naturally, from the outside, and heaven forbid indeed that I should try too closely to reconstruct the possible strange intercourse of these good friends at home.

My anecdote, however, would lose half such point as it may possess were I to omit all mention of the charming turn that her ladyship appeared gradually to have found herself able to give to her deportment. She had made it impossible I should myself bring up our old, our original question, but there was real distinction in her manner of now accepting certain other possibilities. Let me do her that justice; her effort at magnanimity must have been immense. There couldn't fail, of course, to be ways in which poor Mrs Brash paid for it. How much she had to pay we were, in fact, soon enough to see; and it is my intimate conviction that, as a climax, her life at last was the price. But while she lived, at least – and it was with an intensity, for those wondrous weeks, of which she had never dreamed – Lady Beldonald herself faced the music. This is what I mean by the possibilities, by the sharp actualities indeed, that she accepted. She took our friend out, she showed her at home, never attempted to hide or to betray her, played her no trick whatever so long as the ordeal lasted. She drank deep, on *her* side too, of the cup – the cup that for her own lips could only be bitterness. There was, I think, scarce a special success of her companion's at which she was not personally present. Mrs Munden's theory of the silence in which all this would be muffled for them was, none the less, and in abundance, confirmed by our observations. The whole thing was to be the death of one or the other of them, but they never spoke of it at tea. I remember even that Nina went so far as to say to me once, looking me full in the eyes, quite sublimely, 'I've made out what you mean – she *is* a picture.' The beauty of this, moreover, was that, as I am persuaded, she hadn't really made it out at all – the words were the mere hypocrisy of her reflective endeavour for virtue. She couldn't possibly have made it out; her friend was as much as ever 'dreadfully plain' to her; she must have wondered to the last what on earth possessed us. Wouldn't it in fact have been, after all, just this failure of vision, this supreme stupidity in short, that kept the catastrophe so long at bay? There was a certain sense of greatness for her in seeing so many of us so absurdly mistaken; and I recall that on various occasions, and in particular when she uttered the words just quoted, this high serenity, as a sign of the relief of her soreness, if not of the effort of her conscience, did something quite visible to my eyes, and also quite unprecedented, for the beauty of her face. She got a real lift from it – such a momentary discernible sublimity that I recollect coming out on the spot with a queer, crude, amused 'Do you know I believe I could paint you *now*?'

She was a fool not to have closed with me then and there; for what has happened since has altered everything – what was to happen a little later was so much more than I could swallow. This was the disappearance of the famous Holbein from one day to the other – producing a consternation among us all as great as if the Venus of Milo had suddenly vanished from the Louvre. 'She has simply shipped her straight back' – the explanation was given in that form by Mrs Munden, who added that any cord pulled tight enough would end at last by snapping. At the snap, in any case, we mightily jumped, for the masterpiece we had for three or four months been living with had made us feel its presence as a luminous lesson and a daily need. We recognized more than ever that it had been, for high finish, the gem of our collection – we found what a blank it left on the wall. Lady Beldonald might fill up the blank, but *we* couldn't. That she did soon fill it up – and, heaven help us *how*? – was put before me after an interval of no great length, but during which I had not seen her. I dined on the Christmas of last year at Mrs Munden's, and Nina, with a 'scratch lot', as our hostess said, was there, and, the preliminary wait being longish, approached me very sweetly. 'I'll come to you tomorrow if you like,' she said; and the effect of it, after a first stare at her, was to make me look all round. I took in, in these two motions, two things; one of which was that, though now again so satisfied herself of her high state, she could give me nothing comparable to what I should have got had she taken me up at the moment of my meeting her on her distinguished concession; the other that she was 'suited' afresh, and that Mrs Brash's successor was fully installed. Mrs Brash's successor was at the other side of the room, and I became conscious that Mrs Munden was waiting to see my eyes seek her. I guessed the meaning of the wait; what *was* one, this time, to say? Oh, first and foremost, assuredly, that it was immensely droll, for this time, at least, there was no mistake. The lady I looked upon, and as to whom my friend, again quite at sea, appealed to me for a formula, was as little a Holbein, or a

## The Beldonald Holbein

specimen of any other school, as she was, like Lady Beldonald herself, a Titian. The formula was easy to give, for the amusement was that her prettiness – yes, literally, prodigiously, her prettiness – was distinct. Lady Beldonald had been magnificent – had been almost intelligent. Miss What's-her-name continues pretty, continues even young, and doesn't matter a straw! She matters so ideally little that Lady Beldonald is practically safer, I judge, than she has ever been. There has not been a symptom of chatter about this person, and I believe her protectress is much surprised that we are not more struck.

It was, at any rate, strictly impossible to me to make an appointment for the day as to which I have just recorded Nina's proposal; and the turn of events since then has not quickened my eagerness. Mrs Munden remained in correspondence with Mrs Brash – to the extent, that is, of three letters, each of which she showed me. They so told, to our imagination, her terrible little story that we were quite prepared – or thought we were – for her going out like a snuffed candle. She resisted, on her return to her original conditions, less than a year; the taste of the tree, as I had called it, had been fatal to her; what she had contentedly enough lived without before for half a century she couldn't now live without for a day. I know nothing of her original conditions – some minor American city – save that for her to have gone back to them was clearly to have stepped out of her frame. We performed, Mrs Munden and I, a small funeral service for her by talking it all over and making it all out. It wasn't – the minor American city – a market for Holbeins, and what had occurred was that the poor old picture, banished from its museum and refreshed by the rise of no new movement to hang it, was capable of the miracle of a silent revolution, of itself turning, in its dire dishonour, its face to the wall. So it stood, without the intervention of the ghost of a critic, till they happened to pull it round again and find it mere dead paint. Well, it had had, if that is anything, its season of fame, its name on a thousand tongues and printed in capitals in the catalogue. *We* had not been at fault. I haven't, all the same, the least note of her – not a scratch. And I did her so in intention! Mrs Munden continues to remind me, however, that this is not the sort of rendering with which, on the other side, after all, Lady Beldonald proposes to content herself. She has come back to the question of her own portrait. Let me settle it then at last. Since she *will* have the real thing – well, hang it, she shall!

# The Story in It

## I

THE WEATHER HAD turned so much worse that the rest of the day was certainly lost. The wind had risen and the storm gathered force; they gave from time to time a thump at the firm windows and dashed even against those protected by the verandah their vicious splotches of rain. Beyond the lawn, beyond the cliff, the great wet brush of the sky dipped deep into the sea. But the lawn, already vivid with the touch of May, showed a violence of watered green; the budding shrubs and trees repeated the note as they tossed their thick masses, and the cold, troubled light, filling the pretty drawing-room, marked the spring afternoon as sufficiently young. The two ladies seated there in silence could pursue without difficulty – as well as, clearly, without interruption – their respective tasks; a confidence expressed, when the noise of the wind allowed it to be heard, by the sharp scratch of Mrs Dyott's pen at the table where she was busy with letters.

Her visitor, settled on a small sofa that, with a palm-tree, a screen, a stool, a stand, a bowl of flowers and three photographs in silver frames, had been arranged near the light wood-fire as a choice 'corner' – Maud Blessingbourne, her guest, turned audibly, though at intervals neither brief nor regular, the leaves of a book covered in lemon-coloured paper and not yet despoiled of a certain fresh crispness. This effect of the volume, for the eye, would have made it, as presumably the newest French novel – and evidently, from the attitude of the reader, 'good' – consort happily with the special tone of the room, a consistent air of selection and suppression, one of the finer aesthetic evolutions. If Mrs Dyott was fond of ancient French furniture, and distinctly difficult about it, her inmates could be fond – with whatever critical cocks of charming dark-braided heads over slender sloping shoulders – of modern French authors. Nothing had passed for half an hour – nothing, at least, to be exact, but that each of the companions occasionally and covertly intermitted her pursuit in such a manner as to ascertain the degree of absorption of the other without turning round. What their silence was charged with, therefore, was not only a sense of the weather, but a sense, so to speak, of its own nature. Maud Blessingbourne, when she lowered her book into her lap, closed her eyes with a conscious patience that seemed to say she waited; but it was nevertheless she who at last made the movement representing a snap of their tension. She got up and stood by the fire, into which she looked a minute; then came round and approached the window as if to see what was really going on. At this Mrs Dyott wrote with refreshed intensity. Her little pile of letters had grown, and if a look of determination was compatible with her fair and slightly faded beauty, the habit of attending to her business could always keep pace with any excursion of her thought. Yet she was the first who spoke.

'I trust your book has been interesting.'

'Well enough; a little mild.'

A louder throb of the tempest had blurred the sound of the words. 'A little wild?'

'Dear, no – timid and tame; unless I've quite lost my sense.'

'Perhaps you have,' Mrs Dyott placidly suggested – 'reading so many.'

Her companion made a motion of feigned despair. 'Ah, you take away my courage for going to my room, as I was just meaning to, for another.'

'Another French one?'

'I'm afraid.'

'Do you carry them by the dozen—'

'Into innocent British homes?' Maud tried to remember. 'I believe I brought three – seeing them in a shop-window as I passed through town. It never rains but it pours! But I've already read two.'

'And are they the only ones you do read?'

'French ones?' Maud considered. 'Oh, no. D'Annunzio.'

'And what's that?' Mrs Dyott asked as she affixed a stamp.

'Oh, you dear thing!' Her friend was amused, yet almost

showed pity. 'I know you don't read,' Maud went on; 'but why should you? *You* live!'

'Yes – wretchedly enough,' Mrs Dyott returned, getting her letters together. She left her place, holding them as a neat, achieved handful, and came over to the fire, while Mrs Blessingbourne turned once more to the window, where she was met by another flurry.

Maud spoke then as if moved only by the elements. 'Do you expect him through all this?'

Mrs Dyott just waited, and it had the effect, indescribably, of making everything that had gone before seem to have led up to the question. This effect was even deepened by the way she then said, 'Whom do you mean?'

'Why, I thought you mentioned at luncheon that Colonel Voyt was to walk over. Surely he can't.'

'Do you care very much?' Mrs Dyott asked.

Her friend now hesitated. 'It depends on what you call "much". If you mean should I like to see him – then certainly.'

'Well, my dear, I think he understands you're here.'

'So that as he evidently isn't coming,' Maud laughed, 'it's particularly flattering! Or rather,' she added, giving up the prospect again, 'it would be, I think, quite extraordinarily flattering if he did. Except that, of course,' she subjoined, 'he might come partly for you.'

'"Partly" is charming. Thank you for "partly". If you *are* going upstairs, will you kindly,' Mrs Dyott pursued, 'put these into the box as you pass?'

The younger woman, taking the little pile of letters, considered them with envy. 'Nine! You *are* good. You're always a living reproach!'

Mrs Dyott gave a sigh. 'I don't do it on purpose. The only thing, this afternoon,' she went on, reverting to the other question, 'would be their not having come down.'

'And as to that you don't know.'

'No – I don't know.' But she caught even as she spoke a rat-tat-tat of the knocker, which struck her as a sign. 'Ah, there!'

'Then I go.' And Maud whisked out.

Mrs Dyott, left alone, moved with an air of selection to the window, and it was as so stationed, gazing out at the wild weather, that the visitor, whose delay to appear spoke of the wiping of boots and the disposal of drenched mackintosh and cap, finally found her. He was tall, lean, fine, with little in him, on the whole, to confirm the titular in the 'Colonel Voyt' by which he was announced. But he had left the army, and his reputation for gallantry mainly depended now on his fighting Liberalism in the House of Commons. Even these facts, however, his aspect scantly matched; partly, no doubt, because he looked, as was usually said, un-English. His black hair, cropped close, was lightly powdered with silver, and his dense glossy beard, that of an emir or a caliph, and grown for civil reasons, repeated its handsome colour and its somewhat foreign effect. His nose had a strong and shapely arch, and the dark grey of his eyes was tinted with blue. It had been said of him – in relation to these signs – that he would have struck you as a Jew had he not, in spite of his nose, struck you so much as an Irishman. Neither responsibility could in fact have been fixed upon him, and just now, at all events, he was only a pleasant, weather-washed, wind-battered Briton, who brought in from a struggle with the elements that he appeared quite to have enjoyed a certain amount of unremoved mud and an unusual quantity of easy expression. It was exactly the silence ensuing on the retreat of the servant and the closed door that marked between him and his hostess the degree of this ease. They met, as it were, twice: the first time while the servant was there and the second as soon as he was not. The difference was great between the two encounters, though we must add in justice to the second that its marks were at first mainly negative. This communion consisted only in their having drawn each other for a minute as close as possible – as possible, that is, with no help but the full clasp of hands. Thus they were mutually held, and the closeness was at any rate such that, for a little, though it took account of dangers, it did without words. When words presently came the pair were talking by the fire, and she had rung for tea. He had by this time asked if the note he had despatched to her after breakfast had been safely delivered.

'Yes, before luncheon. But I'm always in a state when – except for some extraordinary reason – you send such things by hand. I knew, without it, that you had come. It never fails. I'm sure when you're there – I'm sure when you're not.'

He wiped, before the glass, his wet moustache. 'I see. But this morning I had an impulse.'

'It was beautiful. But they make me as uneasy, sometimes, your impulses, as if they were calculations; make me wonder what you have in reserve.'

'Because when small children are too awfully good they die? Well, I *am* a small child compared to you – but I'm not dead yet. I cling to life.'

He had covered her with his smile, but she continued grave. 'I'm not half so much afraid when you're nasty.'

'Thank you! What then did you do,' he asked, 'with my note?'

'You deserve that I should have spread it out on my dressing-table – or left it, better still, in Maud Blessingbourne's room.'

He wondered while he laughed. 'Oh, but what does *she* deserve?'

It was her gravity that continued to answer. 'Yes – it would probably kill her.'

'She believes so in you?'

'She believes so in *you*. So don't be *too* nice to her.'

He was still looking, in the chimney-glass, at the state of his beard – brushing from it, with his handkerchief, the traces of wind and wet. 'If she also then prefers me when I'm nasty, it seems to me I ought to satisfy her. Shall I now, at any rate, see her?'

'She's so like a pea on a pan over the possibility of it that she's pulling herself together in her room.'

'Oh then, we must try and keep her together. But why, graceful, tender, pretty too – quite, or almost – as she is, doesn't she remarry?'

Mrs Dyott appeared – and as if the first time – to look for the reason. 'Because she likes too many men.'

It kept up his spirits. 'And how many *may* a lady like—?'

'In order not to like any of them too much? Ah, that, you know, I never found out – and it's too late now. When,' she presently pursued, 'did you last see her?'

He really had to think. 'Would it have been since last November or so? – somewhere or other where we spent three days.'

'Oh, at Surredge? I know all about that. I thought you also met afterwards.'

He had again to recall. 'So we did! Wouldn't it have been somewhere at Christmas? But it wasn't by arrangement!' he laughed, giving with his forefinger a little pleasant nick to his hostess's chin. Then as if something in the way she received this attention put him back to his question of a moment before, 'Have you kept my note?'

She held him with her pretty eyes. 'Do you want it back?'

'Ah, don't speak as if I did take things—!'

She dropped her gaze to the fire. 'No, you don't; not even the hard things a really generous nature often would.' She quitted, however, as if to forget that, the chimney-place. 'I put it *there*!'

'You've burnt it? Good!' It made him easier, but he noticed the next moment on a table the lemon-coloured volume left there by Mrs Blessingbourne, and, taking it up for a look, immediately put it down. 'You might, while you were about it, have burnt that too.'

'You've read it?'

'Dear, yes. And you?'

'No,' said Mrs Dyott; 'it wasn't for me Maud brought it.'

It pulled her visitor up. 'Mrs Blessingbourne brought it?'

'For such a day as this.' But she wondered. 'How you look! Is it so awful?'

'Oh, like his others.' Something had occurred to him; his thought was already far. 'Does she know?'

'Know what?'

'Why, anything.'

But the door opened too soon for Mrs Dyott, who could only murmur quickly:

'Take care!'

# II

IT WAS IN fact Mrs Blessingbourne, who had under her arm the book she had gone up for – a pair of covers that this time showed a pretty, a candid blue. She was followed next minute by the servant, who brought in tea, the consumption of which, with the passage of greetings, inquiries and other light civilities between the two visitors, occupied a quarter of an hour. Mrs Dyott meanwhile, as a contribution to so much amenity, mentioned to Maud that her fellow-guest wished to scold her for the books she read – a statement met by this friend with the remark that he must first be sure about them. But as soon as he had picked up the new volume he broke out into a frank 'Dear, dear!'

'Have you read that too?' Mrs Dyott inquired. 'How much you'll have to talk over together! The other one,' she explained to him, 'Maud speaks of as terribly tame.'

'Ah, I must have that out with her! You don't feel the extraordinary force of the fellow?' Voyt went on to Mrs Blessingbourne.

And so, round the hearth, they talked – talked soon, while they warmed their toes, with zest enough to make it seem as happy a chance as any of the quieter opportunities their imprisonment might have involved. Mrs Blessingbourne did feel, it then appeared, the force of the fellow, but she had her reserves and reactions, in which Voyt was much interested. Mrs Dyott rather detached herself, mainly gazing, as she leaned back, at the fire; she intervened, however, enough to relieve Maud of the sense of being listened to. That sense, with Maud, was too apt to convey that one was listened to for a fool. 'Yes, when I read a novel I mostly read a French one,' she had said to Voyt in answer to a question about her usual practice; 'for I seem with it to get hold more of the real thing – to get more life for my money. Only I'm not so infatuated with them but that sometimes for months and months on end I don't read any fiction at all.'

The two books were now together beside them. 'Then when you begin again you read a mass?'

'Dear, no. I only keep up with three or four authors.'

He laughed at this over the cigarette he had been allowed to light. 'I like your "keeping up", and keeping up in particular with "authors".'

'One must keep up with somebody,' Mrs Dyott threw off.

'I daresay I'm ridiculous,' Mrs Blessingbourne conceded without heeding it; 'but that's the way we express ourselves in my part of the country.'

'I only alluded,' said Voyt, 'to the tremendous conscience of your sex. It's more than mine can keep up with. You take everything too hard. But if you can't read the novel of British and American manufacture, heaven knows I'm at one with you. It seems really to show our sense of life as the sense of puppies and kittens.'

'Well,' Maud more patiently returned, 'I'm told all sorts of people are now doing wonderful things; but somehow I remain outside.'

'Ah, it's *they*, it's our poor twangers and twaddlers who remain outside. They pick up a living in the street. And who indeed would want them in?'

Mrs Blessingbourne seemed unable to say, and yet at the same time to have her idea. The subject, in truth, she evidently found, was not so easy to handle. 'People lend me things, and I try; but at the end of fifty pages—'

'There you are! Yes – heaven help us!'

'But what I mean,' she went on, 'isn't that I don't get woefully weary of the eternal French thing. What's *their* sense of life?'

'Ah, *voilà!*' Mrs Dyott softly sounded.

'Oh, but it *is* one; you can make it out,' Voyt promptly

declared. 'They do what they feel, and they feel more things than we. They strike so many more notes, and with so different a hand. When it comes to any account of a relation, say, between a man and a woman – I mean an intimate or a curious or a suggestive one – where are we compared to them? They don't exhaust the subject, no doubt,' he admitted; 'but we don't touch it, don't even skim it. It's as if we denied its existence, its possibility. You'll doubtless tell me, however,' he went on, 'that as all such relations *are* for us, at the most, much simpler, we can only have all round less to say about them.'

She met this imputation with the quickest amusement. 'I beg your pardon. I don't think I shall tell you anything of the sort. I don't know that I even agree with your premise.'

'About such relations?' He looked agreeably surprised. 'You think we make them larger? – or subtler?'

Mrs Blessingbourne leaned back, not looking, like Mrs Dyott, at the fire, but at the ceiling. 'I don't know what I think.'

'It's not that she doesn't know,' Mrs Dyott remarked. 'It's only that she doesn't say.'

But Voyt had this time no eye for their hostess. For a moment he watched Maud. 'It sticks out of you, you know, that you've yourself written something. Haven't you – and published? I've a notion I could read *you*.'

'When I do publish,' she said without moving, 'you'll be the last one I shall tell. I *have*,' she went on, 'a lovely subject, but it would take an amount of treatment—!'

'Tell us then at least what it is.'

At this she again met his eyes. 'Oh, to tell it would be to express it, and that's just what I can't do. What I meant to say just now,' she added, 'was that the French, to my sense, give us only again and again, for ever and ever, the same couple. There they are once more, as one has had them to satiety, in that yellow thing, and there I shall certainly again find them in the blue.'

'Then why do you keep reading about them?' Mrs Dyott demanded.

Maud hesitated. 'I don't!' she sighed. 'At all events, I shan't any more. I give it up.'

'You've been looking for something, I judge,' said Colonel Voyt, 'that you're not likely to find. It doesn't exist.'

'What is it?' Mrs Dyott inquired.

'I never look,' Maud remarked, 'for anything but an interest.'

'Naturally. But your interest,' Voyt replied, 'is in something different from life.'

'Ah, not a bit! I *love* life – in art, though I hate it anywhere else. It's the poverty of the life those people show, and the awful bounders, of both sexes, that they represent.'

'Oh, now we have you!' her interlocutor laughed. 'To me, when all's said and done, they seem to be – as near as art can come – in the truth of the truth. It can only take what life gives it, though it certainly may be a pity that that isn't better. Your complaint of their monotony is a complaint of their conditions. When you say we get always the same couple what do you mean but that we get always the same passion? Of course we do!'

Voyt declared. 'If what you're looking for is another, that's what you won't anywhere find.'

Maud for a while said nothing, and Mrs Dyott seemed to wait. 'Well, I suppose I'm looking, more than anything else, for a decent woman.'

'Oh then, you mustn't look for her in pictures of passion. That's not her element nor her whereabouts.'

Mrs Blessingbourne weighed the objection. 'Doesn't it depend on what you mean by passion?'

'I think one can mean only one thing: the enemy to behaviour.'

'Oh, I can imagine passions that are, on the contrary, friends to it.'

Her interlocutor thought. 'Doesn't it depend perhaps on what you mean by behaviour?'

'Dear, no. Behaviour is just behaviour – the most definite thing in the world.'

'Then what do you mean by the "interest" you just now spoke of? The picture of that definite thing?'

'Yes – call it that. Women aren't *always* vicious, even when they're—'

'When they're what?' Voyt asked.

'When they're unhappy. They can be unhappy and good.'

'That one doesn't for a moment deny. But can they be "good" and interesting?'

'That must be Maud's subject!' Mrs Dyott explained. 'To show a woman who *is*. I'm afraid, my dear,' she continued, 'you could only show yourself.'

'You'd show then the most beautiful specimen conceivable' – and Voyt addressed himself to Maud. 'But doesn't it prove that life is, against your contention, more interesting than art? Life you embellish and elevate; but art would find itself able to do nothing with you, and, on such impossible terms, would ruin you.'

The colour in her faint consciousness gave beauty to her stare. '"Ruin" me?'

'He means,' Mrs Dyott again indicated, 'that you would ruin "art".'

'Without, on the other hand –' Voyt seemed to assent – 'its giving at all a coherent impression of you.'

'She wants her romance cheap!' said Mrs Dyott.

'Oh, no – I should be willing to pay for it. I don't see why the romance – since you give it that name – should be all, as the French inveterately make it, for the women who are bad.'

'Oh, they pay for it!' said Mrs Dyott.

'*Do* they?'

'So, at least –' Mrs Dyott a little corrected herself – 'one has gathered (for I don't read your books, you know!) that they're usually shown as doing.'

Maud wondered, but looking at Voyt, 'They're shown often, no doubt, as paying for their badness. But are they shown as paying for their romance?'

'My dear lady,' said Voyt, 'their romance *is* their badness. There isn't any other. It's a hard law, if you will, and a strange, but goodness has to go without that luxury. Isn't to *be* good just exactly, all round, to go without?' He put it before her kindly and clearly – regretfully too, as if he were sorry the truth should be so sad. He and she, his pleasant eyes seemed to say, would, had they had the making of it, have made it better. 'One has heard it before – at least *I* have; one has heard your question put. But always, when put to a mind not merely muddled, for an inevitable answer. "Why don't you, *cher monsieur*, give us the drama of virtue?" "Because, *chère madame*, the high privilege of virtue is precisely to avoid drama." The adventures of the honest lady? The honest lady hasn't – can't possibly have adventures.'

Mrs Blessingbourne only met his eyes at first, smiling with a certain intensity. 'Doesn't it depend a little on what you call adventures?'

'My poor Maud,' said Mrs Dyott, as if in compassion for sophistry so simple, 'adventures are just adventures. That's all you can make of them!'

But her friend went on, for their companion, as if without hearing. 'Doesn't it depend a good deal on what you call drama?' Maud spoke as one who had already thought it out. 'Doesn't it depend on what you call romance?'

Her listener gave these arguments his very best attention. 'Of course you may call things anything you like – speak of them as one thing and mean quite another. But why should it depend on anything? Behind these words we use – the adventure, the novel, the drama, the romance, the situation, in short, as we most comprehensively say – behind them all stands the same sharp fact that they all, in their different ways, represent.'

'Precisely!' Mrs Dyott was full of approval.

Maud, however, was full of vagueness. 'What great fact?'

'The fact of a relation. The adventure's a relation; the relation's an adventure. The romance, the novel, the drama are the picture of one. The subject the novelist treats is the rise, the formation, the development, the climax, and for the most part the decline, of one. And what is the honest lady doing on that side of the town?'

Mrs Dyott was more pointed. 'She doesn't so much as *form* a relation.'

But Maud bore up. 'Doesn't it depend, again, on what you call a relation?'

'Oh,' said Mrs Dyott, 'if a gentleman picks up her pocket-handkerchief—'

'Ah, even that's one,' their friend laughed, 'if she has thrown it to him. We can only deal with one that *is* one.'

'Surely,' Maud replied. 'But if it's an innocent one—?'

'Doesn't it depend a good deal,' Mrs Dyott asked, 'on what you call innocent?'

'You mean that the adventures of innocence have so often been the material of fiction? Yes,' Voyt replied; 'that's exactly what the bored reader complains of. He has asked for bread and been given a stone. What is it but, with absolute directness, a question of interest, or, as people say, of the story? What's a situation undeveloped but a subject lost? If a relation stops, where's the story? If it doesn't stop, where's the innocence? It seems to me you must choose. It would be very pretty if it were otherwise, but that's how we flounder. Art is our flounderings shown.'

Mrs Blessingbourne — and with an air of deference scarce supported perhaps by its sketchiness — kept her deep eyes on this definition. 'But sometimes we flounder out.'

It immediately touched in Colonel Voyt the spring of a genial derision. 'That's just where I expected *you* would! One always sees it come.'

'He has, you notice,' Mrs Dyott parenthesized to Maud, 'seen it come so often; and he has always waited for it and met it.'

'Met it, dear lady, simply enough! It's the old story, Mrs Blessingbourne. The relation is innocent that the heroine gets out of. The book is innocent that's the story of her getting out. But what the devil — in the name of innocence — was she doing *in?*'

Mrs Dyott promptly echoed the question. 'You have to be in, you know, to *get* out. So there you are already with your relation. It's the end of your goodness.'

'And the beginning,' said Voyt, 'of your play!'

'Aren't they all, for that matter, even the worst,' Mrs Dyott pursued, 'supposed *some* time or other to get out? But if, meanwhile, they've been in, however briefly, long enough to adorn a tale—'

'They've been in long enough to point a moral. That is to point ours!' With which, and as if a sudden flush of warmer light had moved him, Colonel Voyt got up. The veil of the storm had parted over a great red sunset.

Mrs Dyott also was on her feet, and they stood before his charming antagonist, who, with eyes lowered and a somewhat fixed smile, had not moved. 'We've spoiled her subject!' the elder lady sighed.

'Well,' said Voyt, 'it's better to spoil an artist's subject than to spoil his reputation. I mean,' he explained to Maud with his indulgent manner, 'his appearance of knowing what he has got hold of, for that, in the last resort, is his happiness.'

She slowly rose at this, facing him with an aspect as handsomely mild as his own. 'You can't spoil my happiness.'

He held her hand an instant as he took leave. 'I wish I could add to it!'

## III

WHEN HE HAD quitted them and Mrs Dyott had candidly asked if her friend had found him rude or crude, Maud replied – though not immediately – that she had feared showing only too much that she found him charming. But if Mrs Dyott took this, it was to weigh the sense. 'How could you show it too much?'

'Because I always feel that that's my only way of showing anything. It's absurd, if you like,' Mrs Blessingbourne pursued, 'but I never know, in such intense discussions, what strange impression I may give.'

Her companion looked amused. 'Was it intense?'

'*I* was,' Maud frankly confessed.

'Then it's a pity you were so wrong. Colonel Voyt, you know, is right.' Mrs Blessingbourne at this gave one of the slow, soft, silent head-shakes to which she often resorted and which, mostly accompanied by the light of cheer, had somehow, in spite of the small obstinacy that smiled in them, a special grace. With this grace, for a moment, her friend, looking her up and down, appeared impressed, yet not too much so to take, the next minute, a decision. 'Oh, my dear, I'm sorry to differ from anyone so lovely – for you're awfully beautiful tonight, and your frock's the very nicest I've ever seen you wear. But he's as right as he can be.'

Maud repeated her motion. 'Not so right, at all events, as he thinks he is. Or perhaps I can say,' she went on, after an instant, 'that I'm not so wrong. I do know a little what I'm talking about.'

Mrs Dyott continued to study her. 'You *are* vexed. You naturally don't like it – such destruction.'

'Destruction?'

'Of your illusion.'

'I *have* no illusion. If I had, moreover, it wouldn't be destroyed. I have, on the whole, I think, my little decency.'

Mrs Dyott stared. 'Let us grant it for argument. What, then?'

'Well, I've also my little drama.'

'An attachment?'

'An attachment.'

'That you shouldn't have?'

'That I shouldn't have.'

'A passion?'

'A passion.'

'Shared?'

'Ah, thank goodness, no!'

Mrs Dyott continued to gaze. 'The object's unaware—?'

'Utterly.'

Mrs Dyott turned it over. 'Are you sure?'

'Sure.'

'That's what you call your decency? But isn't it,' Mrs Dyott asked, 'rather *his*?'

'Dear, no. It's only his good fortune.'

Mrs Dyott laughed. 'But yours, darling – your good fortune: where does *that* come in?'

'Why, in my sense of the romance of it.'

'The romance of what? Of his not knowing?'

'Of my not wanting him to. If I did –' Maud had touchingly worked it out – 'where would be my honesty?'

The inquiry, for an instant, held her friend; yet only, it seemed, for a stupefaction that was almost amusement. 'Can you want or not want as you like? Where in the world, if you don't want, is your romance?'

Mrs Blessingbourne still wore her smile, and she now, with a light gesture that matched it, just touched the region of her heart. 'There!'

Her companion admiringly marvelled. 'A lovely place for it, no doubt! – but not quite a place, that I can see, to make the sentiment a relation.'

'Why not? What more is required for a relation for *me*?'

'Oh, all sorts of things, I should say! And many more, added to those, to make it one for the person you mention.'

'Ah, that I don't pretend it either should be or *can* be. I only speak for myself.'

It was said in a manner that made Mrs Dyott, with a visible mixture of impressions, suddenly turn away. She indulged in a vague movement or two, as if to look for something, then again found herself near her friend, on whom with the same abruptness, in fact with a strange sharpness, she conferred a kiss that might have represented either her tribute to exalted consistency or her idea of a graceful close of the discussion. 'You deserve that one should speak *for* you!'

Her companion looked cheerful and secure. 'How *can* you, without knowing—?'

'Oh, by guessing! It's not—?'

But that was as far as Mrs Dyott could get. 'It's not,' said Maud, 'anyone you've ever seen.'

'Ah then, I give you up!'

And Mrs Dyott conformed, for the rest of Maud's stay, to the spirit of this speech. It was made on a Saturday night, and Mrs Blessingbourne remained till the Wednesday following, an interval during which, as the return of fine weather was confirmed by the Sunday, the two ladies found a wider range of action. There were drives to be taken, calls made, objects of interest seen, at a distance; with the effect of much easy talk and still more easy silence. There had been a question of

Colonel Voyt's probable return on the Sunday, but the whole time passed without a sign from him, and it was merely mentioned by Mrs Dyott, in explanation, that he must have been suddenly called, as he was so liable to be, to town. That this in fact was what had happened he made clear to her on Thursday afternoon, when, walking over again late, he found her alone. The consequence of his Sunday letters had been his taking, that day, the 4.15. Mrs Voyt had gone back on Thursday, and he now, to settle on the spot the question of a piece of work begun at his place, had rushed down for a few hours in anticipation of the usual collective move for the week's end. He was to go up again by the late train, and had to count a little – a fact accepted by his hostess with the hard pliancy of practice – his present happy moments. Too few as these were, however, he found time to make of her an inquiry or two not directly bearing on their situation. The first was a recall of the question for which Mrs Blessingbourne's entrance on the previous Saturday had arrested her answer. Did that lady know of anything between them?

'No. I'm sure. There's one thing she does know,' Mrs Dyott went on; 'but it's quite different and not so very wonderful.'

'What, then, is it?'

'Well, that she's herself in love.'

Voyt showed his interest. 'You mean she told you?'

'I got it out of her.'

He showed his amusement. 'Poor thing! And with whom?'

'With you.'

His surprise, if the distinction might be made, was less than his wonder. 'You got that out of her too?'

'No – it remains in. Which is much the best way for it. For you to know it would be to end it.'

He looked rather cheerfully at sea. 'Is that then why you tell me?'

'I mean for her to know you know it. Therefore it's in your interest not to let her.'

'I see,' Voyt after a moment returned. 'Your real calculation is that my interest will be sacrificed to my vanity – so that, if your other idea is just, the flame will in fact, and thanks to her morbid conscience, expire by her taking fright at seeing me so pleased. But I promise you,' he declared, 'that she shan't see it. So there you are!' She kept her eyes on him and had evidently to admit, after a little, that there she was. Distinct as he had made the case, however, he was not yet quite satisfied. 'Why are you so sure that I'm the man?'

'From the way she denies you.'

'You put it to her?'

'Straight. If you hadn't been she would, of course, have confessed to you – to keep me in the dark about the real one.'

Poor Voyt laughed out again. 'Oh, you dear souls!'

'Besides,' his companion pursued, 'I was not in want of that evidence.'

'Then what other had you?'

'Her state before you came – which was what made me ask you how much you had seen her. And her state after it,' Mrs

Dyott added. 'And her state,' she wound up, 'while you were here.'

'But her state while I was here was charming.'

'Charming. That's just what I say.'

She said it in a tone that placed the matter in its right light – a light in which they appeared kindly, quite tenderly, to watch Maud wander away into space with her lovely head bent under a theory rather too big for it. Voyt's last word, however, was that there was just enough in it – in the theory – for them to allow that she had not shown herself, on the occasion of their talk, wholly bereft of sense. Her consciousness, if they let it alone – as they of course after this mercifully must – *was*, in the last analysis, a kind of shy romance. Not a romance like their own, a thing to make the fortune of any author up to the mark – one who should have the invention or who *could* have the courage; but a small, scared, starved, subjective satisfaction that would do her no harm and nobody else any good. Who but a duffer – he stuck to his contention – would see the shadow of a 'story' in it?

# *Flickerbridge*

## I

FRANK GRANGER HAD arrived from Paris to paint a portrait — an order given him, as a young compatriot with a future, whose early work would some day have a price, by a lady from New York, a friend of his own people and also, as it happened, of Addie's, the young woman to whom it was publicly both affirmed and denied that he was engaged. Other young women in Paris — fellow-members there of the little tight transpontine world of art-study — professed to know that the pair had been 'several times' over so closely contracted. This, however, was their own affair; the last phase of the relation, the last time of the times, had passed into vagueness; there was perhaps even an impression that if they were inscrutable to their friends they were not wholly crystalline to each other and themselves. What had occurred for Granger, at all events, in connection with the portrait was that Mrs Bracken, his intending model, whose return to America was at hand, had suddenly been called to London by her husband, occupied there with pressing business, but had yet desired that her displacement should not interrupt her sittings. The young man, at her request, had followed her to England and profited by all she could give him, making shift with a small studio lent him by a London painter whom he had known and liked, a few years before, in the French *atelier* that then cradled, and that continued to cradle, so many of their kind.

The British capital was a strange, grey world to him, where people walked, in more ways than one, by a dim light; but he was happily of such a turn that the impression, just as it came, could nowhere ever fail him, and even the worst of these things was almost as much an occupation – putting it only at that – as the best. Mrs Bracken, moreover, passed him on, and while the darkness ebbed a little in the April days he found himself consolingly committed to a couple of fresh subjects. This cut him out work for more than another month, but meanwhile, as he said, he saw a lot – a lot that, with frequency and with much expression, he wrote about to Addie. She also wrote to her absent friend, but in briefer snatches, a meagreness to her reasons for which he had long since assented. She had other play for her pen, as well as, fortunately, other remuneration; a regular correspondence for a 'prominent Boston paper', fitful connections with public sheets perhaps also, in cases, fitful, and a mind, above all, engrossed at times, to the exclusion of everything else, with the study of the short story. This last was what she had mainly come out to go into, two or three years after he had found himself engulfed in the mystery of Carolus. She was indeed, on her own deep sea, more engulfed than he had ever been, and he had grown to accept the sense that, for progress too, she sailed under more canvas. It had not been particularly present to him till now that he had in the least got on, but the way in which Addie had – and evidently, still more, would – was the theme, as it were, of every tongue. She had thirty short stories out and nine descriptive articles. His three or four portraits of fat American ladies – they were all fat, all ladies and all American – were a poor show compared with these triumphs; especially as Addie had begun to throw out that it was about time they should go home. It kept perpetually coming up in Paris, in the transpontine world, that, as the phrase was, America had grown more interesting since they left. Addie was attentive to the rumour, and, as full of conscience as she was of taste, of patriotism as of curiosity, had often put it to him frankly, with what he, who was of New York, recognized as her New England emphasis: 'I'm not sure, you know, that we do *real* justice to our country.' Granger felt he would do it on the day – if the day ever came – he should irrevocably marry her. No other country could possibly have produced her.

# Flickerbridge

## II

BUT MEANWHILE it befell, in London, that he was stricken with influenza and with subsequent sorrow. The attack was short but sharp – had it lasted Addie would certainly have come to his aid; most of a blight, really, in its secondary stage. The good ladies his sitters – the ladies with the frizzled hair, with the diamond earrings, with the chins tending to the massive – left for him, at the door of his lodgings, flowers, soup and love, so that with their assistance he pulled through; but his convalescence was slow and his weakness out of proportion to the muffled shock. He came out, but he went about lame; it tired him to paint – he felt as if he had been ill for a month. He strolled in Kensington Gardens when he should have been at work; he sat long on penny chairs and helplessly mused and mooned. Addie desired him to return to Paris, but there were chances under his hand that he felt he had just wit enough left not to relinquish. He would have gone for a week to the sea – he would have gone to Brighton; but Mrs Bracken had to be finished – Mrs Bracken was so soon to sail. He just managed to finish her in time – the day before the date fixed for his breaking ground on a greater business still, the circumvallation of Mrs Dunn. Mrs Dunn duly waited on him, and he sat down before her, feeling, however, ere he rose, that he must take a long breath before the attack. While asking himself that night, therefore, where he should best replenish his lungs, he received from Addie, who had had from

Mrs Bracken a poor report of him, a communication which, besides being of sudden and startling interest, applied directly to his case.

His friend wrote to him under the lively emotion of having from one day to another become aware of a new relative, an ancient cousin, a sequestered gentlewoman, the sole survival of 'the English branch of the family', still resident, at Flickerbridge, in the 'old family home', and with whom, that he might immediately betake himself to so auspicious a quarter for change of air, she had already done what was proper to place him, as she said, in touch. What came of it all, to be brief, was that Granger found himself so placed almost as he read: he was in touch with Miss Wenham of Flickerbridge, to the extent of being in correspondence with her, before twenty-four hours had sped. And on the second day he was in the train, settled for a five-hours' run to the door of this amiable woman, who had so abruptly and kindly taken him on trust and of whom but yesterday he had never so much as heard. This was an oddity – the whole incident was – of which, in the corner of his compartment, as he proceeded, he had time to take the size. But the surprise, the incongruity, as he felt, could but deepen as he went. It was a sufficiently queer note, in the light, or the absence of it, of his late experience, that so complex a product as Addie should have *any* simple insular tie; but it was a queerer note still that she should have had one so long only to remain unprofitably unconscious of it. Not to have done something with it, used it, worked it, talked about it at least, and perhaps even written – these things, at the rate she moved, represented a loss of opportunity under which, as he saw her, she was peculiarly formed to wince. She was at any rate, it was clear, doing something with it now; using it, working it, certainly, already talking – and, yes, quite possibly writing – about it. She was, in short, smartly making up what she had missed, and he could take such comfort from his own action as he had been helped to by the rest of the facts, succinctly reported from Paris on the very morning of his start.

It was the singular story of a sharp split – in a good English house – that dated now from years back. A worthy Briton, of the best middling stock, had, early in the forties, as a very young man, in Dresden, whither he had been despatched to qualify in German for a stool in an uncle's counting-house, met, admired, wooed and won an American girl, of due attractions, domiciled at that period with her parents and a sister, who was also attractive, in the Saxon capital. He had married her, taken her to England, and there, after some years of harmony and happiness, lost her. The sister in question had, after her death, come to him, and to his young child, on a visit, the effect of which, between the pair, eventually defined itself as a sentiment that was not to be resisted. The bereaved husband, yielding to a new attachment and a new response, and finding a new union thus prescribed, had yet been forced to reckon with the unaccommodating law of the land. Encompassed with frowns in his own country, however, marriages of this particular type were wreathed in smiles in his sister's-in-law, so that his remedy was not forbidden. Choosing between two allegiances he had let the one go that seemed the least close, and had, in brief, transplanted his possibilities to an easier air. The knot was tied for the couple in New York, where, to protect the legitimacy of such other children as might come to them, they settled and prospered. Children came, and one of the daughters, growing up and marrying in her turn, was, if Frank rightly followed, the mother of his own Addie, who had been deprived of the knowledge of her indeed, in childhood, by death, and been brought up, though without undue tension, by a stepmother – a character thus, in the connection, repeated.

The breach produced in England by the invidious action, as it was there held, of the girl's grandfather, had not failed to widen – all the more that nothing had been done on the American side to close it. Frigidity had settled, and hostility had only been arrested by indifference. Darkness, therefore, had fortunately supervened, and a cousinship completely divided. On either side of the impassable gulf, of the impenetrable curtain, each branch had put forth its leaves – a foliage wanting, in the American quarter, it was distinct enough to Granger, in no sign or symptom of climate and environment. The graft in New York had taken, and Addie was a vivid, an unmistakable flower. At Flickerbridge, or wherever, on the other hand, strange to say, the parent stem had had a fortune comparatively meagre. Fortune, it was true, in the vulgarest sense, had attended neither party. Addie's immediate belongings were as poor as they were numerous, and he gathered that Miss Wenham's pretensions to wealth were not so marked as to expose the claim of kinship to the imputation of motive. To this lady's single identity, at all events, the original stock had dwindled, and our young man was properly warned that he would find her shy and solitary. What was singular was that, in these conditions, she should desire, she should endure, to receive him. But that was all another story, lucid enough when mastered. He kept Addie's letters, exceptionally copious, in his lap; he conned them at intervals; he held the threads.

He looked out between whiles at the pleasant English land, an April *aquarelle* washed in with wondrous breadth. He knew the French thing, he knew the American, but he had known nothing of this. He saw it already as the remarkable Miss Wenham's setting. The doctor's daughter at Flickerbridge, with nippers on her nose, a palette on her thumb and innocence in her heart, had been the miraculous link. She had become aware, even there, in our world of wonders, that the current fashion for young women so equipped was to enter the Parisian lists. Addie had accordingly chanced upon her, on the slopes of Montparnasse, as one of the English girls in one of the thorough-going sets. They had met in some easy collocation and had fallen upon common ground; after which the young woman, restored to Flickerbridge for an interlude and retailing there her adventures and impressions, had mentioned to Miss Wenham, who had known and protected her from babyhood, that that lady's own name of Adelaide was, as well as the surname conjoined with it, borne, to her knowledge, in Paris, by an extraordinary American specimen. She had then recrossed the Channel with a wonderful message, a courteous challenge, to her friend's duplicate, who had in turn granted through her every satisfaction. The duplicate had, in other words, bravely let Miss Wenham know exactly who she was. Miss Wenham, in whose personal tradition the flame of resentment appeared to have been reduced by time to the palest ashes – for whom, indeed, the story of the great schism was now but a legend only needing a little less dimness to make it romantic – Miss Wenham had promptly responded by a letter fragrant with the hope that old threads might be taken up. It was a relationship that they must puzzle out together, and she had earnestly sounded the other party to it on the subject of a possible visit. Addie had met her with a definite promise; she would come soon, she would come when free, she would come in July; but meanwhile she sent her deputy. Frank asked himself by what name she had described, by what character introduced him to Flickerbridge. He felt mainly, on the whole, as if he were going there to find out if he were engaged to her. He was at sea, really, now, as to which of the various views Addie herself took of it. To Miss Wenham she must definitely have taken one, and perhaps Miss Wenham would reveal it. This expectation was really his excuse for a possible indiscretion.

# Flickerbridge

## III

HE WAS INDEED to learn on arrival to what he had been committed; but that was for a while so much a part of his first general impression that the fact took time to detach itself, the first general impression demanding verily all his faculties of response. He almost felt, for a day or two, the victim of a practical joke, a gross abuse of confidence. He had presented himself with the moderate amount of flutter involved in a sense of due preparation; but he had then found that, however primed with prefaces and prompted with hints, he had not been prepared at all. How *could* he be, he asked himself, for anything so foreign to his experience, so alien to his proper world, so little to be preconceived in the sharp north light of the newest impressionism, and yet so recognized, after all, really, in the event, so noted and tasted and assimilated? It was a case he would scarce have known how to describe – could doubtless have described best with a full, clean brush, supplemented by a play of gesture; for it was always his habit to see an occasion, of whatever kind, primarily as a picture, so that he might get it, as he was wont to say, so that he might keep it, well together. He had been treated of a sudden, in this adventure, to one of the sweetest, fairest, coolest impressions of his life – one, moreover, visibly, from the start, complete and homogeneous. Oh, it was *there*, if that was all one wanted of a thing! It was so 'there' that, as had befallen him in Italy, in Spain, confronted at last, in dusky side-chapel or rich museum, with great things dreamed of or with greater ones unexpectedly presented, he had held his breath for fear of breaking the spell; had almost, from the quick impulse to respect, to prolong, lowered his voice and moved on tiptoe. Supreme beauty suddenly revealed is apt to strike us as a possible illusion, playing with our desire – instant freedom with it to strike us as a possible rashness.

This fortunately, however – and the more so as his freedom for the time quite left him – didn't prevent his hostess, the evening of his advent and while the vision was new, from being exactly as queer and rare and *impayable*, as improbable, as impossible, as delightful at dinner at eight (she appeared to keep these immense hours) as she had overwhelmingly been at tea at five. She was in the most natural way in the world one of the oddest apparitions, but that the particular means to such an end *could* be natural was an inference difficult to make. He failed in fact to make it for a couple of days; but then – though then only – he made it with confidence. By this time indeed he was sure of everything, including, luckily, himself. If we compare his impression, with slight extravagance, to some of the greatest he had ever received, this is simply because the image before him was so rounded and stamped. It expressed with pure perfection, it exhausted its character. It was so absolutely and so unconsciously what it was. He had been floated by the strangest of chances out of the rushing stream into a clear, still backwater – a deep and quiet pool in which objects were sharply mirrored. He had hitherto in life known nothing that was old except a few statues and pictures; but here everything was old, was immemorial, and nothing so much so as the very freshness itself. Vaguely to have supposed there were such nooks in the world had done little enough, he now saw, to temper the glare of their opposites. It was the fine touches that counted, and these had to be seen to be believed.

Miss Wenham, fifty-five years of age, and unappeasably timid, unaccountably strange, had, on her reduced scale, an almost Gothic grotesqueness; but the final effect of one's sense of it was an amenity that accompanied one's steps like wafted gratitude. More flurried, more spasmodic, more apologetic, more completely at a loss at one moment and more precipitately abounding at another, he had never before in all his days seen any maiden lady; yet for no maiden lady he had ever seen had he so promptly conceived a private enthusiasm. Her eyes protruded, her chin receded and her nose carried on in conversation a queer little independent motion. She wore on the top of her head an upright circular cap that made her resemble a caryatid disburdened, and on other parts of her person strange combinations of colours, stuffs, shapes, of metal, mineral and plant. The tones of her voice rose and fell, her facial convulsions, whether tending – one could scarce make out – to expression or *re*pression, succeeded each other by a law of their own; she was embarrassed at nothing and at everything, frightened at everything and at nothing, and she approached objects, subjects, the simplest questions and answers and the whole material of intercourse, either with the indirectness of terror or with the violence of despair. These things, none the less, her refinements of oddity and intensities of custom, her suggestion at once of conventions and simplicities, of ease and of agony, her roundabout, retarded suggestions and perceptions, still permitted her to strike her guest as irresistibly charming. He didn't know what to call it; she was a fruit of time. She had a queer distinction. She had been expensively produced, and there would be a good deal more of her to come.

The result of the whole quality of her welcome, at any rate, was that the first evening, in his room, before going to bed, he relieved his mind in a letter to Addie, which, if space allowed us to embody it in our text, would usefully perform the office of a 'plate'. It would enable us to present ourselves as profusely illustrated. But the process of reproduction, as we say, costs. He wished his friend to know how grandly their affair turned out. She had put him in the way of something absolutely special – an old house untouched, untouchable, indescribable, an old corner such as one didn't believe existed, and the holy calm of which made the chatter of studios, the smell of paint, the slang of critics, the whole sense and sound of Paris, come back as so many signs of a huge monkey-cage. He moved about, restless, while he wrote; he lighted cigarettes and, nervous and suddenly scrupulous, put them out again; the night was mild and one of the windows of his large high room, which stood over the garden, was up. He lost himself in the things about him, in the type of the room, the last century with not a chair moved, not a point stretched. He hung over the objects and ornaments, blissfully few and adorably good, perfect pieces all, and never one, for a change, French. The scene was as rare as some fine old print with the best bits down in the corners. Old books and old pictures, allusions remembered and aspects conjectured, reappeared to him; he knew now what anxious islanders had been trying for in their backward hunt for the homely. But the homely at Flickerbridge was all style, even as style at the same time was mere honesty. The larger, the smaller past – he scarce knew which to call it – was at all events so hushed to sleep round him as he wrote that he had almost a bad conscience about having come. How one might love it, but how one might spoil it! To look at it too hard was positively to make it conscious, and to make it conscious was positively to wake it up. Its only safety, of a truth, was to be left still to sleep – to sleep in its large, fair chambers, and under its high, clean canopies.

He added thus restlessly a line to his letter, maundered round the room again, noted and fingered something else, and then, dropping on the old flowered sofa, sustained by the tight cubes of its cushions, yielded afresh to the cigarette, hesitated, stared, wrote a few words more. He wanted Addie to know, that was what he most felt, unless he perhaps felt more how much she herself would want to. Yes, what he supremely saw was all that Addie would make of it. Up to his neck in it there he fairly turned cold at the sense of suppressed opportunity, of the outrage of privation, that his correspondent would retrospectively and, as he even divined with a vague shudder, almost vindictively nurse. Well, what had happened was that the acquaintance had been kept for her, like a packet enveloped and sealed for delivery, till her attention was free. He saw her there, heard her and felt her — felt how she would feel and how she would, as she usually said, 'rave'. Some of her young compatriots called it 'yell', and in the reference itself, alas! illustrated their meaning. She would understand the place, at any rate, down to the ground; there wasn't the slightest doubt of that. Her sense of it would be exactly like his own, and he could see, in anticipation, just the terms of recognition and rapture in which she would abound. He knew just what she would call quaint, just what she would call bland, just what she would call weird, just what she would call wild. She would take it all in with an intelligence much more fitted than his own, in fact, to deal with what he supposed he must regard as its literary relations. She would have read the obsolete, long-winded memoirs and novels that both the figures and the setting ought clearly to remind one of; she would know about the past generations — the lumbering county magnates and their turbaned wives and round-eyed daughters, who, in other days, had treated the ruddy, sturdy, tradeless town, the solid square houses and wide, walled gardens, the streets today all grass and gossip, as the scene of a local 'season'. She would have warrant for the assemblies, dinners, deep potations; for the smoked sconces in the dusky parlours; for the long, muddy century of family coaches, 'holsters', highwaymen. She would put a finger, in short, just as he had done, on the vital spot — the rich humility of the whole thing, the fact that neither Flickerbridge in general nor Miss

Wenham in particular, nor anything nor anyone concerned, had a suspicion of their character and their merit. Addie and he would have to come to let in light.

He let it in then, little by little, before going to bed, through the eight or ten pages he addressed to her; assured her that it was the happiest case in the world, a little picture – yet full of 'style' too – absolutely composed and transmitted, with tradition, and tradition only, in every stroke, tradition still noiselessly breathing and visibly flushing, marking strange hours in the tall mahogany clocks that were never wound up and that yet audibly ticked on. All the elements, he was sure he should see, would hang together with a charm, presenting his hostess – a strange iridescent fish for the glazed exposure of an aquarium – as floating in her native medium. He left his letter open on the table, but, looking it over next morning, felt of a sudden indisposed to send it. He would keep it to add more, for there would be more to know; yet when three days had elapsed he had still not sent it. He sent instead, after delay, a much briefer report, which he was moved to make different and, for some reason, less vivid. Meanwhile he learned from Miss Wenham how Addie had introduced him. It took time to arrive with her at that point, but after the Rubicon was crossed they went far afield.

## IV

'OH YES, she said you were engaged. That was why – since I *had* broken out so – she thought I would like to see you; as I assure you I've been so delighted to. But *aren't* you?' the good lady asked as if she saw in his face some ground for doubt.

'Assuredly – if she says so. It may seem very odd to you, but I haven't known, and yet I've felt that, being nothing whatever to you directly, I need some warrant for consenting thus to be thrust on you. We *were*,' the young man explained, 'engaged a year ago; but since then (if you don't mind my telling you such things; I feel now as if I could tell you anything!) I haven't quite known how I stand. It hasn't seemed that we were in a position to marry. Things are better now, but I haven't quite known how she would see them. They were so bad six months ago that I understood her, I thought, as breaking off. I haven't broken; I've only accepted, for the time – because men must be easy with women – being treated as "the best of friends". Well, I try to be. I wouldn't have come here if I hadn't been. I thought it would be charming for her to know you – when I heard from her the extraordinary way you had dawned upon her, and charming therefore if I could help her to it. And if I'm helping you to know *her*,' he went on, 'isn't that charming too?'

'Oh, I so want to!' Miss Wenham murmured, in her unpractical, impersonal way. 'You're so different!' she wistfully declared.

'It's *you*, if I may respectfully, ecstatically say so, who are different. That's the point of it all. I'm not sure that anything so terrible really ought to happen to you as to know us.'

'Well,' said Miss Wenham, 'I do know you a little, by this time, don't I? And I don't find it terrible. It's a delightful change for me.'

'Oh, I'm not sure you ought to have a delightful change!'

'Why not – if you do?'

'Ah, I can bear it. I'm not sure that you can. I'm too bad to spoil – I *am* spoiled. I'm nobody, in short; I'm nothing. I've no type. You're *all* type. It has taken long, delicious years of security and monotony to produce you. You fit your frame with a perfection only equalled by the perfection with which your frame fits you. So this admirable old house, all time-softened white within and time-faded red without, so everything that surrounds you here and that has, by some extraordinary mercy, escaped the inevitable fate of exploitation: so it all, I say, is the sort of thing that, if it were the least bit to fall to pieces, could never, ah, never more, be put together again. I have, dear Miss Wenham,' Granger went on, happy himself in his extravagance, which was yet all sincere, and happier still in her deep, but altogether pleased, mystification – 'I've found, do you know, just the thing one has ever heard of that you most resemble. You're the Sleeping Beauty in the wood.'

He still had no compunction when he heard her bewilderedly sigh: 'Oh, you're too delightfully droll!'

'No, I only put things just as they are, and as I've also learned a little, thank heaven, to see them – which isn't, I quite agree with you, at all what anyone does. You're in the deep doze of the spell that has held you for long years, and it would be a shame, a crime, to wake you up. Indeed I already feel, with a thousand scruples, that I'm giving you the fatal shake. I say it even though it makes me sound a little as if I thought myself the fairy prince.'

She gazed at him with her queerest, kindest look, which he was getting used to, in spite of a faint fear, at the back of his head, of the strange things that sometimes occurred when lonely ladies, however mature, began to look at interesting young men from over the seas as if the young men desired to flirt. 'It's so wonderful,' she said, 'that you should be so very odd and yet so very good-natured.' Well, it all came to the same thing – it was so wonderful that *she* should be so simple and yet so little of a bore. He accepted with gratitude the theory of his languor – which moreover was real enough and partly perhaps why he was so sensitive; he let himself go as a convalescent, let her insist on the weakness that always remained after fever. It helped him to gain time, to preserve the spell even while he talked of breaking it; saw him through slow strolls and soft sessions, long gossips, fitful, hopeless questions – there was so much more to tell than, by any contortion, she *could* – and explanations addressed gallantly and patiently to her understanding, but not, by good fortune, really reaching it. They were perfectly at cross-purposes, and it was all the better, and they wandered together in the silver haze with all communication blurred.

When they sat in the sun in her formal garden he was quite aware that the tenderest consideration failed to disguise his treating her as the most exquisite of curiosities. The term of comparison most present to him was that of some obsolete musical instrument. The old-time order of her mind and her air had the stillness of a painted spinet that was duly dusted, gently rubbed, but never tuned nor played on. Her opinions were like dried rose-leaves; her attitudes like British sculpture; her voice was what he imagined of the possible tone of the old gilded, silver-stringed harp in one of the corners of the drawing-room. The lonely little decencies and modest dignities of her life, the fine grain of its conservatism, the innocence of its ignorance, all its monotony of stupidity and salubrity, its cold dullness and dim brightness, were there before him. Meanwhile, within him, strange things took place. It was literally true that his impression began again, after a lull, to make him nervous and anxious, and for reasons peculiarly confused, almost grotesquely mingled, or at least comically sharp. He was distinctly an agitation and a new taste – that he could see; and he saw quite as much therefore the excitement she already drew from the vision of Addie, an image intensified by the sense of closer kinship and presented to her, clearly, with various erratic enhancements, by her friend the doctor's daughter. At the end of a few days he said to her: 'Do you know she wants to come without waiting any longer? She wants to come while I'm here. I received this morning her letter proposing it, but I've been thinking it over and have waited to speak to you. The thing is, you see, that if she writes to *you* proposing it—'

'Oh, I shall be so particularly glad!'

## V

THEY WERE, as usual, in the garden, and it had not yet been so present to him that if he were only a happy cad there would be a good way to protect her. As she wouldn't hear of his being yet beyond precautions she had gone into the house for a particular shawl that was just the thing for his knees, and, blinking in the watery sunshine, had come back with it across the fine little lawn. He was neither fatuous nor asinine, but he had almost to put it to himself as a small task to resist the sense of his absurd advantage with her. It filled him with horror and awkwardness, made him think of he didn't know what, recalled something of Maupassant's – the smitten 'Miss Harriet' and her tragic fate. There was a preposterous possibility – yes, he held the strings quite in his hands – of keeping the treasure for himself. That was the art of life – what the real artist would consistently do. He would close the door on his impression, treat it as a private museum. He would see that he could lounge and linger there, live with wonderful things there, lie up there to rest and refit. For himself he was sure that after a little he should be able to paint there – do things in a key he had never thought of before. When she brought him the rug he took it from her and made her sit down on the bench and resume her knitting; then, passing behind her with a laugh, he placed it over her own shoulders; after which he moved to and fro before her, his hands in his pockets and his cigarette in his teeth. He was ashamed of the cigarette – a villainous false note; but she allowed, liked, begged him to smoke, and what he said to her on it, in one of the pleasantries she benevolently missed, was that he did so for fear of doing worse. That only showed that the end was really in sight. 'I daresay it will strike you as quite awful, what I'm going to say to you, but I can't help it. I speak out of the depths of my respect for you. It will seem to you horrid disloyalty to poor Addie. Yes – there we are; there *I* am, at least, in my naked monstrosity.' He stopped and looked at her till she might have been almost frightened. 'Don't let her come. Tell her not to. I've tried to prevent it, but she suspects.'

The poor woman wondered. 'Suspects?'

'Well, I drew it, in writing to her, on reflection, as mild as I could – having been visited, in the watches of the night, by the instinct of what might happen. Something told me to keep back my first letter – in which, under the first impression, I myself rashly "raved"; and I concocted instead of it an insincere and guarded report. But guarded as I was I clearly didn't keep you "down", as we say, enough. The wonder of your colour – daub you over with grey as I might – must have come through and told the tale. She scents battle from afar – by which I mean she scents "quaintness". But keep her off. It's hideous, what I'm saying – but I owe it to you. I owe it to the world. She'll kill you.'

'You mean I shan't get on with her?'

'Oh, fatally! See how *I* have. She's intelligent, remarkably pretty, remarkably good. And she'll adore you.'

'Well then?'

'Why, that will be just how she'll do for you.'

'Oh, I can hold my own!' said Miss Wenham with the head-shake of a horse making his sleigh-bells rattle in frosty air.

'Ah, but you can't hold hers! She'll rave about you. She'll write about you. You're Niagara before the first white traveller – and you know, or rather you can't know, what Niagara became *after* that gentleman. Addie will have discovered Niagara. She will understand you in perfection; she will feel you down to the ground; not a delicate shade of you will she lose or let anyone else lose. You'll be too weird for words, but the words will nevertheless come. You'll be too exactly the real thing and to be left too utterly just as you are, and all Addie's friends and all Addie's editors and contributors and readers will cross the Atlantic and flock to Flickerbridge, so, unanimously, universally, vociferously, to leave you. You'll be in the magazines with illustrations; you'll be in the papers with headings; you'll be everywhere with everything. You don't understand – you think you do, but you don't. Heaven forbid you *should* understand! That's just your beauty – your "sleeping" beauty. But you needn't. You can take me on trust. Don't have her. Say, as a pretext, as a reason, anything in the world you like. Lie to her – scare her away. I'll go away and give you up – I'll sacrifice everything myself.' Granger pursued his exhortation, convincing himself more and more. 'If I saw my way out, my way completely through, *I* would pile up some fabric of fiction for her – I should only want to be sure of its not tumbling down.

One would have, you see, to keep the thing up. But I would throw dust in her eyes. I would tell her that you don't do at all — that you're not, in fact, a desirable acquaintance. I'd tell her you're vulgar, improper, scandalous; I'd tell her you're mercenary, designing, dangerous; I'd tell her the only safe course is immediately to let you drop. I would thus surround you with an impenetrable legend of conscientious misrepresentation, a circle of pious fraud, and all the while privately keep you for myself.'

She had listened to him as if he were a band of music and she a small shy garden-party. 'I shouldn't like you to go away. I shouldn't in the least like you not to come again.'

'Ah, there it is!' he replied. 'How can I come again if Addie ruins you?'

'But how will she ruin me — even if she does what you say? I know I'm too old to change and really much too queer to please in any of the extraordinary ways you speak of. If it's a question of quizzing me I don't think my cousin, or anyone else, will have quite the hand for it that *you* seem to have. So that if *you* haven't ruined me—!'

'But I *have* — that's just the point!' Granger insisted. 'I've undermined you at least. I've left, after all, terribly little for Addie to do.'

She laughed in clear tones. 'Well, then, we'll admit that you've done everything but frighten me.'

He looked at her with surpassing gloom. 'No — that again is one of the most dreadful features. You'll positively like it — what's to come. You'll be caught up in a chariot of fire like the prophet – wasn't there, was there, one? – of old. That's exactly why – if one could but have done it – you would have been to be kept ignorant and helpless. There's something or other in Latin that says that it's the finest things that change the most easily for the worse. You already enjoy your dishonour and revel in your shame. It's too late – you're lost!'

# VI

ALL THIS WAS as pleasant a manner of passing the time as any other, for it didn't prevent his old-world corner from closing round him more entirely, nor stand in the way of his making out, from day to day, some new source, as well as some new effect, of its virtue. He was really scared at moments at some of the liberties he took in talk – at finding himself so familiar, for the great note of the place was just that a certain modern ease had never crossed its threshold, that quick intimacies and quick oblivions were a stranger to its air. It had known, in all its days, no rude, no loud invasion. Serenely unconscious of most contemporary things, it had been so of nothing so much as of the diffused social practice of running in and out. Granger held his breath, on occasions, to think how Addie would run. There were moments when, for some reason, more than at others, he heard her step on the staircase and her cry in the hall. If he played freely, none the less, with the idea with which we have shown him as occupied, it was not that in every measurable way he didn't sacrifice, to the utmost, to stillness. He only hovered, ever so lightly, to take up again his thread. She wouldn't hear of his leaving her, of his being in the least fit again, as she said, to travel. She spoke of the journey to London – which was in fact a matter of many hours – as an experiment fraught with lurking complications. He added then day to day, yet only hereby, as he reminded her, giving other complications a larger chance to multiply. He kept it before her, when there was nothing else to do, that she must consider; after which he had his times of fear that she perhaps really would make for him this sacrifice.

He knew that she had written again to Paris, and knew that he must himself again write – a situation abounding for each in the elements of a quandary. If he stayed so long, why then he wasn't better, and if he wasn't better Addie might take it into her head—! They must make it clear that he *was* better, so that, suspicious, alarmed at what was kept from her, she shouldn't suddenly present herself to nurse him. If he was better, however, why did he stay so long? If he stayed only for the attraction the sense of the attraction might be contagious. This was what finally grew clearest for him, so that he had for his mild disciple hours of still sharper prophecy. It consorted with his fancy to represent to her that their young friend had been by this time unsparingly warned; but nothing could be plainer than that this was ineffectual so long as he himself resisted the ordeal. To plead that he remained because he was too weak to move was only to throw themselves back on the other horn of their dilemma. If he was too weak to move Addie would bring him her strength – of which, when she got there, she would give them specimens enough. One morning he broke out at breakfast with an intimate conviction. They would see that she was actually starting – they would receive a wire by noon. They didn't receive it, but by his theory the portent was only the stronger. It had, moreover, its grave as well as its gay side, for Granger's paradox and pleasantry were only the most convenient way for him of saying what he felt. He literally heard the knell sound, and in expressing this to Miss Wenham with the conversational freedom that seemed best to pay his way he the more vividly faced the contingency. He could never return, and though he announced it with a despair that did what might be to make it pass as a joke, he saw that, whether or no she at last understood, she quite at last believed him. On this, to his knowledge, she wrote again to Addie, and the contents of her letter excited his curiosity. But that sentiment, though not assuaged, quite dropped when, the day after, in the evening, she let him know that she had had, an hour before, a telegram.

'She comes Thursday.'

He showed not the least surprise. It was the deep calm of the fatalist. It *had* to be. 'I must leave you then tomorrow.'

She looked, on this, as he had never seen her; it would have been hard to say whether what was in her face was the last failure to follow or the first effort to meet. 'And really not to come back?'

'Never, never, dear lady. Why should I come back? You can

never be again what you *have* been. I shall have seen the last of you.'

'Oh!' she touchingly urged.

'Yes, for I should next find you simply brought to self-consciousness. You'll be exactly what you are, I charitably admit – nothing more or less, nothing different. But you'll be it all in a different way. We live in an age of prodigious machinery, all organized to a single end. That end is publicity – a publicity as ferocious as the appetite of a cannibal. The thing therefore is not to have any illusions – fondly to flatter yourself, in a muddled moment, that the cannibal will spare you. He spares nobody. He spares nothing. It will be all right. You'll have a lovely time. You'll be only just a public character – blown about the world for all you are and proclaimed for all you are on the house-tops. It will be for *that*, mind, I quite recognize – because Addie is superior – as well as for all you aren't. So good-bye.'

He remained, however, till the next day, and noted at intervals the different stages of their friend's journey; the hour, this time, she would really have started, the hour she would reach Dover, the hour she would get to town, where she would alight at Mrs Dunn's. Perhaps she would bring Mrs Dunn, for Mrs Dunn would swell the chorus. At the last, on the morrow, as if in anticipation of this, stillness settled between them; he became as silent as his hostess. But before he went she brought out, shyly and anxiously, as an appeal, the question that, for hours, had clearly been giving her thought. 'Do you meet her then tonight in London?'

'Dear, no. In what position am I, alas! to do that? When can I *ever* meet her again?' He had turned it all over. 'If I could meet Addie after this, you know, I could meet *you*. And if I do meet Addie,' he lucidly pursued, 'what will happen, by the same stroke, is that I *shall* meet you. And that's just what I've explained to you that I dread.'

'You mean that she and I will be inseparable?'

He hesitated. 'I mean that she'll tell me all about you. I can hear her, and her ravings, now.'

She gave again – and it was infinitely sad – her little whinnying laugh. 'Oh, but if what you say is true, you'll know.'

'Ah, but Addie won't! Won't, I mean, know that *I* know – or at least won't believe it. Won't believe that anyone knows. Such,' he added, with a strange, smothered sigh, '*is* Addie. Do you know,' he wound up, 'that what, after all, has most definitely happened is that you've made me see her as I've never done before?'

She blinked and gasped, she wondered and despaired. 'Oh, no, it will be *you*. I've had nothing to do with it. Everything's *all* you!'

But for all it mattered now! 'You'll see,' he said, 'that she's charming. I shall go, for tonight, to Oxford. I shall almost cross her on the way.'

'Then, if she's charming, what am I to tell her from you in explanation of such strange behaviour as your flying away just as she arrives?'

'Ah, you needn't mind about that – you needn't tell her anything.'

She fixed him as if as never again. 'It's none of my business, of course I feel; but isn't it a little cruel if you're engaged?'

Granger gave a laugh almost as odd as one of her own. 'Oh, you've cost me that!' and he put out his hand to her.

She wondered while she took it. 'Cost you—?'

'We're not engaged. Good-bye.'

# *The Beast in the Jungle*

## I

WHAT DETERMINED THE speech that startled him in the course of their encounter scarcely matters, being probably but some words spoken by himself quite without intention – spoken as they lingered and slowly moved together after their renewal of acquaintance. He had been conveyed by friends, an hour or two before, to the house at which she was staying; the party of visitors at the other house, of whom he was one, and thanks to whom it was his theory, as always, that he was lost in the crowd, had been invited over to luncheon. There had been after luncheon much dispersal, all in the interest of the original motive, a view of Weatherend itself and the fine things, intrinsic features, pictures, heirlooms, treasures of all the arts, that made the place almost famous; and the great rooms were so numerous that guests could wander at their will, hang back from the principal group, and, in cases where they took such matters with the last seriousness, give themselves up to mysterious appreciations and measurements. There were persons to be observed, singly or in couples, bending toward objects in out-of-the-way corners with their hands on their knees and their heads nodding quite as with the emphasis of an excited sense of smell. When they were two they either mingled their sounds of ecstasy or melted into silences of even deeper import, so that there were aspects of the occasion that gave it for Marcher much the air of the 'look round', previous to a sale highly advertised, that excites or quenches, as may be, the dream of acquisition. The dream of acquisition at Weatherend would have had to be wild indeed, and John Marcher found himself, among such suggestions, disconcerted almost equally by the presence of those who knew too much and by that of those who knew nothing. The great rooms caused so much poetry and history to press upon him that he needed to wander apart to feel in a proper relation with them, though his doing so was not, as happened, like the gloating of some of his companions, to be compared to the movements of a dog sniffing a cupboard. It had an issue promptly enough in a direction that was not to have been calculated.

It led, in short, in the course of the October afternoon, to his closer meeting with May Bartram, whose face, a reminder, yet not quite a remembrance, as they sat, much separated, at a very long table, had begun merely by troubling him rather pleasantly. It affected him as the sequel of something of which he had lost the beginning. He knew it, and for the time quite welcomed it, as a continuation, but didn't know what it continued, which was an interest, or an amusement, the greater as he was also somehow aware – yet without a direct sign from her – that the young woman herself had not lost the thread. She had not lost it, but she wouldn't give it back to him, he saw, without some putting forth of his hand for it; and he not only saw that, but saw several things more, things odd enough in the light of the fact that at the moment some accident of grouping brought them face to face he was still merely fumbling with the idea that any contact between them in the past would have had no importance. If it had had no importance he scarcely knew why his actual impression of her should so seem to have so much; the answer to which, however, was that in such a life as they all appeared to be leading for the moment one could but take things as they came. He was satisfied, without in the least being able to say why, that this young lady might roughly have ranked in the house as a poor relation; satisfied also that she was not there on a brief visit, but was more or less a part of the establishment – almost a working, a remunerated part. Didn't she enjoy at periods a protection that she paid for by helping, among other services, to show the place and explain it, deal with the tiresome people, answer questions about the dates of the buildings, the styles of the furniture, the authorship of the pictures, the favourite haunts of the ghost? It wasn't that she looked as if you could have given her shillings – it was impossible to look less so. Yet when she finally drifted toward him, distinctly handsome, though ever so much older – older than when he had seen her before – it might have been as an effect of her guessing that he had, within the couple of hours, devoted more imagination to her than to all the others put together, and had thereby penetrated to a kind of truth that the others were too stupid for. She *was* there on harder terms than anyone; she was there as a consequence of things suffered, in one way and another, in the interval of years; and she remembered him very much as she was remembered – only a good deal better.

By the time they at last thus came to speech they were alone in one of the rooms – remarkable for a fine portrait over the chimney-place – out of which their friends had passed, and the charm of it was that even before they had spoken they had practically arranged with each other to stay behind for talk. The charm, happily, was in other things too; it was partly in there being scarce a spot at Weatherend without something to stay behind for. It was in the way the autumn day looked into the high windows as it waned; in the way the red light, breaking at the close from under a low, sombre sky, reached out in a long shaft and played over old wainscots, old tapestry, old gold, old colour. It was most of all perhaps in the way she came to him as if, since she had been turned on to deal with the simpler sort, he might, should he choose to keep the whole thing down, just take her mild attention for a part of her general business. As soon as he heard her voice, however, the gap was filled up and the missing link supplied; the slight irony he divined in her attitude lost its advantage. He almost jumped at it to get there before her. 'I met you years and years ago in Rome. I remember all about it.' She confessed to disappointment – she had been so sure he didn't; and to prove how well he did he began to pour forth the particular recollections that popped up as he called for them. Her face and her voice, all at his service now, worked the miracle – the impression operating like the torch of a lamplighter who touches into flame, one by one, a long row of gas jets. Marcher flattered himself that the illumination was brilliant, yet he was really still more pleased on her showing him, with amusement, that in his haste to make everything right he had got most things rather wrong. It hadn't been at Rome – it had been at Naples; and it hadn't been seven years before – it had been more nearly ten. She hadn't been either with her uncle and aunt, but with her mother and her brother; in addition to which it was not with the Pembles that *he* had been, but with the Boyers, coming down in their company from Rome – a point on which she insisted, a little to his confusion, and as to which she had her evidence in hand. The Boyers she had known, but she didn't know the Pembles, though she had heard of them, and it was the people he was with who had made them acquainted. The incident of the thunderstorm that had raged round them with such violence as to drive them for refuge into an excavation – this incident had not occurred at the Palace of the Caesars, but at Pompeii, on an occasion when they had been present there at an important find.

He accepted her amendments, he enjoyed her corrections, though the moral of them was, she pointed out, that he *really* didn't remember the least thing about her; and he only felt it as a drawback that when all was made conformable to the truth there didn't appear much of anything left. They lingered together still, she neglecting her office – for from the moment he was so clever she had no proper right to him – and both neglecting the house, just waiting as to see if a memory or two more wouldn't again breathe upon them. It had not taken them many minutes, after all, to put down on the table, like the cards of a pack, those that constituted their respective hands; only what came out was that the pack was unfortunately not perfect – that the past, invoked, invited, encouraged, could give them, naturally, no more than it had. It had made them meet – her at twenty, him at twenty-five; but nothing was so strange, they seemed to say to each other, as that, while so occupied, it hadn't done a little more for them. They looked at each other as with the feeling of an occasion missed; the present one would have been so much better if the other, in the far distance, in the foreign land, hadn't been so stupidly meagre. There weren't, apparently, all counted, more than a dozen little old things that had succeeded in coming to pass between them; trivialities of youth, simplicities of freshness, stupidities of ignorance, small possible germs, but too deeply buried – too deeply (didn't it seem?) to sprout after so many years. Marcher said to himself that he ought to have rendered her some service – saved her from a capsized boat in the Bay, or at least recovered her dressing-bag, filched from her cab, in the streets of Naples, by a *lazzarone* with a stiletto. Or it would have been nice if he could have been taken with fever, alone, at his hotel, and she could have come to look after him, to write to his people, to drive him out in convalescence. *Then* they would be in possession of the something or other that their actual show seemed to lack. It yet somehow presented itself, this show, as too good to be spoiled; so that they were reduced for a few minutes more to wondering a little helplessly why – since they seemed to know a certain number of the same people – their reunion had been so long averted. They didn't use that name for it, but their delay from minute to minute to join the others was a kind of confession that they didn't quite want it to be a failure. Their attempted supposition of reasons for their not having met but showed how little they knew of each other. There came in fact a moment when Marcher felt a positive pang. It was vain to pretend she was an old friend, for all the communities were wanting, in spite of which it was as an old friend that he saw she would have suited him. He had new ones enough – was surrounded with them, for instance, at that hour at the other house; as a new one he probably wouldn't have so much as noticed her. He would have liked to invent something, get her to make-believe with him that some passage of a romantic or critical kind *had* originally occurred. He was really almost reaching out in imagination – as against time – for something that would do, and saying to himself that if it didn't come this new incident would simply and rather awkwardly close. They would separate, and now for no second or for no third chance. They would have tried and not succeeded. Then it was, just at the turn, as he afterwards made it out to himself, that, everything else failing, she herself decided to take up the case and, as it were, save the situation. He felt as soon as she spoke that she had been consciously keeping back what she said and hoping to get on without it; a scruple in her that immensely touched him when, by the end of three or four minutes more, he was able to measure it. What she brought out, at any rate, quite cleared the air and supplied the link – the link it was such a mystery he should frivolously have managed to lose.

'You know you told me something that I've never forgotten and that again and again has made me think of you since; it was that tremendously hot day when we went to Sorrento, across the bay, for the breeze. What I allude to was what you said to me, on the way back, as we sat, under the awning of the boat, enjoying the cool. Have you forgotten?'

He had forgotten, and he was even more surprised than ashamed. But the great thing was that he saw it was no vulgar reminder of any 'sweet' speech. The vanity of women had long memories, but she was making no claim on him of a compliment or a mistake. With another woman, a totally different one, he might have feared the recall possibly even of some imbecile 'offer'. So, in having to say that he had indeed forgotten, he was conscious rather of a loss than of a gain; he already saw an interest in the matter of her reference. 'I try to think – but I give it up. Yet I remember the Sorrento day.'

'I'm not very sure you do,' May Bartram after a moment said; 'and I'm not very sure I ought to want you to. It's dreadful to bring a person back, at any time, to what he was ten years before. If you've lived away from it,' she smiled, 'so much the better.'

'Ah, if *you* haven't why should I?' he asked.

'Lived away, you mean, from what I myself was?'

'From what *I* was. I was of course an ass,' Marcher went on; 'but I would rather know from you just the sort of ass I was than – from the moment you have something in your mind – not know anything.'

Still, however, she hesitated. 'But if you've completely ceased to be that sort—?'

'Why, I can then just so all the more bear to know. Besides, perhaps I haven't.'

'Perhaps. Yet if you haven't,' she added, 'I should suppose you would remember. Not indeed that *I* in the least connect with my impression the invidious name you use. If I had only thought you foolish,' she explained, 'the thing I speak of wouldn't so have remained with me. It was about yourself.' She waited, as if it might come to him; but as, only meeting her eyes in wonder, he gave no sign, she burned her ships. 'Has it ever happened?'

Then it was that, while he continued to stare, a light broke for him and the blood slowly came to his face, which began to burn with recognition. 'Do you mean I told you—?' But he faltered, lest what came to him shouldn't be right, lest he should only give himself away.

'It was something about yourself that it was natural one shouldn't forget – that is if one remembered you at all. That's why I ask you,' she smiled, 'if the thing you then spoke of has ever come to pass?'

Oh, then he saw, but he was lost in wonder and found himself embarrassed. This, he also saw, made her sorry for him, as if her allusion had been a mistake. It took him but a moment, however, to feel that it had not been, much as it had been a surprise. After the first little shock of it her knowledge on the contrary began, even if rather strangely, to taste sweet to him. She was the only other person in the world then who would have it, and she had had it all these years, while the fact of his having so breathed his secret had unaccountably faded from him. No wonder they couldn't have met as if nothing had happened. 'I judge,' he finally said, 'that I know what you mean. Only I had strangely enough lost the consciousness of having taken you so far into my confidence.'

'Is it because you've taken so many others as well?'

'I've taken nobody. Not a creature since then.'

'So that I'm the only person who knows?'

'The only person in the world.'

'Well,' she quickly replied, 'I myself have never spoken. I've never, never repeated of you what you told me.' She looked at him so that he perfectly believed her. Their eyes met over it in such a way that he was without a doubt. 'And I never will.'

She spoke with an earnestness that, as if almost excessive, put him at ease about her possible derision. Somehow the whole question was a new luxury to him – that is, from the moment she was in possession. If she didn't take the ironic view she clearly took the sympathetic, and that was what he had had, in all the long time, from no one whomsoever. What he felt was that he couldn't at present have begun to tell her and yet could profit perhaps exquisitely by the accident of having done so of old. 'Please don't then. We're just right as it is.'

'Oh, I am,' she laughed, 'if you are!' To which she added: 'Then you do still feel in the same way?'

It was impossible to him not to take to himself that she was really interested, and it all kept coming as a sort of revelation. He had thought of himself so long as abominably alone, and, lo, he wasn't alone a bit. He hadn't been, it appeared, for an hour – since those moments on the Sorrento boat. It was *she* who had been, he seemed to see as he looked at her – she who had been made so by the graceless fact of his lapse of fidelity. To tell her what he had told her – what had it been but to ask something of her? something that she had given, in her charity, without his having, by a remembrance, by a return of the spirit, failing another encounter, so much as thanked her. What he had asked of her had been simply at first not to laugh at him. She had beautifully not done so for ten years, and she was not doing so now. So he had endless gratitude to make up. Only for that he must see just how he had figured to her. 'What, exactly, was the account I gave——?'

'Of the way you did feel? Well, it was very simple. You said you had had from your earliest time, as the deepest thing within you, the sense of being kept for something rare and strange, possibly prodigious and terrible, that was sooner or later to happen to you, that you had in your bones the foreboding and the conviction of, and that would perhaps overwhelm you.'

'Do you call that very simple?' John Marcher asked.

She thought a moment. 'It was perhaps because I seemed, as you spoke, to understand it.'

'You do understand it?' he eagerly asked.

Again she kept her kind eyes on him. 'You still have the belief?'

'Oh!' he exclaimed helplessly. There was too much to say.

'Whatever it is to be,' she clearly made out, 'it hasn't yet come.'

He shook his head in complete surrender now. 'It hasn't yet come. Only, you know, it isn't anything I'm to *do*, to achieve in the world, to be distinguished or admired for. I'm not such an ass as *that*. It would be much better, no doubt, if I were.'

'It's to be something you're merely to suffer?'

'Well, say to wait for – to have to meet, to face, to see suddenly break out in my life; possibly destroying all further consciousness, possibly annihilating me; possibly, on the other hand, only altering everything, striking at the root of all my world and leaving me to the consequences, however they shape themselves.'

She took this in, but the light in her eyes continued for him not to be that of mockery. 'Isn't what you describe perhaps but the expectation – or, at any rate, the sense of danger, familiar to so many people – of falling in love?'

John Marcher thought. 'Did you ask me that before?'

'No – I wasn't so free-and-easy then. But it's what strikes me now.'

'Of course,' he said after a moment, 'it strikes you. Of course it strikes *me*. Of course what's in store for me may be no more than that. The only thing is,' he went on, 'that I think that if it had been that, I should by this time know.'

'Do you mean because you've *been* in love?' And then as he but looked at her in silence: 'You've been in love, and it hasn't meant such a cataclysm, hasn't proved the great affair?'

'Here I am, you see. It hasn't been overwhelming.'

'Then it hasn't been love,' said May Bartram.

'Well, I at least thought it was. I took it for that – I've taken it till now. It was agreeable, it was delightful, it was miserable,' he explained. 'But it wasn't strange. It wasn't what *my* affair's to be.'

'You want something all to yourself – something that nobody else knows or *has* known?'

'It isn't a question of what I "want" – God knows I don't want anything. It's only a question of the apprehension that haunts me – that I live with day by day.'

He said this so lucidly and consistently that, visibly, it further imposed itself. If she had not been interested before she would have been interested now. 'Is it a sense of coming violence?'

Evidently now too, again, he liked to talk of it. 'I don't think of it as – when it does come – necessarily violent. I only think of it as natural and as of course, above all, unmistakable. I think of it simply as *the* thing. *The* thing will of itself appear natural.'

'Then how will it appear strange?'

Marcher bethought himself. 'It won't – to *me*.'

'To whom then?'

'Well,' he replied, smiling at last, 'say to you.'

'Oh then, I'm to be present?'

'Why, you *are* present – since you know.'

'I see.' She turned it over. 'But I mean at the catastrophe.'

At this, for a minute, their lightness gave way to their gravity; it was as if the long look they exchanged held them together. 'It will only depend on yourself – if you'll watch with me.'

'Are you afraid?' she asked.

'Don't leave me *now*,' he went on.

'Are you afraid?' she repeated.

'Do you think me simply out of my mind?' he pursued instead of answering. 'Do I merely strike you as a harmless lunatic?'

'No,' said May Bartram. 'I understand you. I believe you.'

'You mean you feel how my obsession – poor old thing! – may correspond to some possible reality?'

'To some possible reality.'

'Then you *will* watch with me?'

She hesitated, then for the third time put her question. 'Are you afraid?'

'Did I tell you I was – at Naples?'

'No, you said nothing about it.'

'Then I don't know. And I should *like* to know,' said John Marcher. 'You'll tell me yourself whether you think so. If you'll watch with me you'll see.'

'Very good then.' They had been moving by this time across the room, and at the door, before passing out, they paused as if for the full wind-up of their understanding. 'I'll watch with you,' said May Bartram.

## II

THE FACT THAT she 'knew' – knew and yet neither chaffed him nor betrayed him – had in a short time begun to constitute between them a sensible bond, which became more marked when, within the year that followed their afternoon at Weatherend, the opportunities for meeting multiplied. The event that thus promoted these occasions was the death of the ancient lady, her great-aunt, under whose wing, since losing her mother, she had to such an extent found shelter, and who, though but the widowed mother of the new successor to the property, had succeeded – thanks to a high tone and a high temper – in not forfeiting the supreme position at the great house. The deposition of this personage arrived but with her death, which, followed by many changes, made in particular a difference for the young woman in whom Marcher's expert attention had recognized from the first a dependant with a pride that might ache though it didn't bristle. Nothing for a long time had made him easier than the thought that the aching must have been much soothed by Miss Bartram's now finding herself able to set up a small home in London. She had acquired property, to an amount that made that luxury just possible, under her aunt's extremely complicated will, and when the whole matter began to be straightened out, which indeed took time, she let him know that the happy issue was at last in view. He had seen her again before that day, both because she had more than once accompanied the ancient lady to town and because he had paid another visit to the friends who so conveniently made of Weatherend one of the charms of their own hospitality. These friends had taken him back there; he had achieved there again with Miss Bartram some quiet detachment; and he had in London succeeded in persuading her to more than one brief absence from her aunt. They went together, on these latter occasions, to the National Gallery and the South Kensington Museum, where, among vivid reminders, they talked of Italy at large – not now attempting to recover, as at first, the taste of their youth and their ignorance. That recovery, the first day at Weatherend, had served its purpose well, had given them quite enough; so that they were, to Marcher's sense, no longer hovering about the head-waters of their stream, but had felt their boat pushed sharply off and down the current.

They were literally afloat together; for our gentleman this was marked, quite as marked as that the fortunate cause of it was just the buried treasure of her knowledge. He had with his own hands dug up this little hoard, brought to light – that is to within reach of the dim day constituted by their discretions and privacies – the object of value the hiding-place of which he had, after putting it into the ground himself, so strangely, so long forgotten. The exquisite luck of having again just stumbled on the spot made him indifferent to any other question; he would doubtless have devoted more time to the odd accident of his lapse of memory if he had not been moved to devote so much to the sweetness, the comfort, as he felt, for the future, that this accident itself had helped to keep fresh. It had never entered into his plan that anyone should 'know', and mainly for the reason that it was not in him to tell anyone. That would have been impossible, since nothing but the amusement of a cold world would have waited on it. Since, however, a mysterious fate had opened his mouth in youth, in spite of him, he would count that a compensation and profit by it to the utmost. That the right person *should* know tempered the asperity of his secret more even than his shyness had permitted him to imagine; and May Bartram was clearly right, because – well, because there she was. Her knowledge simply settled it; he would have been sure enough by this time had she been wrong. There was that in his situation, no doubt, that disposed him too much to see her as a mere confidant, taking all her light for him from the fact – the fact only – of her interest in his predicament, from her mercy, sympathy, seriousness, her consent not to regard him as the funniest of the funny. Aware, in fine, that her price for him was just in her giving him this constant sense of his being admirably spared, he was careful to remember that she had, after all, also a life of her own, with things that might happen to *her*, things that in friendship one should likewise take account of. Something fairly remarkable came to pass with him, for that matter, in this connection – something represented by a certain passage of his consciousness, in the suddenest way, from one extreme to the other.

He had thought himself, so long as nobody knew, the most disinterested person in the world, carrying his concentrated burden, his perpetual suspense, ever so quietly, holding his tongue about it, giving others no glimpse of it nor of its effect upon his life, asking of them no allowance and only making on his side all those that were asked. He had disturbed nobody with the queerness of having to know a haunted man, though he had had moments of rather special temptation on hearing people say that they were 'unsettled'. If they were as unsettled as he was – he who had never been settled for an hour in his life – they would know what it meant. Yet it wasn't, all the same, for him to make them, and he listened to them civilly enough. This was why he had such good – though possibly such rather colourless – manners; this was why, above all, he could regard himself, in a greedy world, as decently – as, in fact, perhaps even a little sublimely – unselfish. Our point is accordingly that he valued this character quite sufficiently to measure his present danger of letting it lapse, against which he promised himself to be much on his guard. He was quite ready, none the less, to be selfish just a little, since, surely, no more charming occasion for it had come to him. 'Just a little', in a word, was just as much as Miss Bartram, taking one day with another, would let him. He never would be in the least coercive, and he would keep well before him the lines on which consideration for her – the very highest – ought to proceed. He would thoroughly establish the heads under which her affairs, her requirements, her peculiarities – he went so far as to give them the latitude of that name – would come into their intercourse. All this naturally was a sign of how much he took the intercourse itself for granted. There was nothing more to be done about *that*. It simply existed; had sprung into being with her first penetrating question to him in the autumn light there at Weatherend. The real form it should have taken on the basis that stood out large was the form of their marrying. But the devil in this was that the very basis itself put marrying out of the question. His conviction, his apprehension, his obsession, in short, was not a condition he could invite a woman to share; and that consequence of it was precisely what was the matter with him. Something or other lay in wait for him, amid the twists and the turns of the months and the years, like a crouching beast in the jungle. It signified little whether the crouching beast were destined to slay him or to be slain. The definite point was the inevitable spring of the creature; and the definite lesson from that was that a man of feeling didn't cause himself to be accompanied by a lady on a tiger-hunt. Such was the image under which he had ended by figuring his life.

They had at first, none the less, in the scattered hours spent together, made no allusion to that view of it; which was a sign he was handsomely ready to give that he didn't expect, that he in fact didn't care always to be talking about it. Such a feature in one's outlook was really like a hump on one's back. The difference it made every minute of the day existed quite independently of discussion. One discussed, of course, *like* a hunchback, for there was always, if nothing else, the hunchback face. That remained, and she was watching him; but people watched best, as a general thing, in silence, so that such would be predominantly the manner of their vigil. Yet he didn't want, at the same time, to be solemn; solemn was what he imagined he too much tended to be with other people. The thing to be, with the one person who knew, was easy and natural – to make the reference rather than be seeming to avoid it, to avoid it rather than be seeming to make it, and to keep it, in any case, familiar, facetious even, rather than pedantic and portentous. Some such consideration as the latter was doubtless in his mind, for instance, when he wrote pleasantly to Miss Bartram that perhaps the great thing he had so long felt as in the lap of the gods was no more than this circumstance, which touched him so nearly, of her acquiring a house in London. It was the first allusion they had yet again made, needing any other hitherto so little; but when she replied, after having given him the news, that she was by no means satisfied with such a trifle, as the climax to so special a suspense, she almost set him wondering if she hadn't even a larger conception of singularity for him than he had for himself. He was at all events destined to become aware little by little, as time went by, that she was all the while looking at his life, judging it, measuring it, in the light of the thing she knew, which grew to be at last, with the consecration of the years, never mentioned between them save as 'the real truth' about him. That had always been his own form of reference to it, but she adopted the form so quietly that, looking back at the end of a period, he knew there was no moment at which it was traceable that she had, as he might say, got inside his condition, or exchanged the attitude of beautifully indulging for that of still more beautifully believing him.

It was always open to him to accuse her of seeing him but as the most harmless of maniacs, and this, in the long run – since it covered so much ground – was his easiest description of their friendship. He had a screw loose for her, but she liked him in spite of it, and was practically, against the rest of the world, his kind, wise keeper, unremunerated, but fairly amused and, in the absence of other near ties, not disreputably occupied. The rest of the world of course thought him queer, but she, she only, knew how, and above all why, queer; which was precisely what enabled her to dispose the concealing veil in the right folds. She took his gaiety from him – since it had to pass with them for gaiety – as she took everything else; but she certainly so far justified by her unerring touch his finer sense of the degree to which he had ended by convincing her. *She* at least never spoke of the secret of his life except as 'the real truth about you', and she had in fact a wonderful way of making it seem, as such, the secret of her own life too. That was in fine how he so constantly felt her as allowing for him; he couldn't on the whole call it anything else. He allowed for himself, but she, exactly, allowed still more; partly because, better placed for a sight of the matter, she traced his unhappy perversion through portions of its course into which he could scarce follow it. He knew how he felt, but, besides knowing that, she knew how he *looked* as well; he knew each of the things of importance he was insidiously kept from doing, but she could add up the amount they made, understand how much, with a lighter weight on his spirit, he might have done, and thereby establish how, clever as he was, he fell short. Above all she was in the secret of the difference between the forms he went through – those of his little office under Government, those of caring for his modest patrimony, for his library, for his garden in the country, for the people in London whose invitations he accepted and repaid – and the detachment that reigned beneath them and that made of all behaviour, all that could in the least be called behaviour, a long act of dissimulation. What it had come to was that he wore a mask painted with the social simper, out of the eye-holes of which there looked eyes of an expression not in the least matching the other features. This the stupid world, even after years, had never more than half discovered. It was only May Bartram who had, and she achieved, by an art indescribable, the feat of at once – or perhaps it was only alternately – meeting the eyes from in front and mingling her own vision, as from over his shoulder, with their peep through the apertures.

So, while they grew older together, she did watch with him, and so she let this association give shape and colour to her own existence. Beneath *her* forms as well detachment had learned to sit, and behaviour had become for her, in the social sense, a false account of herself. There was but one account of her that would have been true all the while, and that she could give, directly, to nobody, least of all to John Marcher. Her whole attitude was a virtual statement, but the perception of that only seemed destined to take its place for him as one of the many things necessarily crowded out of his consciousness. If she had, moreover, like himself, to make sacrifices to their real truth, it was to be granted that her compensation might have affected her as more prompt and more natural. They had long periods, in this London time, during which, when they were together, a stranger might have listened to them without in the least pricking up his ears; on the other hand, the real truth was equally liable at any moment to rise to the surface, and the auditor would then have wondered indeed what they were talking about. They had from an early time made up their mind that society was, luckily, unintelligent, and the margin that this gave them had fairly become one of their commonplaces. Yet there were still moments when the situation turned almost fresh – usually under the effect of some expression drawn from herself. Her expressions doubtless repeated themselves, but her intervals were generous. 'What saves us, you know, is that we answer so completely to so usual an appearance: that of the man and woman whose friendship has become such a daily habit, or almost, as to be at last indispensable.' That, for instance, was a remark she had frequently enough had occasion to make, though she had given it at different times different developments. What we are especially concerned with is the turn it happened to take from her one afternoon when he had come to see her in honour of her birthday. This anniversary had fallen on a Sunday, at a season of thick fog and general outward gloom; but he had brought her his customary offering, having known her now long enough to have established a hundred little customs. It was one of his proofs to himself, the present he made her on her birthday, that he had not sunk into real selfishness. It was mostly nothing more than a small trinket, but it was always fine of its kind, and he was regularly careful to pay for it more than he thought he could afford. 'Our habit saves you, at least, don't you see? because it makes you, after all, for the vulgar, indistinguishable from other men. What's the most inveterate mark of men in general? Why, the capacity to spend endless time with dull women – to spend it, I won't say without being bored, but without minding that they are, without being driven off at a tangent by it; which comes to the same thing. I'm your dull woman, a part of the daily bread for which you pray at church. That covers your tracks more than anything.'

'And what covers yours?' asked Marcher, whom his dull woman could mostly to this extent amuse. 'I see of course what you mean by your saving me, in one way and another, so far as other people are concerned – I've seen it all along. Only, what is it that saves *you*? I often think, you know, of that.'

She looked as if she sometimes thought of that too, but in rather a different way. 'Where other people, you mean, are concerned?'

'Well, you're really so in with me, you know – as a sort of result of my being so in with yourself. I mean of my having such an immense regard for you, being so tremendously grateful for all you've done for me. I sometimes ask myself if it's quite fair. Fair I mean to have so involved and – since one may say it – interested you. I almost feel as if you hadn't really had time to do anything else.'

'Anything else but be interested?' she asked. 'Ah, what else does one ever want to be? If I've been "watching" with you, as we long ago agreed that I was to do, watching is always in itself an absorption.'

'Oh, certainly,' John Marcher said, 'if you hadn't had your curiosity—! Only, doesn't it sometimes come to you, as time goes on, that your curiosity is not being particularly repaid?'

May Bartram had a pause. 'Do you ask that, by any chance, because you feel at all that yours isn't? I mean because you have to wait so long.'

Oh, he understood what she meant. 'For the thing to happen that never does happen? For the beast to jump out? No, I'm just where I was about it. It isn't a matter as to which I can *choose*, I can decide for a change. It isn't one as to which there *can* be a change. It's in the lap of the gods. One's in the hands of one's law – there one is. As to the form the law will take, the way it will operate, that's its own affair.'

'Yes,' Miss Bartram replied; 'of course one's fate is coming, of course it *has* come, in its own form and its own way, all the while. Only, you know, the form and the way in your case were to have been – well, something so exceptional and, as one may say, so particularly *your* own.'

Something in this made him look at her with suspicion. 'You

say "were to *have* been", as if in your heart you had begun to doubt.'

'Oh!' she vaguely protested.

'As if you believed,' he went on, 'that nothing will now take place.'

She shook her head slowly, but rather inscrutably. 'You're far from my thought.'

He continued to look at her. 'What then is the matter with you?'

'Well,' she said after another wait, 'the matter with me is simply that I'm more sure than ever my curiosity, as you call it, will be but too well repaid.'

They were frankly grave now; he had got up from his seat, had turned once more about the little drawing-room to which, year after year, he brought his inevitable topic; in which he had, as he might have said, tasted their intimate community with every sauce, where every object was as familiar to him as the things of his own house and the very carpets were worn with his fitful walk very much as the desks in old counting-houses are worn by the elbows of generations of clerks. The generations of his nervous moods had been at work there, and the place was the written history of his whole middle life. Under the impression of what his friend had just said he knew himself, for some reason, more aware of these things, which made him, after a moment, stop again before her. 'Is it, possibly, that you've grown afraid?'

'Afraid?' He thought, as she repeated the word, that his

question had made her, a little, change colour; so that, lest he should have touched on a truth, he explained very kindly, 'You remember that that was what you asked *me* long ago – that first day at Weatherend.'

'Oh yes, and you told me you didn't know – that I was to see for myself. We've said little about it since, even in so long a time.'

'Precisely,' Marcher interposed – 'quite as if it were too delicate a matter for us to make free with. Quite as if we might find, on pressure, that I *am* afraid. For then,' he said, 'we shouldn't, should we? quite know what to do.'

She had for the time no answer to this question. 'There have been days when I thought you were. Only, of course,' she added, 'there have been days when we have thought almost anything.'

'Everything. Oh!' Marcher softly groaned as with a gasp, half spent, at the face, more uncovered just then than it had been for a long while, of the imagination always with them. It had always had its incalculable moments of glaring out, quite as with the very eyes of the very Beast, and, used as he was to them, they could still draw from him the tribute of a sigh that rose from the depths of his being. All that they had thought, first and last, rolled over him; the past seemed to have been reduced to mere barren speculation. This in fact was what the place had just struck him as so full of – the simplification of everything but the state of suspense. That remained only by seeming to hang in the void surrounding it. Even his original fear, if fear it had been, had lost itself in the desert. 'I judge, however,' he continued, 'that you see I'm not afraid now.'

'What I see is, as I make it out, that you've achieved something almost unprecedented in the way of getting used to danger. Living with it so long and so closely, you've lost your sense of it; you know it's there, but you're indifferent, and you cease even, as of old, to have to whistle in the dark. Considering what the danger is,' May Bartram wound up, 'I'm bound to say that I don't think your attitude could well be surpassed.'

John Marcher faintly smiled. 'It's heroic?'

'Certainly – call it that.'

He considered. 'I *am*, then, a man of courage?'

'That's what you were to show me.'

He still, however, wondered. 'But doesn't the man of courage know what he's afraid of – or *not* afraid of? I don't know *that*, you see. I don't focus it. I can't name it. I only know I'm exposed.'

'Yes, but exposed – how shall I say? – so directly. So intimately. That's surely enough.'

'Enough to make you feel, then – as what we may call the end of our watch – that I'm not afraid?'

'You're not afraid. But it isn't,' she said, 'the end of our watch. That is, it isn't the end of yours. You've everything still to see.'

'Then why haven't you?' he asked. He had had, all along, today, the sense of her keeping something back, and he still had it. As this was his first impression of that, it made a kind of date.

The case was the more marked as she didn't at first answer; which in turn made him go on. 'You know something I don't.' Then his voice, for that of a man of courage, trembled a little. 'You know what's to happen.' Her silence, with the face she showed, was almost a confession – it made him sure. 'You know, and you're afraid to tell me. It's so bad that you're afraid I'll find out.'

All this might be true, for she did look as if, unexpectedly to her, he had crossed some mystic line that she had secretly drawn round her. Yet she might, after all, not have worried; and the real upshot was that he himself, at all events, needn't. 'You'll never find out.'

# III

IT WAS ALL to have made, none the less, as I have said, a date; as came out in the fact that again and again, even after long intervals, other things that passed between them wore, in relation to this hour, but the character of recalls and results. Its immediate effect had been indeed rather to lighten insistence – almost to provoke a reaction; as if their topic had dropped by its own weight and as if moreover, for that matter, Marcher had been visited by one of his occasional warnings against egotism. He had kept up, he felt, and very decently on the whole, his consciousness of the importance of not being

## The Beast in the Jungle

selfish, and it was true that he had never sinned in that direction without promptly enough trying to press the scales the other way. He often repaired his fault, the season permitting, by inviting his friend to accompany him to the opera; and it not infrequently thus happened that, to show he didn't wish her to have but one sort of food for her mind, he was the cause of her appearing there with him a dozen nights in the month. It even happened that, seeing her home at such times, he occasionally went in with her to finish, as he called it, the evening, and, the better to make his point, sat down to the frugal but always careful little supper that awaited his pleasure. His point was made, he thought, by his not eternally insisting with her on himself; made for instance, at such hours, when it befell that, her piano at hand and each of them familiar with it, they went over passages of the opera together. It chanced to be on one of these occasions, however, that he reminded her of her not having answered a certain question he had put to her during the talk that had taken place between them on her last birthday. 'What is it that saves *you*?' – saved her, he meant, from that appearance of variation from the usual human type. If he had practically escaped remark, as she pretended, by doing, in the most important particular, what most men do – find the answer to life in patching up an alliance of a sort with a woman no better than himself – how had she escaped it, and how could the alliance, such as it was, since they must suppose it had been more or less noticed, have failed to make her rather positively talked about?

'I never said,' May Bartram replied, 'that it hadn't made me talked about.'

'Ah well then, you're not "saved".'

'It has not been a question for me. If you've had your woman, I've had,' she said, 'my man.'

'And you mean that makes you all right?'

She hesitated. 'I don't know why it shouldn't make me — humanly, which is what we're speaking of — as right as it makes you.'

'I see,' Marcher returned. '"Humanly", no doubt, as showing that you're living for something. Not, that is, just for me and my secret.'

May Bartram smiled. 'I don't pretend it exactly shows that I'm not living for you. It's my intimacy with you that's in question.'

He laughed as he saw what she meant. 'Yes, but since, as you say, I'm only, so far as people make out, ordinary, you're — aren't you? — no more than ordinary either. You help me to pass for a man like another. So if I *am*, as I understand you, you're not compromised. Is that it?'

She had another hesitation, but she spoke clearly enough. 'That's it. It's all that concerns me — to help you to pass for a man like another.'

He was careful to acknowledge the remark handsomely. 'How kind, how beautiful, you are to me! How shall I ever repay you?'

She had her last grave pause, as if there might be a choice of ways. But she chose. 'By going on as you are.'

It was into this going on as he was that they relapsed, and really for so long a time that the day inevitably came for a further sounding of their depths. It was as if these depths, constantly bridged over by a structure that was firm enough in spite of its lightness and of its occasional oscillation in the somewhat vertiginous air, invited on occasion, in the interest of their nerves, a dropping of the plummet and a measurement of the abyss. A difference had been made moreover, once for all, by the fact that she had, all the while, not appeared to feel the need of rebutting his charge of an idea within her that she didn't dare to express, uttered just before one of the fullest of their later discussions ended. It had come up for him then that she 'knew' something and that what she knew was bad – too bad to tell him. When he had spoken of it as visibly so bad that she was afraid he might find it out, her reply had left the matter too equivocal to be let alone and yet, for Marcher's special sensibility, almost too formidable again to touch. He circled about it at a distance that alternately narrowed and widened and that yet was not much affected by the consciousness in him that there was nothing she could 'know', after all, any better than he did. She had no source of knowledge that he hadn't equally – except of course that she might have finer nerves. That was what women had where they were interested; they made out things, where people were concerned, that the people often couldn't have made out for themselves. Their nerves, their sensibility, their imagination, were conductors and revealers, and the beauty of May Bartram was in particular that she had given herself so to his case. He felt in these days what, oddly enough, he had never felt before, the growth of a dread of losing her by some catastrophe – some catastrophe that yet wouldn't at all be *the* catastrophe: partly because she had, almost of a sudden, begun to strike him as useful to him as never yet, and partly by reason of an appearance of uncertainty in her health, coincident and equally new. It was characteristic of the inner detachment he had hitherto so successfully cultivated and to which our whole account of him is a reference, it was characteristic that his complications, such as they were, had never yet seemed so as at this crisis to thicken about him, even to the point of making him ask himself if he were, by any chance, of a truth, within sight or sound, within touch or reach, within the immediate jurisdiction of the thing that waited.

When the day came, as come it had to, that his friend confessed to him her fear of a deep disorder in her blood, he felt somehow the shadow of a change and the chill of a shock. He immediately began to imagine aggravations and disasters, and above all to think of her peril as the direct menace for himself of personal privation. This indeed gave him one of those partial recoveries of equanimity that were agreeable to him – it showed him that what was still first in his mind was the loss she herself might suffer. 'What if she should have to die before knowing, before seeing——?' It would have been brutal, in the early stages of her trouble, to put that question to her; but it had immediately sounded for him to his own concern, and the possibility was what most made him sorry for her. If she did 'know', moreover, in the sense of her having had some — what should he think? — mystical, irresistible light, this would make the matter not better, but worse, inasmuch as her original adoption of his own curiosity had quite become the basis of her life. She had been living to see what would *be* to be seen, and it would be cruel to her to have to give up before the accomplishment of the vision. These reflections, as I say, refreshed his generosity; yet, make them as he might, he saw himself, with the lapse of the period, more and more disconcerted. It lapsed for him with a strange, steady sweep, and the oddest oddity was that it gave him, independently of the threat of much inconvenience, almost the only positive surprise his career, if career it could be called, had yet offered him. She kept the house as she had never done; he had to go to her to see her — she could meet him nowhere now, though there was scarce a corner of their loved old London in which she had not in the past, at one time or another, done so; and he found her always seated by her fire in the deep, old-fashioned chair she was less and less able to leave. He had been struck one day, after an absence exceeding his usual measure, with her suddenly looking much older to him than he had ever thought of her being; then he recognized that the suddenness was all on his side — he had just been suddenly struck. She looked older because inevitably, after so many years, she *was* old, or almost; which was of course true in still greater measure of her companion. If she was old, or almost, John Marcher assuredly was, and yet it was her showing of the lesson, not his own, that brought the truth home to him. His surprises began here; when once they had begun they multiplied; they came rather with a rush: it was as if, in the oddest way in the world, they had all been kept back, sown in a thick cluster, for the late afternoon of life, the time at which, for people in general, the unexpected has died out.

One of them was that he should have caught himself – for he *had* so done – *really* wondering if the great accident would take form now as nothing more than his being condemned to see this charming woman, this admirable friend, pass away from him. He had never so unreservedly qualified her as while confronted in thought with such a possibility; in spite of which there was small doubt for him that as an answer to his long riddle the mere effacement of even so fine a feature of his situation would be an abject anticlimax. It would represent, as connected with his past attitude, a drop of dignity under the shadow of which his existence could only become the most grotesque of failures. He had been far from holding it a failure – long as he had waited for the appearance that was to make it a success. He had waited for a quite other thing, not for such a one as that. The breath of his good faith came short, however, as he recognized how long he had waited, or how long, at least, his companion had. That she, at all events, might be recorded as having waited in vain – this affected him sharply, and all the more because of his at first having done little more than amuse himself with the idea. It grew more grave as the gravity of her condition grew, and the state of mind it produced in him, which he ended by watching, himself, as if it had been some definite disfigurement of his outer person, may pass for another of his surprises. This conjoined itself still with another, the really stupefying consciousness of a question that he would have allowed to shape itself had he dared. What did everything mean – what, that is, did *she* mean, she and her vain waiting and her probable death and the soundless admonition of it all – unless that, at this time of day, it was simply, it was overwhelmingly too late? He had never, at any stage of his queer consciousness, admitted the whisper of such a correction; he had never, till within these last few months, been so false to his conviction as not to hold that what was to come to him had time, whether *he* struck himself as having it or not. That at last, at last, he certainly hadn't it, to speak of, or had it but in the scantiest measure – such, soon enough, as things went with him, became the inference with which his old obsession had to reckon: and this it was not helped to do by the more and more confirmed appearance that the great vagueness casting the long shadow in which he had lived had, to attest itself, almost no margin left. Since it was in Time that he was to have met his fate, so it was in Time that his fate was to have acted; and as he waked up to the sense of no longer being young, which was exactly the sense of being stale, just as that, in turn, was the sense of being weak, he waked up to another matter beside. It all hung together; they were subject, he and the great vagueness, to an equal and indivisible law. When the possibilities themselves had, accordingly, turned stale, when the secret of the gods had grown faint, had perhaps even quite evaporated, that, and that only, was failure. It wouldn't have been failure to be bankrupt, dishonoured, pilloried, hanged; it was failure not to be anything. And so, in the dark valley into which his path had taken its unlooked-for twist, he wondered not a little as he groped. He didn't care what awful crash might overtake him, with what ignominy or what monstrosity he might yet be associated — since he wasn't, after all, too utterly old to suffer — if it would only be decently proportionate to the posture he had kept, all his life, in the promised presence of it. He had but one desire left — that he shouldn't have been 'sold'.

# IV

THEN IT WAS that one afternoon, while the spring of the year was young and new, she met, all in her own way, his frankest betrayal of these alarms. He had gone in late to see her, but evening had not settled, and she was presented to him in that long, fresh light of waning April days which affects us often with a sadness sharper than the greyest hours of autumn. The week had been warm, the spring was supposed to have begun early, and May Bartram sat, for the first time in the year, without a fire, a fact that, to Marcher's sense, gave the scene of which she formed part a smooth and ultimate look, an air of knowing, in its immaculate order and its cold, meaningless cheer, that it would never see a fire again. Her own aspect — he could scarce have said why — intensified this note. Almost as white as wax, with the marks and signs in her face as numerous and as fine as if they had been etched by a needle, with soft white draperies relieved by a faded green scarf, the delicate tone of which had been consecrated by the years, she was the picture of a serene, exquisite, but impenetrable sphinx, whose head, or indeed all whose person, might have been powdered with silver. She was a sphinx, yet with her white petals and green fronds she might have been a lily too – only an artificial lily, wonderfully imitated and constantly kept, without dust or stain, though not exempt from a slight droop and a complexity of faint creases, under some clear glass bell. The perfection of household care, of high polish and finish, always reigned in her rooms, but they especially looked to Marcher at present as if everything had been wound up, tucked in, put away, so that she might sit with folded hands and with nothing more to do. She was 'out of it', to his vision; her work was over; she communicated with him as across some gulf, or from some island of rest that she had already reached, and it made him feel strangely abandoned. Was it – or, rather, wasn't it – that if for so long she had been watching with him the answer to their question had swum into her ken and taken on its name, so that her occupation was verily gone? He had as much as charged her with this in saying to her, many months before, that she even then knew something she was keeping from him. It was a point he had never since ventured to press, vaguely fearing, as he did, that it might become a difference, perhaps a disagreement, between them. He had in short, in this later time, turned nervous, which was what, in all the other years, he had never been; and the oddity was that his nervousness should have waited till he had begun to doubt, should have held off so long as he was sure. There was something, it seemed to him, that the wrong word would bring down on his head, something that would so at least put an end to his suspense. But he wanted not to speak the wrong word; that would make everything ugly. He wanted the knowledge he lacked to drop on him, if drop it could, by its own august weight. If she was to forsake him it was surely for her to take leave. This was why he didn't ask her again, directly, what she knew; but it was also why, approaching the matter from another side, he said to her in the course of his visit: 'What do you regard as the very worst that, at this time of day, *can* happen to me?'

He had asked her that in the past often enough; they had, with the odd, irregular rhythm of their intensities and avoidances, exchanged ideas about it and then had seen the ideas washed away by cool intervals, washed like figures traced in sea-sand. It had ever been the mark of their talk that the oldest allusions in it required but a little dismissal and reaction to come out again, sounding for the hour as new. She could thus at present meet his inquiry quite freshly and patiently. 'Oh yes, I've repeatedly thought, only it always seemed to me of old that I couldn't quite make up my mind. I thought of dreadful things, between which it was difficult to choose; and so must you have done.'

'Rather! I feel now as if I had scarce done anything else. I appear to myself to have spent my life in thinking of nothing *but* dreadful things. A great many of them I've at different times named to you, but there were others I couldn't name.'

'They were too, too dreadful?'

'Too, too dreadful – some of them.'

She looked at him a minute, and there came to him as he met it an inconsequent sense that her eyes, when one got their full clearness, were still as beautiful as they had been in youth, only beautiful with a strange, cold light – a light that somehow was a part of the effect, if it wasn't rather a part of the cause, of the pale, hard sweetness of the season and the hour. 'And yet,' she said at last, 'there are horrors we have mentioned.'

It deepened the strangeness to see her, as such a figure in such a picture, talk of 'horrors', but she was to do, in a few minutes, something stranger yet – though even of this he was to take the full measure but afterwards – and the note of it was already in the air. It was, for the matter of that, one of the signs that her eyes were having again such a high flicker of their prime. He had to admit, however, what she said. 'Oh yes, there were times when we did go far.' He caught himself in the act of speaking as if it all were over. Well, he wished it were; and the consummation depended, for him, clearly, more and more on his companion.

But she had now a soft smile. 'Oh, far—!'

It was oddly ironic. 'Do you mean you're prepared to go further?'

She was frail and ancient and charming as she continued to look at him, yet it was rather as if she had lost the thread. 'Do you consider that we went so far?'

'Why, I thought it the point you were just making – that we *had* looked most things in the face.'

'Including each other?' She still smiled. 'But you're quite right. We've had together great imaginations, often great fears; but some of them have been unspoken.'

'Then the worst – we haven't faced that. I *could* face it, I believe, if I knew what you think it. I feel,' he explained, 'as if I had lost my power to conceive such things.' And he wondered if he looked as blank as he sounded. 'It's spent.'

'Then why do you assume,' she asked, 'that mine isn't?'

'Because you've given me signs to the contrary. It isn't a question for you of conceiving, imagining, comparing. It isn't a question now of choosing.' At last he came out with it. 'You know something that I don't. You've shown me that before.'

These last words affected her, he could see in a moment, remarkably, and she spoke with firmness. 'I've shown you, my dear, nothing.'

He shook his head. 'You can't hide it.'

'Oh, oh!' May Bartram murmured over what she couldn't hide. It was almost a smothered groan.

'You admitted it months ago, when I spoke of it to you as of something you were afraid I would find out. Your answer was that I couldn't, that I wouldn't, and I don't pretend I have. But you had something therefore in mind, and I see now that it must have been, that it still is, the possibility that, of all possibilities, has settled itself for you as the worst. This,' he went on, 'is why I appeal to you. I'm only afraid of ignorance now – I'm not afraid of knowledge.' And then as for a while she said nothing: 'What makes me sure is that I see in your face and feel here, in this air and amid these appearances, that you're out of it. You've done. You've had your experience. You leave me to my fate.'

Well, she listened, motionless and white in her chair, as if she had in fact a decision to make, so that her whole manner was a virtual confession, though still with a small, fine, inner stiffness, an imperfect surrender. 'It *would* be the worst,' she finally let herself say. 'I mean the thing that I've never said.'

It hushed him a moment. 'More monstrous than all the monstrosities we've named?'

'More monstrous. Isn't that what you sufficiently express,' she asked, 'in calling it the worst?'

Marcher thought. 'Assuredly – if you mean, as I do, something that includes all the loss and all the shame that are thinkable.'

'It would if it *should* happen,' said May Bartram. 'What we're speaking of, remember, is only my idea.'

'It's your belief,' Marcher returned. 'That's enough for me. I feel your beliefs are right. Therefore if, having this one, you give me no more light on it, you abandon me.'

'No, no!' she repeated. 'I'm with you – don't you see? – still.' And as if to make it more vivid to him she rose from her chair – a movement she seldom made in these days – and showed herself, all draped and all soft, in her fairness and slimness. 'I haven't forsaken you.'

It was really, in its effort against weakness, a generous

assurance, and had the success of the impulse not, happily, been great, it would have touched him to pain more than to pleasure. But the cold charm in her eyes had spread, as she hovered before him, to all the rest of her person, so that it was, for the minute, almost like a recovery of youth. He couldn't pity her for that; he could only take her as she showed – as capable still of helping him. It was as if, at the same time, her light might at any instant go out; wherefore he must make the most of it. There passed before him with intensity the three or four things he wanted most to know; but the question that came of itself to his lips really covered the others. 'Then tell me if I shall consciously suffer.'

She promptly shook her head. 'Never!'

It confirmed the authority he imputed to her, and it produced on him an extraordinary effect. 'Well, what's better than that? Do you call that the worst?'

'You think nothing is better?' she asked.

She seemed to mean something so special that he again sharply wondered, though still with the dawn of a prospect of relief. 'Why not, if one doesn't *know*?' After which, as their eyes, over his question, met in a silence, the dawn deepened and something to his purpose came, prodigiously, out of her very face. His own, as he took it in, suddenly flushed to the forehead, and he gasped with the force of a perception to which, on the instant, everything fitted. The sound of his gasp filled the air; then he became articulate. 'I see – if I don't suffer!'

In her own look, however, was doubt. 'You see what?'

'Why, what you mean – what you've always meant.'

She again shook her head. 'What I mean isn't what I've always meant. It's different.'

'It's something new?'

She hesitated. 'Something new. It's not what you think. I see what you think.'

His divination drew breath then; only her correction might be wrong. 'It isn't that I *am* a donkey?' he asked between faintness and grimness. 'It isn't that it's all a mistake?'

'A mistake?' she pityingly echoed. *That* possibility, for her, he saw, would be monstrous; and if she guaranteed him the immunity from pain it would accordingly not be what she had in mind. 'Oh, no,' she declared; 'it's nothing of that sort. You've been right.'

Yet he couldn't help asking himself if she weren't, thus pressed, speaking but to save him. It seemed to him he should be most lost if his history should prove all a platitude. 'Are you telling me the truth, so that I shan't have been a bigger idiot than I can bear to know? I *haven't* lived with a vain imagination, in the most besotted illusion? I haven't waited but to see the door shut in my face?'

She shook her head again. 'However the case stands *that* isn't the truth. Whatever the reality, it *is* a reality. The door isn't shut. The door's open,' said May Bartram.

'Then something's to come?'

She waited once again, always with her cold, sweet eyes on him. 'It's never too late.' She had, with her gliding step, diminished the distance between them, and she stood nearer to him, close to him, a minute, as if still full of the unspoken. Her movement might have been for some finer emphasis of what she was at once hesitating and deciding to say. He had been standing by the chimney-piece, fireless and sparely adorned, a small, perfect old French clock and two morsels of rosy Dresden constituting all its furniture; and her hand grasped the shelf while she kept him waiting, grasped it a little as for support and encouragement. She only kept him waiting, however; that is he only waited. It had become suddenly, from her movement and attitude, beautiful and vivid to him that she had something more to give him; her wasted face delicately shone with it, and it glittered, almost as with the white lustre of silver, in her expression. She was right, incontestably, for what he saw in her face was the truth, and strangely, without consequence, while their talk of it as dreadful was still in the air, she appeared to present it as inordinately soft. This, prompting bewilderment, made him but gape the more gratefully for her revelation, so that they continued for some minutes silent, her face shining at him, her contact imponderably pressing, and his stare all kind, but all expectant. The end, none the less, was that what he had expected failed to sound. Something else took place instead, which seemed to consist at first in the mere closing of her eyes. She gave way at the same instant to a slow, fine shudder, and though he remained staring – though he stared, in fact, but the harder – she turned off and regained her chair. It was the end of what she had been intending, but it left him thinking only of that.

'Well, you don't say—?'

She had touched in her passage a bell near the chimney and had sunk back, strangely pale. 'I'm afraid I'm too ill.'

'Too ill to tell me?' It sprang up sharp to him, and almost to his lips, the fear that she would die without giving him light. He checked himself in time from so expressing his question, but she answered as if she had heard the words.

'Don't you know – now?'

'"Now"—?' She had spoken as if something that had made a difference had come up within the moment. But her maid, quickly obedient to her bell, was already with them. 'I know nothing.' And he was afterwards to say to himself that he must have spoken with odious impatience, such an impatience as to show that, supremely disconcerted, he washed his hands of the whole question.

'Oh!' said May Bartram.

'Are you in pain?' he asked, as the woman went to her.

'No,' said May Bartram.

Her maid, who had put an arm round her as if to take her to her room, fixed on him eyes that appealingly contradicted her; in spite of which, however, he showed once more his mystification. 'What then has happened?'

She was once more, with her companion's help, on her feet, and, feeling withdrawal imposed on him, he had found, blankly, his hat and gloves and had reached the door. Yet he waited for her answer. 'What *was* to,' she said.

## V

HE CAME BACK the next day, but she was then unable to see him, and as it was literally the first time this had occurred in the long stretch of their acquaintance he turned away, defeated and sore, almost angry – or feeling at least that such a break in their custom was really the beginning of the end – and wandered alone with his thoughts, especially with one of them that he was unable to keep down. She was dying, and he would lose her; she was dying, and his life would end. He stopped in the park, into which he had passed, and stared before him at his recurrent doubt. Away from her the doubt pressed again; in her presence he had believed her, but as he felt his forlornness he threw himself into the explanation that, nearest at hand, had most of a miserable warmth for him and least of a cold torment. She had deceived him to save him – to put him off with something in which he should be able to rest. What could the thing that was to happen to him be, after all, but just this thing that had begun to happen? Her dying, her death, his consequent solitude – *that* was what he had figured as the beast in the jungle, that was what had been in the lap of the gods. He had had her word for it as he left her; for what else, on earth, could she have meant? It wasn't a thing of a monstrous order; not a fate rare and distinguished; not a stroke of fortune that overwhelmed and immortalized; it had only the stamp of the common doom. But poor Marcher, at this hour, judged the common doom sufficient. It would serve his turn, and even as the consummation of infinite waiting he would bend his pride to accept it. He sat down on a bench in the twilight. He hadn't been a fool. Something had *been*, as she had said, to come. Before he rose indeed it had quite struck him that the final fact really matched with the long avenue through which he had had to reach it. As sharing his suspense, and as giving herself all, giving her life, to bring it to an end, she had come with him every step of the way. He had lived by her aid, and to leave her behind would be cruelly, damnably to miss her. What could be more overwhelming than that?

Well, he was to know within the week, for though she kept him a while at bay, left him restless and wretched during a series of days on each of which he asked about her only again to have to turn away, she ended his trial by receiving him where she had always received him. Yet she had been brought out at some hazard into the presence of so many of the things that were, consciously, vainly, half their past, and there was scant service left in the gentleness of her mere desire, all too visible, to check his obsession and wind up his long trouble. That was clearly what she wanted; the one thing more, for her own peace, while she could still put out her hand. He was so affected by her state that, once seated by her chair, he was moved to let everything go; it was she herself therefore who brought him back, took up again, before she dismissed him, her last word of the other time. She showed how she wished to leave their affair in order. 'I'm not sure you understood. You've nothing to wait for more. It *has* come.'

Oh, how he looked at her! 'Really?'

'Really.'

'The thing that, as you said, *was* to?'

'The thing that we began in our youth to watch for.'

Face to face with her once more he believed her; it was a claim to which he had so abjectly little to oppose. 'You mean that it has come as a positive, definite occurrence, with a name and a date?'

'Positive. Definite. I don't know about the "name", but, oh, with a date!'

He found himself again too helplessly at sea. 'But come in the night – come and passed me by?'

May Bartram had her strange, faint smile. 'Oh no, it hasn't passed you by!'

'But if I haven't been aware of it, and it hasn't touched me——?'

'Ah, your not being aware of it,' and she seemed to hesitate an instant to deal with this – 'your not being aware of it is the strangeness *in* the strangeness. It's the wonder *of* the wonder.' She spoke as with the softness almost of a sick child, yet now at last, at the end of all, with the perfect straightness of a sibyl. She visibly knew that she knew, and the effect on him was of something co-ordinate, in its high character, with the law that had ruled him. It was the true voice of the law; so on her lips would the law itself have sounded. 'It *has* touched you,' she went on. 'It has done its office. It has made you all its own.'

'So utterly without my knowing it?'

'So utterly without your knowing it.' His hand, as he leaned to her, was on the arm of her chair, and, dimly smiling always now, she placed her own on it. 'It's enough if *I* know it.'

'Oh!' he confusedly sounded, as she herself of late so often had done.

'What I long ago said is true. You'll never know now, and I think you ought to be content. You've *had* it,' said. May Bartram.

'But had what?'

'Why, what was to have marked you out. The proof of your law. It has acted. I'm too glad,' she then bravely added, 'to have been able to see what it's *not*.'

He continued to attach his eyes to her, and with the sense that it was all beyond him, and that *she* was too, he would still have sharply challenged her, had he not felt it an abuse of her weakness to do more than take devoutly what she gave him, take it as hushed as to a revelation. If he did speak, it was out of the foreknowledge of his loneliness to come. 'If you're glad of what it's "not", it might then have been worse?'

She turned her eyes away, she looked straight before her with which, after a moment: 'Well, you know our fears.'

He wondered. 'It's something then we never feared?'

On this, slowly, she turned to him. 'Did we ever dream, with all our dreams, that we should sit and talk of it thus?'

He tried for a little to make out if they had; but it was as if their dreams, numberless enough, were in solution in some thick, cold mist, in which thought lost itself. 'It might have been that we couldn't talk?'

'Well—' she did her best for him — 'not from this side. This, you see,' she said, 'is the *other* side.'

'I think,' poor Marcher returned, 'that all sides are the same to me.' Then, however, as she softly shook her head in correction: 'We mightn't, as it were, have got across—?'

'To where we are — no. We're *here*' — she made her weak emphasis.

'And much good does it do us!' was her friend's frank comment.

'It does us the good it can. It does us the good that *it* isn't here. It's past. It's behind,' said May Bartram. 'Before—' but her voice dropped.

He had got up, not to tire her, but it was hard to combat his yearning. She after all told him nothing but that his light had failed – which he knew well enough without her. 'Before—?' he blankly echoed.

'Before, you see, it was always to *come*. That kept it present.'

'Oh, I don't care what comes now! Besides,' Marcher added, 'it seems to me I liked it better present, as you say, than I can like it absent with *your* absence.'

'Oh, mine!' — and her pale hands made light of it.

'With the absence of everything.' He had a dreadful sense of standing there before her for — so far as anything but this proved, this bottomless drop was concerned — the last time of their life. It rested on him with a weight he felt he could scarce bear, and this weight it apparently was that still pressed out what remained in him of speakable protest. 'I believe you; but I can't begin to pretend I understand. *Nothing*, for me, is past; nothing *will* pass until I pass myself, which I pray my stars may be as soon as possible. Say, however,' he added, 'that I've eaten my cake, as you contend, to the last crumb – how can the thing I've never felt at all be the thing I was marked out to feel?'

She met him, perhaps, less directly, but she met him unperturbed. 'You take your "feelings" for granted. You were to suffer your fate. That was not necessarily to know it.'

'How in the world – when what is such knowledge but suffering?'

She looked up at him a while, in silence. 'No – you don't understand.'

'I suffer,' said John Marcher.

'Don't, don't!'

'How can I help at least *that*?'

'*Don't!*' May Bartram repeated.

She spoke it in a tone so special, in spite of her weakness, that he stared an instant – stared as if some light, hitherto hidden, had shimmered across his vision. Darkness again closed over it, but the gleam had already become for him an idea. 'Because I haven't the right——?'

'Don't *know* – when you needn't,' she mercifully urged. 'You needn't – for we shouldn't.'

'Shouldn't?' If he could but know what she meant!

'No – it's too much.'

'Too much?' he still asked – but with a mystification that was the next moment, of a sudden, to give way. Her words, if they meant something, affected him in this light – the light also of her wasted face – as meaning *all*, and the sense of what knowledge had been for herself came over him with a rush which broke through into a question. 'Is it of that, then, you're dying?'

She but watched him, gravely at first, as if to see, with this, where he was, and she might have seen something, or feared something, that moved her sympathy. 'I would live for you still – if I could.' Her eyes closed for a little, as if, withdrawn into herself, she were, for a last time, trying. 'But I can't!' she said as she raised them again to take leave of him.

She couldn't indeed, as but too promptly and sharply appeared, and he had no vision of her after this that was anything but darkness and doom. They had parted forever in that strange talk; access to her chamber of pain, rigidly guarded, was almost wholly forbidden him; he was feeling now moreover, in the face of doctors, nurses, the two or three relatives attracted doubtless by the presumption of what she had to 'leave', how few were the rights, as they were called in such cases, that he had to put forward, and how odd it might even seem that their intimacy shouldn't have given him more of them. The stupidest fourth cousin had more, even though she had been nothing in such a person's life. She had been a feature of features in *his*, for what else was it to have been so indispensable? Strange beyond saying were the ways of existence, baffling for him the anomaly of his lack, as he felt it to be, of producible claim. A woman might have been, as it were, everything to him, and it might yet present him in no connection that anyone appeared obliged to recognize. If this was the case in these closing weeks it was the case more sharply on the occasion of the last offices rendered, in the great grey London cemetery, to what had been mortal, to what had been precious, in his friend. The concourse at her grave was not numerous, but he saw himself treated as scarce more nearly concerned with it than if there had been a thousand others. He was in short from this moment face to face with the fact that he was to profit extraordinarily little by the interest May Bartram had taken in him. He couldn't quite have said what he expected, but he had somehow not expected this approach to a double privation. Not only had her interest failed him, but he seemed to feel himself unattended – and for a reason he couldn't sound – by the distinction, the dignity, the propriety, if nothing else, of the man markedly bereaved. It was as if, in the view of society, he had not *been* markedly bereaved, as if there still failed some sign or proof of it, and as if, none the less, his character could never be affirmed, nor the deficiency ever made up. There were moments, as the weeks went by, when he would have liked, by some almost aggressive act, to take his stand on the intimacy of his loss, in order that it *might* be questioned and his retort, to the relief of his spirit, so recorded; but the moments of an irritation more helpless followed fast on these, the moments during which, turning things over with a good conscience but with a bare horizon, he found himself wondering if he oughtn't to have begun, so to speak, further back.

He found himself wondering indeed at many things, and this

last speculation had others to keep it company. What could he have done, after all, in her lifetime, without giving them both, as it were, away? He couldn't have made it known she was watching him, for that would have published the superstition of the Beast. This was what closed his mouth now – now that the Jungle had been threshed to vacancy and that the Beast had stolen away. It sounded too foolish and too flat; the difference for him in this particular, the extinction in his life of the element of suspense, was such in fact as to surprise him. He could scarce have said what the effect resembled; the abrupt cessation, the positive prohibition, of music perhaps, more than anything else, in some place all adjusted and all accustomed to sonority and to attention. If he could at any rate have conceived lifting the veil from his image at some moment of the past (what had he done, after all, if not lift it to *her*?), so to do this today, to talk to people at large of the jungle cleared and confide to them that he now felt it as safe, would have been not only to see them listen as to a good-wife's tale, but really to hear himself tell one. What it presently came to in truth was that poor Marcher waded through his beaten grass, where no life stirred, where no breath sounded, where no evil eye seemed to gleam from a possible lair, very much as if vaguely looking for the Beast, and still more as if missing it. He walked about in an existence that had grown strangely more spacious, and, stopping fitfully in places where the undergrowth of life struck him as closer, asked himself yearningly, wondered secretly, and sorely, if it would have lurked here or there. It would have at all events *sprung*; what was at least complete was his belief in the truth itself of the assurance given him. The change from his old sense to his new was absolute and final: what was to happen *had* so absolutely and finally happened that he was as little able to know a fear for his future as to know a hope; so absent in short was any question of anything still to come. He was to live entirely with the other question, that of his unidentified past, that of his having to see his fortune impenetrably muffled and masked.

The torment of this vision became then his occupation; he couldn't perhaps have consented to live but for the possibility of guessing. She had told him, his friend, not to guess; she had forbidden him, so far as he might, to know, and she had even in a sort denied the power in him to learn: which were so many things, precisely, to deprive him of rest. It wasn't that he wanted, he argued for fairness, that anything that had happened to him should happen over again; it was only that he shouldn't, as an anticlimax, have been taken sleeping so sound as not to be able to win back by an effort of thought the lost stuff of consciousness. He declared to himself at moments that he would either win it back or have done with consciousness for ever; he made this idea his one motive, in fine, made it so much his passion that none other, to compare with it, seemed ever to have touched him. The lost stuff of consciousness became thus for him as a strayed or stolen child to an unappeasable father; he hunted it up and down very much as if he were knocking at doors and inquiring of the police. This was the spirit in which, inevitably, he set himself to travel; he started on a journey that was to be as long as he could make it; it danced before him that, as the other side of the globe couldn't possibly have less to say to him, it might, by a possibility of suggestion, have more. Before he quitted London, however, he made a pilgrimage to May Bartram's grave, took his way to it through the endless avenues of the grim suburban necropolis, sought it out in the wilderness of tombs, and, though he had come but for the renewal of the act of farewell, found himself, when he had at last stood by it, beguiled into long intensities. He stood for an hour, powerless to turn away and yet powerless to penetrate the darkness of death; fixing with his eyes her inscribed name and date, beating his forehead against the fact of the secret they kept, drawing his breath, while he waited as if, in pity of him, some sense would rise from the stones. He kneeled on the stones, however, in vain; they kept what they concealed; and if the face of the tomb did become a face for him it was because her two names were like a pair of eyes that didn't know him. He gave them a last long look, but no palest light broke.

# VI

HE STAYED AWAY, after this, for a year; he visited the depths of Asia, spending himself on scenes of romantic interest, of superlative sanctity; but what was present to him everywhere was that for a man who had known what *he* had known the world was vulgar and vain. The state of mind in which he had lived for so many years shone out to him, in reflection, as a light that coloured and refined, a light beside which the glow of the East was garish, cheap and thin. The terrible truth was that he had lost – with everything else – a distinction as well; the things he saw couldn't help being common when he had become common to look at them. He was simply now one of them himself – he was in the dust, without a peg for the sense of difference; and there were hours when, before the temples of gods and the sepulchres of kings, his spirit turned, for nobleness of association, to the barely discriminated slab in the London suburb. That had become for him, and more intensely with time and distance, his one witness of a past glory. It was all that was left to him for proof or pride, yet the past glories of Pharaohs were nothing to him as he thought of it. Small wonder then that he came back to it on the morrow of his return. He was drawn there this time as irresistibly as the other, yet with a confidence, almost, that was doubtless the effect of the many months that had elapsed. He had lived, in spite of himself, into his change of feeling, and in wandering over the earth had wandered, as might be said, from the circumference to the centre of his desert. He had settled to his safety and accepted perforce his extinction; figuring to himself, with some colour, in the likeness of certain little old men he remembered to have seen, of whom, all meagre and wizened as they might look, it was related that they had in their time fought twenty duels or been loved by ten princesses. They indeed had been wondrous for others, while he was but wondrous for himself; which, however, was exactly the cause of his haste to renew the wonder by getting back, as he might put it, into his own presence. That had quickened his steps and checked his delay. If his visit was prompt it was because he had been separated so long from the part of himself that alone he now valued.

It is accordingly not false to say that he reached his goal wlth a certain elation and stood there again with a certain assurance. The creature beneath the sod *knew* of his rare experience, so that, strangely now, the place had lost for him its mere blankness of expression. It met him in mildness – not, as before, in mockery; it wore for him the air of conscious greeting that we find, after absence, in things that have closely belonged to us and which seem to confess of themselves to the connection. The plot of ground, the graven tablet, the tended flowers affected him so as belonging to him that he quite felt for the hour like a contented landlord reviewing a piece of property. Whatever had happened – well, had happened. He had not come back this time with the vanity of that question, his former worrying, 'What, *what*?' now practically so spent. Yet he would, none the less, never again so cut himself off from the spot; he would come back to it every month, for if he did nothing else by its aid he at least held up his head. It thus grew for him, in the oddest way, a positive resource; he carried out his idea of periodical returns, which took their place at last among the most inveterate of his habits. What it all amounted to, oddly enough, was that, in his now so simplified world, this garden of death gave him the few square feet of earth on which he could still most live. It was as if, being nothing anywhere else for anyone, nothing even for himself, he were just everything here, and if not for a crowd of witnesses, or indeed for any witness but John Marcher, then by clear right of the register that he could scan like an open page. The open page was the tomb of his friend, and *there* were the facts of the past, there the truth of his life, there the backward reaches in which he could lose himself. He did this, from time to time, with such effect that he seemed to wander through the old years with his hand in the arm of a companion who was, in the most extraordinary manner, his other, his younger self; and to wander, which was more extraordinary yet, round and round a third presence – not wandering she, but stationary, still, whose eyes, turning with his revolution, never ceased to follow him, and whose seat was his point, so to speak, of orientation. Thus in short he settled to live – feeding only on the sense that he once *had* lived, and dependent on it not only for a support but for an identity.

It sufficed him, in its way, for months, and the year elapsed; it would doubtless even have carried him further but for an accident, superficially slight, which moved him, in a quite other direction, with a force beyond any of his impressions of Egypt or of India. It was a thing of the merest chance – the turn, as he afterwards felt, of a hair, though he was indeed to live to believe that if light hadn't come to him in this particular fashion it would still have come in another. He was to live to believe this, I say, though he was not to live, I may not less definitely mention, to do much else. We allow him at any rate the benefit of the conviction, struggling up for him at the end, that, whatever might have happened or not happened, he would have come round of himself to the light. The incident of an autumn day had put the match to the train laid from of old by his misery. With the light before him he knew that even of late his ache had only been smothered. It was strangely drugged, but it throbbed; at the touch it began to bleed. And the touch, in the event, was the face of a fellow-mortal. This face, one grey afternoon when the leaves were thick in the alleys, looked into Marcher's own, at the cemetery, with an expression like the cut of a blade. He felt it, that is, so deep down that he winced at the steady thrust. The person who so mutely assaulted him was a figure he had noticed, on reaching his own goal, absorbed by a grave a short distance away, a grave apparently fresh, so that the emotion of the visitor would probably match it for frankness. This fact alone forbade further attention, though during the time he stayed he remained vaguely conscious of his neighbour, a middle-aged man apparently, in mourning, whose bowed back, among the clustered monuments and mortuary yews, was constantly presented. Marcher's theory that these were elements in contact with which he himself revived, had suffered, on this occasion, it may be granted, a sensible though inscrutable check. The autumn day was dire for him as none had recently been, and he rested with a heaviness he had not yet known on the low stone table that bore May Bartram's name. He rested without power to move, as if some spring in him, some spell vouchsafed, had suddenly been broken forever. If he could have done that moment as he wanted he would simply have stretched himself on the slab that was ready to take him, treating it as a place prepared to receive his last sleep. What in all the wide world had he now to keep awake for? He stared before him with the question, and it was then that, as one of the cemetery walks passed near him, he caught the shock of the face.

His neighbour at the other grave had withdrawn, as he himself, with force in him to move, would have done by now, and was advancing along the path on his way to one of the gates. This brought him near, and his pace was slow, so that – and all the more as there was a kind of hunger in his look – the two men were for a minute directly confronted. Marcher felt him on the spot as one of the deeply stricken – a perception so sharp that nothing else in the picture lived for it, neither his dress, his age, nor his presumable character and class; nothing lived but the deep ravage of the features that he showed. He *showed* them – that was the point; he was moved, as he passed, by some impulse that was either a signal for sympathy or, more possibly, a challenge to another sorrow. He might already have been aware of our friend, might, at some previous hour, have noticed in him the smooth habit of the scene, with which the state of his own senses so scantly consorted, and might thereby have been stirred as by a kind of overt discord. What Marcher was at all events conscious of was, in the first place, that the image of scarred passion presented to him was conscious too – of something that profaned the air; and, in the second, that, roused, startled, shocked, he was yet the next moment looking after it, as it went, with envy. The most extraordinary thing that had happened to him – though he had given that name to other matters as well – took place, after his immediate vague stare, as a consequence of this impression. The stranger passed, but the raw glare of his grief remained, making our friend wonder in pity what wrong, what wound it expressed, what injury not to be healed. What had the man *had* to make him, by the loss of it, so bleed and yet live?

Something – and this reached him with a pang – that *he*, John Marcher, hadn't; the proof of which was precisely John Marcher's arid end. No passion had ever touched him, for this was what passion meant; he had survived and maundered and pined, but where had been *his* deep ravage? The extraordinary thing we speak of was the sudden rush of the result of this question. The sight that had just met his eyes named to him, as in letters of quick flame, something he had utterly, insanely missed, and what he had missed made these things a train of fire, made them mark themselves in an anguish of inward throbs. He had seen *outside* of his life, not learned it within, the way a woman was mourned when she had been loved for herself; such was the force of his conviction of the meaning of the stranger's face, which still flared for him like a smoky torch. It had not come to him, the knowledge, on the wings of experience; it had brushed him, jostled him, upset him, with the disrespect of chance, the insolence of an accident. Now that the illumination had begun, however, it blazed to the zenith, and what he presently stood there gazing at was the sounded void of his life. He gazed, he drew breath, in pain; he turned in his dismay, and, turning, he had before him in sharper incision than ever the open page of his story. The name on the table smote him as the passage of his neighbour had done, and what it said to him, full in the face, was that *she* was what he had missed. This was the awful thought, the answer to all the past, the vision at the dread clearness of which he turned as cold as the stone beneath him. Everything fell together, confessed, explained, overwhelmed; leaving him most of all stupefied at the blindness he had cherished. The fate he had been marked for he had met with a vengeance – he had emptied the cup to the lees; he had been the man of his time, *the* man, to whom nothing on earth was to have happened. That was the rare stroke – that was his visitation. So he saw it, as we say, in pale horror, while the pieces fitted and fitted. So *she* had seen it, while he didn't, and so she served at this hour to drive the truth home. It was the truth, vivid and monstrous, that all the while he had waited the wait was itself his portion. This the companion of his vigil had at a given moment perceived, and she had then offered him the chance to baffle his doom. One's doom, however, was never baffled, and on the day she had told him that his own had come down she had seen him but stupidly stare at the escape she offered him.

The escape would have been to love her; then, *then* he would have lived. *She* had lived – who could say now with what passion? – since she had loved him for himself; whereas he had never thought of her (ah, how it hugely glared at him!) but in the chill of his egotism and the light of her use. Her spoken words came back to him, and the chain stretched and stretched. The beast had lurked indeed, and the beast, at its hour, had sprung; it had sprung in that twilight of the cold April when, pale, ill, wasted, but all beautiful, and perhaps even then recoverable, she had risen from her chair to stand before him and let him imaginably guess. It had sprung as he didn't guess; it had sprung as she hopelessly turned from him, and the mark, by the time he left her, had fallen where it *was* to fall. He had justified his fear and achieved his fate; he had failed, with the last exactitude, of all he was to fail of; and a moan now rose to his lips as he remembered she had prayed he mightn't know. This horror of waking — *this* was knowledge, knowledge under the breath of which the very tears in his eyes seemed to freeze. Through them, none the less, he tried to fix it and hold it; he kept it there before him so that he might feel the pain. That at least, belated and bitter, had something of the taste of life. But the bitterness suddenly sickened him, and it was as if, horribly, he saw, in the truth, in the cruelty of his image, what had been appointed and done. He saw the Jungle of his life and saw the lurking Beast; then, while he looked, perceived it, as by a stir of the air, rise, huge and hideous, for the leap that was to settle him. His eyes darkened — it was close; and, instinctively turning, in his hallucination, to avoid it, he flung himself, on his face, on the tomb.

# *The Papers*

## I

THERE WAS A longish period – the dense duration of a London winter, cheered, if cheered it could be called, with lurid electric, with fierce 'incandescent' flares and glares – when they repeatedly met, at feeding-time, in a small and not quite savoury pot-house a stone's-throw from the Strand. They talked always of pot-houses, of feeding-time – by which they meant any hour between one and four of the afternoon; they talked of most things, even of some of the greatest, in a manner that gave, or that they desired to show as giving, in respect to the conditions of their life, the measure of their detachment, their contempt, their general irony. Their general irony, which they tried at the same time to keep gay and to make amusing at least to each other, was their refuge from the want of savour, the want of napkins, the want, too often, of shillings, and of many things besides that they would have liked to have. Almost all they had with any security was their youth, complete, admirable, very nearly invulnerable, or as yet inattackable; for they didn't count their talent, which they had originally taken for granted and had since then lacked freedom of mind, as well indeed as any offensive reason, to reappraise. They were taken up with other questions and other estimates – the remarkable limits, for instance, of their luck, the remarkable smallness of the talent of their friends. They were above all in that phase of youth and in that state of aspiration in which 'luck' is the subject of most frequent reference, as definite as the colour red, and in which it is the elegant name for money when people are as refined as they are poor. She was only a suburban young woman in a sailor hat, and he a young man destitute, in strictness, of occasion for a 'topper'; but they felt that they had in a peculiar way the freedom of the town, and the town, if it did nothing else, gave a range to the spirit. They sometimes went, on excursions that they groaned at as professional, far afield from the Strand, but the curiosity with which they came back was mostly greater than any other, the Strand being for them, with its ampler alternative Fleet Street, overwhelmingly the Papers, and the Papers being, at a rough guess, all the furniture of their consciousness.

The Daily Press played for them the part played by the embowered nest on the swaying bough for the parent birds that scour the air. It was, as they mainly saw it, a receptacle, owing its form to the instinct more remarkable, as they held the journalistic, than that even of the most highly organized animal, into which, regularly, breathlessly, contributions had to be dropped – odds and ends, all grist to the mill, all somehow digestible and convertible, all conveyed with the promptest possible beak and the flutter, often, of dreadfully fatigued little wings. If there had been no Papers there would have been no young friends for us of the figure we hint at, no chance mates, innocent and weary, yet acute even to penetration, who were apt to push off their plates and rest their elbows on the table in the interval between the turn-over of the pint-pot and the call for the awful glibness of their score. Maud Blandy drank beer – and welcome, as one may say; and she smoked cigarettes when privacy permitted, though she drew the line at this in the right place, just as she flattered herself she knew how to draw it, journalistically, where other delicacies were concerned. She was fairly a product of the day – so fairly that she might have been born afresh each morning, to serve, after the fashion of certain agitated ephemeral insects, only till the morrow. It was as if a past had been wasted on her and a future were not to be fitted; she was really herself, so far at least as her great preoccupation went, an edition, an 'extra special', coming out at the loud hours and living its life, amid the roar of vehicles, the hustle of pavements, the shriek of newsboys, according to the quantity of shock to be proclaimed and distributed, the quantity to be administered, thanks to the varying temper of Fleet Street, to the nerves of the nation. Maud was a shocker, in short, in petticoats, and alike for the thoroughfare, the club, the suburban train and the humble home; though it must honestly be added that petticoats were not of her essence. This was one of the reasons, in an age of 'emancipations', of her intense actuality, as well as, positively, of a good fortune to which, however impersonal she might have appeared, she was not herself in a position to do full justice; the felicity of her having about her naturally so much of the young bachelor that she was saved the disfigurement of any marked straddling or elbowing. It was literally true of her that she would have pleased less, or at least have offended more, had she been obliged, or been prompted, to assert – all too vainly, as it would have been sure to be – her superiority to sex. Nature, constitution, accident, whatever we happen to call it, had relieved her of this care; the struggle for life, the competition with men, the taste of the day, the fashion of the hour had *made* her superior, or had at any rate made her indifferent, and she had no difficulty in remaining so. The thing was therefore, with the aid of an extreme general flatness of person, directness of step and simplicity of motive, quietly enough done, without a grace, a weak inconsequence, a stray reminder to interfere with the success; and it is not too much to say that the success – by which I mean the plainness of the type – would probably never have struck you as so great as at the moments of our young lady's chance comradeship with Howard Bight. For the young man, though his personal signs had not, like his friend's, especially the effect of one of the stages of an evolution, might have been noted as not so fiercely or so freshly a male as to distance Maud in the show.

She presented him in truth, while they sat together, as

comparatively girlish. She fell naturally into gestures, tones, expressions, resemblances, that he either suppressed, from sensibility to her personal predominance, or that were merely latent in him through much taking for granted. Mild, sensitive, none too solidly nourished, and condemned, perhaps by a deep delusion as to the final issue of it, to perpetual coming and going, he was so resigned to many things, and so disgusted even with many others, that the least of his cares was the cultivation of a bold front. What mainly concerned him was its being bold enough to get him his dinner, and it was never more void of aggression than when he solicited in person those scraps of information, snatched at those floating particles of news, on which his dinner depended. Had he had time a little more to try his case, he would have made out that if he liked Maud Blandy it was partly by the impression of what she could do for him: what she could do for herself had never entered into his head. The positive quantity, moreover, was vague to his mind; it existed, that is, for the present, but as the proof of how, in spite of the want of encouragement, a fellow could keep going. She struck him in fact as the only encouragement he had, and this altogether by example, since precept, frankly, was deterrent on her lips, as speech was free, judgement prompt, and accent not absolutely pure. The point was that, as the easiest thing to be with her, he was so passive that it almost made him graceful and so attentive that it almost made him distinguished. She was herself neither of these things, and they were not of course what a man had most to be; whereby she contributed to their common view the impatiences required by a proper reaction, forming thus for him a kind of protective hedge behind which he could wait. Much waiting, for either, was, I hasten to add, always in order, inasmuch as their novitiate seemed to them interminable and the steps of their ladder fearfully far apart. It rested – the ladder – against the great stony wall of the public attention – a sustaining mass which apparently wore somewhere, in the upper air, a big, thankless, expressionless face, a countenance equipped with eyes, ears, an uplifted nose and a gaping mouth – all convenient if they could only be reached. The ladder groaned meanwhile, swayed and shook with the weight of the close-pressed climbers, tier upon tier, occupying the upper, the middle, the nethermost rounds and quite preventing, for young persons placed as our young friends were placed, any view of the summit. It was meanwhile moreover only Howard Bight's perverse view – he was confessedly perverse – that Miss Blandy had arrived at a perch superior to his own.

She had hitherto recognized in herself indeed but a tighter clutch and a grimmer purpose; she had recognized, she believed, in keen moments, a vocation; she had recognized that there had been eleven of them at home, with herself as youngest, and distinctions by that time so blurred in her that she might as easily have been christened John. She had recognized truly, most of all, that if they came to talk they both were nowhere; yet this was compatible with her insisting that Howard had as yet comparatively had the luck. When he wrote to people they consented, or at least they answered; almost always, for that matter, they answered with greed, so that he was not without something of some sort to hawk about to buyers. Specimens indeed of human greed – *the* greed, the great one, the eagerness to figure, the snap at the bait of publicity, he had collected in such store as to stock, as to launch, a museum. In this museum the prize object, the high rare specimen, had been for some time established; a celebrity of the day enjoying, uncontested, a glass case all to himself, more conspicuous than any other, before which the arrested visitor might rebound from surprised recognition. Sir A. B. C. Beadel-Muffet, K.C.B., M.P., stood forth there as large as life, owing indeed his particular place to the shade of direct acquaintance with him that Howard Bight could boast, yet with his eminent presence in such a collection but too generally and notoriously justified. He was universal and ubiquitous, commemorated, under some rank rubric, on every page of every public print every day in every year, and as inveterate a feature of each issue of any self-respecting sheet as the name, the date, the tariffed advertisements. He had always done something, or was about to do something, round which the honours of announcement clustered, and indeed, as he had inevitably thus become a subject of fallacious report, one half of his chronicle appeared to consist of official contradiction of the other half. His activity – if it had not better been called his passivity – was beyond any other that figured in the public eye, for no other assuredly knew so few or such brief intermittences. Yet, as there was the inside as well as the outside view of his current history, the quantity of it was easy to analyse for the possessor of the proper crucible. Howard Bight, with his arms on the table, took it apart and put it together again most days in the year, so that an amused comparison of notes on the subject often added a mild spice to his colloquies with Maud Blandy. They knew, the young pair, as they considered, many secrets, but they liked to think that they knew none quite so scandalous as the way that, to put it roughly, this distinguished person maintained his distinction.

It was known certainly to all who had to do with the Papers, a brotherhood, a sisterhood of course interested — for what was it, in the last resort, but the interest of their bread and butter? — in shrouding the approaches to the oracle, in not telling tales out of school. They all lived alike on the solemnity, the sanctity of the oracle, and the comings and goings, the doings and undoings, the intentions and retractations of Sir A. B. C. Beadel-Muffet, K.C.B., M.P., were in their degree a part of that solemnity. The Papers, taken together the glory of the age, were, though superficially multifold, fundamentally one, so that any revelation of their being procured or procurable to float an object not intrinsically buoyant would very logically convey discredit from the circumference — where the revelation would be likely to be made — to the centre. Of so much as this our grim neophytes, in common with a thousand others, were perfectly aware; but something in the nature of their wit, such as it was, or in the condition of their nerves, such as it easily might become, sharpened almost to acerbity their relish of so artful an imitation of the voice of fame. The fame was *all* voice, as they could guarantee who had an ear always glued to the speaking-tube; the items that made the sum were individually of the last vulgarity, but the accumulation was a triumph – one of the greatest the age could show – of industry and vigilance. It was after all not true that a man had done nothing who for ten years had so fed, so dyked and directed and distributed the fitful sources of publicity. He had laboured, in his way, like a navvy with a spade; he might be said to have earned by each night's work the reward, each morning, of his small spurt of glory. Even for such a matter as its not being true that Sir A. B. C. Beadel-Muffet, K.C.B., M.P., was to start on his visit to the Sultan of Samarcand on the 23rd, *but* being true that he was to start on the 29th, the personal attention required was no small affair, taking the legend with the fact, the myth with the meaning, the original artless error with the subsequent earnest truth – allowing in fine for the statement still to come that the visit would have to be relinquished in consequence of the visitor's other pressing engagements, and bearing in mind the countless channels to be successively watered. Our young man, one December afternoon, pushed an evening paper across to his companion, keeping his thumb on a paragraph at which she glanced without eagerness. She might, from her manner, have known by instinct what it would be, and her exclamation had the note of satiety. 'Oh, he's working *them* now?'

'If he has begun he'll work them hard. By the time that has gone round the world there'll be something else to say. "We are authorized to state that the marriage of Miss Miranda

Beadel-Muffet to Captain Guy Devereux, of the Fiftieth Rifles, will not take place." Authorized to state – rather! when every wire in the machine has been pulled over and over. They're authorized to state something every day in the year, and the authorization is not difficult to get. Only his daughters, now that they're coming on, poor things – and I believe there are many – will have to be chucked into the pot and produced on occasions when other matter fails. How pleasant for them to find themselves hurtling through the air, clubbed by the paternal hand, like golf-balls in a suburb! Not that I suppose they don't like it – why should one suppose anything of the sort?' Howard Bight's impression of the general appetite appeared today to be especially vivid, and he and his companion were alike prompted to one of those slightly violent returns on themselves and the work they were doing which none but the vulgar-minded altogether avoid. 'People – as I see them – would almost rather be jabbered about unpleasantly than not be jabbered about at all: whenever you try them – whenever, at least, I do – I'm confirmed in that conviction. It isn't only that if one holds out the mere tip of the perch they jump at it like starving fish; it is that they leap straight out of the water themselves, leap in their thousands and come flopping, open-mouthed and goggle-eyed, to one's very door. What is the sense of the French expression about a person's making *des yeux de carpe*? It suggests the eyes that a young newspaper-man seems to see all round him, and I declare I sometimes feel that, if one has the courage not to blink at the show, the gilt is a good deal rubbed off the gingerbread of one's early illusions. They all do it, as the song is at the music-halls, and it's some of one's surprises that tell one most. You've thought there were some high souls that didn't do it — that wouldn't, I mean, to work the oracle, lift a little finger of their own. But, Lord bless you, give them a chance — you'll find some of the greatest the greediest. I give you my word for it, I haven't a scrap of faith left in a single human creature. Except, of course,' the young man added, 'the grand creature that *you* are, and the cold, calm, comprehensive one whom you thus admit to your familiarity. *We* face the music. We see, we understand; we know we've got to live, and how we do it. But at least, like this, alone together, we take our intellectual revenge, we escape the indignity of being fools dealing with fools. I don't say we shouldn't enjoy it more if we *were*. But it can't be helped; we haven't the gift — the gift, I mean, of not seeing. We do the worst we can for the money.'

'*You* certainly do the worst you can,' Maud Blandy soon replied, 'when you sit there, with your wanton wiles, and take the spirit out of me. I require a working faith, you know. If one isn't a fool, in our world, where *is* one?'

'Oh, I say!' her companion groaned without alarm. 'Don't you fail *me*, mind you.'

They looked at each other across their clean platters, and, little as the light of romance seemed superficially to shine in them or about them, the sense was visibly enough in each of being involved in the other. He would have been sharply alone, the softly sardonic young man, if the somewhat dry young woman hadn't affected him, in a way he was even too nervous to put to the test, as saving herself up for him; and the consciousness of absent resources that was on her own side quite compatible with this economy grew a shade or two less dismal with the imagination of his somehow being at costs for her. It wasn't an expense of shillings – there was not much question of that; what it came to was perhaps nothing more than that, being, as he declared himself, 'in the know', he kept pulling her in too, as if there had been room for them both. He told her everything, all his secrets. He talked and talked, often making her think of herself as a lean, stiff person, destitute of skill or art, but with ear enough to be performed to, sometimes strangely touched, at moments completely ravished, by a fine violinist. He was her fiddler and genius; she was sure neither of her taste nor of his tunes, but if she could do nothing else for him she could hold the case while he handled the instrument. It had never passed between them that they could draw nearer, for they seemed near, near verily for pleasure, when each, in a decent young life, was so much nearer to the other than to anything else. There was no pleasure known to either that wasn't further off. What held them together was in short that they were in the same boat, a cockle-shell in a great rough sea, and that the movements required for keeping it afloat not only were what the situation safely permitted, but also made for reciprocity and intimacy. These talks over greasy white slabs, repeatedly mopped with moist grey cloths by young women in black uniforms, with inexorable braided 'buns' in the nape of weak necks, these sessions, sometimes prolonged, in halls of oilcloth, among penal-looking tariffs and pyramids of scones, enabled them to rest on their oars; the more that they were on terms with the whole families, chartered companies, of food-stations, each a race of innumerable and indistinguishable members, and had mastered those hours of comparative elegance, the earlier and the later, when the little weary ministrants were limply sitting down and the occupants of the red benches bleakly interspaced. So it was, that, at times, they renewed their understanding, and by signs, mannerless and meagre, that would have escaped the notice of witnesses. Maud Blandy had no need to kiss her hand across to him to show she felt what he meant; she had moreover never in her life kissed her hand to anyone, and her companion couldn't have imagined it of her. His romance was so grey that it wasn't romance at all; it was a reality arrived at without stages, shades, forms. If he had been ill or stricken she would have taken him – other resources failing – into her lap; but would that, which would scarce even have been motherly, have been romantic? She nevertheless at this moment put in her plea for the general element. 'I can't help it, about Beadel-Muffet; it's too magnificent – it appeals to me. And then I've a particular feeling about him – I'm waiting to see what will happen. It *is* genius, you know, to get yourself so celebrated for nothing – to carry out your idea in the face of everything. I mean your idea of *being* celebrated. It isn't as if he had done even one little thing. What *has* he done when you come to look?'

'Why, my dear chap, he has done everything. He has missed

nothing. He has been in everything, *of* everything, *at* everything, *over* everything, *under* everything, that has taken place for the last twenty years. He's *always* present, and, though he never makes a speech, he never fails to get alluded to in the speeches of others. That's doing it cheaper than anyone else does it, but it's thoroughly doing it – which is what we're talking about. And so far,' the young man contended, 'from its being "in the face" of anything, it's positively with the help of everything, since the Papers are everything and more. They're made for such people, though no doubt he's the person who has known best how to use them. I've gone through one of the biggest sometimes, from beginning to end – it's quite a thrilling little game – to catch him once out. It has happened to me to think I was near it when, on the last column of the last page – I count "advertisements", heaven help us, out! – I've found him as large as life and as true as the needle to the pole. But at last, in a way, it goes, it can't help going, of itself. He comes in, he breaks out, of himself; the letters, under the compositor's hand, form themselves, from the force of habit, into his name – any connection for it, any context, being as good as any other, and the wind, which he has originally "raised", but which continues to blow, setting perpetually in his favour. The thing would really be now, don't you see, for him to keep himself out. That would be, on my honour, it strikes me – his *getting* himself out – the biggest fact in his record.'

The girl's attention, as her friend developed the picture, had become more present. 'He *can't* get himself out. There he is.' She had a pause; she had been thinking. 'That's just my idea.'

'Your idea? Well, an idea's always a blessing. What do you want for it?'

She continued to turn it over as if weighing its value. 'Something perhaps *could* be done with it – only it would take imagination.'

He wondered, and she seemed to wonder that he didn't see. 'Is it a situation for a "ply"?'

'No, it's too good for a ply – yet it isn't quite good enough for a short story.'

'It would do then for a novel?'

'Well, I seem to see it,' Maud said – 'and with a lot *in* it to be got out. But I seem to see it as a question not of what you or I might be able to do with it, but of what the poor man himself may. That's what I meant just now,' she explained, 'by my having a creepy sense of what may happen for him. It has already more than once occurred to me. *Then*,' she wound up, 'we shall have real life, the case itself.'

'Do you know *you've* got imagination?' Her friend, rather interested, appeared by this time to have seized her thought.

'I see him having for some reason, very imperative, to seek retirement, lie low, to hide, in fact, like a man "wanted", but pursued all the while by the lurid glare that he has himself so started and kept up, and at last literally devoured ("like Frankenstein", of course!) by the monster he has created.'

'I say, you *have* got it!' – and the young man flushed, visibly, artistically, with the recognition of elements which his eyes had for a minute earnestly fixed. 'But it will take a lot of doing.'

'Oh,' said Maud, '*we* shan't have to do it. He'll do it himself.'

'I wonder.' Howard Bight really wondered. 'The fun would be for him to do it *for* us. I mean for him to want us to help him somehow to get out.'

'Oh, "us"!' the girl mournfully sighed.

'Why not, when he comes to us to get in?'

Maud Blandy stared. 'Do you mean to you personally? You surely know by this time that no one ever "comes" to me.'

'Why, I went to him in the first instance; I made up to him straight, I did him "at home", somewhere, as I've surely mentioned to you before, three years ago. He liked, I believe – for he's really a delightful old ass – the way I did it; he knows my name and has my address, and has written me three or four times since, with his own hand, a request to be so good as to make use of my (he hopes) still close connection with the daily Press to rectify the rumour that he has reconsidered his opinion on the subject of the blankets supplied to the Upper Tooting Workhouse Infirmary. He has reconsidered his opinion on no subject whatever – which he mentions, in the interest of historic truth, without further intrusion on my valuable time. And he regards that sort of thing as a commodity that I can dispose of – thanks to my "close connection" – for several shillings.'

'And can you?'

'Not for several pence. They're all tariffed, but he's tariffed low – having a value, apparently, that money doesn't represent. He's always welcome, but he isn't always paid for. The beauty, however, is in his marvellous memory, his keeping us all so apart and not muddling the fellow to whom he has written that he hasn't done this, that or the other with the fellow to whom he has written that he has. He'll write to me again some day about something else – about his alleged position on the date of the next school-treat of the Chelsea Cabmen's Orphanage. I shall seek a market for the precious item, and that will keep us in touch; so that if the complication you have the sense of in your bones does come into play – the thought's too beautiful! – he may once more remember me. Fancy his coming to one with a "What can you do for me *now*?"' Bight lost himself in the happy vision; it gratified so his cherished consciousness of the 'irony of fate' – a consciousness so cherished that he never could write ten lines without use of the words.

Maud showed however at this point a reserve which appeared to have grown as the possibility opened out. 'I believe in it – it must come. It can't not. It's the only end. He doesn't know; nobody knows – the simple-minded all: only you and I know. But it won't be nice, remember.'

'It won't be funny?'

'It will be pitiful. There'll have to be a reason.'

'For his turning round?' The young man nursed the vision. 'More or less – I see what you mean. But except for a "ply" will that so much matter? His reason will concern himself. What will concern us will be his funk and his helplessness, his having to stand there in the blaze, with nothing and nobody to put it out. We shall see him, shrieking for a bucket of water, wither up in the central flame.'

Her look had turned sombre. 'It makes one cruel. That is it makes *you*. I mean our trade does.'

'I daresay – I see too much. But I'm willing to chuck it.'

'Well,' she presently replied, 'I'm not willing to, but it seems pretty well on the cards that I shall have to. *I* don't see too much. I don't see enough. So, for all the good it does me—!'

She had pushed back her chair and was looking round for her umbrella. 'Why, what's the matter?' Howard Bight too blankly inquired.

She met his eyes while she pulled on her rusty old gloves. 'Well, I'll tell you another time.'

He kept his place, still lounging, contented where she had again become restless. 'Don't you call it seeing enough to see – to have had so luridly revealed to you – the doom of Beadel-Muffet?'

'Oh, he's not my business, he's yours. You're his man, or one of his men – he'll come back to you. Besides, he's a special case, and, as I say, I'm too sorry for him.'

'That's a proof then of what you do see.'

Her silence for a moment admitted it, though evidently she was making, for herself, a distinction, which she didn't express. 'I don't then see what I want, what I require. And *he*,' she added, 'if he does have some reason, will have to have an awfully strong one. To be strong enough it will have to be awful.'

'You mean he'll have done something?'

'Yes, that may remain undiscovered if he can only drop out of the papers, sit for a while in darkness. You'll know what it is;

you'll not be able to help yourself. But I shan't want to, for anything.'

She had got up as she said it, and he sat looking at her, thanks to her odd emphasis, with an interest that, as he also rose, passed itself off as a joke. 'Ah, then, you sweet sensitive thing, I promise to keep it from you.'

# II

THEY MET AGAIN a few days later, and it seemed the law of their meetings that these should take place mainly within moderate eastward range of Charing Cross. An afternoon performance of a play translated from the Finnish, already several times given, on a series of Saturdays, had held Maud for an hour in a small, hot, dusty theatre where the air hung as heavy about the great 'trimmed' and plumed hats of the ladies as over the flora and fauna of a tropical forest; at the end of which she edged out of her stall in the last row, to join a small band of unattached critics and correspondents, spectators with ulterior views and pencilled shirtcuffs, who, coming together in the lobby for an exchange of ideas, were ranging from 'Awful rot' to 'Rather jolly'. Ideas, of this calibre, rumbled and flashed, so that, lost in the discussion, our young woman failed at first to make out that a gentleman on the other side of the group, but standing a little off, had his eyes on her for some extravagant, though apparently quite respectable, purpose. He had been waiting for her to recognize him, and as soon as he had caught her attention he came round to her with an eager bow. She had by this time entirely placed him – placed him as the smoothest and most shining subject with which, in the exercise of her profession, she had yet experimented; but her recognition was accompanied with a pang that his amiable address made but the sharper. She had her reason for awkwardness in the presence of a rosy, glossy, kindly, but discernibly troubled personage whom she had waited on 'at home' at her own suggestion – promptly welcomed – and the sympathetic element in whose 'personality', the Chippendale, the photographic, the autographic elements in whose flat in the Earl's Court Road, she had commemorated in the liveliest prose of which she was capable. She had described with humour his favourite pug, she had revealed with permission his favourite make of Kodak, she had touched upon his favourite manner of spending his Sundays and had extorted from him the shy confession that he preferred after all the novel of adventure to the novel of subtlety. Her embarrassment was therefore now the greater as, touching to behold, he so clearly had approached her with no intention of asperity, not even at first referring at all to the matter that couldn't have been gracefully explained.

She had seen him originally – had had the instinct of it in making up to him – as one of the happy of the earth, and the impression of him 'at home', on his proving so good-natured about the interview, had begotten in her a sharper envy, a hungrier sense of the invidious distinctions of fate, than any her literary conscience, which she deemed rigid, had yet had to reckon with. He must have been rich, rich by such estimates as hers; he at any rate had everything, while she had nothing – nothing but the vulgar need of offering him to brag, on his behalf, for money, if she could get it, about his luck. She hadn't in fact got money, hadn't so much as managed to work in her stuff anywhere; a practical comment sharp enough on her having represented to him – with wasted pathos, she was indeed soon to perceive – how 'important' it was to her that people should let her get at them. This dim celebrity had not needed that argument; he had not only, with his alacrity, allowed her, as she had said, to try her hand, but had tried *with* her, quite feverishly, and all to the upshot of showing her that there were even greater outsiders than herself. He could have put down money, could have published, as the phrase was – a bare two columns – at his own expense; but it was just a part of his rather irritating luxury that he had a scruple about that, wanted intensely to taste the sweet, but didn't want to owe it to any wire-pulling. He wanted the golden apple straight from the tree, where it yet seemed so unable to grow for him by any exuberance of its own. He had breathed to her his real secret – that to be inspired, to work with effect, he had to feel he was appreciated, to have it all somehow come back to him. The artist, necessarily sensitive, lived on encouragement, on knowing and being reminded that people cared for him a little, cared even just enough to flatter him a wee bit. They had talked that over, and he had really, as he called it, quite put himself in her power. He had whispered in her ear that it might be very weak and silly, but that positively to be himself, to do anything, certainly to do his best, he required the breath of sympathy. He did love notice, let alone praise – there it was. To be systematically ignored – well, blighted him at the root. He was afraid she would think he had said too much, but she left him with his leave, none the less, to repeat a part of it. They had agreed that she was to bring in prettily, somehow, that he did love praise; for just the right way he was sure he could trust to her taste.

She had promised to send him the interview in proof, but she had been able, after all, to send it but in type-copy. If *she*, after all, had had a flat adorned – as to the drawing-room alone – with eighty-three photographs, and all in plush frames; if she had lived in the Earl's Court Road, had been rosy and glossy and well filled out; and if she had looked withal, as she always made a point of calling it when she wished to refer without vulgarity to the right place in the social scale, 'unmistakably gentle' – if she had achieved these things she would have snapped her fingers at all other sweets, have sat as tight as possible and let the world wag, have spent her Sundays in silently thanking her stars, and not have cared to know one Kodak, or even one novelist's 'methods', from another. Except for his unholy itch he was in short so just the person she would have liked to be that the last consecration was given for her to his character by his speaking quite as if he had accosted her only to secure her view of the strange Finnish 'soul'. He had come each time – there had been four Saturdays; whereas Maud herself had

had to wait till today, though her bread depended on it, for the roundabout charity of her publicly bad seat. It didn't matter *why* he had come – so that he might see it somewhere printed of him that he was 'a conspicuously faithful attendant' at the interesting series; it only mattered that he was letting her off so easily, and yet that there was a restless hunger, odd on the part of one of the filled-out, in his appealing eye, which she now saw not to be a bit intelligent, though that didn't matter either. Howard Bight came into view while she dealt with these impressions, whereupon she found herself edging a little away from her patron. Her other friend, who had but just arrived and was apparently waiting to speak to her, would be a pretext for a break before the poor gentleman should begin to accuse her of having failed him. She had failed herself so much more that she would have been ready to reply to him that *he* was scarce the one to complain; fortunately, however, the bell sounded the end of the interval and her tension was relaxed. They all flocked back to their places, and her *camarade* – she knew enough often so to designate him – was enabled, thanks to some shifting of other spectators, to occupy a seat beside her. He had brought with him the breath of business; hurrying from one appointment to another he might have time but for a single act. He had seen each of the others by itself, and the way he now crammed in the third, after having previously snatched the fourth, brought home again to the girl that he was leading the real life. Her own was a dull imitation of it. Yet it happened at the same time that before the curtain rose again he had, with a 'Who's your fat friend?' professed to have caught her in the act of making her own brighter.

'"Mortimer Marshal"?' he echoed after she had, a trifle dryly, satisfied him. 'Never heard of him.'

'Well, I shan't tell him that. But you *have*,' she said; 'you've only forgotten. I told you after I had been to him.'

Her friend thought – it came back to him. 'Oh yes, and showed me what you had made of it. I remember your stuff was charming.'

'I see you remember nothing,' Maud a little more dryly said. 'I didn't show you what I had made of it. I've never made anything. You've not seen my stuff, and nobody has. They won't have it.'

She spoke with a smothered vibration, but, as they were still waiting, it had made him look at her; by which she was slightly the more disconcerted. 'Who won't?'

'Everyone, everything won't. Nobody, nothing will. He's hopeless, or rather *I* am. I'm no good. And he knows it.'

'O – oh!' the young man kindly but vaguely protested. 'Has he been making that remark to you?'

'No – that's the worst of it. He's too dreadfully civil. He thinks I can do something.'

'Then why do you say he knows you can't?'

She was impatient; she gave it up. 'Well, I don't know what he knows – except that he does want to be loved.'

'Do you mean he has proposed to you to love him?'

'Loved by the great heart of the public – speaking through

its natural organ. He wants to be – well, where Beadel-Muffet is.'

'Oh, I hope not!' said Bight with grim amusement.

His friend was struck with his tone. 'Do you mean it's coming on for Beadel-Muffet – what we talked about?' And then as he looked at her so queerly that her curiosity took a jump: 'It really and truly *is*? Has anything happened?'

'The rummest thing in the world – since I last saw you. We're wonderful, you know, you and I together – we *see*. And what we see always takes place, usually within the week. It wouldn't be believed. But it will do for *us*. At any rate it's high sport.'

'Do you mean,' she asked, 'that his scare has literally begun?'

He meant, clearly, quite as much as he said. 'He has written to me again he wants to see me, and we've an appointment for Monday.'

'Then why isn't it the old game?'

'Because it isn't. He wants to gather from me, as I *have* served him before, if something can't be done. *On a souvent besoin d'un plus petit que soi.* Keep quiet, and we shall see something.'

This was very well; only his manner visibly had for her the effect of a chill in the air. 'I hope,' she said, 'you're going at least to be decent to him.'

'Well, you'll judge. Nothing at all can be done – it's too ridiculously late. And it serves him right. I shan't deceive him, certainly, but I might as well enjoy him.'

The fiddles were still going, and Maud had a pause. 'Well,

you know you've more or less lived on him. I mean it's the kind of thing you *are* living on.'

'Precisely – that's just why I loathe it.'

Again she hesitated. 'You mustn't quarrel, you know, with your bread and butter.'

He looked straight before him, as if she had been consciously, and the least bit disagreeably, sententious. 'What in the world's that but what I shall just be *not* doing? If our bread and butter is the universal push I consult our interest by not letting it trifle with us. They're not to blow hot and cold – it won't do. There he is – let him get out himself. What I call sport is to see if he can.'

'And not – poor wretch – to help him?'

But Bight was ominously lucid. 'The devil is that he can't *be* helped. His one idea of help, from the day he opened his eyes, has been to be prominently – damn the word! – mentioned: it's the only kind of help that exists in connection with him. What therefore is a fellow to do when he happens to want it to stop – wants a special sort of prominence that will work like a trap in a pantomime and enable him to vanish when the situation requires it? Is one to mention that he wants *not* to be mentioned – never, never, please, any more? Do you see the success of that, all over the place, do you see the headlines in the American papers? No, he must die as he has lived – the Principal Public Person of his time.'

'Well,' she sighed, 'it's all horrible.' And then without a transition: 'What do you suppose has happened to him?'

'The dreadfulness I wasn't to tell you?'

'I only mean if you suppose him in a really bad hole.'

The young man considered. 'It can't certainly be that he has had a change of heart – never. It may be nothing worse than that the woman he wants to marry has turned against it.'

'But I supposed him – with his children all so boomed – to *be* married.'

'Naturally; else he couldn't have got such a boom from the poor lady's illness, death and burial. Don't you remember two years ago? – "We are given to understand that Sir A. B. C. Beadel-Muffet, K.C.B., M.P., particularly desires that no flowers be sent for the late Hon. Lady Beadel-Muffet's funeral." And then, the next day: "We are authorized to state that the impression, so generally prevailing, that Sir A. B. C. Beadel-Muffet has expressed an objection to flowers in connection with the late Hon. Lady Beadel-Muffet's obsequies, rests on a misapprehension of Sir A. B. C. Beadel-Muffet's markedly individual views. The floral tributes already delivered in Queen's Gate Gardens, and remarkable for number and variety, have been the source of such gratification to the bereaved gentleman as his situation permits." With a wind-up of course for the following week – the inevitable few heads of remark, on the part of the bereaved gentleman, on the general subject of Flowers at Funerals as a Fashion, vouchsafed, under pressure possibly indiscreet, to a rising young journalist always thirsting for the authentic word.'

'I guess now,' said Maud, after an instant, 'the rising young journalist. You egged him on.'

'Dear, no. I panted in his rear.'

'It makes you,' she added, 'more than cynical.'

'And what do you call "more than" cynical?'

'It makes you sardonic. Wicked,' she continued; 'devilish.'

'That's it — that *is* cynical. Enough's as good as a feast.' But he came back to the ground they had quitted. 'What were you going to say *he's* prominent for, Mortimer Marshal?'

She wouldn't, however, follow him there yet, her curiosity on the other issue not being spent. 'Do you know then as a fact, that he's marrying again, the bereaved gentleman?'

Her friend, at this, showed impatience. 'My dear fellow, do you *see* nothing? We had it all, didn't we, three months ago, and then we didn't have it, and then we had it again; and goodness knows where we are. But I throw out the possibility. I forget her bloated name, but she may be rich, and she may be decent. She may make it a condition that he keeps out — out, I mean, of the only things he has really ever been "in".'

'The Papers?'

'The dreadful, nasty, vulgar Papers. She may put it to him — I see it dimly and queerly, but I see it — that he must get out first, and then they'll talk; then she'll say yes, then he'll have the money. I see it — and much more sharply — that he *wants* the money, needs it, I mean, badly, desperately, so that this necessity may very well make the hole in which he finds himself. Therefore he must do something — what he's trying to do. It supplies the motive that our picture, the other day, rather missed.'

Maud Blandy took this in, but it seemed to fail to satisfy her. 'It must be something worse. You make it out *that*, so that your practical want of mercy, which you'll not be able to conceal from me, shall affect me as less in human.'

'I don't make it out anything, and I don't care what it is; the queerness, the grand "irony" of the case is itself enough for me. You, on your side, however, I think, make it out what you call "something worse", because of the romantic bias of your mind. You "see red". Yet isn't it, after all, sufficiently lurid that he shall lose his blooming bride?'

'You're sure,' Maud appealed, 'that he'll lose her?'

'Poetic justice screams for it; and my whole interest in the matter is staked on it.'

But the girl continued to brood. 'I thought you contend that nobody's half "decent". Where do you find a woman to make such a condition?'

'Not easily, I admit.' The young man thought. 'It will be *his* luck to have found her. That's his tragedy, say, that she can financially save him, but that she happens to be just the one freak, the creature whose stomach has turned. The spark – I mean of decency – has got, after all, somehow to be kept alive; and it may be lodged in this particular female form.'

'I see. But why should a female form that's so particular confess to an affinity with a male form that's so fearfully general? As he's *all* self-advertisement, why isn't it much more natural to her simply to loathe him?'

'Well, because, oddly enough, it seems that people don't.'

'*You* do,' Maud declared. 'You'll kill him.'

He just turned a flushed cheek to her, and she saw that she had touched something that lived in him. 'We *can*,' he consciously smiled, 'deal death. And the beauty is that it's in a perfectly straight way. We can lead them on. But have you ever seen Beadel-Muffet for yourself?' he continued.

'No. How often, please, need I tell you that I've seen nobody and nothing?'

'Well, if you had you'd understand.'

'You mean he's so fetching?'

'Oh, he's great. He's not "all" self-advertisement – or at least he doesn't seem to be: that's his pull. But I see, you female humbug,' Bight pursued, 'how much you'd like him yourself.'

'I want, while I'm about it, to pity him in sufficient quantity.'

'Precisely. Which means, for a woman, with extravagance and to the point of immorality.'

'I ain't a woman,' Maud Blandy sighed. 'I wish I were!'

'Well, about the pity,' he went on; 'you shall be immoral, I promise you, before you've done. Doesn't Mortimer Marshal,' he asked, 'take you for a woman?'

'You'll have to ask him. How,' she demanded, 'does one know those things?' And she stuck to her Beadel-Muffet. 'If you're to see him on Monday shan't you then get to the bottom of it?'

'Oh, I don't conceal from you that I promise myself larks, but I won't tell you, positively I won't,' Bight said, 'what I see. You're morbid. If it's only bad enough – I mean his motive – you'll want to save him.'

'Well, isn't that what you're to profess to him that *you* want?'

'Ah,' the young man returned, 'I believe you'd really invent a way.'

'I would if I could.' And with that she dropped it. 'There's my fat friend,' she presently added, as the entr'acte still hung heavy and Mortimer Marshal, from a row much in advance of them, screwed himself round in his tight place apparently to keep her in his eye.

'He does then,' said her companion, 'take you for a woman. I seem to guess he's "littery".'

'That's it; so badly that he wrote that "littery" ply *Corisanda*, you must remember, with Beatrice Beaumont in the principal part, which was given at three matinées in this very place and which hadn't even the luck of being slated. Every creature connected with the production, from the man himself and Beatrice *her*self down to the mothers and grandmothers of the sixpenny young women, the young women of the programmes, was interviewed both before and after, and he promptly published the piece, pleading guilty to the "littery" charge – which is the great stand he takes and the subject of the discussion.'

Bight had wonderingly followed. 'Of what discussion?'

'Why, the one he thinks there ought to have been. There hasn't been any, of course, but he wants it, dreadfully misses it. People won't keep it up – whatever they *did* do, though I don't myself make out that they did anything. His state of mind requires something to start with, which has got somehow to be provided. There must have been a noise made, don't you see? to make him prominent; and in order to remain prominent he has got to go for his enemies. The hostility to his ply, and all *because* it's "littery", we can do nothing without that; but it's uphill work to come across it. We sit up nights trying, but we seem to get no for'arder. The public attention would seem to abhor the whole matter even as nature abhors a vacuum. We've nothing to go upon, otherwise we might go far. But there we are.'

'I see,' Bight commented. 'You're nowhere at all.'

'No; it isn't even that, for we're just where *Corisanda*, on the stage and in the closet, put us at a stroke. Only there we stick fast nothing seems to happen, nothing seems to come or to be capable of being made to come. We wait.'

'Oh, if he waits with *you*!' Bight amicably gibed.

'He may wait for ever?'

'No, but resignedly. You'll make him forget his wrongs.'

'Ah, I'm not of that sort, and I could only do it by making him come into his rights. And I recognize now that that's impossible. There are different cases, you see, whole different classes of them, and his is the opposite to Beadel-Muffet's.'

Howard Bight gave a grunt. 'Why the opposite if you also pity him? I'll be hanged,' he added, 'if you won't save *him* too.'

But she shook her head. She knew. 'No; but it's nearly, in its way, as lurid. Do you know,' she asked, 'what he has done?'

'Why, the difficulty appears to be that he can't have done anything. He should strike once more – hard, and in the same place. He should bring out another ply.'

'Why so? You can't be more than prominent, and he *is* prominent. You can't do more than subscribe, in your prominence, to thirty-seven "press-cutting" agencies in England and America, and, having done so, you can't do more than sit at home with your ear on the postman's knock, looking out for results. *There* comes in the tragedy – there are no results. Mortimer Marshal's postman doesn't knock; the press-cutting agencies can't find anything to cut. With thirty-seven, in the whole English-speaking world, scouring millions of papers for him in vain, and with a big slice of his private income all the while going to it, the "irony" is too cruel, and the way he looks at one, as in one's degree responsible, does make one wince. He expected, naturally, most from the Americans, but it's they who have failed him worst. Their silence is that of the tomb, and it seems to grow, if the silence of the tomb *can* grow. He won't admit that the thirty-seven look far enough or long enough, and he writes them, I infer, angry letters, wanting to know what the deuce they suppose he has paid them for. But what are they either, poor things, to do?'

'Do? They can print his angry letters. That, at least, will break the silence, and he'll like it better than nothing.'

This appeared to strike our young woman. 'Upon my word, I really believe he would.' Then she thought better of it. 'But they'd be afraid, for they do guarantee, you know, that there's something for everyone. They claim it's their strength – that there's enough to go round. They won't want to show that they break down.'

'Oh, well,' said the young man, 'if he can't manage to smash a pane of glass somewhere—!'

'That's what he thought *I* would do. And it's what *I* thought I might,' Maud added; 'otherwise I wouldn't have approached him. I did it on spec, but I'm no use. I'm a fatal influence. I'm a non-conductor.'

She said it with such plain sincerity that it quickly took her companion's attention. 'I *say*!' he covertly murmured. 'Have you a secret sorrow?'

'Of course I've a secret sorrow.' And she stared at it, stiff and a little sombre, not wanting it to be too freely handled, while the curtain at last rose to the lighted stage.

# III

SHE WAS LATER ON more open about it, sundry other things, not wholly alien, having meanwhile happened. One of these had been that her friend had waited with her to the end of the Finnish performance and that it had then, in the lobby, as they went out, not been possible for her not to make him acquainted with Mr Mortimer Marshal. This gentleman had clearly waylaid her and had also clearly divined that her companion was of the Papers – papery all through; which doubtless had something to do with his having handsomely proposed to them to accompany him somewhere to tea. They hadn't seen why they shouldn't, it being an adventure, all in their line, like another; and he had carried them, in a four-wheeler, to a small and refined club in a region which was as the fringe of the Piccadilly region, where even their own presence scarce availed to contradict the implication of the exclusive. The whole occasion, they were further to feel, was essentially a tribute to their professional connection, especially that side of it which flushed and quavered, which panted and pined in their host's personal nervousness. Maud Blandy now saw it vain to contend with his delusion that *she*, underfed and unprinted, who had never been so conscious as during these bribed moments of her non-conducting quality, was papery to any purpose – a delusion that exceeded, by her measure, every other form of pathos. The decoration of the tea-room was a pale, aesthetic green, the liquid in the delicate cups a copious potent amber; the bread and butter was thin and golden, the muffins a revelation to her that she was barbarously hungry. There were ladies at other tables with other gentlemen – ladies with long feather boas and hats not of the sailor pattern, and gentlemen whose straight collars were doubled up much higher than Howard Bight's and their hair parted far more at the side. The talk was so low, with pauses somehow so not of embarrassment that it could only have been earnest, and the air, an air of privilege and privacy to our young woman's sense, seemed charged with fine things taken for granted. If it hadn't been for Bight's company she would have grown almost frightened, so much seemed to be offered her for something she couldn't do. That word of Bight's about smashing a window-pane had lingered with her; it had made her afterwards wonder, while they sat in their stalls, if there weren't some brittle surface in range of her own elbow. She had to fall back on the consciousness of how her elbow, in spite of her type, lacked practical point, and that was just why the terms in which she saw her services now, as she believed, bid for, had the effect of scaring her. They came out most, for that matter, in Mr Mortimer Marshal's dumbly insistent eyes, which seemed to be perpetually saying: 'You know what I mean when I'm too refined – like everything here, don't you see? – to say it out. You know there ought to be something about me somewhere, and that really, with the opportunities, the facilities you enjoy, it wouldn't be so much out of your way just to – well, reward this little attention.'

The fact that he was probably every day, in just the same anxious flurry and with just the same superlative delicacy, paying little attentions with an eye to little rewards, this fact by itself but scantily eased her, convinced as she was that no luck but her own was as hopeless as his. He squared the clever young wherever he could get at them, but it was the clever young, taking them generally, who fed from his hand and then forgot him. She didn't forget him; she pitied him too much, pitied herself, and was more and more, as she found, now pitying everyone; only she didn't know how to say to him that she could do, after all, nothing for him. She oughtn't to have come, in the first place, and wouldn't if it hadn't been for her companion. Her companion was increasingly sardonic – which was the way in which, at best, she now increasingly saw him; he was shameless in acceptance, since, as she knew, as she felt at his side, he had come only, at bottom, to mislead and to mystify. *He* was, as she wasn't, on the Papers and of them, and their baffled entertainer knew it without either a hint on the subject from herself or a need, on the young man's own lips, of the least vulgar allusion. Nothing was so much as named, the whole connection was sunk; they talked about clubs, muffins, afternoon performances, the effect of the Finnish soul upon the appetite, quite as if they had met in society. Nothing could have been less like society – she innocently supposed at least – than the real spirit of their meeting; yet Bight did nothing that he might do to keep the affair within bounds. When looked at by their friend so hard and so hintingly, he only looked back, just as dumbly, but just as intensely and, as might be said, portentously; ever so impenetrably, in fine, and ever so wickedly. He didn't smile – as if to cheer – the least little bit; which he might be abstaining from on purpose to make his promises solemn: so, as he tried to smile – she couldn't, it was all too dreadful – she wouldn't meet her friend's eyes, but kept looking, heartlessly, at the 'notes' of the place, the hats of the ladies, the tints of the rugs, the intenser Chippendale, here and there, of the chairs and tables, of the very guests, of the very waitresses. It had come to her early: 'I've done him, poor man, at home, and the obvious thing now will be to do him at his club.' But this inspiration plumped against her fate even as an imprisoned insect against the window-glass. She couldn't do him at his club without decently asking leave; whereby he would know of her feeble feeler, feeble because she was so sure of refusals. She would rather tell him, desperately, what she thought of him than expose him to see again that she was herself nowhere, herself nothing. Her one comfort was that, for the half-hour – it had made the situation quite possible – he seemed fairly hypnotized by her colleague; so that when they took leave he as good as thanked her for what she had this time done for him. It was one of the signs of his infatuated state that he clearly viewed Bight as a mass of helpful cleverness, though the cruel creature, uttering scarce a sound, had only fixed him in a manner that might have been taken for the fascination of deference. He might perfectly have been an idiot for all the poor gentleman knew. But the poor gentleman saw a possible 'leg up' in every bush; and nothing but impertinence would have convinced him that she hadn't brought him, compunctiously as to the past, a master of the proper art. Now, more than ever, how he would listen for the postman!

The whole occasion had broken so, for busy Bight, into matters to be attended to before Fleet Street warmed to its work, that the pair were obliged, outside, to part company on the spot, and it was only on the morrow, a Saturday, that they could taste again of that comparison of notes which made for each the main savour, albeit slightly acrid, of their current consciousness. The air was full, as from afar, of the grand indifference of spring, of which the breath could be felt so much before the face could be seen, and they had bicycled side by side out to Richmond Park as with the impulse to meet it on its way. They kept a Saturday, when possible, sacred to the Suburbs as distinguished from the Papers — when possible being largely when Maud could achieve the use of the somewhat fatigued family machine. Many sisters contended for it, under whose flushed pressure it might have been seen spinning in many different directions. Superficially, at Richmond, our young couple rested — found a quiet corner to lounge deep in the Park, with their machines propped by one side of a great tree and their associated backs sustained by another. But agitation, finer than the finest scorching, was in the air for them; it was made sharp, rather abruptly, by a vivid outbreak from Maud. It was very well, she observed, for her friend to be clever at the expense of the general 'greed'; he saw it in the light of his own jolly luck, and what she saw, as it happened, was nothing but the general art of letting you starve, yourself, in your hole. At the end of five minutes her companion had turned quite pale with having to face the large extent of her confession. It was a confession for the reason that in the first place it evidently cost her an effort that pride had again and again successfully prevented, and because in the second she had thus the air of having lived overmuch on swagger. She could scarce have said at this moment what, for a good while, she had really lived on, and she didn't let him know now to complain either of her privation or of her disappointments. She did it to show why she couldn't go with him when he was so awfully sweeping. There were at any rate apparently, all over, two wholly different sets of people. If everyone rose to his bait no creature had ever risen to hers; and that was the grim truth of her position, which proved at the least that there were two quite different kinds of luck. They told two different stories of human vanity; they couldn't be reconciled. And the poor girl put it in a nutshell. 'There's but one person I've *ever* written to who has so much as noticed my letter.'

He wondered, painfully affected – it rather overwhelmed him; he took hold of it at the easiest point. 'One person—?'

'The misguided man we had tea with. He alone – *he* rose.'

'Well then, you see that when they do rise they *are* misguided. In other words they're donkeys.'

'What I see is that I don't strike the right ones and that I haven't therefore your ferocity; that is my ferocity, if I have any, rests on a different ground. You'll say that I go for the wrong people; but I don't, God knows – witness Mortimer Marshall – fly too high. I picked him out, after prayer and fasting, as just the likeliest of the likely – not anybody a bit grand and yet not quite a nobody; and by an extraordinary chance I was justified. Then I pick out others who seem just as good, I pray and fast, and no sound comes back. But I work through my ferocity too,' she stiffly continued, 'though at first it was great, feeling as I did that when my bread and butter was in it people had no right not to oblige me. It was their duty – what they were prominent *for* – to be interviewed, so as to keep me going; and I did as much for them any day as they would be doing for me.'

Bight heard her, but for a moment said nothing. 'Did you tell them that? I mean say to them it was your little all?'

'Not vulgarly – I know how. There are ways of saying it's

"important"; and I hint it just enough to see that the importance fetches them no more than anything else. It isn't important to *them*. And I, in their place,' Maud went on, 'wouldn't answer either; I'll be hanged if ever I would. That's what it comes to, that there *are* two distinct lots, and that my luck, being born so, is always to try the snubbers. You were born to know by instinct the others. But it makes me more tolerant.'

'More tolerant of what?' her friend asked.

'Well, of what you described to me. Of what you rail at.'

'Thank you for *me*!' Bight laughed.

'Why not? Don't you live on it?'

'Not in such luxury – you surely must see for yourself – as the distinction you make seems to imply. It isn't luxury to be nine-tenths of the time sick of everything. People moreover are worth to me but tuppence apiece; there are too many, confound them – so many that I don't see really how any can be left over for *your* superior lot. It *is* a chance,' he pursued – 'I've had refusals too – though I confess they've sometimes been of the funniest. Besides, I'm getting out of it,' the young man wound up. 'God knows I want to. My advice to you,' he added in the same breath, 'is to sit tight. There are as good fish in the sea—!'

She waited a moment. 'You're sick of everything and you're getting out of it; it's not good enough for you, in other words, but it's still good enough for me. Why am I to sit tight when you sit so loose?'

'Because what you want will come – can't help coming.

Then, in time, you'll also get out of it. But then you'll have had it, as I have, and the good of it.'

'But what, really, if it breeds nothing but disgust,' she asked, 'do you *call* the good of it?'

'Well, two things. First the bread and butter, and then the fun. I repeat it – sit tight.'

'Where's the fun,' she asked again, 'of learning to despise people?'

'You'll see when it comes. It will all be upon you, it will change for you any day. Sit tight, sit tight.'

He expressed such confidence that she might for a minute have been weighing it. 'If you get out of it, what will you do?'

'Well, imaginative work. This job has made me at least *see*. It has given me the loveliest tips.'

She had still another pause. 'It has given me – *my* experience has – a lovely tip too.'

'And what's that?'

'I've told you before – the tip of pity. I'm so much sorrier for them all – panting and gasping for it like fish out of water – than I am anything else.'

He wondered. 'But I thought that was what just isn't your experience.'

'Oh, I mean then,' she said impatiently, 'that my tip is from yours. It's only a different tip. I want to save them.'

'Well,' the young man replied, and as if the idea had had a meaning for him, 'saving them may perhaps work out as a branch. The question is can you be paid for it?'

'Beadel-Muffet would pay me,' Maud suddenly suggested.

'Why, that's just what I'm expecting,' her companion laughed, 'that he will, after tomorrow – directly or indirectly – do *me*.'

'Will you take it from him then only to get him in deeper, as that's what you perfectly know you'll do? You won't save him; you'll lose him.'

'What then would you, in the case,' Bight asked, 'do for your money?'

Well, the girl thought. 'I'd get him to see me – I should have first, I recognize, to catch my hare – and then I'd work up my stuff. Which would be boldly, quite by a masterstroke, a statement of his fix – of the fix, I mean, of his wanting, his supplicating to be dropped. I'd give out that it would really oblige. Then I'd send my copy about, and the rest of the matter would take care of itself. I don't say *you* could do it that way – you'd have a different effect. But I should be able to trust the thing, being mine, not to be looked at, or, if looked at, chucked straight into the basket. I should so have, to that extent, handled the matter, and I should so, by merely touching it, have broken the spell. That's my one line – I stop things off by touching them. There'd never be a word about him more.'

Her friend, with his legs out and his hands locked at the back of his neck, had listened with indulgence. 'Then hadn't I better arrange it for you that Beadel-Muffet shall see you?'

'Oh, not after you've damned him!'

'You want to see him first?'

'It will be the only way – to be of any use to him. You ought to wire him in fact not to open his mouth till he has seen me.'

'Well, I will,' said Bight at last. 'But, you know, we shall lose something very handsome – his struggle, all in vain, with his fate. Noble sport, the sight of it all.' He turned a little, to rest on his elbow, and, cycling suburban young man as he was, he might have been, outstretched under his tree, melancholy Jacques looking off into a forest glade, even as sailor-hatted Maud, in – for elegance – a new cotton blouse and a long-limbed angular attitude, might have prosefully suggested the mannish Rosalind. He raised his face in appeal to her. 'Do you really ask me to sacrifice it?'

'Rather than sacrifice *him*? Of course I do.'

He said for a while nothing more; only, propped on his elbow, lost himself again in the Park. After which he turned back to her. Will you have me?' he suddenly asked.

'"Have you"—?'

'Be my bonny bride. For better, for worse. I hadn't, upon my honour,' he explained with obvious sincerity, 'understood you were so down.'

'Well, it isn't so bad as that,' said Maud Blandy.

'So bad as taking up with *me*?'

'It isn't as bad as having let you know – when I didn't want you to.'

He sank back again with his head dropped, putting himself more at his ease. 'You're too proud – that's what's the matter with you. And I'm too stupid.'

'No, you're not,' said Maud grimly. 'Not stupid.'

'Only cruel, cunning, treacherous, cold-blooded, vile?' He drawled the words out softly, as if they sounded fair.

'And I'm not stupid either,' Maud Blandy went on. 'We just, poor creatures – well, we just *know*.'

'Of course we do. So why do you want us to drug ourselves with rot? to go on as if we didn't know?'

She made no answer for a moment; then she said: 'There's good to be known too.'

'Of course, again. There are all sorts of things, and some much better than others. That's why,' the young man added, 'I just put that question to you.'

'Oh no, it isn't. You put it to me because you think I feel I'm no good.'

'How so, since I keep assuring you that you've only to wait? How so, since I keep assuring you that if you do wait it will all come with a rush? But say I *am* sorry for you,' Bight lucidly pursued; 'how does that prove either that my motive is base or that I do you a wrong?'

The girl waived this question, but she presently tried another. 'Is it your idea that we should live on all the people——?'

'The people we catch? Yes, old man, till we can do better.'

'My conviction is,' she soon returned, 'that if I were to marry you I should dish you. I should spoil the business. It would fall off; and, as I can do nothing myself, then where should we be?'

'Well,' said Bight, 'we mightn't be quite so high up in the scale of the morbid.'

'It's you that are morbid,' she answered. 'You've, in your way – like everyone else, for that matter, all over the place – "sport" on the brain.'

'Well,' he demanded, 'what is sport but success? What is success but sport?'

'Bring that out somewhere. If it be true,' she said, 'I'm glad I'm a failure.'

After which, for a longish space, they sat together in silence, a silence finally broken by a word from the young man. 'But about Mortimer Marshal – how do you propose to save *him*?'

It was a change of subject that might, by its so easy introduction of matter irrelevant, have seemed intended to dissipate whatever was left of his proposal of marriage. That proposal, however, had been somehow both too much in the tone of familiarity to linger and too little in that of vulgarity to drop. It had had no form, but the mild air kept perhaps thereby the better the taste of it. This was sensibly moreover in what the girl found to reply. 'I think, you know, that he'd be no such bad friend. I mean that, with his appetite, there would be something to be done. He doesn't half hate me.'

'Ah, my dear,' her friend ejaculated, 'don't, for God's sake, be low.'

But she kept it up. 'He clings to me. You saw. It's hideous, the way he's able to "do" himself.'

Bight lay quiet, then spoke as with a recall of the Chippendale Club. 'Yes, I couldn't "do" you as he could. But if you don't bring it off—?'

'Why then does he cling? Oh, because, all the same, I'm potentially the Papers still. I'm at any rate the nearest he has got to them. And then I'm other things.'

'I see.'

'I'm so awfully attractive,' said Maud Blandy. She got up with this and, shaking out her frock, looked at her resting bicycle, looked at the distances possibly still to be gained. Her companion paused, but at last also rose, and by that time she was awaiting him, a little gaunt and still not quite cool, as an illustration of her last remark. He stood there watching her, and she followed this remark up. 'I do, you know, really pity him.'

It had almost a feminine fineness, and their eyes continued to meet. 'Oh, you'll work it!' And the young man went to his machine.

## IV

IT WAS NOT till five days later that they again came together, and during these days many things had happened. Maud Blandy had, with high elation, for her own portion, a sharp sense of this; if it had at the time done nothing more intimate for her the Sunday of bitterness just spent with Howard Bight had started, all abruptly, a turn of the tide of her luck. This turn had not in the least been in the young man's having spoken to her of marriage — since she hadn't even, up to the late hour of their parting, so much as answered him straight: she dated the sense of difference much rather from the throb of a happy thought that had come to her while she cycled home to Kilburnia in the darkness. The throb had made her for the few minutes, tired as she was, put on speed, and it had been the cause of still further proceedings for her the first thing the next morning. The active step that was the essence of these proceedings had almost got itself taken before she went to bed; which indeed was what had happened to the extent of her writing, on the spot, a meditated letter. She sat down to it by the light of the guttering candle that awaited her on the dining-room table and in the stale air of family food that only *had* been – a residuum so at the mercy of mere ventilation that she didn't so much as peep into a cupboard; after which she had been on the point of nipping over, as she would have said, to drop it into that opposite pillar-box whose vivid maw, opening out through thick London nights, had received so many of her fruitless little ventures. But she had checked herself and waited, waited to be sure, with the morning, that her fancy wouldn't fade; posting her note in the end, however, with a confident jerk, as soon as she was up. She had, later on, had business, or at least had sought it, among the haunts that she had taught herself to regard as professional; but neither on the Monday nor on either of the days that directly followed had she encountered there the friend whom it would take a difference in more matters than could as yet be dealt with to enable her to regard, with proper assurance or with proper modesty, as a lover. Whatever he was, none the less, it couldn't otherwise have come to her that it was possible to feel lonely in the Strand. That showed, after all, how thick they must constantly have been – which *was* perhaps a thing to begin to think of in a new, in a steadier light. But it showed doubtless still more that her companion was probably up to something rather awful; it made her wonder, holding her breath a little, about Beadel-Muffet, made her certain that he and his affairs would partly account for Bight's whirl of absence.

Ever conscious of empty pockets, she had yet always a penny, or at least a ha'penny, for a paper, and those she now scanned, she quickly assured herself, were edited quite as usual. Sir A. B. C. Beadel-Muffet, K.C.B., M.P., had returned on Monday from Undertone, where Lord and Lady Wispers had, from the previous Friday, entertained a very select party; Sir A. B. C. Beadel-Muffet, K.C.B., M.P., was to attend on Tuesday the weekly meeting of the society of the Friends of Rest; Sir A. B. C. Beadel-Muffet, K.C.B., M.P., had kindly consented to preside on Wednesday, at Samaritan House, at the opening of the Sale of Work of the Middlesex Incurables. These familiar announcements, however, far from appeasing her curiosity, had an effect upon her nerves; she read into them mystic meanings that she had never read before. Her freedom of mind in this direction was indeed at the same time limited, for her own horizon was already, by the Monday night, bristling with new possibilities, and the Tuesday itself – well, what had the Tuesday itself become, with this eruption, from within, of interest amounting really to a revelation, what had the Tuesday itself become but the greatest day yet of her life? Such a description of it would have appeared to apply predominantly to the morning had she not, under the influence, precisely, of the morning's thrill, gone, towards evening, with her design, into the Charing Cross Station. There, at the bookstall, she bought them all, every rag that was hawked; and there, as she unfolded one at a venture, in the crowd and under the lamps, she felt her consciousness further, felt it for the moment quite impressively, enriched. 'Personal Peeps – Number Ninety-Three: A Chat with the New Dramatist' needed neither the 'H. B.' as a terminal signature nor a text spangled, to the exclusion of almost everything else, with Mortimer Marshals that looked as tall as if lettered on posters, to help to account for her young man's use of his time. And yet, as she soon made out, it had been used with an economy that caused her both to wonder and to wince; the 'peep' commemorated being none other than their tea with the artless creature the previous Saturday, and the meagre incidents and pale impressions of that occasion furnishing forth the picture.

Bight had solicited no new interview; he hadn't been such a fool – for she saw, soon enough, with all her intelligence, that this was what he would have been, and that a repetition of contact would have dished him. What he *had* done, she found herself perceiving – and perceiving with an emotion that caused her face to glow – was journalism of the intensest essence; a column concocted of nothing, an omelette made, as it were, without even the breakage of the egg or two that might have been expected to be the price. The poor gentleman's whereabouts at five o'clock was the only egg broken, and this light and delicate crash was the sound in the world that would be sweetest to him. What stuff it had to be, since the writer really knew nothing about him, yet how its being just such stuff made it perfectly serve its purpose! She might have marvelled afresh, with more leisure, at such purposes, but she was lost in the wonder of seeing how, without matter, without thought, without an excuse, without a fact and yet at the same time sufficiently without a fiction, he had managed to be as resonant as if he had beaten a drum on the platform of a booth. And he had not been too personal, not made anything awkward for *her*, had given nothing and nobody away, had tossed the Chippendale Club into the air with such a turn that it had fluttered down again, like a blown feather, miles from its site. The thirty-seven agencies would already be posting to their subscriber thirty-seven copies, and their subscriber, on his side, would be posting, to his acquaintance, many times thirty-seven, and thus at least getting something for his money; but this didn't tell her why her friend had taken the trouble – if it had *been* a trouble; why at all events he had taken the time, pressed as he apparently was for that commodity. These things she was indeed presently to learn, but they were meanwhile part of a suspense composed of more elements than any she had yet tasted. And the suspense was prolonged, though other affairs too, that were not part of it, almost equally crowded upon her; the week having almost waned when relief arrived in the form of a cryptic post-card. The post-card bore the H. B., like the precious 'Peep', which had already had a wondrous sequel, and it appointed, for the tea-hour, a place of meeting familiar to Maud, with the simple addition of the significant word 'Larks!'

When the time he had indicated came she waited for him, at their small table, swabbed like the deck of a steam-packet, nose to nose with a mustard-pot and a price-list, in the consciousness of perhaps after all having as much to tell him as to hear from him. It appeared indeed at first that this might well be the case, for the questions that came up between them when he had taken his place were overwhelmingly those he himself insisted on putting. 'What has he done, what *has* he, and what will he?' – that inquiry, not loud but deep, had met him as he sat down; without however producing the least recognition. Then she as soon felt that his silence and his manner were enough for her, or that, if they hadn't been, his wonderful look, the straightest she had ever had from him, would instantly have made them so. He looked at her hard, hard, as if he had meant 'I say, mind your eyes!' and it amounted really to a glimpse, rather fearful, of the subject. It was no joke, the subject, clearly, and her friend had fairly gained age, as he had certainly lost weight, in his recent dealings with it. It struck her even, with everything else, that this was positively the way she would have liked him to show if their union had taken the form they hadn't reached the point of discussing; wearily coming back to her from the thick of things, wanting to put on his slippers and have his tea, all prepared by her and in their place, and beautifully to be trusted to regale her in his turn. He was excited, disavowedly, and it took more disavowal still after she had opened her budget – which she did, in truth, by saying to him as her first alternative: 'What did you do him *for*, poor Mortimer Marshal? It isn't that he's not in the seventh heaven—!'

'He *is* in the seventh heaven!' Bight quickly broke in. 'He doesn't want my blood?'

'Did you do him,' she asked, 'that he should want it? It's splendid how you could – simply on that show.'

'That show? Why,' said Howard Bight, 'that show was an immensity. That show was volumes, stacks, abysses.'

He said it in such a tone that she was a little at a loss. 'Oh, you don't want abysses.'

'Not much, to knock off such twaddle. There isn't a breath in it of what I saw. What I saw is my own affair. I've got the abysses for myself. They're in my head – it's always something. But the monster,' he demanded, 'has written you?'

'How couldn't he – that night? I got it the next morning, telling me how much he wanted to thank me and asking me where he might see me. So I went,' said Maud, 'to see him.'

'At his own place again?'

'At his own place again. What do I yearn for but to be received at people's own places?'

'Yes, for the stuff. But when you've had – as you had had from him – the stuff?'

'Well, sometimes, you see, I get more. He gives me all I can take.' It was in her head to ask if by chance Bight were jealous, but she gave it another turn. 'We had a big palaver, partly about you. He appreciates.'

'Me?'

'Me – first of all, I think. All the more that I've had – fancy! – a proof of my stuff, the despised and rejected, as originally concocted, and that he has now seen it. I tried it on again with *Brains*, the night of your thing – sent it off with your thing enclosed as a rouser. They took it, by return, like a shot – you'll see on Wednesday. And if the dear man lives till then, for impatience, I'm to lunch with him that day.'

'I see,' said Bight. 'Well, that was what I did it for. It shows how right I was.'

They faced each other, across their thick crockery, with eyes that said more than their words, and that, above all, said, and asked, other things. So she went on in a moment: 'I don't know what he doesn't expect. And he thinks I can keep it up.'

'Lunch with him *every* Wednesday?'

'Oh, he'd give me my lunch, and more. It was last Sunday that you were right – about my sitting close,' she pursued. 'I'd have been a pretty fool to jump. Suddenly, I see, the music begins. I'm awfully obliged to you.'

'You feel,' he presently asked, 'quite differently – so differently that I've missed my chance? I don't care for *that* serpent, but there's something else that you don't tell me.' The young man, detached and a little spent, with his shoulder against the wall and a hand vaguely playing over the knives, forks and spoons, dropped his succession of sentences without an apparent direction. 'Something else has come up, and you're as pleased as Punch. Or, rather, you're not quite entirely so, because you can't goad me to fury. You can't worry me as much as you'd like. Marry me first, old man, and *then* see if I mind. Why shouldn't you keep it up? — I mean lunching with him?' His questions came as in play that was a little pointless, without his waiting more than a moment for answers; though it was not indeed that she might not have answered even in the moment, had not the pointless play been more what she wanted. 'Was it at the place,' he went on, 'that he took us to?'

'Dear no — at his flat, where I've been before. You'll see, in *Brains*, on Wednesday. I don't think I've muffed it — it's really rather there. But he showed me everything this time — the bathroom, the refrigerator, and the machines for stretching his trousers. He has nine, and in constant use.'

'Nine?' said Bight gravely.

'Nine.'

'Nine trousers?'

'Nine machines. I don't know how many trousers.'

'Ah, my dear,' he said, 'that's a grave omission; the want of the information will be felt and resented. But does it all, at any rate,' he asked, 'sufficiently fetch you?' After which, as she didn't speak, he lapsed into helpless sincerity. 'Is it really, you think, his dream to secure you?'

She replied, on this, as if his tone made it too amusing, 'Quite. There's no mistaking it. He sees me as, most days in the year, pulling the wires and beating the drum somewhere; that is he sees me of course not exactly as writing about "our home" – once I've got one – myself, but as procuring others to do it through my being (as *you've* made him believe) in with the Organs of Public Opinion. He doesn't see, if I'm half decent, why there shouldn't be something about him every day in the week. He's all right, and he's all ready. And who, after all, *can* do him so well as the partner of his flat? It's like making, in one of those big domestic siphons, the luxury of the poor, your own soda-water. It comes cheaper, and it's always on the sideboard. "*Vichy chez soi.*" The interviewer at home.'

Her companion took it in. 'Your place is on *my* sideboard – you're really a first-class fizz! He steps then, at any rate, into Beadel-Muffet's place.'

'That,' Maud assented, 'is what he would like to do.' And she knew more than ever there was something to wait for.

'It's a lovely opening,' Bight returned. But he still said, for the moment, nothing else; as if, charged to the brim though he had originally been, she had rather led his thought away.

'What have you done with poor Beadel?' she consequently asked. 'What is it, in the name of goodness, you're doing *to* him? It's worse than ever.'

'Of course it's worse than ever.'

'He capers,' said Maud, 'on every house-top – he jumps out of every bush.' With which her anxiety really broke out. '*Is* it you that are doing it?'

'If you mean am I seeing him, I certainly am. I'm seeing nobody else. I assure you he's spread thick.'

'But you're acting for him?'

Bight waited. 'Five hundred people are acting for him; but the difficulty is that what he calls the "terrific forces of publicity" – by which he means ten thousand *other* persons – are acting against him. We've all in fact been turned on – to turn everything off, and that's exactly the job that makes the biggest noise. It appears everywhere, in every kind of connection and every kind of type, that Sir A. B. C. Beadel-Muffet, K.C.B., M.P., desires to cease to appear *anywhere*; and then it appears that his desiring to cease to appear is observed to conduce directly to his more tremendously appearing, or certainly, and in the most striking manner, to his not in the least *dis*appearing. The workshop of silence roars like the Zoo at dinner-time. He *can't* disappear; he hasn't weight enough to sink; the splash the diver makes, you know, tells where he is. If you ask me what I'm doing,' Bight wound up, 'I'm holding him under water. But we're in the middle of the pond, the banks are thronged with spectators, and I'm expecting from day to day to see stands erected and gate-money taken. There,' he wearily smiled, 'you have it. Besides,' he then added with an odd change of tone, 'I rather think you'll see tomorrow.'

He had made her at last horribly nervous. 'What shall I see?'

'It will all be out.'

'Then why shouldn't you tell me?'

'Well,' the young man said, 'he *has* disappeared. There you are. I mean personally. He's not to be found. But nothing could make more, you see, for ubiquity. The country will ring with it.

He vanished on Tuesday night – was then last seen at his club. Since then he has given no sign. How can a man disappear who does *that* sort of thing? It is, as you say, to caper on the housetops. But it will only be known tonight.'

'Since when, then,' Maud asked, 'have you known it?'

'Since three o'clock today. But I've kept it. I *am* – a while longer – keeping it.'

She wondered; she was full of fears. 'What do you expect to get for it?'

'Nothing – if you spoil my market. I seem to make out that you want to.'

She gave this no heed; she had her thought. 'Why then did you three days ago wire me a mystic word?'

'Mystic—?'

'What do you call "Larks"?'

'Oh, I remember. Well, it was because I saw larks coming; because I saw, I mean, what has happened. I was sure it would have to happen.'

'And what the mischief *is* it?'

Bight smiled. 'Why, what I tell you. That he has gone.'

'Gone where?'

'Simply bolted to parts unknown. "Where" is what nobody who belongs to him is able in the least to say, or seems likely to be able.'

'Any more than why?'

'Any more than why.'

'Only *you* are able to say that?'

'Well,' said Bight, 'I can say what has so lately stared me in the face, what he has been thrusting at me in all its grotesqueness: his desire for a greater privacy worked through the Papers themselves. He came to me with it,' the young man presently added. 'I didn't go to *him*.'

'And he trusted you,' Maud replied.

'Well, you see what I have given him – the very flower of my genius. What more do you want? I'm spent, seedy, sore. I'm sick,' Bight declared, 'of his beastly funk.'

Maud's eyes, in spite of it, were still a little hard. 'Is he thoroughly sincere?'

'Good God, no! How *can* he be? Only trying it – as a cat, for a jump, tries too smooth a wall. He drops straight back.'

'Then isn't his funk real?'

'As real as he himself is.'

Maud wondered. 'Isn't his flight——?'

'That's what we shall see!'

'Isn't,' she continued, 'his reason?'

'Ah,' he laughed out, 'there you are again!'

But she had another thought and was not discouraged. 'Mayn't he be, honestly, mad?'

'Mad – oh yes. But not, I think, honestly. He's not honestly anything in the world but the Beadel-Muffet of our delight.'

'Your delight,' Maud observed after a moment, 'revolts me.' And then she said: 'When did you last see him?'

'On Tuesday at six, love. I was one of the last.'

'Decidedly, too, then, I judge, one of the worst.' She gave him her idea. 'You hounded him on.'

'I reported,' said Bight, 'success. Told him how it was going.'

'Oh, I can see you! So that if he's dead——'

'Well?' asked Bight blandly.

'His blood is on your hands.'

He eyed his hands a moment. 'They *are* dirty for him! But now, darling,' he went on, 'be so good as to show me yours.'

'Tell me first,' she objected, 'what you believe. *Is* it suicide?'

'I think that's the thing for us to make it. Till somebody,' he smiled, 'makes it something else.' And he showed how he warmed to the view. 'There are weeks of it, dearest, yet.'

He leaned more toward her, with his elbows on the table, and in this position, moved by her extreme gravity, he lightly flicked her chin with his finger. She threw herself, still grave, back from his touch, but they remained thus a while closely confronted. 'Well,' she at last remarked, 'I shan't pity you.'

'You make it, then, everyone except me?'

'I mean,' she continued, 'if you do have to loathe yourself.'

'Oh, I shan't miss it.' And then as if to show how little, 'I did mean it, you know, at Richmond,' he declared.

'I won't have you if you've killed him,' she presently returned.

'You'll decide in that case for the *nine*?' And as the allusion, with its funny emphasis, left her blank: 'You want to wear *all* the trousers?'

'You deserve,' she said, when light came, 'that I should take him.' And she kept it up. 'It's a lovely flat.'

Well, he could do as much. 'Nine, I suppose, appeals to you as the number of the muses?'

This short passage, remarkably, for all its irony, brought them together again, to the extent at least of leaving Maud's elbows on the table and of keeping her friend, now a little back in his chair, firm while he listened to her. So the girl came out. 'I've seen Mrs Chorner three times. I wrote that night, after our talk at Richmond, asking her to oblige. And I put on cheek as I had never, never put it. I said the public would be so glad to hear from her "on the occasion of her engagement".'

'Do you call that cheek?' Bight looked amused. 'She at any rate rose straight.'

'No, she rose crooked; but she rose. What you had told me there in the Park – well, immediately happened. She did consent to see me, and so far you had been right in keeping me up to it. But what do you think it was for?'

'To show you *her* flat, *her* tub, *her* petticoats?'

'She doesn't live in a flat; she lives in a house of her own, and a jolly good one, in Green Street, Park Lane; though I did, as happened, see her tub, which is a dream – all marble and silver, like a kind of a swagger sarcophagus, a thing for the Wallace Collection; and though her petticoats, as she first shows, seem all that, if you wear petticoats yourself, you can look at. There's no doubt of her money – given her place and her things, and given her appearance too, poor dear, which would take some doing.'

'She squints?' Bight sympathetically asked.

'She's so ugly that she *has* to be rich – she couldn't afford it on less than five thousand a year. As it is, I could well see, she can afford anything – even such a nose. But she's funny and decent; sharp, but a really good sort. And they're *not* engaged.'

'She told you so? Then there you are!'

'It all depends,' Maud went on; 'and you don't know where I am at all. *I* know what it depends on.'

'Then there you are again! It's a mine of gold.'

'Possibly, but not in your sense. She wouldn't give me the first word of an interview – it wasn't for that she received me. It was for something much better.'

Well, Bight easily guessed. 'For *my* job?'

'To see what can be done. She loathes his publicity.'

The young man's face lighted. 'She told you so?'

'She received me on purpose to tell me.'

'Then why do you question my "larks"? What do you want more?'

'I want nothing – with what I have: nothing, I mean, but to help her. We made friends – I like her. And she likes *me*,' said Maud Blandy.

'Like Mortimer Marshal, precisely.'

'No, precisely not like Mortimer Marshal. I caught, on the spot, her idea – *that* was what took her. Her idea is that I can help her – help her to keep them quiet about Beadel: for which purpose I seem to have struck her as falling from the skies, just at the right moment, into her lap.'

Howard Bight followed, yet lingered by the way. 'To keep *whom* quiet——?'

'Why, the beastly Papers – what we've been talking about. She wants him straight out of them – *straight*.'

'She too?' Bight wondered. 'Then *she's* in terror?'

'No, not in terror – or it wasn't that when I last saw her. But in mortal disgust. She feels it has gone too far – which is what she wanted me, as an honest, decent, likely young woman, up to my neck in it, as she supposed, to understand from her. My relation with her is now that I do understand and that if an improvement takes place I shan't have been the worse for it. Therefore you see,' Maud went on, 'you simply cut my throat when you prevent improvement.'

'Well, my dear,' her friend returned, 'I won't let you bleed to death.' And he showed, with this, as confessedly struck. 'She doesn't then, you think, *know*—?'

'Know what?'

'Why, what, about him, there may *be* to be known. Doesn't know of his flight.'

'She didn't – certainly.'

'Nor of anything to make it likely?'

'What you call his queer reason? No – she named it to me no more than you have; though she does mention, distinctly, that he himself hates, or pretends to hate, the exhibition daily made of him.'

'She speaks of it,' Bight asked, 'as pretending—?'

Maud straightened it out. 'She feels him – *that* she practically told me – as rather ridiculous. She honestly has her feeling; and, upon my word, it's what I like her for. Her stomach has turned and she has made it her condition. "Muzzle your Press," she says; "*then* we'll talk." She gives him three months – she'll give him even six. And this, meanwhile – when he comes to *you* – is how you forward the muzzling.'

'The Press, my child,' Bight said, 'is the watchdog of civilization, and the watchdog happens to be – it can't be helped – in a chronic state of *rabies*. Muzzling is easy talk; one can but keep the animal on the run. Mrs Chorner, however,' he added, 'seems a figure of fable.'

'It's what I told you she would have to be when, some time back, you threw out, as a pure hypothesis, to supply the man with a motive, your exact vision of her. Your motive has come true,' Maud went on – 'with the difference only, if I understand you, that this doesn't appear the whole of it. That doesn't matter' – she frankly paid him a tribute. 'Your forecast was inspiration.'

'A stroke of genius' – he had been the first to feel it. But there were matters less clear. 'When did you see her last?'

'Four days ago. It was the third time.'

'And even then she didn't imagine the truth about him?'

'I don't know, you see,' said Maud, 'what you *call* the truth.'

'Well, that he – quite by that time – didn't know where the deuce to turn. That's truth enough.'

Maud made sure. 'I don't see how she can have known it and not have been upset. She wasn't,' said the girl, 'upset. She *isn't* upset. But she's original.'

'Well, poor thing,' Bight remarked, 'she'll have to be.'

'Original?'

'Upset. Yes, and original too, if she doesn't give up the job.' It had held him an instant — but there were many things. 'She sees the wild ass he is, and yet she's willing—?'

'"Willing" is just what I asked *you* three months ago,' Maud returned, 'how she *could* be.'

He had lost it — he tried to remember. 'What then did I say?'

'Well, practically, that women are idiots. Also, I believe, that he's a dazzling beauty.'

'Ah yes, he *is*, poor wretch, though beauty today in distress.'

'Then there you are,' said Maud. They had got up, as at the end of their story, but they stood a moment while he waited for change. 'If it comes out,' the girl dropped, '*that* will save him. If he's dishonoured — as I see her — she'll have him, because then he won't be ridiculous. And I can understand it.'

Bight looked at her in such appreciation that he forgot, as he pocketed it, to glance at his change. 'Oh, you creatures—!'

'Idiots, aren't we?'

Bight let the question pass, but still with his eyes on her, 'You ought to want him to *be* dishonoured.'

'I can't want him, then — if he's to get the good of it — to be dead.'

Still for a little he looked at her. 'And if *you're* to get the good?' But she had turned away, and he went with her to the door, before which, when they had passed out, they had in the side-street, a backwater to the flood of the Strand, a further sharp colloquy. They were alone, the small street for a moment empty, and they felt at first that they had adjourned to a greater privacy, of which, for that matter, he took prompt advantage. 'You're to lunch again with the man of the flat?'

'Wednesday, as I say; 1.45.'

'Then oblige me by stopping away.'

'You don't like it?' Maud asked.

'Oblige me, oblige me,' he repeated.

'And disoblige *him*?'

'Chuck him. We've started him. It's enough.'

Well, the girl but wanted to be fair. 'It's *you* who started him; so I admit you're quits.'

'That then started *you* – made *Brains* repent; so you see what you both owe me. I let the creature off, but I hold you to your debt. There's only one way for you to meet it.' And then as she but looked into the roaring Strand: 'With worship.' It made her, after a minute, meet his eyes, but something just then occurred that stayed any word on the lips of either. A sound reached their ears, as yet unheeded, the sound of newsboys in the great thoroughfare shouting 'extra-specials' and mingling with the shout a catch that startled them. The expression in their eyes quickened as they heard, borne on the air, 'Mysterious Disappearance—!' and then lost it in the hubbub. It was easy to complete the cry, and Bight himself gasped. 'Beadel-Muffet? Confound them!'

'Already?' Maud had turned positively pale.

'They've got it first – be hanged to them!'

Bight gave a laugh – a tribute to their push – but her hand

was on his arm for a sign to listen again. It was there, in the raucous throats; it was there, for a penny, under the lamps and in the thick of the stream that stared and passed and left it. They caught the whole thing – 'Prominent Public Man!' And there was something brutal and sinister in the way it was given to the flaring night, to the other competing sounds, to the general hardness of hearing and sight which was yet, on London pavements, compatible with an interest sufficient for cynicism. He had been, poor Beadel, public and prominent, but he had never affected Maud Blandy at least as so marked with this character as while thus loudly committed to extinction. It was horrid – it was tragic; yet her lament for him was dry. 'If he's gone I'm dished.'

'Oh, he's gone – now,' said Bight.

'I mean if he's dead.'

'Well, perhaps he isn't. I see,' Bight added, 'what you do mean. If he's dead you can't kill him.'

'Oh, she wants him alive,' said Maud.

'Otherwise she can't chuck him?'

To which the girl, however, anxious and wondering, made no direct reply. 'Good-bye to Mrs Chorner. And I owe it to *you*.'

'Ah, my love!' he vaguely appealed.

'Yes, it's you who have destroyed him, and it makes up for what you've done *for* me.'

'I've done it, you mean, against you? I didn't know,' he said, 'you'd take it so hard.'

Again, as he spoke, the cries sounded out: 'Mysterious

Disappearance of Prominent Public Man!' It seemed to swell as they listened; Maud started with impatience. 'I hate it too much,' she said, and quitted him to join the crowd.

He was quickly at her side, however, and before she reached the Strand he had brought her again to a pause. 'Do you mean you hate it so much you won't have me?'

It had pulled her up short, and her answer was proportionately straight. 'I won't have you if he's dead.'

'Then will you if he's not?'

At this she looked at him hard. 'Do you *know*, first?'

'No – blessed if I do.'

'On your honour?'

'On my honour.'

'Well,' she said after a hesitation, 'if *she* doesn't drop me—'

'It's an understood thing?' he pressed.

But again she hung fire. 'Well, produce him first.'

They stood there striking their bargain, and it was made, by the long look they exchanged, a question of good faith. 'I'll produce him,' said Howard Bight.

# V

IF IT HAD NOT been a disaster, Beadel-Muffet's plunge into the obscure, it would have been a huge success; so large a space did the prominent public man occupy, for the next few days, in the

Papers, so near did he come, nearer certainly than ever before, to supplanting other topics. The question of his whereabouts, of his antecedents, of his habits, of his possible motives, of his probable, or improbable, embarrassments, fairly raged, from day to day and from hour to hour, making the Strand, for our two young friends, quite fiercely, quite cruelly vociferous. They met again promptly, in the thick of the uproar, and no other eyes could have scanned the current rumours and remarks so eagerly as Maud's unless it had been those of Maud's companion. The rumours and remarks were mostly very wonderful, and all of a nature to sharpen the excitement produced in the comrades by their being already, as they felt, 'in the know'. Even for the girl this sense existed, so that she could smile at wild surmises; she struck herself as knowing much more than she did, especially as, with the alarm once given, she abstained, delicately enough, from worrying, from catechizing Bight. She only looked at him as to say, 'See, while the suspense lasts, how generously I spare you,' and her attitude was not affected by the interested promise he had made her. She believed he knew more than he said, though he had sworn as to what he didn't; she saw him in short as holding some threads but having lost others, and his state of mind, so far as she could read it, represented in equal measure assurances unsupported and anxieties unconfessed. He would have liked to pass for having, on cynical grounds, and for the mere ironic beauty of it, believed that the hero of the hour was only, as he had always been, 'up to' something from which he would emerge more than ever glorious, or at least conspicuous;

but, knowing the gentleman was more than anything, more than all else, asinine, he was not deprived of ground in which fear could abundantly grow. If Beadel, in other words, was ass enough, as was conceivable, to be working the occasion, he was by the same token ass enough to have lost control of it, to have committed some folly from which even fools don't rebound. That was the spark of suspicion lurking in the young man's ease, and that, Maud knew, explained something else.

The family and friends had but too promptly been approached, been besieged; yet Bight, in all the promptness, had markedly withdrawn from the game – had had, one could easily judge, already too much to do with it. Who but he, otherwise, would have been so naturally let loose upon the forsaken home, the bewildered circle, the agitated club, the friend who had last conversed with the eminent absentee, the waiter, in exclusive halls, who had served him with five-o'clock tea, the porter, in august Pall Mall, who had called his last cab, the cabman, supremely privileged, who had driven him – where? 'The Last Cab' would, as our young woman reflected, have been a heading so after her friend's own heart, and so consonant with his genius, that it took all her discretion not to ask him how he had resisted it. She didn't ask, she but herself noted the title for future use – she would have at least got that, 'The Last Cab', out of the business; and, as the days went by and the extra-specials swarmed, the situation between them swelled with all the unspoken. Matters that were grave depended on it for each – and nothing so much, for instance, as her seeing Mrs Chorner again.

To see that lady as things *had* been had meant that the poor woman might have been helped to believe in her. Believing in her she would have paid her, and Maud, disposed as she was, really had felt capable of earning the pay. Whatever, as the case stood, was caused to hang in the air, nothing dangled more free than the profit derivable from muzzling the Press. With the watchdog to whom Bight had compared it barking for dear life, the moment was scarcely adapted for calling afresh upon a person who had offered a reward for silence. The only silence, as we say, was in the girl's not mentioning to her friend how these embarrassments affected her. Mrs Chorner was a person she liked – a connection more to her taste than any she had professionally made, and the thought of her now on the rack, tormented with suspense, might well have brought to her lips a 'See *there* what you've done!'

There was, for that matter, in Bight's face – he couldn't keep it out – precisely the look of seeing it; which was one of her reasons too for not insisting on her wrong. If he couldn't conceal it this was a part of the rest of the unspoken; he didn't allude to the lady lest it might be too sharply said to him that it was on *her* account he should most blush. Last of all he was hushed by the sense of what he had himself said when the news first fell on their ears. His promise to 'produce' the fugitive was still in the air, but with every day that passed the prospect turned less to redemption. Therefore if her own promise, on a different head, depended on it, he was naturally not in a hurry to bring the question to a test. So it was accordingly that they but read the

Papers and looked at each other. Maud felt in truth that these organs had never been so worth it, nor either she or her friend – whatever the size of old obligations – so much beholden to them. They helped them to wait, and the better, really, the longer the mystery lasted. It grew of course daily richer, adding to its mass as it went and multiplying its features, looming especially larger through the cloud of correspondence, communication, suggestion, supposition, speculation, with which it was presently suffused. Theories and explanations sprouted at night and bloomed in the morning, to be overtopped at noon by a still thicker crop and to achieve by evening the density of a tropical forest. These, again, were the green glades in which our young friends wandered.

Under the impression of the first night's shock Maud had written to Mortimer Marshal to excuse herself from her engagement to luncheon – a step of which she had promptly advised Bight as a sign of her playing fair. He took it, she could see, for what it was worth, but she could see also how little he now cared. He was thinking of the man with whose strange agitation he had so cleverly and recklessly played, and, in the face of the catastrophe of which they were still so likely to have news, the vanities of smaller fools, the conveniences of first-class flats, the memory of Chippendale teas, ceased to be actual or ceased at any rate to be importunate. Her old interview, furbished into freshness, had appeared, on its Wednesday, in *Brains*, but she had not received in person the renewed homage of its author – she had only, once more, had the vision of his inordinate purchase and diffusion of the precious number. It was a vision, however, at which neither Bight nor she smiled; it was funny on so poor a scale compared with their other show. But it befell that when this latter had, for ten days, kept being funny to the tune that so lengthened their faces, the poor gentleman glorified in *Brains* succeeded in making it clear that he was not easily to be dropped. He wanted now, evidently, as the girl said to herself, to live at concert pitch, and she gathered, from three or four notes, to which, at short intervals, he treated her, that he was watching in anxiety for reverberations not as yet perceptible. His expectation of results from what our young couple had done for him would, as always, have been a thing for pity with a young couple less imbued with the comic sense; though indeed it would also have been a comic thing for a young couple less attentive to a different drama. Disappointed of the girl's company at home the author of *Corisanda* had proposed fresh appointments, which she had desired at the moment, and indeed more each time, not to take up; to the extent even that, catching sight of him, unperceived, on one of these occasions, in her inveterate Strand, she checked on the spot a first impulse to make herself apparent. He was before her, in the crowd, and going the same way. He had stopped a little to look at a shop, and it was then that she swerved in time not to pass close to him. She turned and reversed, conscious and convinced that he was, as she mentally put it, on the prowl for her.

She herself, poor creature – as she also mentally put it – she herself was shamelessly on the prowl, but it wasn't, for her self-respect, to get herself puffed, it wasn't to pick up a personal advantage. It was to pick up news of Beadel-Muffet, to be near the extra-specials, and it was, also – as to this she was never blind – to cultivate that nearness by chances of Howard Bight. The blessing of blindness, in truth, at this time, she scantily enjoyed – being perfectly aware of the place occupied, in her present attitude to that young man, by the simple impossibility of not seeing him. She had done with him, certainly, if he *had* killed Beadel, and nothing was now growing so fast as the presumption in favour of some catastrophe, yet shockingly to be revealed, enacted somewhere in desperate darkness – though probably 'on lines', as the Papers said, anticipated by none of the theorists in their own columns, any more than by clever people at the clubs, where the betting was so heavy. She had done with him, indubitably, but she had not – it was equally unmistakable – done with letting him see how thoroughly she *would* have done; or, to feel about it otherwise, she was laying up treasure in time – as against the privations of the future. She was affected moreover – perhaps but half-consciously – by another consideration; her attitude to Mortimer Marshal had turned a little to fright; she wondered, uneasily, at impressions she might have given him; and she had it, finally, on her mind that, whether or no the vain man believed in them, there must be a limit to the belief she had communicated to her friend. He *was* her friend, after all – whatever should happen; and there were things that, even in that hampered character, she couldn't allow him to suppose. It was a queer business now, in fact, for her to ask herself if she, Maud Blandy, had produced on any sane human sense an effect of flirtation.

She saw herself in this possibility as in some grotesque reflector, a full-length looking-glass of the inferior quality that deforms and discolours. It made her, as a flirt, a figure for frank derision, and she entertained, honest girl, none of the self-pity that would have spared her a shade of this sharpened consciousness, have taken an inch from facial proportion where it would have been missed with advantage, or added one in such other quarters as would have welcomed the gift. She might have counted the hairs of her head, for any wish she could have achieved to remain vague about them, just as she might have rehearsed, disheartened, postures of grace, for any dream she could compass of having ever accidentally struck one. Void, in short, of a personal illusion, exempt with an exemption which left her not less helplessly aware of where her hats and skirts and shoes failed, than of where her nose and mouth and complexion, and, above all, where her poor figure, without a scrap of drawing, did, she blushed to bethink herself that she might have affected her young man as really bragging of a conquest. Her *other* young man's pursuit of her, what was it but rank greed – not in the least for her person, but for the connection of which he had formed so preposterous a view? She was ready now to say to herself that she had swaggered to Bight for the joke – odd indeed though the wish to undeceive him at the moment when he would have been more welcome than ever to think what he liked. The only thing she wished him not to think, as she believed, was that she thought Mortimer Marshal thought her – or anyone on earth thought her – intrinsically charming. She didn't want to put to him 'Do you suppose I suppose that if it came to the point—?' her reasons for such avoidance being easily conceivable. He was not to suppose that, in any such quarter, she struck herself as either casting a spell or submitting to one; only, while their crisis lasted, rectifications were scarce in order. She couldn't remind him even, without a mistake, that she had but wished to worry him; because in the first place that suggested again a pretension in her (so at variance with the image in the mirror) to put forth arts – suggested possibly even that she used similar ones when she lunched, in bristling flats, with the pushing; and because in the second it would have seemed a sort of challenge to him to renew his appeal.

Then, further and most of all, she had a doubt which by itself would have made her wary, as it distinctly, in her present suspended state, made her uncomfortable; she was haunted by the after-sense of having perhaps been fatuous. A spice of conviction, in respect to what was open to her, an element of elation, in her talk to Bight about Marshal, had there not, after all, been? Hadn't she a little liked to think the wretched man *could* cling to her? and hadn't she also a little, for herself, filled out the future, in fancy, with the picture of the droll relation? She had seen it as droll, evidently; but had she seen it as impossible, unthinkable? It had become unthinkable now, and she was not wholly unconscious of how the change had worked. Such workings were queer – but there they were; the foolish man had become odious to her precisely *because* she was hardening her face for Bight. The latter was no foolish man, but this it was that made it the more a pity he should have placed the impassable between them. That was what, as the days went on, she felt herself take in. It was there, the impassable – she couldn't lucidly have said why, couldn't have explained the thing on the real scale of the wrong her comrade had done. It was a wrong, it was a wrong – she couldn't somehow get out of that; which was a proof, no doubt, that she confusedly tried. The author of *Corisanda* was sacrificed in the effort – for ourselves it may come to that. Great to poor Maud Blandy as well, for that matter, great, yet also attaching, were the obscurity and ambiguity in which some impulses lived and moved – the rich gloom of their combinations, contradictions, inconsistencies, surprises. It rested her verily a little from her straightness – the line of a character, she felt, markedly like the line of the Edgware Road and of Maida Vale – that she *could* be queerly inconsistent, and inconsistent in the hustling Strand, where, if anywhere, you had, under pain of hoofs and wheels, to decide whether or no you would cross. She had moments, before shop-windows, into which she looked without seeing, when all the unuttered came over her. She had once told her friend that she pitied everyone, and at these moments, in sharp unrest, she pitied Bight for their tension, in which nothing was relaxed.

It was all too mixed and too strange – each of them in a different corner with a different impossibility. There was her own, in far Kilburnia; and there was her friend's, everywhere – for where didn't he go? and there was Mrs Chorner's, on the very edge of Park 'Line', in spite of all petticoats and marble baths; and there was Beadel-Muffet's, the wretched man, God only knew where — which was what made the whole show supremely incoherent: he ready to give his head, if, as seemed so unlikely, he still *had* a head, to steal into cover and keep under, out of the glare; he having scoured Europe, it might so well be guessed, for some hole in which the Papers wouldn't find him out, and then having — what else was there by this time to presume? — died, in the hole, as the only way not to see, to hear, to know, let alone *be* known, heard, seen. Finally, while he lay there relieved by the only relief, here was poor Mortimer Marshall, undeterred, undismayed, unperceiving, so hungry to be paragraphed in something like the same fashion and published on something like the same scale, that, for the very blindness of it, he couldn't read the lesson that was in the air, and scrambled, to his utmost, toward the boat itself that ferried the warning ghost. Just *that*, beyond everything, was the incoherence that made for rather dismal farce, and on which Bight had put his finger in naming the author of *Corisanda* as a candidate, in turn, for the comic, the tragic vacancy. It was a wonderful moment for such an ideal, and the sight was not really to pass from her till she had seen the whole of the wonder. A fortnight had elapsed since the night of Beadel's disappearance, and the conditions attending the afternoon performances of the Finnish drama had in some degree reproduced themselves — to the extent, that is, of the place, the time and several of the actors involved; the audience, for reasons traceable, being differently composed. A lady of 'high social position', desirous still further to elevate that character by the obvious aid of the theatre, had engaged a playhouse for a series of occasions on which she was to affront in person whatever volume of attention she might succeed in collecting. Her success had not immediately been great, and by the third or the fourth day the public consciousness was so markedly astray that the means taken to recover it penetrated, in the shape of a complimentary ticket, even to our young woman. Maud had communicated with Bight, who could be sure of a ticket, proposing to him that they should go together and offering to await him in the porch of the theatre. He joined her there, but with so queer a face – for her subtlety – that she paused before him, previous to their going in, with a straight 'You *know* something!'

'About that rank idiot?' He shook his head, looking kind enough; but it didn't make him, she felt, more natural. 'My dear, it's all beyond me.'

'I mean,' she said with a shade of uncertainty, 'about poor dear Beadel.'

'So do I. So does everyone. No one now, at any moment, means anything about anyone else. But I've lost intellectual control – of the extraordinary case. I flattered myself I still had a certain amount. But the situation at last escapes me. I break down. Non comprenny? I give it up.'

She continued to look at him hard. 'Then what's the matter with you?'

'Why, just *that*, probably – that I feel like a clever man

"done", and that your tone with me adds to the feeling. Or, putting it otherwise, it's perhaps only just one of the ways in which I'm so interesting; that, with the life we lead and the age we live in, there's *always* something the matter with me – there can't help being: some rage, some disgust, some fresh amazement against which one hasn't, for all one's experience, been proof. That sense – of having been sold again – produces emotions that may well, on occasion, be reflected in the countenance. There you are.'

Well, he might say that, 'There you are,' as often as he liked without, at the pass they had come to, making her in the least see where she was. She was only just where she stood, a little apart in the lobby, listening to his words, which she found eminently characteristic of him, struck with an odd impression of his talking against time, and, most of all, tormented to recognize that she could fairly do nothing better, at such a moment, than feel he was awfully nice. The moment – that of his most blandly (she would have said in the case of another most impudently) failing, all round, to satisfy her – was appropriate only to some emotion consonant with her dignity. It was all crowded and covered, hustled and interrupted now; but what really happened in this brief passage, and with her finding no words to reply to him, was that dignity quite appeared to collapse and drop from her, to sink to the floor, under the feet of people visibly bristling with 'paper', where the young man's extravagant offer of an arm, to put an end and help her in, had the effect of an invitation to leave it lying to be trampled on.

Within, once seated, they kept their places through two intervals, but at the end of the third act – there were to be no less than five – they fell in with a movement that carried half the audience to the outer air. Howard Bight desired to smoke, and Maud offered to accompany him, for the purpose, to the portico, where, somehow, for both of them, the sense was immediately strong that *this*, the squalid Strand, damp yet incandescent, ugly yet eloquent, familiar yet fresh, was life, palpable, ponderable, possible, much more than the stuff, neither scenic nor cosmic, they had quitted. The difference came to them, from the street, in a most mild blast, which they simply took in, at first, in a long draught, as more amusing than their play, and which, for the moment, kept them conscious of the voices of the air as of something mixed and vague. The next thing, of course, however, was that they heard the hoarse newsmen, though with the special sense of the sound not standing out – which, so far as it did come, made them exchange a look. There was no hawker just then within call.

'What are they crying?'

'Blessed if I care!' Bight said while he got his light – which he had but just done when they saw themselves closely approached. The Papers had come into sight in the form of a small boy bawling the 'Winner' of something, and at the same moment they recognized their reprieve they recognized also the presence of Mortimer Marshal.

He had no shame about it. 'I fully believed I should find you.'

'But you haven't been,' Bight asked, 'inside?'

'Not at today's performance – I only just thought I'd pass. But at each of the others,' Mortimer Marshal confessed.

'Oh, you're a devotee,' said Bight, whose reception of the poor man contended, for Maud's attention, with this extravagance of the poor man's own importunity. Their friend had sat through the piece three times on the chance of her being there for one or other of the acts, and if he had given that up in discouragement he still hovered and waited. Who now, moreover, was to say he wasn't rewarded? To find her companion as well as at last to find herself gave the reward a character that it took, somehow, for her eye, the whole of this misguided person's curiously large and flat, but distinctly bland, sweet, solicitous countenance to express. It came over the girl with horror that here was a material object – the incandescence, on the edge of the street, didn't spare it – which she had had perverse moments of seeing fixed before her for life. She asked herself, in this agitation, what she would have likened it to; more than anything perhaps to a large clean china plate, with a neat 'pattern', suspended, to the exposure of hapless heads, from the centre of the domestic ceiling. Truly she was, as by the education of the strain undergone, learning something every hour – it seemed so to be the case that a strain enlarged the mind, formed the taste, enriched, even, the imagination. Yet in spite of this last fact, it must be added, she continued rather mystified by the actual pitch of her comrade's manner, Bight really behaving as if he enjoyed their visitor's 'note'. He treated him so decently, as they said, that he might suddenly have taken to liking his company; which was an odd appearance till Maud understood it – whereupon it became for her a slightly sinister one. For the effect of the honest gentleman, she by that time saw, was to make her friend nervous and vicious, and the form taken by his irritation was just this dangerous candour, which encouraged the candour of the victim. She had for the latter a residuum of pity, whereas Bight, she felt, had none, and she didn't want him, the poor man, absolutely to pay with his life.

It was clear, however, within a few minutes, that this was what he was bent on doing, and she found herself helpless before his smug insistence. She had taken his measure; he was *made* incorrigibly to try, irredeemably to fail – to be, in short, eternally defeated and eternally unaware. He wouldn't rage – he *couldn't*, for the citadel might, in that case, have been carried by his assault; he would only spend his life in walking round and round it, asking everyone he met how in the name of goodness one did get in. And everyone would make a fool of him – though no one so much as her companion now – and everything would fall from him but the perfection of his temper, of his tailor, of his manners, of his mediocrity. He evidently rejoiced at the happy chance which had presented him again to Bight, and he lost as little time as possible in proposing, the play ended, an adjournment again to tea. The spirit of malice in her comrade, now inordinately excited, met this suggestion with an amendment that fairly made her anxious; Bight threw out, in a word, the idea that he himself surely, this time, should entertain Mr Marshal.

'Only I'm afraid I can take you but to a small pot-house that we poor journalists haunt.'

'They're just the places I delight in – it would be of an extraordinary interest. I sometimes venture into them – feeling awfully strange and wondering, I do assure you, who people are. But to go there with *you*—!' And he looked from Bight to Maud and from Maud back again with such abysses of appreciation that she knew him as lost indeed.

# VI

IT WAS DEMONIC of Bight, who immediately answered that he would tell him with pleasure who everyone was, and she felt this the more when her friend, making light of the rest of the entertainment they had quitted, advised their sacrificing it and proceeding to the other scene. He was really too eager for his victim – she wondered what he wanted to do with him. He could only play him at the most a practical joke – invent appetizing identities, once they were at table, for the dull consumers around. No one, at the place they most frequented, had an identity in the least appetizing, no one was anyone or anything. It was apparently of the essence of existence on such terms – the terms, at any rate, to which *she* was reduced – that people comprised in it couldn't even minister to each other's curiosity, let alone to envy or awe. She would have wished therefore, for their pursuer, to intervene a little, to warn him against beguilement; but they had moved together along the Strand and then out of it, up a near cross street, without her opening her mouth. Bight, as she felt, was acting to prevent this; his easy talk redoubled, and he led his lamb to the shambles. The talk had jumped to poor Beadel – her friend had startled her by causing it, almost with violence, at a given moment, to take that direction, and he thus quite sufficiently stayed her speech. The people she lived with mightn't make you curious, but there was of course always a sharp exception for *him*. She kept still, in fine, with the wonder of what he wanted; though indeed she might, in the presence of their guest's response, have felt he was already getting it. He was getting, that is – and *she* was, into the bargain – the fullest illustration of the ravage of a passion; so sublimely Marshal rose to the proposition, infernally thrown off, that, in whatever queer box or tight place Beadel might have found himself, it was something, after all, to have so powerfully interested the public. The insidious artless way in which Bight made his point! – 'I don't know that I've ever known the public (and I watch it, as in my trade we have to, day and night) *so* consummately interested.' They had that phenomenon – the present consummate interest – well before them while they sat at their homely meal, served with accessories so different from those of the sweet Chippendale (another chord on which the young man played with just the right effect!), and it would have been hard to say if the guest were, for the first moments, more under the spell of the marvellous 'hold' on the town achieved by the great absentee, or of that of the delicious coarse table-cloth, the extraordinary form of the salt-cellars, and the fact that he had within range of sight, at the other end of the room, in the person of the little quiet man with blue spectacles and an obvious wig, the greatest authority in London about the inner life of the criminal classes. Beadel, none the less, came up again and stayed up – would clearly so have been *kept* up, had there been need, by their host, that the girl couldn't at last fail to see how much it was for herself that his intention worked. What *was* it, all the same – since it couldn't be anything so simple as to expose their hapless visitor? What had she to learn about *him*? – especially at the hour of seeing what there was still to learn about Bight. She ended by deciding – for his appearance bore her out – that his explosion was but the form taken by an inward fever. The fever, on this theory, was the result of the final pang of responsibility. The mystery of Beadel had grown too dark to be borne – which they would presently feel; and he was meanwhile in the phase of bluffing it off, precisely because it was to overwhelm him.

'And do you mean you too would pay with your *life*?' He put the question, agreeably, across the table to his guest; agreeably of course in spite of his eye's dry glitter.

His guest's expression, at this, fairly became beautiful. 'Well, it's an awfully nice point. Certainly one would like to *feel* the great murmur surrounding one's name, to *be* there, more or less, so as not to lose the sense of it, and as I really think, you know, the pleasure; the great city, the great empire, the world itself for the moment, hanging literally on one's personality and giving a start, in its suspense, whenever one is mentioned. Big sensation, you know, that,' Mr Marshal pleadingly smiled, 'and of course if one were dead one wouldn't enjoy it. One would have to come to life for that.'

'Naturally,' Bight rejoined – 'only that's what the dead don't do. You can't eat your cake and have it. The question is,' he good-naturedly explained, 'whether you'd be willing, for the certitude of the great murmur you speak of, to part with your life under circumstances of extraordinary mystery.'

His guest earnestly fixed it. 'Whether *I* would be willing?'

'Mr Marshal wonders,' Maud said to Bight, 'if you are, as a person interested in his reputation, definitely proposing to him some such possibility.'

He looked at her, on this, with mild, round eyes, and she felt, wonderfully, that he didn't quite see her as joking. He smiled – he always smiled, but his anxiety showed, and he turned it again to their companion. 'You mean – a – the knowing how it might be *going* to be felt?'

'Well, yes – call it that. The consciousness of what one's unexplained extinction – given, to start with, one's high position – would mean, wouldn't be able to *help* meaning, for millions and millions of people. The point is – and I admit it's, as you call it, a "nice" one – if you can think of the impression so made as worth the purchase. *Naturally*, naturally, there's but the impression you make. You don't receive any. You can't. You've only your confidence – so far as that's an impression.

Oh, it *is* indeed a nice point; and I only put it to you,' Bight wound up, 'because, you know, you do like to be recognized.'

Mr Marshal was bewildered, but he was not so bewildered as not to be able, a trifle coyly, but still quite bravely, to confess to that. Maud, with her eyes on her friend, found herself thinking of him as of some plump, innocent animal, more or less of the pink-eyed rabbit or sleek guinea-pig order, involved in the slow spell of a serpent of shining scales. Bight's scales, truly, had never so shone as this evening, and he used to admiration – which was just a part of the lustre – the right shade of gravity. He was neither so light as to fail of the air of an attractive offer, nor yet so earnest as to betray a gibe. He might conceivably have been, as an undertaker of improvements in defective notorieties, placing before his guest a practical scheme. It was really quite as if he were ready to guarantee the 'murmur' if Mr Marshal was ready to pay the price. And the price wouldn't of course be only Mr Marshal's existence. All this, at least, if Mr Marshal felt moved to take it so. The prodigious thing, next, was that Mr Marshal *was* so moved – though, clearly, as was to be expected, with important qualifications. 'Do you really mean,' he asked, 'that one would excite *this* delightful interest?'

'You allude to the charged state of the air on the subject of Beadel?' Bight considered, looking volumes. 'It would depend a good deal upon who one *is*.'

He turned, Mr Marshal, again to Maud Blandy, and his eyes seemed to suggest to her that she should put his question for him. They forgave her, she judged, for having so oddly forsaken him, but they appealed to her now not to leave him to struggle alone. Her own difficulty was, however, meanwhile, that she feared to serve him as he suggested without too much, by way of return, turning his case to the comic; whereby she only looked at him hard and let him revert to their friend. 'Oh,' he said, with a rich wistfulness from which the comic was not absent, 'of course everyone can't pretend to be Beadel.'

'Perfectly. But we're speaking, after all, of those who do count.'

There was quite a hush, for the minute, while the poor man faltered. 'Should you say that *I* – in any appreciable way – count?'

Howard Bight distilled honey. 'Isn't it a little a question of how much we should find you *did*, or, for that matter, might, as it were, be made to, in the event of a real catastrophe?'

Mr Marshal turned pale, yet he met it too with sweetness. 'I like the way –' and he had a glance for Maud – 'you talk of catastrophes!'

His host did the comment justice. 'Oh, it's only because, you see, we're so peculiarly in the presence of one. Beadel shows so tremendously what a catastrophe does for the right person. His absence, you may say, doubles, quintuples, his presence.'

'I see, I see!' Mr Marshal was all there. 'It's awfully interesting to be so present. And yet it's rather dreadful to be so absent.' It had set him fairly musing; for couldn't the opposites be reconciled? 'If he *is*,' he threw out, 'absent—!'

'Why, he's absent, of course,' said Bight, 'if he's dead.'

'And really dead is what you believe him to be?'

He breathed it with a strange break, as from a mind too full. It was on the one hand a grim vision for his own case, but was on the other a kind of clearance of the field. With Beadel out of the way his own case could live, and he was obviously thinking what it might be to be as dead as that and yet as much alive. What his demand first did, at any rate, was to make Howard Bight look straight at Maud. Her own look met him, but she asked nothing now. She felt him somehow fathomless, and his practice with their infatuated guest created a new suspense. He might indeed have been looking at her to learn how to reply, but even were this the case she had still nothing to answer. So in a moment he had spoken without her. 'I've quite given him up.'

It sank into Marshal, after which it produced something. 'He ought then to come back. I mean,' he explained, 'to see for himself – to *have* the impression.'

'Of the noise he has made? Yes –' Bight weighed it – 'that would be the ideal.'

'And it would, if one must call it "noise",' Marshal limpidly pursued, 'make – a – more.'

'Oh, but if you *can't*!'

'Can't, you mean, through having already made so much, add to the quantity?'

'Can't –' Bight was a wee bit sharp – 'come back, confound it, at all. Can't return from the dead!'

Poor Marshal had to take it. 'No – not if you *are* dead.'

'Well, that's what we're talking about.'

Maud, at this, for pity, held out a perch. 'Mr Marshal, I think, is talking a little on the basis of the possibility of your not being!' He threw her an instant glance of gratitude, and it gave her a push. 'So long as you're not quite too utterly, you *can* come back.'

'Oh,' said Bight, 'in time for the fuss?'

'Before –' Marshal met it – 'the interest has subsided. It naturally then *wouldn't* – would it? – subside!'

'No,' Bight granted; 'not if it hadn't, through wearing out – I mean your being lost too long – already died out.'

'Oh, of course,' his guest agreed, 'you mustn't be lost *too* long.' A vista had plainly opened to him, and the subject led him on. He had, before its extent, another pause. 'About how long, do you think—?'

Well, Bight *had* to think. 'I should say Beadel had rather overdone it.'

The poor gentleman stared. 'But if he can't help himself—?'

Bight gave a laugh. 'Yes; but in case he could.'

Maud again intervened, and, as her question was for their host, Marshal was all attention. 'Do you consider Beadel has overdone it?'

Well, once more, it took consideration. The issue of Bight's, however, was not of the clearest. 'I don't think we can tell unless he *were* to. I don't think that, without seeing it, and judging by the special case, one can quite know how it would be taken. He might, on the one side, have spoiled, so to speak, his market; and he might, on the other, have scored as never before.'

'It might be,' Maud threw in, 'just the making of him.'

'Surely –' Marshal glowed – 'there's just that chance.'

'What a pity then,' Bight laughed, 'that there isn't someone to take it! For the light it would throw, I mean, on the laws – so mysterious, so curious, so interesting – that govern the great currents of public attention. They're not wholly whimsical – wayward and wild; they have their strange logic, their obscure reason – if one could only get *at* it! The man who does, you see – and who can keep his discovery to himself! – will make his everlasting fortune, as well, no doubt, as that of a few others. It's *our* branch, *our* preoccupation, in fact, Miss Blandy's and mine – this pursuit of the incalculable, this study, to that end, of the great forces of publicity. Only, of course, it must be remembered,' Bight went on, 'that in the case we're speaking of – the man disappearing as Beadel has now disappeared, and supplanting for the time every other topic – must have someone on the spot for him, to keep the pot boiling, someone acting, with real intelligence, in his interest. I mean if he's to get the good of it when he does turn up. It would never do, you see, that *that* should be flat!'

'Oh no, not *flat*, never!' Marshal quailed at the thought. Held as in a vice by his host's high lucidity, he exhaled his interest at every pore. 'It wouldn't be flat for Beadel, would it? – I mean if he *were* to come.'

'Not much! It wouldn't be flat for Beadel – I think I can undertake.' And Bight undertook so well that he threw himself back in his chair with his thumbs in the armholes of his waistcoat and his head very much up. 'The only thing is that for poor Beadel it's a luxury, so to speak, wasted – and so dreadfully, upon my word, that one quite regrets there's no one to step in.'

'To step in?' His visitor hung upon his lips.

'To do the thing better, so to speak – to do it right; to – having raised the whirlwind – really *ride* the storm. To seize the psychological hour.'

Marshal met it, yet he wondered. 'You speak of the reappearance? I see. But the man of the reappearance would have, wouldn't he? – or perhaps I don't follow? – to be the same as the man of the *dis*appearance. It wouldn't do as well – would it? – for *somebody else* to turn up?'

Bight considered him with attention – as if there were fine possibilities. 'No; unless such a person should turn up, say – well, with news of him.'

'But what news?'

'With lights – the more lurid the better – *on* the darkness. With the facts, don't you see, *of* the disappearance.'

Marshal, on his side, threw himself back. 'But he'd have to know them!'

'Oh,' said Bight, with prompt portentousness, 'that could be managed.'

It was too much, by this time, for his victim, who simply turned on Maud a dilated eye and a flushed cheek. 'Mr Marshal,' it made her say – 'Mr Marshal would like to turn up.'

Her hand was on the table, and the effect of her words,

combined with this, was to cause him, before responsive speech could come, to cover it respectfully but expressively with his own. 'Do you mean,' he panted to Bight, 'that you have, amid the general collapse of speculation, facts to give?'

'I've always facts to give.'

It begot in the poor man a large hot smile. 'But – how shall I say? – authentic, or as I believe you clever people say, "inspired" ones?'

'If I should undertake such a case as we're supposing, I would of course by that circumstance undertake that my facts should be – well, worthy of it. I would take,' Bight on his own part modestly smiled, 'pains with them.'

It finished the business. 'Would you take pains for *me*?'

Bight looked at him now hard. 'Would you like to appear?'

'Oh, "appear"!' Marshal weakly murmured.

'Is it, Mr Marshal, a real proposal? I mean are you prepared—?'

Wonderment sat in his eyes – an anguish of doubt and desire. 'But wouldn't you prepare me—?'

'Would you prepare *me* – that's the point,' Bight laughed – '*to* prepare you?'

There was a minute's mutual gaze, but Marshal took it in. 'I don't know what you're making me say; I don't know what you're making me *feel*. When one is with people so up in these things –' and he turned to his companions, alternately, a look as of conscious doom lighted with suspicion, a look that was like a cry for mercy – 'one feels a little as if one ought to be saved from one's self. For I daresay one's foolish enough with one's poor little wish—'

'The little wish, my dear sir' – Bight took him up – 'to stand out in the world! Your wish is the wish of all high spirits.'

'It's dear of you to say it.' Mr Marshal was all response. 'I shouldn't want, even if it *were* weak or vain, to have lived wholly unknown. And if what you ask is whether I understand you to speak, as it were, professionally—'

'You *do* understand me?' Bight pushed back his chair.

'Oh, but so well! – when I've already seen what you can do. I need scarcely say, that having seen it, I shan't bargain.'

'Ah, then, *I* shall,' Bight smiled. 'I mean with the Papers. It must be half profits.'

'"Profits"?' His guest was vague.

'Our friend,' Maud explained to Bight, 'simply wants the position.'

Bight threw her a look. 'Ah, he must take what I give him.'

'But what you give me,' their friend handsomely contended, '*is* the position.'

'Yes; but the terms that I shall get! I don't produce you, of course,' Bight went on, 'till I've prepared you. But when I do produce you it will be as a value.'

'You'll get so much for me?' the poor gentleman quavered.

'I shall be able to get, I think, anything I ask. So we divide.' And Bight jumped up.

Marshal did the same, and, while, with his hands on the back of his chair, he steadied himself from the vertiginous view, they faced each other across the table. 'Oh, it's too wonderful!'

'You're not afraid?'

He looked at a card on the wall, framed, suspended and marked with the word 'Soups'. He looked at Maud, who had not moved. 'I don't know; I may be; I must feel. What I *should* fear,' he added, 'would be his coming back.'

'Beadel's? Yes, that would dish you. But since he can't—!'

'I place myself,' said Mortimer Marshal, 'in your hands.'

Maud Blandy still hadn't moved; she stared before her at the cloth. A small sharp sound, unheard, she saw, by the others, had reached her from the street, and with her mind instinctively catching at it, she waited, dissimulating a little, for its repetition or its effect. It was the howl of the Strand, it was news of the absent, and it would have a bearing. She had a hesitation, for she winced even now with the sense of Marshal's intensest look at her. He couldn't be saved from himself, but he might be, still, from Bight; though it hung of course, her chance to warn him, on what the news would be. She thought with concentration, while her friends unhooked their overcoats, and by the time these garments were donned she was on her feet. Then she spoke. 'I don't want you to be "dished".'

He allowed for her alarm. 'But how *can* I be?'

'Something has come.'

'Something—?' The men had both spoken.

They had stopped where they stood; she again caught the sound. 'Listen! They're crying.'

They waited then, and it came – came, of a sudden, with a burst and as if passing the place. A hawker, outside, with his 'extra', called by someone and hurrying, bawled it as he moved. 'Death of Beadel-Muffet – Extraordinary News!'

They all gasped, and Maud, with her eyes on Bight, saw him, to her satisfaction at first, turn pale. But his guest drank it in. 'If it's true then?' – Marshal triumphed at her – 'I'm *not* dished.'

But she only looked hard at Bight, who struck her as having, at the sound, fallen to pieces, and as having above all, on the instant, turned cold for his worried game. 'Is it true?' she austerely asked.

His white face answered. 'It's true.'

## VII

THE FIRST THING, on the part of our friends – after each interlocutor, producing a penny, had plunged into the unfolded 'Latest' – was this very evidence of their dispensing with their companion's further attendance on their agitated state, and all the more that Bight was to have still, in spite of agitation, his function with him to accomplish: a result much assisted by the insufflation of wind into Mr Marshal's sails constituted by the fact before them. With Beadel publicly dead this gentleman's opportunity, on the terms just arranged, opened out; it was quite as if they had seen him, then and there, step, with a kind of spiritual splash, into the empty seat of the boat so launched, scarcely even taking time to master the essentials before he gave himself to the breeze. The essentials indeed he was, by their understanding, to receive in full from Bight at their earliest leisure; but nothing could so vividly have marked his confidence in the young man as the promptness with which he appeared now ready to leave him to his inspiration. The news moreover, as yet, was the rich, grim fact – a sharp flare from an Agency, lighting into blood-colour the locked room, finally, with the police present, forced open, of the first hotel at Frankfort-on-the-Oder; but there was enough of it, clearly, to bear scrutiny, the scrutiny represented in our young couple by the act of perusal prolonged, intensified, repeated, so repeated that it was exactly perhaps with this suggestion of doubt that poor Mr Marshal had even also a little lost patience. He vanished, at any rate, while his supporters, still planted in the side-street into which they had lately issued, stood extinguished, as to any facial communion, behind the array of printed columns. It was only after he had gone that, whether aware or not, the other lowered, on either side, the absorbing page and knew that their eyes had met. A remarkable thing, for Maud Blandy, then happened, a thing quite as remarkable at least as poor Beadel's suicide, which we recall her having so considerably discounted.

Present as they thus were at the tragedy, present in far Frankfort just where they stood, by the door of their stale pot-house and in the thick of London air, the logic of her situation, she was sharply conscious, would have been an immediate rupture with Bight. He was scared at what he had done – he looked his scare so straight out at her that she might almost have seen in it the dismay of his question of how far his responsibility, given the facts, might, if pried into, be held – and not only at the judgement-seat of mere morals – to reach. The dismay was to that degree illuminating that she had had from him no such avowal of responsibility as this amounted to, and the limit to any laxity on her own side had therefore not been set for her with any such sharpness. It put her at last in the right, his scare – quite richly in the right; and as that was naturally but where she had waited to find herself, everything that now silently passed between them had the merit, if it had none other, of simplifying. Their hour had struck, the hour after which she was definitely not to have forgiven him. Yet what occurred, as I say, was that, if, at the end of five minutes, she had moved much further, it proved to be, in spite of logic, not in the sense away from him, but in the sense nearer. He showed to her, at these strange moments, as blood-stained and literally hunted; the yell of the hawkers, repeated and echoing round them, was like a cry for his life; and there was in particular a minute during which, gazing down into the roused Strand, all equipped both with mob and with constables, she asked herself whether she had best get off with him through the crowd, where they would be least noticed, or get him away through quiet Covent Garden, empty at that hour, but with policemen to watch a furtive couple, and with the news, more bawled at their heels in the stillness, acquiring the sound of the very voice of justice. It was this last sudden terror that presently determined her, and determined with it an impulse of protection that had somehow to do with pity without having to do with tenderness. It settled, at all events, the question of leaving him; she couldn't leave him there and so; she must see at least what would have come of his own sense of the shock.

The way he took it, the shock, gave her afresh the measure of how perversely he had played with Marshal – of how he had tried so, on the very edge of his predicament, to cheat his fears and beguile his want of ease. He had insisted to his victim on the truth he had now to reckon with, but had insisted only because he didn't believe it. Beadel, by that attitude, was but lying low; so that he would have no promise really to redeem. At present he had one, indeed, and Maud could ask herself if the redemption of it, with the leading of their wretched friend a further fantastic dance, would be what he depended on to drug the pain of remorse. By the time she had covered as much ground as this, however, she had also, standing before him, taken his special out of his hand and, folding it up carefully with her own and smoothing it down, packed the two together into such a small tight ball as she might toss to a distance without the air, which she dreaded, of having, by any looser proceeding, disowned or evaded the news. Howard Bight, helpless and passive, putting on the matter no governed face, let her do with him as she liked, let her, for the first time in their acquaintance, draw his hand into her arm as if he were an invalid or as if she were a snare. She took with him, thus guided and sustained, their second plunge; led him, with decision, straight to where their shock was shared and amplified, pushed her way, guarding him, across the dense thoroughfare and through the great westward current which fairly seemed to meet and challenge them, and then, by reaching Waterloo Bridge with him and descending the granite steps, set him down at last on the Embankment. It was a fact, none the less, that she had in her eyes, all the while, and too strangely for speech, the vision of the scene in the little German city: the smashed door, the exposed horror, the wondering, insensible group, the English gentleman, in the disordered room, driven to bay among the scattered personal objects that only too floridly announced and emblazoned him, and several of which the Papers were already naming — the poor English gentleman, hunted and hiding, done to death by the thing he yet, for so long, always *would* have, and stretched on the floor with his beautiful little revolver still in his hand and the effusion of his blood, from a wound taken, with rare resolution, full in the face, extraordinary and dreadful.

She went on with her friend, eastward and beside the river, and it was as if they both, for that matter, had, in their silence, the dire material vision. Maud Blandy, however, presently stopped short — one of the connections of the picture so brought her to a stand. It had come over her, with a force she couldn't check, that the catastrophe itself would have been, with all the unfathomed that yet clung to it, just the thing for her companion's professional hand; so that, queerly but absolutely, while she looked at him again in reprobation and pity, it was as much as she could do not to feel it for him as something missed, not to wish he might have been there to snatch his chance, and not, above all, to betray to him this reflection. It had really risen to her lips – 'Why aren't *you*, old man, on the spot?' and indeed the question, had it broken forth, might well have sounded as a provocation to him to start without delay. Such was the effect, in poor Maud, for the moment, of the habit, so confirmed in her, of seeing time marked only by the dial of the Papers. She had admired in Bight the true journalist that she herself was so clearly not – though it was also not what she had *most* admired in him; and she might have felt, at this instant, the charm of putting true journalism to the proof. She might have been on the point of saying: 'Real business, you know, would be for you to start *now*, just as you are, before anyone else, sure as you can so easily be of having the pull'; and she might, after a moment, while they paused, have been looking back, through the river-mist, for a sign of the hour, at the blurred face of Big Ben. That she grazed this danger yet avoided it was partly the result in truth of her seeing for herself quickly enough that the last thing Bight could just then have thought of, even under provocation of the most positive order, was the chance thus failing him, or the train, the boat, the advantage, that the true journalist wouldn't have missed. He quite, under her eyes, while they stood together, ceased to be the true journalist; she saw him, as she felt, put off the character as definitely as she might have seen him remove his coat, his hat, or the contents of his pockets, in order to lay them on the parapet before jumping into the river. Wonderful was the difference that this transformation, marked by no word and supported by no sign, made in the man she had hitherto known. Nothing, again, could have so expressed for her his continued inward dismay. It was as if, for that matter, she couldn't have asked him a question without adding to it; and she didn't wish to add to it, since she was by this time more fully aware that she wished to be generous. When she at last uttered other words it, was precisely so that she mightn't press him.

'I think of *her* – poor thing: that's what it makes me do. I think of her there at this moment – just out of the "Line" – with this stuff shrieked at her windows.' With which, having so at once contained and relieved herself, she caused him to walk on.

'Are you talking of Mrs Chorner?' he after a moment asked. And then, when he had had her quick 'Of course – of who else?' he said what she didn't expect. 'Naturally one thinks of her. But she has herself to blame. I mean she drove him—' What he meant, however, Bight suddenly dropped, taken as he was with another idea, which had brought them the next minute to a halt. 'Mightn't you, by the way, see her?'

'See her *now*—?'

'"Now" or never – for the good of it. Now's just your time.'

'But how can it be hers, in the very midst—?'

'*Because* it's in the very midst. She'll tell you things tonight that she'll never tell again. Tonight she'll be great.'

Maud gaped almost wildly. 'You want me, at such an hour, to *call*—?'

'And send up your card with the word – oh, of course the right one! – on it.'

'What do you suggest,' Maud asked, 'as the right one?'

'Well, "The world *wants* you" – that usually does. I've seldom known it, even in deeper distress than is, after all, here supposable, to fail. Try it, at any rate.'

The girl, strangely touched, intensely wondered. 'Demand of her, you mean, to let me explain for her?'

'There you are. You catch on. Write *that* – if you like – "Let me explain." She'll want to explain.'

Maud wondered at him more – he had somehow so turned the tables on her. 'But she doesn't. It's exactly *what* she doesn't; she never *has*. And that he, poor wretch, was always wanting to—'

'Was precisely what made her hold off? I grant it.' He had waked up. 'But that was before she had killed him. Trust me, she'll chatter now.'

This, for his companion, simply forced it out. 'It wasn't *she* who killed him. That, my dear, you know.'

'You mean it was I who did? Well then, my child, interview *me*.' And, with his hands in his pockets and his idea apparently genuine, he smiled at her, by the grey river and under the high lamps, with an effect strange and suggestive. '*That* would be a go!'

'You mean –' she jumped at it – 'you'll tell me what you know?'

'Yes, and even what I've done! But – if you'll take it so – for the Papers. Oh, for the Papers only!'

She stared. 'You mean you want me to get it in—?'

'I don't "want" you to do anything, but I'm ready to help you, ready to get it in for you, like a shot, myself, if it's a thing you yourself want.'

'A thing I want – to give you away?'

'Oh,' he laughed, 'I'm just now worth giving! You'd really do it, you know. And, to help you, here I am. It *would* be for you – only judge! – a leg up.'

It would indeed, she really saw; somehow, on the spot, she believed it. But his surrender made her tremble. It wasn't a joke – she *could* give him away; or rather she could sell him for money. Money, thus, was what he offered her, or the value of money, which was the same; it was what he wanted her to have. She was conscious already, however, that she could have it only as he offered it, and she said therefore, but half-heartedly, 'I'll keep your secret.'

He looked at her more gravely. 'Ah, as a secret I can't give it.' Then he hesitated. 'I'll get you a hundred pounds for it.'

'Why don't you,' she asked, 'get them for yourself?'

'Because I don't care for myself. I care only for you.'

She waited again. 'You mean for my taking you?' And then as he but looked at her: 'How should I take you if I had dealt with you that way?'

'What do I lose by it,' he said, 'if, by our understanding of the other day, since things have so turned out, you're not to take me at all? So, at least, on my proposal, you get something else.'

'And what,' Maud returned, 'do you get?'

'I *don't* "get"; I lose. I *have* lost. So I don't matter.' The eyes with which she covered him at this might have signified either that he didn't satisfy her or that his last word – *as* his word – rather imposed itself. Whether or no, at all events, she decided that he still did matter. She presently moved again, and they walked some minutes more. He had made her tremble, and she continued to tremble. So unlike anything that had ever come to her was, if seriously viewed, his proposal. The quality of it, while she walked, grew intenser with each step. It struck her as, when one came to look at it, unlike any offer any man could ever have made or any woman ever have received; and it began accordingly, on the instant, to affect her as almost inconceivably romantic, absolutely, in a manner, and quite out of the blue, *dramatic*; immeasurably more so, for example, than the sort of thing she had come out to hear in the afternoon – the sort of thing that was already so far away. If he was joking it was poor, but if he was serious it was, properly, sublime. And he wasn't joking. He was, however, after an interval, talking again, though, trembling still, she had not been attentive; so that she was unconscious of what he had said until she heard him once more sound Mrs Chorner's name. 'If you don't, you know, someone else will, and someone much worse. You told me she likes you.' She had at first no answer for him, but it presently made her stop again. It was beautiful, if she would, but it was odd – this pressure for *her* to push at the very hour he himself had renounced pushing. A part of the whole sublimity of his attitude, so far as she was concerned, it clearly was; since, obviously, he was not now to profit by anything she might do. She seemed to see that, as the last service he could render, he wished to launch her and leave her. And that came out the more as he kept it up. 'If she likes you, you know, she really wants you. Go to her as a friend.'

'And bruit her abroad as one?' Maud Blandy asked.

'Oh, as a friend *from* the Papers – from them and *for* them, and with just your half-hour to give her before you rush back to them. Take it even – oh, you can safely' – the young man developed – 'a little high with her. That's the way – the real way.' And he spoke the next moment as if almost losing his patience. 'You ought by this time, you know, to understand.'

There was something in her mind that it still charmed – his mastery of the horrid art. He could see, always, the superior way, and it was as if, in spite of herself, she were getting the truth from him. Only she didn't want the truth – at least not that one. 'And if she simply, for my impudence, chucks me out of the window? A short way is easy for them, you know, when one doesn't scream or kick, or hang on to the furniture or the banisters. And I usually, you see –' she said it pensively – 'don't. I've always, from the first, had my retreat prepared for any occasion, and flattered myself that, whatever hand I might, or mightn't, become at getting in, no one would ever be able so beautifully to get out. Like a flash, simply. And if she does, as I say, chuck me, it's *you* who fall to the ground.'

He listened to her without expression, only saying 'If you feel for her, as you insist, it's your duty.' And then later, as if he had made an impression, 'Your duty, I mean, to try. I admit, if you will, that there's a risk, though I don't, with my experience, feel it. Nothing venture, at any rate, nothing have; and it's all, isn't it? at the worst, in the day's work. There's but one thing you can go on, but it's enough. The greatest probability.'

She resisted, but she was taking it in. 'The probability that she will throw herself on my neck?'

'It will be either one thing or the other,' he went on as if he had not heard her. 'She'll not receive you, or she will. But if she does your fortune's made, and you'll be able to look higher than the mere *common* form of donkey.' She recognized the reference to Marshal, but that was a thing she needn't mind now, and he had already continued. 'She'll keep *nothing* back. And you mustn't either.'

'Oh, won't I?' Maud murmured.

'Then you'll break faith with her.'

And, as if to emphasize it, he went on, though without leaving her an infinite time to decide, for he looked at his watch as they proceeded, and when they came, in their spacious walk, abreast of another issue, where the breadth of the avenue, the expanses of stone, the stretch of the river, the dimness of the distance, seemed to isolate them, he appeared, by renewing their halt and looking up afresh toward the town, to desire to speed her on her way. Many things meanwhile had worked within her, but it was not till she had kept him on past the Temple Station of the Underground that she fairly faced her opportunity. Even then too there were still other things, under the assault of which she dropped, for the moment, Mrs Chorner. 'Did you really,' she asked, 'believe he'd turn up alive?'

With his hands in his pockets he continued to gloom at her. 'Up there, just now, with Marshal – what did you take me as believing?'

'I gave you up. And I do give you. You're beyond me. Only,' she added, 'I seem to have made you out since then as really staggered. Though I don't say it,' she ended, 'to bear hard upon you.'

'Don't bear hard,' said Howard Bight very simply.

It moved her, for all she could have said; so that she had for a moment to wonder if it were bearing hard to mention some features of the rest of her thought. If she was to have him, certainly, it couldn't be without knowing, as she said to herself, something – something she might perhaps mitigate a little the solitude of his penance by possessing. 'There were moments when I even imagined that, up to a certain point, you were still in communication with him. Then I seemed to see that you lost touch – though you braved it out for me; that you had begun to be really uneasy and were giving him up. I seemed to see,' she pursued after a hesitation, 'that it was coming home to you that you had worked him up too high – that you were feeling, if I may say it, that you had better have stopped short. I mean short of *this*.'

'You may say it,' Bight answered. 'I *had* better.'

She looked at him a moment. 'There was more of him than you believed.'

'There was more of him. And now,' Bight added, looking across the river, 'here's *all* of him.'

'Which you feel you have on your heart?'

'I don't know where I have it.' He turned his eyes to her. 'I must wait.'

'For more facts?'

'Well,' he returned after a pause, 'hardly perhaps for "more" if – with what we have – this *is* all. But I've things to think out. I must wait to see how I feel. I did nothing but what he wanted. But we were behind a bolting horse – whom neither of us could have stopped.'

'And *he*,' said Maud, 'is the one dashed to pieces.'

He had his grave eyes on her. 'Would you like it to have been me?'

'Of course not. But you enjoyed it – the bolt; everything up to the smash. Then, with that ahead, you were nervous.'

'I'm nervous still,' said Howard Bight.

Even in his unexpected softness there was something that escaped her, and it made in her, just a little, for irritation. 'What I mean is that you enjoyed his terror. That was what led you on.'

'No doubt – it was so grand a case. But do you call charging me with it,' the young man asked, '*not* bearing hard—?'

'No –' she pulled herself up – 'it *is*. I don't charge you. Only I feel how little – about what has been, all the while, *behind* – you tell me. Nothing explains.'

'Explains what?'

'Why, his act.'

He gave a sign of impatience. 'Isn't the explanation what I offered a moment ago to give you?'

It came, in effect, back to her. 'For use?'

'For use.'

'Only?'

'Only.' It was sharp.

They stood a little, on this, face to face; at the end of which she turned away. 'I'll go to Mrs Chorner.' And she was off while he called after her to take a cab. It was quite as if she were to come upon him, in his strange insistence, for the fare.

# VIII

IF SHE KEPT to herself, from the morrow on, for three days, her adoption of that course was helped, as she thankfully felt, by the great other circumstance and the great public commotion under cover of which it so little mattered what became of private persons. It was not simply that she had her reasons, but she couldn't during this time have descended again to Fleet Street even had she wished, though she said to herself often enough that her behaviour was rank cowardice. She left her friend alone with what he had to face, since, as she found, she could in absence from him a little recover herself. In his presence, the night of the news, she knew she had gone to pieces, had yielded, all too vulgarly, to a weakness proscribed by her original view.

Her original view had been that if poor Beadel, worked up, as she inveterately kept seeing him, *should* embrace the tragic remedy, Howard Bight wouldn't be able not to show as practically compromised. He wouldn't be able not to smell of the wretched man's blood, morally speaking, too strongly for condonations or complacencies. There were other things, truly, that, during their minutes on the Embankment, he *had* been able to do, but they constituted just the sinister subtlety to which it was well that she should not again, yet awhile, be exposed. They were of the order – from the safe summit of Maida Hill she could make it out – that had proved corrosive to the muddled mind of the Frankfort fugitive, deprived, in the midst of them, of any honest issue. Bight, of course, rare youth, had *meant* no harm; but what was precisely queerer, what, when you came to judge, less human, than to be formed for offence, for injury, by the mere inherent play of the spirit of observation, of criticism, by the inextinguishable flame, in fine, of the ironic passion? The ironic passion, in such a world as surrounded one, might assert itself as half the dignity, the decency, of life; yet, none the less, in cases where one had seen it prove gruesomely fatal (and not to one's self, which was nothing, but to others, even the stupid and the vulgar) one was plainly admonished to – well, stand off a little and think.

This was what Maud Blandy, while the Papers roared and resounded more than ever with the new meat flung to them, tried to consider that she was doing; so that the attitude held her fast during the freshness of the event. The event grew, as she had felt it would, with every further fact from Frankfort and with every extra-special, and reached its maximum, inevitably, in the light of comment and correspondence. These features, before the catastrophe, had indubitably, at the last, flagged a little, but they revived so prodigiously, under the well-timed shock, that, for the period we speak of, the poor gentleman seemed, with a continuance, with indeed an enhancement, of his fine old knack, to have the successive editions *all* to himself. They had been always of course, the Papers, very largely about him, but it was not too much to say that at this crisis they were about nothing else worth speaking of; so that our young woman could but groan in spirit at the direful example set to the emulous. She spared an occasional moment to the vision of Mortimer Marshal, saw him drunk, as she might have said, with the mere fragrance of the wine of glory, and asked herself what art Bight would now use to furnish him forth as he had promised. The mystery of Beadel's course loomed, each hour, so much larger and darker that the plan would have to be consummate, or the private knowledge alike beyond cavil and beyond calculation, which should attempt either to sound or to mask the appearances. Strangely enough, none the less, she even now found herself thinking of her rash colleague as attached, for the benefit of his surviving victim, to this idea; she went in fact so far as to imagine him half-upheld, while the public wonder spent itself, by the prospect of the fun he might still have with Marshal. This implied, she was not unconscious, that his notion of fun was infernal, and would of course be especially so were his knowledge as real as she supposed it. He would inflate their foolish friend with knowledge that was false and so start him as a balloon for the further gape of the world. This was the image, in turn, that would yield the last sport – the droll career of the wretched man as wandering forever through space under the apprehension, in time duly gained, that the least touch of earth would involve the smash of his car. Afraid, thus, to drop, but at the same time equally out of conceit of the chill air of the upper and increasing solitudes to which he had soared, he would become such a diminishing speck, though traceably a prey to wild human gyrations, as she might conceive Bight to keep in view for future recreation.

It wasn't however the future that was actually so much in question for them all as the immediately near present, offered to her as the latter was in the haunting light of the inevitably unlimited character of any real inquiry. The inquiry of the Papers, immense and ingenious, had yet for her the saving quality that she didn't take it as real. It abounded, truly, in hypotheses, most of them lurid enough, but a certain ease of mind as to what these might lead to was perhaps one of the advantages she owed to her constant breathing of Fleet Street air. She couldn't quite have said why, but she felt it wouldn't be the Papers that, proceeding from link to link, would arrive vindictively at Bight's connection with his late client. The enjoyment of that consummation would rest in another quarter, and if the young man were as uneasy now as she thought he ought to be even while she hoped he wasn't, it would be from the fear in his eyes of such justice as was shared with the vulgar. The Papers held an inquiry, but the Authorities, as they vaguely figured to her, would hold an inquest; which was a matter – even when international, complicated and arrangeable, between Frankfort and London, only on some system unknown to her – more in tune with possibilities of exposure. It was not, as need scarce be said, from the exposure of Beadel that she averted herself; it was from the exposure of the person who had made of Beadel's danger, Beadel's dread – whatever these really represented – the use that the occurrence at Frankfort might be shown to certify. It was well before her, at all events, that if Howard Bight's reflections, so stimulated, kept pace at all with her own, he would at the worst, or even at the best, have been glad to meet her again. It was her knowing that and yet lying low that she privately qualified as cowardice; it was the instinct of watching and waiting till she should see how great the danger might become. And she had moreover another reason, which we shall presently learn. The extra-specials meanwhile were to be had in Kilburnia almost as soon as in the Strand; the little ponied and painted carts, tipped at an extraordinary angle, by which they were disseminated, had for that matter, she observed, never rattled up the Edgware Road at so furious a rate. Each evening, it was true, when the flare of Fleet Street would have begun really to smoke, she had, in resistance to old habit, a little to hold herself; but for three successive days she tided over that crisis. It was not till the fourth night that her reaction suddenly declared itself, determined as it partly was by the latest poster that dangled free at the door of a small shop just out of her own street. The establishment dealt in buttons, pins, tape, and silver bracelets, but the branch of its industry she patronized was that of telegrams, stamps, stationery, and the 'Edinburgh rock' offered to the appetite of the several small children of her next-door neighbour but one. 'The Beadel-Muffet Mystery, Startling Disclosures, Action of the Treasury' – at these words she anxiously gazed; after which she decided. It was as if from her hill-top, from her very house-top, to which the window of her little room was contiguous, she had seen the red light in the east. It *had*, this time, its colour. She went on, she went far, till she met a cab, which she hailed, 'regardless', she felt, as she had hailed one after leaving Bight by the river. 'To Fleet Street' she simply said, and it took her – that she felt too – back into life.

Yes, it was life again, bitter, doubtless, but with a taste, when, having stopped her cab, short of her indication, in Covent Garden, she walked across southward and to the top of the street in which she and her friend had last parted with Mortimer Marshal. She came down to their favoured pot-house, the scene of Bight's high compact with that worthy, and here, hesitating, she paused, uncertain as to where she had best look out. Her conviction, on her way, had but grown; Howard Bight would be looking out – *that* to a certainty; something more, something portentous, had happened (by her evening paper, scanned in the light of her little shop-window, she had taken instant possession of it), and this would have made him know that she couldn't keep up what he would naturally call her 'game'. There were places where they often met, and the diversity of these – not too far apart, however – would be his only difficulty. He was on the prowl, in fine, with his hat over his eyes; and she hadn't known, till this vision of him came, what seeds of romance were in her soul. Romance, the other night, by the river, had brushed them with a wing that was like the blind bump of a bat, but that had been something on *his* part, whereas this thought of bringing him succour as to a Russian anarchist, to some victim of society or subject of extradition, was all her own, and was of this special moment. She *saw* him with his hat over his eyes; she saw him with his overcoat collar turned up; she saw him as a hunted hero cleverly drawn in one of the serializing weeklies or, as they said, in some popular 'ply', and the effect of it was to open to her on the spot a sort of happy sense of all her possible immorality. That was the romantic sense, and everything vanished but the richness of her thrill. She knew little enough what she might have to do for him, but her hope, as sharp as a pang, was that, if anything, it would put her in danger too. The hope, as it happened then, was crowned on the very spot; she had never so felt in danger as when, just now, turning to the glazed door of their cook-shop, she saw a man, within, close behind the glass, still, stiff and ominous, looking at her hard. The light of the place was behind him, so that his face, in the dusk of the side-street, was dark, but it was visible that she showed for him as an object of interest. The next thing, of course, she had seen more – seen she could be such an object, in such a degree, only to her friend himself, and that Bight had been thus sure of her; and the next thing after that had passed straight in and been met by him, as he stepped aside to admit her, in silence. He *had* his hat pulled down and, quite forgetfully, in spite of the warmth within, the collar of his mackintosh up.

It was his silence that completed the perfection of these things – the perfection that came out most of all, oddly, after he had corrected them by removal and was seated with her, in their common corner, at tea, with the room almost to themselves and no one to consider but Marshal's little man in the obvious wig and the blue spectacles, the great authority on the inner life of the criminal classes. Strangest of all, nearly, was it, that, though now essentially belonging, as Maud felt, to this order, they were not conscious of the danger of his presence. What she had wanted most immediately to learn was how Bight had known; but he made, and scarce to her surprise, short work of that. 'I've known every evening – known, that is, that you've wanted to come; and I've been here every evening, waiting just there till I should see you. It was but a question of time. Tonight, however, I was sure – for there's, after all, *something* of me left. Besides, besides—!' He had, in short, another certitude. 'You've been ashamed – I knew, when I saw nothing come, that you would be. But also that that would pass.'

Maud found him, as she would have said, all there. 'I've been ashamed, you mean, of being afraid?'

'You've been ashamed about Mrs Chorner; that is, about *me*. For that you did go to her I know.'

'Have you been then yourself?'

'For what do you take me?' He seemed to wonder. 'What had I to do with her — except *for* you?' And then before she could say: 'Didn't she receive you?'

'Yes, as you said, she "wanted" me.'

'She jumped at you?'

'Jumped at me. She gave me an hour.'

He flushed with an interest that, the next moment, had flared in spite of everything into amusement. 'So that I was right, in my perfect wisdom, up to the hilt?'

'Up to the hilt. She took it from me.'

'That the public wants her?'

'That it won't take a refusal. So she opened up.'

'Overflowed?'

'Prattled.'

'Gushed?'

'Well, recognized and embraced her opportunity. Kept me there till midnight. Told me, as she called it, everything about everything.'

They looked at each other long on it, and it determined in Bight at last a brave clatter of his crockery. 'They're stupendous!'

'It's *you* that are,' Maud replied, 'to have found it out so. You know them down to the ground.'

'Oh, what I've found out—!' But it was more than he could talk of then. 'If I hadn't really felt sure, I wouldn't so have urged you. Only now, if you please, I don't understand your having apparently but kept her in your pocket.'

'Of course you don't,' said Maud Blandy. To which she added, 'And I don't quite myself. I only know that now that I have her there nothing will induce me to take her out.'

'Then you potted her, permit me to say,' he answered, 'on absolutely false pretences.'

'Absolutely; which is precisely why I've been ashamed. I made for home with the whole thing,' she explained, 'and there, that night, in the hours till morning, when, turning it over, I saw all it really was, I knew that I *couldn't* – that I would rather choose *that* shame, that of not doing for her what I had offered, than the hideous honesty of bringing it out. Because, you see,' Maud declared, 'it was – well, it was too much.'

Bight followed her with a sharpness! 'It was so good?'

'Quite beautiful! Awful!'

He wondered. 'Really charming?'

'Charming, interesting, horrible. It was *true* – and it was the whole thing. It was herself – and it was *him*, all of him too. Not a bit made up, but just the poor woman melted and overflowing, yet at the same time raging – like the hot-water tap when it boils. I never saw anything like it; everything, as you guaranteed, came out; it has made me know things. So, to have come down here with it, to have begun to hawk it, either through you, as you kindly proposed, or in my own brazen person, to the highest bidder – well, I felt that I didn't *have* to, after all, if I didn't want to, and that if it's the only way I can get money I would much rather starve.'

'I see.' Howard Bight saw all. 'And that's why you're ashamed?'

She hesitated — she was both so remiss and so firm. 'I knew that by my not coming back to you, you would have guessed, have found me wanting; just, for that matter, as *she* has found me. And I couldn't explain. I can't — I can't to *her*. So that,' the girl went on, 'I shall have done, so far as her attitude to me was to be concerned, something more indelicate, something more indecent, than if I had passed her on. I shall have wormed it all out of her, and then, by not having carried it to market, disappointed and cheated her. She was to have heard it cried like fresh herring.'

Bight was immensely taken. 'Oh, beyond all doubt. You're in a fix. You've played, you see, a most unusual game. The code allows everything *but* that.'

'Precisely. So I must take the consequences. I'm dishonoured, but I shall have to bear it. And I shall bear it by getting *out*. Out, I mean, of the whole thing. I shall chuck them.'

'Chuck the *Papers*?' he asked in his simplicity.

But his wonder, she saw, was overdone — their eyes too frankly met. 'Damn the Papers!' said Maud Blandy.

It produced in his sadness and weariness the sweetest smile that had yet broken through. 'We *shall*, between us, if we keep it up, ruin them! And you make nothing,' he went on, 'of one's having at last so beautifully started you? Your complaint,' he developed, 'was that you couldn't get in. Then suddenly, with a splendid jump, you *are* in. Only, however, to look round you and say with disgust "Oh, *here*?" Where the devil do you *want* to be?'

'Ah, that's another question. At least,' she said, 'I can scrub floors. I can take it out perhaps – my swindle of Mrs Chorner,' she pursued – 'in scrubbing *hers*.'

He only, after this, looked at her a little. 'She has written to you?'

'Oh, in high dudgeon. I was to have attended to the "press-cutting" people as well, and she was to have seen herself, at the furthest, by the second morning (that was day-before-yesterday) all over the place. She wants to know what I mean.'

'And what do you answer?'

'That it's hard, of course, to make her understand, but that I've felt her, since parting with her, simply to be too good.'

'Signifying by it, naturally,' Bight amended, 'that you've felt yourself to be so.'

'Well, that too if you like. But she was exquisite.'

He considered. 'Would she do for a ply?'

'Oh God, no!'

'Then for a tile?'

'Perhaps,' said Maud Blandy at last.

He understood, visibly, the shade, as well as the pause; which, together, held him a moment. But it was of something else he spoke. 'And you who had found they would never bite!'

'Oh, I was wrong,' she simply answered. 'Once they've *tasted* blood—!'

'They want to devour,' her friend laughed, 'not only the bait and the hook, but the line and the rod and the poor fisherman himself? Except,' he continued, 'that poor Mrs Chorner hasn't yet even "tasted". However,' he added, 'she obviously will.'

Maud's assent was full. 'She'll find others. She'll appear.'

He waited a moment – his eye had turned to the door of the street. 'Then she must be quick. These are things of the hour.'

'You hear something?' she asked, his expression having struck her.

He listened again, but it was nothing. 'No – but it's somehow in the air.'

'What is?'

'Well, that she must hurry. She must get in. She must get out.' He had his arms on the table, and, locking his hands and inclining a little, he brought his face nearer to her. 'My sense tonight's of an openness—! I don't know what's the matter. Except, that is, that you're great.'

She looked at him, not drawing back. 'You know everything – so immeasurably more than you admit or than you tell me. You mortally perplex and worry me.'

It made him smile. 'You're great, you're great,' he only repeated. 'You know it's quite awfully swagger, what you've done.'

'What I haven't, you mean; what I never shall. Yes,' she added, but now sinking back – 'of course you see that too. What *don't* you see, and what, with such ways, is to be the end of you?'

'You're great, you're great –' he kept it up. 'And I like you. That's to be the end of me.'

So, for a minute, they left it, while she came to the thing that, for the last half-hour, had most been with her. 'What *is* the "action", announced tonight, of the Treasury?'

'Oh, they've sent somebody out, partly, it would seem, at the request of the German authorities, to take possession.'

'Possession, you mean, of his effects?'

'Yes, and legally, administratively, of the whole matter.'

'Seeing, you mean, that there's still more in it——?'

'Than meets the eye,' said Bight, 'precisely. But it won't be till the case is transferred, as it presently will be, to this country, that they *will* see. Then it will be funny.'

'Funny?' Maud Blandy asked.

'Oh, lovely.'

'Lovely for *you*?'

'Why not? The bigger the whole thing grows, the lovelier.'

'You've odd notions,' she said, 'of loveliness. Do you expect his situation won't be traced to you? Don't you suppose you'll be forced to speak?'

'To "speak"——?'

'Why, if it *is* traced. What do you make, otherwise, of the facts tonight?'

'Do you call them facts?' the young man asked.

'I mean the Astounding Disclosures.'

'Well, do you only read your headlines? "The most astounding disclosures are expected" – *that's* the valuable text. Is *it*,' he went on, 'what fetched you?'

His answer was so little of one that she made her own scant. 'What fetched me is that I can't rest.'

'No more can I,' he returned. 'But in what danger do you think me?'

'In any in which you think yourself. Why not, if I don't mean in danger of hanging?'

He looked at her so that she presently took him for serious at last – which was different from his having been either worried or perverse. 'Of public discredit, you mean – for having so unmercifully baited him? Yes,' he conceded with a straightness that now surprised her, 'I've thought of that. But how can the baiting be proved?'

'If they take possession of his effects won't his effects be partly his papers, and won't they, among them, find letters from you, and won't your letters show it?'

'Well, show what?'

'Why, the frenzy to which you worked him – and thereby your connection.'

'They won't show it to dunderheads.'

'And are they all dunderheads?'

'Every mother's son of them – where anything so beautiful is concerned.'

'Beautiful?' Maud murmured.

'Beautiful, my letters are – gems of the purest ray. I'm covered.'

She let herself go – she looked at him long. 'You're a wonder. But all the same,' she added, 'you don't like it.'

'Well, I'm not sure.' Which clearly meant, however, that he almost *was*, from the way in which, the next moment, he had exchanged the question for another. 'You haven't anything to tell me of Mrs Chorner's explanation?'

Oh, as to this, she had already considered and chosen. 'What do you want of it when you know so much more? So much more, I mean, than even she has known.'

'Then she *hasn't* known—?'

'There you are! What,' asked Maud, 'are you talking about?'

She had made him smile, even though his smile was perceptibly pale; and he continued. 'Of what was behind. Behind any game of mine. Behind everything.'

'So am I then talking of that. No,' said Maud, 'she hasn't known, and she doesn't know I judge, to this hour. Her explanation therefore doesn't bear upon that. It bears upon something else.'

'Well, my dear, on what?'

He was not, however, to find out by simply calling her his dear; for she had not sacrificed the reward of her interview in order to present the fine flower of it, unbribed, even to *him*. 'You know how little you've ever told me, and you see how, at this instant, even while you press me to gratify you, you give me nothing. I give,' she smiled – yet not a little flushed – 'nothing *for* nothing.'

He showed her he felt baffled, but also that she was perverse. 'What you want of me is what, originally, you wouldn't hear of: anything so dreadful, that is, as his predicament must be. You saw that to make him want to keep quiet he must have something to be ashamed of, and that was just what, in pity, you positively objected to learning. You've grown,' Bight smiled, 'more interested since.'

'If I have,' said Maud, 'it's because *you* have. Now, at any rate, I'm not afraid.'

He waited a moment. 'Are you very sure?'

'Yes, for my mystification is greater at last than my delicacy. I don't know till I do know –' and she expressed this even with difficulty – 'what it has been, all the while, that it was a question of, and what, consequently, all the while, we've been talking about.'

'Ah, but why should you know?' the young man inquired. 'I can understand your needing to, or somebody's needing to, if we were in a ply, or even, though in a less degree, if we were in a tile. But since, my poor child, we're only in the delicious muddle of life itself—!'

'You may have all the plums of the pudding, and I nothing but a mouthful of cold suet?' Maud pushed back her chair; she had taken up her old gloves; but while she put them on she kept in view both her friend and her grievance. 'I don't believe,' she at last brought out, 'that there *is*, or that there ever was, anything.'

'Oh, oh, oh!' Bight laughed.

'There's nothing,' she continued, '"behind". There's no horror.'

'You hold, by that,' said Bight, 'that the poor man's deed is *all* me? That does make it, you see, bad for me.'

She got up and, there before him, finished smoothing her

creased gloves. 'Then we *are* – if there's such richness – in a ply.'

'Well, we are not, at all events – so far as we ourselves are concerned – the spectators.' And he also got up. 'The spectators must look out for themselves.'

'Evidently, poor things!' Maud sighed. And as he still stood as if there might be something for him to come from her, she made her attitude clear – which was quite the attitude now of tormenting him a little. 'If you know something about him which she doesn't, and also which *I* don't, she knows something about him – as I do too – which *you* don't.'

'Surely: when it's exactly what I'm trying to get out of you. Are you afraid *I'll* sell it?'

But even this taunt, which she took moreover at its worth, didn't move her. 'You definitely then won't tell me?'

'You mean that if I will you'll tell *me*?'

She thought again. 'Well – yes. But on that condition alone.'

'Then you're safe,' said Howard Bight. 'I *can't*, really, my dear, tell you. Besides, if it's to come out—!'

'I'll wait in that case till it does. But I must warn you,' she added, 'that *my* facts *won't* come out.'

He considered. 'Why not, since the rush at her is probably even now being made? Why not, if she receives others?'

Well, Maud could think too. 'She'll receive them, but they won't receive *her*. Others are like *your* people – dunderheads. Others won't understand, won't count, won't exist.' And she moved to the door. 'There *are* no others.' Opening the door, she had reached the street with it, even while he replied, overtaking her, that there were certainly none such as herself; but they had scarce passed out before her last remark was, to their somewhat disconcerted sense, sharply enough refuted. There was still the other they had forgotten, and that neglected quantity, plainly in search of them and happy in his instinct of the chase, now stayed their steps in the form of Mortimer Marshal.

# IX

HE WAS COMING in as they came out; and his 'I *hoped* I might find you', an exhalation of cool candour that they took full in the face, had the effect, the next moment, of a great soft carpet, all flowers and figures, suddenly unrolled for them to walk upon and before which they felt a scruple. Their ejaculation, Maud was conscious, couldn't have passed for a welcome, and it wasn't till she saw the poor gentleman checked a little, in turn, by their blankness, that she fully perceived how interesting they had just become to themselves. His face, however, while, in their arrest, they neither proposed to re-enter the shop with him nor invited him to proceed with them anywhere else – his face, gaping there, for Bight's promised instructions, like a fair receptacle, shallow but with all the capacity of its flatness, brought back so to our young woman the fond fancy her companion had last excited in him that he profited just a little – and for sympathy in spite of his folly – by her sense that with her too the latter had somehow amused himself. This placed her, for the brief instant, in a strange fellowship with their visitor's plea, under the impulse of which, without more thought, she had turned to Bight. 'Your eager claimant,' she, however, simply said, 'for the opportunity now so beautifully created.'

'I've ventured,' Mr Marshal glowed back, 'to come and remind you that the hours are fleeting.'

Bight had surveyed him with eyes perhaps equivocal. 'You're afraid someone else will step in?'

'Well, with the place so tempting and so empty—!'

Maud made herself again his voice. 'Mr Marshal sees it empty itself perhaps too fast.'

He acknowledged, in his large, bright way, the help afforded him by her easy lightness. 'I do want to get in, you know, before anything happens.'

'And what,' Bight inquired, 'are you afraid *may* happen?'

'Well, to make sure,' he smiled, 'I want myself, don't you see, to happen first.'

Our young woman, at this, fairly fell, for her friend, into his sweetness. '*Do* let him happen!'

'*Do* let me happen!' Mr Marshal followed it up.

They stood there together, where they had paused, in their strange council of three, and their extraordinary tone, in connection with their number, might have marked them, for some passer catching it, as persons not only discussing questions supposedly reserved for the Fates, but absolutely enacting some encounter of these portentous forces. 'Let you – let you?' Bight gravely echoed, while on the sound, for the moment, immensities might have hung. It was as far, however, as he was to have time to speak, for even while his voice was in the air another, at first remote and vague, joined it there on an ominous note and hushed all else to stillness. It came, through the roar of thoroughfares, from the direction of Fleet Street, and it made our interlocutors exchange an altered look. They recognized it, the next thing, as the howl, again, of the Strand, and then but an instant elapsed before it flared into the night. 'Return of Beadel-Muffet! Tremenjous Sensation!'

Tremenjous indeed, so tremenjous that, each really turning as pale with it as they had turned, on the same spot, the other time and with the other news, they stood long enough stricken and still for the cry, multiplied in a flash, again to reach them. They couldn't have said afterwards who first took it up. 'Return—?'

'From the *Dead* – I *say*!' poor Marshal piercingly quavered.

'Then he *hasn't* been—?' Maud gasped it with him at Bight.

But that genius, clearly, was not less deeply affected. 'He's alive?' he breathed in a long, soft wail in which admiration appeared at first to contend with amazement and then the sense of the comic to triumph over both. Howard Bight uncontrollably – it might have struck them as almost hysterically – laughed.

The others could indeed but stare. 'Then who's dead?' piped Mortimer Marshal.

'I'm afraid, Mr Marshal, that *you* are,' the young man returned, more gravely, after a minute. He spoke as if he saw *how* dead.

Poor Marshal was lost. 'But someone was killed—!'

'Someone undoubtedly was, but Beadel somehow has survived it.'

'Has he, then, been playing the game—?' It baffled comprehension.

Yet it wasn't even that what Maud most wondered. 'Have you all the while really known?' she asked of Howard Bight.

He met it with a look that puzzled her for the instant, but that she then saw to mean, half with amusement, half with sadness, that his genius was, after all, simpler. 'I wish I had. I really believed.'

'All along?'

'No; but after Frankfort.'

She remembered things. 'You haven't had a notion this evening?'

'Only from the state of my nerves.'

'Yes, your nerves must be in a state!' And somehow now she had no pity for him. It was almost as if she were, frankly, disappointed. '*I*,' she then boldly said, 'didn't believe.'

'If you had mentioned that then,' Marshal observed to her, 'you would have saved me an awkwardness.'

But Bight took him up. 'She did believe – so that she might punish me.'

'Punish you—?'

Maud raised her hand at her friend. 'He doesn't understand.'

He was indeed, Mr Marshal, fully pathetic now. 'No, I don't understand. Not a wee bit.'

'Well,' said Bight kindly, 'we none of us do. We must give it up.'

'You think *I* really must—?'

'You, sir,' Bight smiled, 'most of all. The places seem so taken.'

His client, however, clung. 'He won't die again—?'

'If he does he'll again come to life. He'll never die. Only *we* shall die. He's immortal.'

He looked up and down, this inquirer; he listened to the howl of the Strand, not yet, as happened, brought nearer to them by one of the hawkers. And yet it was as if, overwhelmed by his lost chance, he knew himself too weak even for *their* fond aid. He still therefore appealed. 'Will *this* be a boom for him?'

'His return? Colossal. For – fancy! – it was exactly what we talked of, you remember, the other day, as the ideal. I mean,' Bight smiled, 'for a man to be lost, and yet at the same time—'

'To be found?' poor Marshal too hungrily mused.

'To be boomed,' Bight continued, 'by his smash and yet never to have been too smashed to know how he was booming.'

It was wonderful for Maud too. 'To have given it all up, and yet to have it all.'

'Oh, better than that,' said her friend: 'to have *more* than all, and more than you gave up. Beadel,' he was careful to explain to their companion, 'will have more.'

Mr Marshal struggled with it. 'More than if he were dead?'

'More,' Bight laughed, 'than if he weren't! It's what *you* would have liked, as I understand you, isn't it? and what you would have got. It's what *I* would have helped you to.'

'But who then,' wailed Marshal, 'helps *him*?'

'Nobody. His star. His genius.'

Mortimer Marshal glared about him as for some sign of such aids in his own sphere. It embraced, his own sphere too, the roaring Strand, yet – mystification and madness! – it was with Beadel the Strand was roaring. A hawker, from afar, at sight of the group, was already scaling the slope. 'Ah, but *how* the devil—?'

Bight pointed to this resource. 'Go and see.'

'But don't *you* want them?' poor Marshal asked as the others retreated.

'The Papers?' They stopped to answer. 'No, never again. We've done with them. We give it up.'

'I mayn't again see you?'

Dismay and a last clutch were in Marshal's face, but Maud, who had taken her friend's meaning in a flash, found the word to meet them. 'We retire from business.'

With which they turned again to move in the other sense, presenting their backs to Fleet Street. They moved together up the rest of the hill, going on in silence, not arrested by another little shrieking boy, not diverted by another extra-special, not pausing again till, at the end of a few minutes, they found themselves in the comparative solitude of Covent Garden, encumbered with the traces of its traffic, but now given over to peace. The howl of the Strand had ceased, their client had vanished for ever, and from the centre of the empty space they could look up and see stars. One of these was of course Beadel-Muffet's, and the consciousness of that, for the moment, kept down any arrogance of triumph. He still hung above them, he ruled, immortal, the night; they were far beneath, and he now transcended their world; but a sense of relief, of escape, of the light, still unquenched, of their old irony, made them stand there face to face. There was more between them now than there had ever been, but it had ceased to separate them, it sustained them in fact like a deep water on which they floated closer. Still, however, there was something Maud needed. 'It had been all the while worked?'

'Ah, not, before God – since I lost sight of him – by *me*.'

'Then by himself?'

'I daresay. But there are plenty for him. He's beyond me.'

'But you thought,' she said, 'it *would* be so. You thought,' she declared, 'something.'

Bight hesitated. 'I thought it would be great if he *could*. And *as* he could – why, it *is* great. But all the same I too was sold. I *am* sold. That's why I give up.'

'Then it's why *I* do. We must do something,' she smiled at him, 'that requires less cleverness.'

'We must love each other,' said Howard Bight.

'But can we live by that?'

He thought again; then he decided. 'Yes.'

'Ah,' Maud amended, 'we must be "littery". We've now got stuff.'

'For the dear old ply, for the rattling good tile? Ah, they take better stuff than this – though this too is good.'

'Yes,' she granted on reflection, 'this is good, but it has bad holes. *Who was the dead man in the locked hotel room?*'

'Oh, I don't mean that. *That*,' said Bight, 'he'll splendidly explain.'

'But how?'

'Why, in the Papers. Tomorrow.'

Maud wondered. 'So soon?'

'If he returned tonight, and it's not yet ten o'clock, there's plenty of time. It will be in *all* of them – while the universe waits. He'll hold us in the hollow of his hand. His chance is just there. And there,' said the young man, 'will be his greatness.'

'Greater than ever then?'

'Quadrupled.'

She followed; then it made her seize his arm. '*Go* to him!'

Bight frowned. '"Go"—?'

'This instant. *You* explain!'

He understood, but only to shake his head. 'Never again. I bow to him.'

Well, she after a little understood; but she thought again. 'You mean that the great hole is that he really had no reason, no funk—?'

'I've wondered,' said Howard Bight.

'Whether he *had* done anything to make publicity embarrassing?'

'I've wondered,' the young man repeated.

'But I thought you knew!'

'So did I. But I thought also I knew he was dead. However,' Bight added, 'he'll explain that too.'

'Tomorrow?'

'No – as a different branch. Say day after.'

'Ah, then,' said Maud, 'if he explains—!'

'There's no hole? I don't know!' – and it forced from him at last a sigh. He was impatient of it, for he had done with it; it would soon bore him. So fast they lived. 'It will take,' he only dropped, 'much explaining.'

His detachment was logical, but she looked a moment at his sudden weariness. 'There's always, remember, Mrs Chorner.'

'Oh yes, Mrs Chorner; we luckily invented *her*.'

'Well, if she drove him to his death—?'

Bight, with a laugh, caught at it. 'Is that it? *Did* she drive him?'

It pulled her up, and, though she smiled, they stood again, a little, as on their guard. 'Now, at any rate,' Maud simply said at last, 'she'll marry him. So you see how right I was.'

With a preoccupation that had grown in him, however, he had already lost the thread. 'How right—?'

'Not to sell my Talk.'

'Oh yes,' – he remembered. 'Quite right.' But it all came to something else. 'Whom will *you* marry?'

She only, at first, for answer, kept her eyes on him. Then she turned them about the place and saw no hindrance, and then, further, bending with a tenderness in which she felt so transformed, so won to something she had never been before, that she might even, to other eyes, well have looked so, she gravely kissed him. After which, as he took her arm, they walked on together. 'That, at least,' she said, 'we'll put in the Papers.'

# The Jolly Corner

## I

'Everyone asks me what I "think" of everything,' said Spencer Brydon; 'and I make answer as I can – begging or dodging the question, putting them off with any nonsense. It wouldn't matter to any of them really,' he went on, 'for, even were it possible to meet in that stand-and-deliver way so silly a demand on so big a subject, my "thoughts" would still be almost altogether about something that concerns only myself.' He was talking to Miss Staverton, with whom for a couple of months now he had availed himself of every possible occasion to talk; this disposition and this resource, this comfort and support, as the situation in fact presented itself, having promptly enough taken the first place in the considerable array of rather unattenuated surprises attending his so strangely belated return to America. Everything was somehow a surprise; and that might be natural when one had so long and so consistently neglected everything, taken pains to give surprises so much margin for play. He had given them more than thirty years – thirty-three, to be exact; and they now seemed to him to have organized their performance quite on the scale of that licence. He had been twenty-three on leaving New York – he was fifty-six today: unless indeed he were to reckon as he had sometimes, since his repatriation, found himself feeling; in which case he would have lived longer than is often allotted to man. It would have taken a century, he repeatedly said to himself, and said also to Alice Staverton, it would have taken a longer absence and a more averted mind than those even of which he had been guilty, to pile up the differences, the newnesses, the queernesses, above all the bignesses, for the better or the worse, that at present assaulted his vision wherever he looked.

The great fact all the while however had been the incalculability; since he *had* supposed himself, from decade to decade, to be allowing, and in the most liberal and intelligent manner, for brilliancy of change. He actually saw that he had allowed for nothing; he missed what he would have been sure of finding, he found what he would never have imagined. Proportions and values were upside-down; the ugly things he had expected, the ugly things of his far-away youth, when he had too promptly waked up to a sense of the ugly – these uncanny phenomena placed him rather, as it happened, under the charm; whereas the 'swagger' things, the modern, the monstrous, the famous things, those he had more particularly, like thousands of ingenuous inquirers every year, come over to see, were exactly his sources of dismay. They were as so many set traps for displeasure, above all for reaction, of which his restless tread was constantly pressing the spring. It was interesting, doubtless, the whole show, but it would have been too disconcerting hadn't a certain finer truth saved the situation. He had distinctly not, in this steadier light, come over *all* for the monstrosities; he had come, not only in the last analysis but quite on the face of the act, under an impulse with which they had nothing to do. He had come – putting the thing pompously – to look at his 'property', which he had thus for a third of a century not been within four thousand miles of; or, expressing it less sordidly, he had yielded to the humour of seeing again his house on the jolly corner, as he usually, and quite fondly, described it – the one in which he had first seen the light, in which various members of his family had lived and had died, in which the holidays of his overschooled boyhood had been passed and the few social flowers of his chilled adolescence gathered, and which, alienated then for so long a period, had, through the successive deaths of his two brothers and the termination of old arrangements, come wholly into his hands. He was the owner of another, not quite so 'good' – the jolly corner having been, from far back, superlatively extended and consecrated; and the value of the pair represented his main capital, with an income consisting, in these later years, of their respective rents which (thanks precisely to their original excellent type) had never been depressingly low. He could live in 'Europe', as he had been in the habit of living, on the product of these flourishing New York leases, and all the better since, that of the second structure, the mere number in its long row, having within a twelvemonth fallen in, renovation at a high advance had proved beautifully possible.

These were items of property indeed, but he had found himself since his arrival distinguishing more than ever between them. The house within the street, two bristling blocks westward, was already in course of reconstruction as a tall mass of flats; he had acceded, some time before, to overtures for this conversion – in which, now that it was going forward, it had been not the least of his astonishments to find himself able, on the spot, and though without a previous ounce of such experience, to participate with a certain intelligence, almost with a certain authority. He had lived his life with his back so turned to such concerns and his face addressed to those of so different an order that he scarce knew what to make of this lively stir, in a compartment of his mind never yet penetrated, of a capacity for business and a sense for construction. These virtues, so common all round him now, had been dormant in his own organism – where it might be said of them perhaps that they had slept the sleep of the just. At present, in the splendid autumn weather – the autumn at least was a pure boon in the terrible place – he loafed about his 'work' undeterred, secretly agitated; not in the least 'minding' that the whole proposition, as they said, was vulgar and sordid, and ready to climb ladders, to walk the plank, to handle materials and look wise about them, to ask questions, in fine, and challenge explanations and really 'go into' figures.

It amused, it verily quite charmed him; and, by the same

stroke, it amused, and even more, Alice Staverton, though perhaps charming her perceptibly less. She wasn't however going to be better-off for it, as *he* was — and so astonishingly much: nothing was now likely, he knew, ever to make her better-off than she found herself, in the afternoon of life, as the delicately frugal possessor and tenant of the small house in Irving Place to which she had subtly managed to cling through her almost unbroken New York career. If he knew the way to it now better than to any other address among the dreadful multiplied numberings which seemed to him to reduce the whole place to some vast ledger-page, overgrown, fantastic, of ruled and criss-crossed lines and figures — if he had formed, for his consolation, that habit, it was really not a little because of the charm of his having encountered and recognized, in the vast wilderness of the wholesale, breaking through the mere gross generalization of wealth and force and success, a small still scene where items and shades, all delicate things, kept the sharpness of the notes of a high voice perfectly trained, and where economy hung about like the scent of a garden. His old friend lived with one maid and herself dusted her relics and trimmed her lamps and polished her silver; she stood off, in the awful modern crush, when she could, but she sallied forth and did battle when the challenge was really to 'spirit', the spirit she after all confessed to, proudly and a little shyly, as to that of the better time, that of *their* common, their quite far-away and antediluvian social period and order. She made use of the street-cars when need be, the terrible things that people scrambled for as the panic-stricken at sea scramble for the boats; she affronted, inscrutably, under stress, all the public concussions and ordeals; and yet, with that slim mystifying grace of her appearance, which defied you to say if she were a fair young woman who looked older through trouble, or a fine smooth older one who looked young through successful indifference; with her precious reference, above all, to memories and histories into which he could enter, she was as exquisite for him as some pale pressed flower (a rarity to begin with), and, failing other sweetnesses, she was a sufficient reward of his effort. They had communities of knowledge, 'their' knowledge (this discriminating possessive was always on her lips) of presences of the other age, presences all overlaid, in his case, by the experience of a man and the freedom of a wanderer, overlaid by pleasure, by infidelity, by passages of life that were strange and dim to her, just by 'Europe' in short, but still unobscured, still exposed and cherished, under that pious visitation of the spirit from which she had never been diverted.

She had come with him one day to see how his 'apartment-house' was rising; he had helped her over gaps and explained to her plans, and while they were there had happened to have, before her, a brief but lively discussion with the man in charge, the representative of the building-firm that had undertaken his work. He had found himself quite 'standing up' to this personage over a failure on the latter's part to observe some detail of one of their noted conditions, and had so lucidly argued his case that, besides ever so prettily flushing, at the time, for sympathy in his triumph, she had afterwards said to him (though to a slightly greater effect of irony) that he had clearly for too many years neglected a real gift. If he had but stayed at home he would have anticipated the inventor of the sky-scraper. If he had but stayed at home he would have discovered his genius in time really to start some new variety of awful architectural hare and run it till it burrowed in a gold-mine. He was to remember these words, while the weeks elapsed, for the small silver ring they had sounded over the queerest and deepest of his own lately most disguised and most muffled vibrations.

It had begun to be present to him after the first fortnight, it had broken out with the oddest abruptness, this particular wanton wonderment: it met him there – and this was the image under which he himself judged the matter, or at least, not a little, thrilled and flushed with it – very much as he might have been met by some strange figure, some unexpected occupant, at a turn of one of the dim passages of an empty house. The quaint analogy quite hauntingly remained with him, when he didn't indeed rather improve it by a still intenser form: that of his opening a door behind which he would have made sure of finding nothing, a door into a room shuttered and void, and yet so coming, with a great suppressed start, on some quite erect confronting presence, something planted in the middle of the place and facing him through the dusk. After that visit to the house in construction he walked with his companion to see the other and always so much the better one, which in the eastward direction formed one of the corners, the 'jolly' one precisely, of the street now so generally dishonoured and disfigured in its westward reaches, and of the comparatively conservative Avenue. The Avenue still had pretensions, as Miss Staverton said, to decency; the old people had mostly gone, the old names were unknown, and here and there an old association seemed to stray, all vaguely, like some very aged person, out too late, whom you might meet and feel the impulse to watch or follow, in kindness, for safe restoration to shelter.

They went in together, our friends; he admitted himself with his key, as he kept no one there, he explained, preferring, for his reasons, to leave the place empty, under a simple arrangement with a good woman living in the neighbourhood and who came for a daily hour to open windows and dust and sweep. Spencer Brydon had his reasons and was growingly aware of them; they seemed to him better each time he was there, though he didn't name them all to his companion, any more than he told her as yet how often, how quite absurdly often, he himself came. He only let her see for the present, while they walked through the great blank rooms, that absolute vacancy reigned and that, from top to bottom, there was nothing but Mrs Muldoon's broomstick, in a corner, to tempt the burglar. Mrs Muldoon was then on the premises, and she loquaciously attended the visitors, preceding them from room to room and pushing back shutters and throwing up sashes – all to show them, as she remarked, how little there was to see. There was little indeed to see in the great gaunt shell where the main dispositions and the general apportionment of space, the style of an age of ampler allowances, had nevertheless for its master their honest pleading message, affecting him as some good old servant's, some lifelong retainer's appeal for a character, or even for a retiring-pension; yet it was also a remark of Mrs Muldoon's that, glad as she was to oblige him by her noon-day round, there was a request she greatly hoped he would never make of her. If he should wish her for any reason to come in after dark she would just tell him, if he 'plased', that he must ask it of somebody else.

The fact that there was nothing to see didn't militate for the worthy woman against what one *might* see, and she put it frankly to Miss Staverton that no lady could be expected to like, could she? 'craping up to thim top storeys in the ayvil hours'. The gas and the electric light were off in the house, and she fairly evoked a gruesome vision of her march through the great grey rooms – so many of them as there were too! – with her glimmering taper. Miss Staverton met her honest glare with a smile and the profession that she herself certainly would recoil from such an adventure. Spencer Brydon meanwhile held his peace – for the moment; the question of the 'evil' hours in his old home had already become too grave for him. He had begun some time since to 'crape', and he knew just why a packet of candles addressed to that pursuit had been stowed by his own hand, three weeks before, at the back of a drawer of the fine old sideboard that occupied, as a 'fixture', the deep recess in the dining-room. Just now he laughed at his companions – quickly however changing the subject; for the reason that, in the first place, his laugh struck him even at that moment as starting the odd echo, the conscious human resonance (he scarce knew how to qualify it) that sounds made while he was there alone sent back to his ear or his fancy; and that, in the second, he imagined Alice Staverton for the instant on the point of asking him, with a divination, if he ever so prowled. There were divinations he was unprepared for, and he had at all events averted inquiry by the time Mrs Muldoon had left them, passing on to other parts.

There was happily enough to say, on so consecrated a spot, that could be said freely and fairly; so that a whole train of declarations was precipitated by his friend's having herself broken out, after a yearning look round: 'But I hope you don't mean they want you to pull *this* to pieces!' His answer came, promptly, with his reawakened wrath: it was of course exactly what they wanted, and what they were 'at' him for, daily, with the iteration of people who couldn't for their life understand a man's liability to decent feelings. He had found the place, just as it stood and beyond what he could express, an interest and a joy. There were values other than the beastly rent-values, and in short, in short—! But it was thus Miss Staverton took him up. 'In short you're to make so good a thing of your sky-scraper that, living in luxury on *those* ill-gotten gains, you can afford for a while to be sentimental here!' Her smile had for him, with the words, the particular mild irony with which he found half her talk suffused; an irony without bitterness and that came, exactly, from her having so much imagination – not, like the cheap sarcasms with which one heard most people, about the world of 'society', bid for the reputation of cleverness, from nobody's really having any. It was agreeable to him at this very moment to be sure that when he had answered, after a brief demur, 'Well yes: so, precisely, you may put it!' her imagination would still do him justice. He explained that even if never a dollar were to come to him from the other house he would nevertheless cherish this one; and he dwelt, further, while they lingered and wandered, on the fact of the stupefaction he was already exciting, the positive mystification he felt himself create.

He spoke of the value of all he read into it, into the mere sight of the walls, mere shapes of the rooms, mere sound of the floors, mere feel, in his hand, of the old silver-plated knobs of the several mahogany doors, which suggested the pressure of the palms of the dead; the seventy years of the past in fine that these things represented, the annals of nearly three generations, counting his grandfather's, the one that had ended there, and the impalpable ashes of his long-extinct youth, afloat in the very air like microscopic motes. She listened to everything; she was a woman who answered intimately but who utterly didn't chatter. She scattered abroad therefore no cloud of words; she could assent, she could agree, above all she could encourage, without doing that. Only at the last she went a little further than he had done himself. 'And then how do you know? You may still, after all, want to live here.' It rather indeed pulled him up, for it wasn't what he had been thinking, at least in her sense of the words. 'You mean I may decide to stay on for the sake of it?'

'Well, *with* such a home—!' But, quite beautifully, she had too much tact to dot so monstrous an *i*, and it was precisely an illustration of the way she didn't rattle. How could anyone

– of any wit – insist on anyone else's 'wanting' to live in New York?

'Oh,' he said, 'I *might* have lived here (since I had my opportunity early in life); I might have put in here all these years. Then everything would have been different enough – and, I daresay, "funny" enough. But that's another matter. And then the beauty of it – I mean of my perversity, of my refusal to agree to a "deal" – is just in the total absence of a reason. Don't you see that if I had a reason about the matter at all it would *have* to be the other way, and would then be inevitably a reason of dollars? There are no reasons here *but* of dollars. Let us therefore have none whatever – not the ghost of one.'

They were back in the hall then for departure, but from where they stood the vista was large, through an open door, into the great square main saloon, with its almost antique felicity of brave spaces between windows. Her eyes came back from that reach and met his own a moment. 'Are you very sure the "ghost" of one doesn't, much rather, serve—?'

He had a positive sense of turning pale. But it was as near as they were then to come. For he made answer, he believed, between a glare and a grin: 'Oh ghosts – of course the place must swarm with them! I should be ashamed of it if it didn't. Poor Mrs Muldoon's right, and it's why I haven't asked her to do more than look in.'

Miss Staverton's gaze again lost itself, and things she didn't utter, it was clear, came and went in her mind. She might even for the minute, off there in the fine room, have imagined some element dimly gathering. Simplified like the death-mask of a handsome face, it perhaps produced for her just then an effect akin to the stir of an expression in the 'set' commemorative plaster. Yet whatever her impression may have been she produced instead a vague platitude. 'Well, if it were only furnished and lived in—!'

She appeared to imply that in case of its being still furnished he might have been a little less opposed to the idea of a return. But she passed straight into the vestibule, as if to leave her words behind her, and the next moment he had opened the house-door and was standing with her on the steps. He closed the door and, while he re-pocketed his key, looking up and down, they took in the comparatively harsh actuality of the Avenue, which reminded him of the assault of the outer light of the Desert on the traveller emerging from an Egyptian tomb. But he risked before they stepped into the street his gathered answer to her speech. 'For me it *is* lived in. For me it *is* furnished.' At which it was easy for her to sigh 'Ah yes—!' all vaguely and discreetly; since his parents and his favourite sister, to say nothing of other kin, in numbers, had run their course and met their end there. That represented, within the walls, ineffaceable life.

It was a few days after this that, during an hour passed with her again, he had expressed his impatience of the too flattering curiosity – among the people he met – about his appreciation of New York. He had arrived at none at all that was socially producible, and as for that matter of his 'thinking' (thinking the better or the worse of anything there) he was wholly taken up with one subject of thought. It was mere vain egoism, and it was moreover, if she liked, a morbid obsession. He found all things come back to the question of what he personally might have been, how he might have led his life and 'turned out', if he had not so, at the outset, given it up. And confessing for the first time to the intensity within him of this absurd speculation – which but proved also, no doubt, the habit of too selfishly thinking – he affirmed the impotence there of any other source of interest, any other native appeal. 'What would it have made of me, what would it have made of me? I keep forever wondering, all idiotically; as if I could possibly know! I see what it has made of dozens of others, those I meet, and it positively aches within me, to the point of exasperation, that it would have made something of me as well. Only I can't make out *what*, and the worry of it, the small rage of curiosity never to be satisfied, brings back what I remember to have felt, once or twice, after judging best, for reasons, to burn some important letter unopened. I've been sorry, I've hated it – I've never known what was in the letter. You may of course say it's a trifle—!'

'I don't say it's a trifle,' Miss Staverton gravely interrupted.

She was seated by her fire, and before her, on his feet and restless, he turned to and fro between this intensity of his idea and a fitful and unseeing inspection, through his single eye-glass, of the dear little old objects on her chimney-piece. Her interruption made him for an instant look at her harder. 'I shouldn't care if you did!' he laughed, however; 'and it's only a figure, at any rate, for the way I now feel. *Not* to have followed my perverse young course – and almost in the teeth of my father's curse, as I may say; not to have kept it up, so, "over there", from that day to this, without a doubt or a pang; not, above all, to have liked it, to have loved it, so much, loved it, no doubt, with such an abysmal conceit of my own preference: some variation from *that*, I say, must have produced some different effect for my life and for my "form". I should have stuck here – if it had been possible; and I was too young, at twenty-three, to judge, *pour deux sous*, whether it *were* possible. If I had waited I might have seen it was, and then I might have been, by staying here, something nearer to one of these types who have been hammered so hard and made so keen by their conditions. It isn't that I admire them so much – the question of any charm in them, or of any charm, beyond that of the rank money-passion, exerted by their conditions *for* them, has nothing to do with the matter: it's only a question of what fantastic, yet perfectly possible, development of my own nature I mayn't have missed. It comes over me that I had then a strange *alter ego* deep down somewhere within me, as the full-blown flower is in the small tight bud, and that I just took the course, I just transferred him to the climate, that blighted him for once and for ever.'

'And you wonder about the flower,' Miss Staverton said. 'So do I, if you want to know; and so I've been wondering these several weeks. I believe in the flower,' she continued, 'I feel it would have been quite splendid, quite huge and monstrous.'

'Monstrous above all!' her visitor echoed; 'and I imagine, by the same stroke, quite hideous and offensive.'

'You don't believe that,' she returned; 'if you did you wouldn't wonder. You'd know, and that would be enough for you. What you feel — and what I feel *for* you — is that you'd have had power.'

'You'd have liked me that way?' he asked.

She barely hung fire. 'How should I not have liked you?'

'I see. You'd have liked me, have preferred me, a billionaire!'

'How should I not have liked you?' she simply again asked.

He stood before her still — her question kept him motionless. He took it in, so much there was of it; and indeed his not otherwise meeting it testified to that. 'I know at least what I am,' he simply went on; 'the other side of the medal's clear enough. I've not been edifying — I believe I'm thought in a hundred quarters to have been barely decent. I've followed strange paths and worshipped strange gods; it must have come to you again and again — in fact you've admitted to me as much — that I was leading, at any time these thirty years, a selfish frivolous scandalous life. And you see what it has made of me.'

She just waited, smiling at him. 'You see what it has made of *me.*'

'Oh you're a person whom nothing can have altered. You were born to be what you are, anywhere, anyway: you've the perfection nothing else could have blighted. And don't you see how, without my exile, I shouldn't have been waiting till now——?' But he pulled up for the strange pang.

'The great thing to see,' she presently said, 'seems to me to be that it has spoiled nothing. It hasn't spoiled your being here at last. It hasn't spoiled this. It hasn't spoiled your speaking—' She also however faltered.

He wondered at everything her controlled emotion might mean. 'Do you believe then – too dreadfully! – that I *am* as good as I might ever have been?'

'Oh no! Far from it!' With which she got up from her chair and was nearer to him. 'But I don't care,' she smiled.

'You mean I'm good enough?'

She considered a little. 'Will you believe it if I say so? I mean will you let that settle your question for you?' And then as if making out in his face that he drew back from this, that he had some idea which, however absurd, he couldn't yet bargain away: 'Oh you don't care either – but very differently: you don't care for anything but yourself.'

Spencer Brydon recognized it – it was in fact what he had absolutely professed. Yet he importantly qualified. '*He* isn't myself. He's the just so totally other person. But I do want to see him,' he added. 'And I can. And I shall.'

Their eyes met for a minute while he guessed from something in hers that she divined his strange sense. But neither of them otherwise expressed it, and her apparent understanding, with no protesting shock, no easy derision, touched him more deeply than anything yet, constituting for his stifled perversity, on the spot, an element that was like breathable air. What she said however was unexpected. 'Well, *I've* seen him.'

'You—?'

'I've seen him in a dream.'

'Oh a "dream"—!' It let him down.

'But twice over,' she continued. 'I saw him as I see you now.'

'You've dreamed the same dream—?'

'Twice over,' she repeated. 'The very same.'

This did somehow a little speak to him, as it also gratified him. 'You dream about me at that rate?'

'Ah about *him*!' she smiled.

His eyes again sounded her. 'Then you know all about him.' And as she said nothing more: 'What's the wretch like?'

She hesitated, and it was as if he were pressing her so hard that, resisting for reasons of her own, she had to turn away. 'I'll tell you some other time!'

## II

IT WAS AFTER this that there was most of a virtue for him, most of a cultivated charm, most of a preposterous secret thrill, in the particular form of surrender to his obsession and of address to what he more and more believed to be his privilege. It was what in these weeks he was living for – since he really felt life to begin but after Mrs Muldoon had retired from the scene and, visiting the ample house from attic to cellar, making sure he was alone, he knew himself in safe possession and, as he tacitly expressed it, let himself go. He sometimes came twice in the twenty-four hours; the moments he liked best were those of gathering dusk, of the short autumn twilight; this was the time of which, again and again, he found himself hoping most. Then he could, as seemed to him, most intimately wander and wait, linger and listen, feel his fine attention, never in his life before so fine, on the pulse of the great vague place: he preferred the lampless hour and only wished he might have prolonged each day the deep crepuscular spell. Later – rarely much before midnight, but then for a considerable vigil – he watched with his glimmering light; moving slowly, holding it high, playing it far, rejoicing above all, as much as he might, in open vistas, reaches of communication between rooms and by passages; the long straight chance or show, as he would have called it, for the revelation he pretended to invite. It was a practice he found he could perfectly 'work' without exciting remark; no one was in the least the wiser for it; even Alice Staverton, who was moreover a well of discretion, didn't quite fully imagine.

He let himself in and let himself out with the assurance of calm proprietorship; and accident so far favoured him that, if a fat Avenue 'officer' had happened on occasion to see him entering at eleven-thirty, he had never yet, to the best of his belief, been noticed as emerging at two. He walked there on the crisp November nights, arrived regularly at the evening's end; it was as easy to do this after dining out as to take his way to a club or to his hotel. When he left his club, if he hadn't been dining out, it was ostensibly to go to his hotel; and when he left his hotel, if he had spent a part of the evening there, it was ostensibly to go to his club. Everything was easy in fine; everything conspired and promoted: there was truly even in the strain of his experience something that glossed over, something that salved and simplified, all the rest of consciousness. He circulated, talked, renewed, loosely and pleasantly, old relations – met indeed, so far as he could, new expectations and seemed to make out on the whole that in spite of the career, of such different contacts, which he had spoken of to Miss Staverton as ministering so little, for those who might have watched it, to edification, he was positively rather liked than not. He was a dim secondary social success – and all with people who had truly not an idea of him. It was all mere surface sound, this murmur of their welcome, this popping of their corks – just as his gestures of response were the extravagant shadows, emphatic in proportion as they meant little, of some game of *ombres chinoises*. He projected himself all day, in thought, straight over the bristling line of hard unconscious heads and into the other, the real, the waiting life; the life that, as soon as he had heard behind him the click of his great house-door, began for him, on the jolly corner, as beguilingly as the slow opening bars of some rich music follows the tap of the conductor's wand.

He always caught the first effect of the steel point of his stick on the old marble of the hall pavement, large black-and-white squares that he remembered as the admiration of his childhood and that had then made in him, as he now saw, for the growth of an early conception of style. This effect was the dim reverberating tinkle as of some far-off bell hung who should say where?

– in the depths of the house, of the past, of that mystical other world that might have flourished for him had he not, for weal or woe, abandoned it. On this impression he did ever the same thing; he put his stick noiselessly away in a corner – feeling the place once more in the likeness of some great glass bowl, all precious concave crystal, set delicately humming by the play of a moist finger round its edge. The concave crystal held, as it were, this mystical other world, and the indescribably fine murmur of its rim was the sigh there, the scarce audible pathetic wail to his strained ear, of all the old baffled forsworn possibilities. What he did therefore by this appeal of his hushed presence was to wake them into such measure of ghostly life as they might still enjoy. They were shy, all but unappeasably shy, but they weren't really sinister; at least they weren't as he had hitherto felt them – before they had taken the Form he so yearned to make them take, the Form he at moments saw himself in the light of fairly hunting on tiptoe, the points of his evening-shoes, from room to room and from storey to storey.

That was the essence of his vision – which was all rank folly, if one would, while he was out of the house and otherwise occupied, but which took on the last verisimilitude as soon as he was placed and posted. He knew what he meant and what he wanted; it was as clear as the figure on a cheque presented in demand for cash. His *alter ego* 'walked' – that was the note of his image of him, while his image of his motive for his own odd pastime was the desire to waylay him and meet him. He roamed, slowly, warily, but all restlessly, he himself did – Mrs Muldoon had been right, absolutely, with her figure of their 'craping'; and the presence he watched for would roam restlessly too. But it would be as cautious and as shifty; the conviction of its probable, in fact its already quite sensible, quite audible evasion of pursuit grew for him from night to night, laying on him finally a rigour to which nothing in his life had been comparable. It had been the theory of many superficially judging persons, he knew, that he was wasting that life in a surrender to sensations, but he had tasted of no pleasure so fine as his actual tension, had been introduced to no sport that demanded at once the patience and the nerve of this stalking of a creature more subtle, yet at bay perhaps more formidable, than any beast of the forest. The terms, the comparisons, the very practices of the chase positively came again into play; there were even moments when passages of his occasional experience as a sportsman, stirred memories, from his younger time, of moor and mountain and desert, revived for him – and to the increase of his keenness – by the tremendous force of analogy. He found himself at moments – once he had placed his single light on some mantel-shelf or in some recess – stepping back into shelter or shade, effacing himself behind a door or in an embrasure, as he had sought of old the vantage of rock and tree; he found himself holding his breath and living in the joy of the instant, the supreme suspense created by big game alone.

He wasn't afraid (though putting himself the question as he believed gentlemen on Bengal tiger-shoots or in close quarters with the great bear of the Rockies had been known to confess to having put it); and this indeed – since here at least he might be frank! – because of the impression, so intimate and so strange, that he himself produced as yet a dread, produced certainly a strain, beyond the liveliest he was likely to feel. They fell for him into categories, they fairly became familiar, the signs, for his own perception, of the alarm his presence and his vigilance created; though leaving him always to remark, portentously, on his probably having formed a relation, his probably enjoying a consciousness, unique in the experience of man. People enough, first and last, had been in terror of apparitions, but who had ever before so turned the tables and become himself, in the apparitional world, an incalculable terror? He might have found this sublime had he quite dared to think of it; but he didn't too much insist, truly, on that side of his privilege. With habit and repetition he gained to an extraordinary degree the power to penetrate the dusk of distances and the darkness of corners, to resolve back into their innocence the treacheries of uncertain light, the evil-looking forms taken in the gloom by mere shadows, by accidents of the air, by shifting effects of perspective; putting down his dim luminary he could still wander on without it, pass into other rooms and, only knowing it was there behind him in case of need, see his way about, visually project for his purpose a comparative clearness. It made him feel, this acquired faculty, like some monstrous stealthy cat; he wondered if he would have glared at these moments with large shining yellow eyes, and what it mightn't verily be, for the poor hard-pressed *alter ego*, to be confronted with such a type.

He liked however the open shutters; he opened everywhere those Mrs Muldoon had closed, closing them as carefully afterwards, so that she shouldn't notice: he liked – on this he did like, and above all in the upper rooms! – the sense of the hard silver of the autumn stars through the window-panes, and scarcely less the flare of the street-lamps below, the white electric lustre which it would have taken curtains to keep out. This was human, actual, social; this was of the world he had lived in, and he was more at his ease certainly for the countenance, coldly general and impersonal, that all the while and in spite of his detachment it seemed to give him. He had support, of course, mostly in the rooms at the wide front and the prolonged side; it failed him considerably in the central shades and the parts at the back. But if he sometimes, on his rounds, was glad of his optical reach, so none the less often the rear of the house affected him as the very jungle of his prey. The place was there more subdivided; a large 'extension' in particular, where small rooms for servants had been multiplied, abounded in nooks and corners, in closets and passages, in the ramifications especially of an ample back staircase over which he leaned, many a time, to look far down – not deterred from his gravity even while aware that he might, for a spectator, have figured some solemn simpleton playing at hide-and-seek. Outside, in fact, he might himself make that ironic *rapprochement*; but within the walls, and in spite of the clear windows, his consistency was proof against the cynical light of New York.

It had belonged to that idea of the exasperated consciousness of his victim to become a real test for him; since he had quite put it to himself from the first that, oh distinctly! he could 'cultivate' his whole perception. He had felt it as above all open to cultivation – which indeed was but another name for his manner of spending his time. He was bringing it on, bringing it to perfection, by practice; in consequence of which it had grown so fine that he was now aware of impressions, attestations of his general postulate, that couldn't have broken upon him at once. This was the case more specifically with a phenomenon at last quite frequent for him in the upper rooms, the recognition – absolutely unmistakable, and by a turn dating from a particular hour, his resumption of his campaign after a diplomatic drop, a calculated absence of three nights – of his being definitely followed, tracked at a distance carefully taken and to the express end that he should the less confidently, less arrogantly, appear to himself merely to pursue. It worried, it finally quite broke him up, for it proved, of all the conceivable impressions, the one least suited to his book. He was kept in sight while remaining himself – as regards the essence of his position – sightless, and his only recourse then was in abrupt turns, rapid recoveries of ground. He wheeled about, retracing his steps, as if he might so catch in his face at least the stirred air of some other quick revolution. It was indeed true that his fully dislocalized thought of these manoeuvres recalled to him Pantaloon, at the Christmas farce, buffeted and tricked from behind by ubiquitous Harlequin; but it left intact the influence of the conditions themselves each time he was re-exposed to them, so that in fact this association, had he suffered it to become constant, would on a certain side have but ministered to his intenser gravity. He had made, as I have said, to create on the premises the baseless sense of a reprieve, his three absences; and the result of the third was to confirm the after-effect of the second.

On his return, that night – the night succeeding his last intermission – he stood in the hall and looked up the staircase with a certainty more intimate than any he had yet known. 'He's *there*, at the top, and waiting – not, as in general, falling back for disappearance. He's holding his ground, and it's the first time – which is a proof, isn't it? that something has happened for him.' So Brydon argued with his hand on the banister and his foot on the lowest stair; in which position he felt as never before the air chilled by his logic. He himself turned cold in it, for he seemed of a sudden to know what now was involved. 'Harder pressed? – yes, he takes it in, with its thus making clear to him that I've come, as they say, "to stay". He finally doesn't like and can't bear it, in the sense, I mean, that his wrath, his menaced interest, now balances with his dread. I've hunted him till he has "turned": that, up there, is what has happened – he's the fanged or the antlered animal brought at last to bay.' There came to him, as I say – but determined by an influence beyond my notation! – the acuteness of this certainty; under which, however, the next moment, he had broken into a sweat that he would as little have consented to attribute to fear as he would have dared immediately to act upon it for enterprise. It marked none the less a prodigious thrill, a thrill that represented sudden dismay, no doubt, but also represented, and with the selfsame throb, the strangest, the most joyous, possibly the next minute almost the proudest, duplication of consciousness.

'He has been dodging, retreating, hiding, but now, worked up to anger, he'll fight!' – this intense impression made a single mouthful, as it were, of terror and applause. But what was wondrous was that the applause, for the felt fact, was so eager, since, if it was his other self he was running to earth, this ineffable identity was thus in the last resort not unworthy of him. It bristled there – somewhere near at hand, however unseen still – as the hunted thing, even as the trodden worm of the adage *must* at last bristle; and Brydon at this instant tasted probably of a sensation more complex than had ever before found itself consistent with sanity. It was as if it would have shamed him that a character so associated with his own should triumphantly succeed in just skulking, should to the end not risk the open; so that the drop of this danger was, on the spot, a great lift of the whole situation. Yet with another rare shift of the same subtlety he was already trying to measure by how much more he himself might now be in peril of fear; so rejoicing that he could, in another form, actively inspire that fear, and simultaneously quaking for the form in which he might passively know it.

The apprehension of knowing it must after a little have grown in him, and the strangest moment of his adventure perhaps, the most memorable or really most interesting, afterwards, of his crisis, was the lapse of certain instants of concentrated conscious *combat*, the sense of a need to hold on to something, even after the manner of a man slipping and slipping on some awful incline; the vivid impulse, above all, to move, to act, to charge, somehow and upon something – to show himself, in a word, that he wasn't afraid. The state of 'holding on' was thus the state to which he was momentarily reduced; if there had been anything, in the great vacancy, to seize, he would presently have been aware of having clutched it as he might under a shock at home have clutched the nearest chair-back. He had been surprised at any rate – of this he *was* aware – into something unprecedented since his original appropriation of the place; he had closed his eyes, held them tight, for a long minute, as with that instinct of dismay and that terror of vision. When he opened them the room, the other contiguous rooms, extraordinarily, seemed lighter – so light, almost, that at first he took the change for day. He stood firm, however that might be, just where he had paused; his resistance had helped him – it was as if there were something he had tided over. He knew after a little what this was – it had been in the imminent danger of flight. He had stiffened his will against going; without this he would have made for the stairs, and it seemed to him that, still with his eyes closed, he would have descended them, would have known how, straight and swiftly, to the bottom.

Well, as he had held out, here he was – still at the top, among the more intricate upper rooms and with the gauntlet of the others, of all the rest of the house, still to run when it should be his time to go. He would go at his time – only at his time: didn't he go every night very much at the same hour? He took out his watch – there was light for that: it was scarcely a quarter past one, and he had never withdrawn so soon. He reached his lodgings for the most part at two – with his walk of a quarter of an hour. He would wait for the last quarter – he wouldn't stir till then; and he kept his watch there with his eyes on it, reflecting while he held it that this deliberate wait, a wait with an effort, which he recognized, would serve perfectly for the attestation he desired to make. It would prove his courage – unless indeed the latter might most be proved by his budging at last from his place. What he mainly felt now was that, since he hadn't originally scuttled, he had his dignities – which had never in his life seemed so many – all to preserve and to carry aloft. This was before him in truth as a physical image, an image almost worthy of an age of greater romance. That remark indeed glimmered for him only to glow the next instant with a finer light; since what age of romance, after all, could have matched either the state of his mind or, 'objectively', as they said, the wonder of his situation? The only difference would have been that, brandishing his dignities over his head as in a parchment scroll, he might then – that is in the heroic time – have proceeded downstairs with a drawn sword in his other grasp.

At present, really, the light he had set down on the mantel of the next room would have to figure his sword; which utensil, in the course of a minute, he had taken the requisite number of steps to possess himself of. The door between the rooms was open, and from the second another door opened to a third. These rooms, as he remembered, gave all three upon a common corridor as well, but there was a fourth, beyond them, without issue save through the preceding. To have moved, to have heard his step again, was appreciably a help; though even in recognizing this he lingered once more a little by the chimney-piece on which his light had rested. When he next moved, just hesitating where to turn, he found himself considering a circumstance that, after his first and comparatively vague apprehension of it, produced in him the start that often attends some pang of recollection, the violent shock of having ceased happily to forget. He had come into sight of the door in which the brief chain of communication ended and which he now surveyed from the nearer threshold, the one not directly facing it. Placed at some distance to the left of this point, it would have admitted him to the last room of the four, the room without other approach or egress, had it not, to his intimate conviction, been closed *since* his former visitation, the matter probably of a quarter of an hour before. He stared with all his eyes at the wonder of the fact, arrested again where he stood and again holding his breath while he sounded its sense. Surely it had been *subsequently* closed — that is, it had been on his previous passage indubitably open!

He took it full in the face that something had happened between — that he couldn't not have noticed before (by which he meant on his original tour of all the rooms that evening) that such a barrier had exceptionally presented itself. He had indeed since that moment undergone an agitation so extraordinary that it might have muddled for him any earlier view; and he tried to convince himself that he might perhaps then have gone into the room and, inadvertently, automatically, on coming out, have drawn the door after him. The difficulty was that this exactly was what he never did; it was against his whole policy, as he might have said, the essence of which was to keep vistas clear. He had them from the first, as he was well aware, quite on the brain: the strange apparition, at the far end of one of them, of his baffled 'prey' (which had become by so sharp an irony so little the term now to apply!) was the form of success his imagination had most cherished, projecting into it always a refinement of beauty. He had known fifty times the start of perception that had afterwards dropped; had fifty times gasped to himself 'There!' under some fond brief hallucination. The house, as the case stood, admirably lent itself; he might wonder at the taste, the native architecture of the particular time, which could rejoice so in the multiplication of doors – the opposite extreme to the modern, the actual almost complete proscription of them; but it had fairly contributed to provoke this obsession of the presence encountered telescopically, as he might say, focused and studied in diminishing perspective and as by a rest for the elbow.

It was with these considerations that his present attention was charged – they perfectly availed to make what he saw portentous. He *couldn't*, by any lapse, have blocked that aperture; and if he hadn't, if it was unthinkable, why what else was clear but that there had been another agent? Another agent? – he had been catching, as he felt, a moment back, the very breath of him; but when had he been so close as in this simple, this logical, this completely personal act? It was so logical, that is, that one might have *taken* it for personal; yet for what did Brydon take it, he asked himself, while, softly panting, he felt his eyes almost leave their sockets. Ah this time at last they *were*, the two, the opposed projections of him, in presence; and this time, as much as one would, the question of danger loomed. With it rose, as not before, the question of courage – for what he knew the blank face of the door to say to him was 'Show us how much you have!' It stared, it glared back at him with that challenge; it put to him the two alternatives: should he just push it open or not? Oh to have this consciousness was to *think* – and to think, Brydon knew, as he stood there, was, with the lapsing moments, not to have acted! Not to have acted – that was the misery and the pang – was even still not to act; was in fact *all* to feel the thing in another, in a new and terrible way. How long did he pause and how long did he debate? There was presently nothing to measure it; for his vibration had already changed – as just by the effect of its intensity. Shut up there, at bay, defiant, and with the prodigy of the thing palpably provably *done*, thus giving notice like some stark signboard – under that accession of accent the situation itself had turned; and Brydon at last remarkably made up his mind on what it had turned to.

It had turned altogether to a different admonition; to a supreme hint, for him, of the value of Discretion! This slowly dawned, no doubt – for it could take its time; so perfectly, on his threshold, had he been stayed, so little as yet had he either advanced or retreated. It was the strangest of all things that now when, by his taking ten steps and applying his hand to a latch, or even his shoulder and his knee, if necessary, to a panel, all the hunger of his prime need might have been met, his high curiosity crowned, his unrest assuaged – it was amazing, but it was also exquisite and rare, that insistence should have, at a touch, quite dropped from him. Discretion – he jumped at that; and yet not, verily, at such a pitch, because it saved his nerves or his skin, but because, much more valuably, it saved the situation. When I say he 'jumped' at it I feel the consonance of this term with the fact that – at the end indeed of I know not how long – he did move again, he crossed straight to the door. He wouldn't touch it – it seemed now that he might *if* he would: he would only just wait there a little, to show, to prove, that he wouldn't. He had thus another station, close to the thin partition by which revelation was denied him; but with his eyes bent and his hands held off in a mere intensity of stillness. He listened as if there had been something to hear, but this attitude, while it lasted, was his own communication. 'If you won't then – good: I spare you and I give up. You affect me as by the appeal positively for pity: you convince me that for reasons rigid and sublime – what do I know? – we both of us should have suffered. I respect them then, and, though moved and privileged as, I believe, it has never been given to man, I retire, I renounce – never, on my honour, to try again. So rest for ever – and let *me*!'

That, for Brydon, was the deep sense of this last demonstration – solemn, measured, directed, as he felt it to be. He brought it to a close, he turned away; and now verily he knew how deeply he had been stirred. He retraced his steps, taking up his candle, burnt, he observed, well-nigh to the socket, and marking again, lighten it as he would, the distinctness of his footfall; after which, in a moment, he knew himself at the other side of the house. He did here what he had not yet done at these hours – he opened half a casement, one of those in the front, and let in the air of the night; a thing he would have taken at any time previous for a sharp rupture of his spell. His spell was broken now, and it didn't matter – broken by his concession and his surrender, which made it idle henceforth that he should ever come back. The empty street – its other life so marked even by the great lamp-lit vacancy – was within call, within touch; he stayed there as to be in it again, high above it though he was still perched; he watched as for some comforting common fact, some vulgar human note, the passage of a scavenger or a thief, some night-bird however base. He would have blessed that sign of life; he would have welcomed positively the slow approach of his friend the policeman, whom he had hitherto only sought to avoid, and was not sure that if the patrol had come into sight he mightn't have felt the impulse to get into relation with it, to hail it, on some pretext, from his fourth floor.

The pretext that wouldn't have been too silly or too compromising, the explanation that would have saved his dignity and kept his name, in such a case, out of the papers, was not definite to him: he was so occupied with the thought of recording his Discretion – as an effect of the vow he had just uttered to his intimate adversary – that the importance of this loomed large and something had overtaken all ironically his sense of proportion. If there had been a ladder applied to the front of the house, even one of the vertiginous perpendiculars employed by painters and roofers and sometimes left standing overnight, he would have managed somehow, astride of the window-sill, to compass by outstretched leg and arm that mode of descent. If there had been some such uncanny thing as he had found in his room at hotels, a workable fire-escape in the form of notched cable or a canvas chute, he would have availed himself of it as a proof – well, of his present delicacy. He nursed that sentiment, as the question stood, a little in vain, and even – at the end of he scarce knew, once more, how long – found it, as by the action on his mind of the failure of response of the outer world, sinking back to vague anguish. It seemed to him he had waited an age for some stir of the great grim hush; the life of the town was itself under a spell – so unnaturally, up and down the whole prospect of known and rather ugly objects, the blankness and the silence lasted. Had they ever, he asked himself, the hard-faced houses, which had begun to look livid in the dim dawn, had they ever spoken so little to any need of his spirit? Great built voids, great crowded stillnesses put on, often, in the heart of cities, for the small hours, a sort of sinister mask, and it was of this large collective negation that Brydon presently became conscious – all the more that the break of day was, almost incredibly, now at hand, proving to him what a night he had made of it.

He looked again at his watch, saw what had become of his

time-values (he had taken hours for minutes – not, as in other tense situations, minutes for hours) and the strange air of the streets was but the weak, the sullen flush of a dawn in which everything was still locked up. His choked appeal from his own open window had been the sole note of life, and he could but break off at last as for a worse despair. Yet while so deeply demoralized he was capable again of an impulse denoting – at least by his present measure – extraordinary resolution; of retracing his steps to the spot where he had turned cold with the extinction of his last pulse of doubt as to there being in the place another presence than his own. This required an effort strong enough to sicken him; but he had his reason, which overmastered for the moment everything else. There was the whole of the rest of the house to traverse, and how should he screw himself to that if the door he had seen closed were at present open? He could hold to the idea that the closing had practically been for him an act of mercy, a chance offered him to descend, depart, get off the ground and never again profane it. This conception held together, it worked; but what it meant for him depended now clearly on the amount of forbearance his recent action, or rather his recent inaction, had engendered. The image of the 'presence', whatever it was, waiting there for him to go – this image had not yet been so concrete for his nerves as when he stopped short of the point at which certainty would have come to him. For, with all his resolution, or more exactly with all his dread, he did stop short – he hung back from really seeing. The risk was too great and his fear too definite: it took at this moment an awful specific form.

He knew – yes, as he had never known anything – that, *should* he see the door open, it would all too abjectly be the end of him. It would mean that the agent of his shame – for his shame was the deep abjection – was once more at large and in general possession; and what glared him thus in the face was the act that this would determine for him. It would send him straight about to the window he had left open, and by that window, be long ladder and dangling rope as absent as they would, he saw himself uncontrollably, insanely, fatally take his way to the street. The hideous chance of this he at least could avert; but he could only avert it by recoiling in time from assurance. He had the whole house to deal with, this fact was still there; only he now knew that uncertainty alone could start him. He stole back from where he had checked himself – merely to do so was suddenly like safety – and, making blindly for the greater staircase, left gaping rooms and sounding passages behind. Here was the top of the stairs, with a fine large dim descent and three spacious landings to mark off. His instinct was all for mildness, but his feet were harsh on the floors, and, strangely, when he had in a couple of minutes become aware of this, it counted somehow for help. He couldn't have spoken, the tone of his voice would have scared him, and the common conceit or resource of 'whistling in the dark' (whether literally or figuratively) have appeared basely vulgar; yet he liked none the less to hear himself go, and when he had reached his first landing – taking it all with no rush, but quite steadily – that stage of success drew from him a gasp of relief.

The house, withal, seemed immense, the scale of space again inordinate; the open rooms, to no one of which his eyes deflected, gloomed in their shuttered state like mouths of caverns; only the high skylight that formed the crown of the deep well created for him a medium in which he could advance, but which might have been, for queerness of colour, some watery under-world. He tried to think of something noble, as that his property was really grand, a splendid possession; but this nobleness took the form too of the clear delight with which he was finally to sacrifice it. They might come in now, the builders, the destroyers – they might come as soon as they would. At the end of two flights he had dropped to another zone, and from the middle of the third, with only one more left, he recognized the influence of the lower windows, of half-drawn blinds, of the occasional gleam of street-lamps, of the glazed spaces of the vestibule. This was the bottom of the sea, which showed an illumination of its own and which he even saw paved – when at a given moment he drew up to sink a long look over the banisters – with the marble squares of his childhood. By that time indubitably he felt, as he might have said in a commoner cause, better; it had allowed him to stop and draw breath, and the ease increased with the sight of the old black-and-white slabs. But what he most felt was that now surely, with the element of impunity pulling him as by hard firm hands, the case was settled for what he might have seen above had he dared that last look. The closed door, blessedly remote now, was still closed – and he had only in short to reach that of the house.

He came down further, he crossed the passage forming the access to the last flight; and if here again he stopped an instant it was almost for the sharpness of the thrill of assured escape. It made him shut his eyes — which opened again to the straight slope of the remainder of the stairs. Here was impunity still, but impunity almost excessive; inasmuch as the side-lights and the high fan-tracery of the entrance were glimmering straight into the hall; an appearance produced, he the next instant saw, by the fact that the vestibule gaped wide, that the hinged halves of the inner door had been thrown far back. Out of that again the *question* sprang at him, making his eyes, as he felt, half-start from his head, as they had done, at the top of the house, before the sign of the other door. If he had left that one open, hadn't he left this one closed, and wasn't he now in *most* immediate presence of some inconceivable occult activity? It was as sharp, the question, as a knife in his side, but the answer hung fire still and seemed to lose itself in the vague darkness to which the thin admitted dawn, glimmering archwise over the whole outer door, made a semicircular margin, a cold silvery nimbus that seemed to play a little as he looked — to shift and expand and contract.

It was as if there had been something within it, protected by indistinctness and corresponding in extent with the opaque surface behind, the painted panels of the last barrier to his escape, of which the key was in his pocket. The indistinctness mocked him even while he stared, affected him as somehow shrouding or challenging certitude, so that after faltering an instant on his step he let himself go with the sense that here *was* at last something to meet, to touch, to take, to know – something all unnatural and dreadful, but to advance upon which was the condition for him either of liberation or of supreme defeat. The penumbra, dense and dark, was the virtual screen of a figure which stood in it as still as some image erect in a niche or as some black-vizored sentinel guarding a treasure. Brydon was to know afterwards, was to recall and make out, the particular thing he had believed during the rest of his descent. He saw, in its great grey glimmering margin, the central vagueness diminish, and he felt it to be taking the very form toward which, for so many days, the passion of his curiosity had yearned. It gloomed, it loomed, it was something, it was somebody, the prodigy of a personal presence.

Rigid and conscious, spectral yet human, a man of his own substance and stature waited there to measure himself with his power to dismay. This only could it be – this only till he recognized, with his advance, that what made the face dim was the pair of raised hands that covered it and in which, so far from being offered in defiance, it was buried as for dark deprecation. So Brydon, before him, took him in; with every fact of him now, in the higher light, hard and acute – his planted stillness, his vivid truth, his grizzled bent head and white masking hands, his queer actuality of evening-dress, of dangling double eye-glass, of gleaming silk lappet and white linen, of pearl button and gold watch-guard and polished shoe. No portrait by a great modern master could have presented him with more intensity, thrust him out of his frame with more art, as if there had been 'treatment', of the consummate sort, in his every shade and salience. The revulsion, for our friend, had become, before he knew it, immense – this drop, in the act of apprehension, to the sense of his adversary's inscrutable manoeuvre. That meaning at least, while he gaped, it offered him; for he could but gape at his other self in this other anguish, gape as a proof that *he*, standing there for the achieved, the enjoyed, the triumphant life, couldn't be faced in his triumph. Wasn't the proof in the splendid covering hands, strong and completely spread? – so spread and so intentional that, in spite of a special verity that surpassed every other, the fact that one of these hands had lost two fingers, which were reduced to stumps, as if accidentally shot away, the face was effectually guarded and saved.

'Saved', though, *would* it be? – Brydon breathed his wonder till the very impunity of his attitude and the very insistence of his eyes produced, as he felt, a sudden stir which showed the next instant as a deeper portent, while the head raised itself, the betrayal of a braver purpose. The hands, as he looked, began to move, to open; then, as if deciding in a flash, dropped from the face and left it uncovered and presented. Horror, with the sight, had leaped into Brydon's throat, gasping there in a sound he couldn't utter; for the bared identity was too hideous as *his*, and his glare was the passion of his protest. The face, *that* face, Spencer Brydon's? – he searched it still, but looking away from it in dismay and denial, falling straight from his height of sublimity. It was unknown, inconceivable, awful, disconnected from any possibility—! He had been 'sold', he inwardly moaned, stalking such game as this: the presence before him was a presence, the horror within him a horror, but the waste of his nights had been only grotesque and the success of his adventure an irony. Such an identity fitted his at *no* point, made its alternative monstrous. A thousand times yes, as it came upon him nearer now – the face was the face of a stranger. It came upon him nearer now, quite as one of those expanding fantastic images projected by the magic lantern of childhood; for the stranger, whoever he might be, evil, odious, blatant, vulgar, had advanced as for aggression, and he knew himself give ground. Then harder pressed still, sick with the force of his shock, and falling back as under the hot breath and the roused passion of a life larger than his own, a rage of personality before which his own collapsed, he felt the whole vision turn to darkness and his very feet give way. His head went round; he was going; he had gone.

## III

WHAT HAD NEXT brought him back, clearly – though after how long? – was Mrs Muldoon's voice, coming to him from quite near, from so near that he seemed presently to see her as kneeling on the ground before him while he lay looking up at her; himself not wholly on the ground, but half-raised and upheld

# The Jolly Corner

– conscious, yes, of tenderness of support and, more particularly, of a head pillowed in extraordinary softness and faintly refreshing fragrance. He considered, he wondered, his wit but half at his service; then another face intervened, bending more directly over him, and he finally knew that Alice Staverton had made her lap an ample and perfect cushion to him, and that she had to this end seated herself on the lowest degree of the staircase, the rest of his long person remaining stretched on his old black-and-white slabs. They were cold, these marble squares of his youth; but *he* somehow was not, in this rich return of consciousness – the most wonderful hour, little by little, that he had ever known, leaving him, as it did, so gratefully, so abysmally passive, and yet as with a treasure of intelligence waiting all round him for quiet appropriation; dissolved, he might call it, in the air of the place and producing the golden glow of a late autumn afternoon. He had come back, yes – come back from further away than any man but himself had ever travelled; but it was strange how with this sense what he had come back *to* seemed really the great thing, and as if his prodigious journey had been all for the sake of it. Slowly but surely his consciousness grew, his vision of his state thus completing itself: he had been miraculously *carried* back – lifted and carefully borne as from where he had been picked up, the uttermost end of an interminable grey passage. Even with this he was suffered to rest, and what had now brought him to knowledge was the break in the long mild motion.

It had brought him to knowledge, to knowledge – yes, this

was the beauty of his state; which came to resemble more and more that of a man who has gone to sleep on some news of a great inheritance, and then, after dreaming it away, after profaning it with matters strange to it, has waked up again to serenity of certitude and has only to lie and watch it grow. This was the drift of his patience – that he had only to let it shine on him. He must moreover, with intermissions, still have been lifted and borne; since why and how else should he have known himself, later on, with the afternoon glow intenser, no longer at the foot of his stairs – situated as these now seemed at that dark other end of his tunnel – but on a deep window-bench of his high saloon, over which had been spread, couch-fashion, a mantle of soft stuff lined with grey fur that was familiar to his eyes and that one of his hands kept fondly feeling as for its pledge of truth. Mrs Muldoon's face had gone, but the other, the second he had recognized, hung over him in a way that showed how he was still propped and pillowed. He took it all in, and the more he took it the more it seemed to suffice: he was as much at peace as if he had had food and drink. It was the two women who had found him, on Mrs Muldoon's having plied, at her usual hour, her latch-key – and on her having above all arrived while Miss Staverton still lingered near the house. She had been turning away, all anxiety, from worrying the vain bell-handle – her calculation having been of the hour of the good woman's visit; but the latter, blessedly, had come up while she was still there, and they had entered together. He had then lain, beyond the vestibule, very much as he was lying now – quite, that is, as he appeared to have fallen, but all so wondrously without bruise or gash; only in a depth of stupor. What he most took in, however, at present, with the steadier clearance, was that Alice Staverton had for a long unspeakable moment not doubted he was dead.

'It must have been that I *was*.' He made it out as she held him. 'Yes – I can only have died. You brought me literally to life. Only,' he wondered, his eyes rising to her, 'only, in the name of all the benedictions, how?'

It took her but an instant to bend her face and kiss him, and something in the manner of it, and in the way her hands clasped and locked his head while he felt the cool charity and virtue of her lips, something in all this beatitude somehow answered everything. 'And now I keep you,' she said.

'Oh keep me, keep me!' he pleaded while her face still hung over him: in response to which it dropped again and stayed close, clingingly close. It was the seal of their situation – of which he tasted the impress for a long blissful moment in silence. But he came back. 'Yet how did you know——?'

'I was uneasy. You were to have come, you remember – and you had sent no word.'

'Yes, I remember – I was to have gone to you at one today.' It caught on to their 'old' life and relation – which were so near and so far. 'I was still out there in my strange darkness – where was it, what was it? I must have stayed there so long.' He could but wonder at the depth and the duration of his swoon.

'Since last night?' she asked with a shade of fear for her possible indiscretion.

'Since this morning – it must have been: the cold dim dawn of today. Where have I been,' he vaguely wailed, 'where have I been?' He felt her hold him close, and it was as if this helped him now to make in all security his mild moan. 'What a long dark day!'

All in her tenderness she had waited a moment. 'In the cold dim dawn?' she quavered.

But he had already gone on piecing together the parts of the whole prodigy. 'As I didn't turn up you came straight—?'

She barely cast about. 'I went first to your hotel – where they told me of your absence. You had dined out last evening and hadn't been back since. But they appeared to know you had been at your club.'

'So you had the idea of *this*—?'

'Of what?' she asked in a moment.

'Well – of what has happened.'

'I believed at least you'd have been here. I've known, all along,' she said, 'that you've been coming.'

'"Known" it—?'

'Well, I've believed it. I said nothing to you after that talk we had a month ago – but I felt sure. I knew you *would*,' she declared.

'That I'd persist, you mean?'

'That you'd see him.'

'Ah but I didn't!' cried Brydon with his long wail. 'There's somebody – an awful beast; whom I brought, too horribly, to bay. But it's not me.'

At this she bent over him again, and her eyes were in his eyes. 'No – it's not you.' And it was as if, while her face hovered, he might have made out in it, hadn't it been so near, some particular meaning blurred by a smile. 'No, thank heaven,' she repeated – 'it's not you! Of course it wasn't to have been.'

'Ah but it *was*,' he gently insisted. And he stared before him now as he had been staring for so many weeks. 'I was to have known myself.'

'You couldn't!' she returned consolingly. And then reverting, and as if to account further for what she had herself done, 'But it wasn't only *that*, that you hadn't been at home,' she went on. 'I waited till the hour at which we had found Mrs Muldoon that day of my going with you; and she arrived, as I've told you, while, failing to bring anyone to the door, I lingered in my despair on the steps. After a little, if she hadn't come, by such a mercy, I should have found means to hunt her up. But it wasn't,' said Alice Staverton, as if once more with her fine intention – 'it wasn't only that.'

His eyes, as he lay, turned back to her. 'What more then?'

She met it, the wonder she had stirred. 'In the cold dim dawn, you say? Well, in the cold dim dawn of this morning I too saw you.'

'Saw *me*—?'

'Saw *him*,' said Alice Staverton. 'It must have been at the same moment.'

He lay an instant taking it in – as if he wished to be quite reasonable. 'At the same moment?'

'Yes – in my dream again, the same one I've named to you. He came back to me. Then I knew it for a sign. He had come to you.'

At this Brydon raised himself; he had to see her better. She helped him when she understood his movement, and he sat up, steadying himself beside her there on the window-bench and with his right hand grasping her left. '*He* didn't come to me.'

'You came to yourself,' she beautifully smiled.

'Ah I've come to myself now – thanks to you, dearest. But this brute, with his awful face – this brute's a black stranger. He's none of *me*, even as I *might* have been,' Brydon sturdily declared.

But she kept the clearness that was like the breath of infallibility. 'Isn't the whole point that you'd have been different?'

He almost scowled for it. 'As different as *that*—?'

Her look again was more beautiful to him than the things of this world. 'Haven't you exactly wanted to know *how* different? So this morning,' she said, 'you appeared to me.'

'Like *him*?'

'A black stranger!'

'Then how did you know it was I?'

'Because, as I told you weeks ago, my mind, my imagination, had worked so over what you might, what you mightn't have been – to show you, you see, how I've thought of you. In the midst of that you came to me – that my wonder might be answered. So I knew,' she went on; 'and believed that, since the question held you too so fast, as you told me that day, you too would see for yourself. And when this morning I again saw I knew it would be because you had – and also then, from the first moment, because you somehow wanted me. *He* seemed to tell me of that. So why,' she strangely smiled, 'shouldn't I like him?'

It brought Spencer Brydon to his feet. 'You "like" that horror—?'

'I *could* have liked him. And to me,' she said, 'he was no horror. I had accepted him.'

'"Accepted"—?' Brydon oddly sounded.

'Before, for the interest of his difference – yes. And as *I* didn't disown him, as *I* knew him – which you at last, confronted with him in his difference, so cruelly didn't, my dear – well, he must have been, you see, less dreadful to me. And it may have pleased him that I pitied him.'

She was beside him on her feet, but still holding his hand – still with her arm supporting him. But though it all brought for him thus a dim light, 'You "pitied" him?' he grudgingly, resentfully asked.

'He has been unhappy, he has been ravaged,' she said.

'And haven't I been unhappy? Am not I – you've only to look at me! – ravaged?'

'Ah I don't say I like him *better*,' she granted after a thought. 'But he's grim, he's worn – and things have happened to him. He doesn't make shift, for sight, with your charming monocle.'

'No' – it struck Brydon: 'I couldn't have sported mine "downtown". They'd have guyed me there.'

'His great convex pince-nez – I saw it, I recognized the kind – is for his poor ruined sight. And his poor right hand—!'

'Ah!' Brydon winced – whether for his proved identity or for his lost fingers. Then, 'He has a million a year,' he lucidly added. 'But he hasn't you.'

'And he isn't – no, he isn't – *you*!' she murmured as he drew her to his breast.

# *A Round of Visits*

## I

He had been out but once since his arrival, Mark Monteith; that was the next day after – he had disembarked by night on the previous; then everything had come at once, as he would have said, everything had changed. He had got in on Tuesday; he had spent Wednesday for the most part downtown, looking into the dismal subject of his anxiety – the anxiety that, under a sudden decision, had brought him across the unfriendly sea at mid-winter, and it was through information reaching him on Wednesday evening that he had measured his loss, measured, above all, his pain. These were two distinct things, he felt, and, though both bad, one much worse than the other. It wasn't till the next three days had pretty well ebbed, in fact, that he knew himself for so badly wounded. He had waked up on Thursday morning, so far as he had slept at all, with the sense, together, of a blinding New York blizzard and of a deep sore inward ache.

The great white savage storm would have kept him at the best within doors, but his stricken state was by itself quite reason enough.

He so felt the blow indeed, so gasped, before what had happened to him, at the ugliness, the bitterness, and, beyond these things, the sinister strangeness, that, the matter of his dismay little by little detaching and projecting itself, settling there face to face with him as something he must now live with always, he might have been in charge of some horrid alien thing, some violent, scared, unhappy creature whom there was small joy, of a truth, in remaining with, but whose behaviour wouldn't perhaps bring him under notice, nor otherwise compromise him, so long as he should stay to watch it. A young jibbering ape of one of the more formidable sorts, or an ominous infant panther smuggled into the great gaudy hotel and whom it might yet be important he shouldn't advertise, couldn't have affected him as needing more domestic attention. The great gaudy hotel – The Pocahontas, but carried out largely on 'Du Barry' lines – made all about him, beside, behind, below, above, in blocks and tiers and superpositions, a sufficient defensive hugeness; so that, between the massive labyrinth and the New York weather, life in a lighthouse during a gale would scarce have kept him more apart. Even when, in the course of that worse Thursday, it had occurred to him for vague relief that the odious certified facts couldn't be all his misery, and that, with his throat and a probable temperature, a brush of the epidemic, which was forever brushing him, accounted for something, even then he couldn't resign himself to bed and broth and dimness, but only circled and prowled the more within his high cage, only watched the more from his tenth storey the rage of the elements.

In the afternoon he had a doctor – the caravanserai, which supplied everything in quantities, had one for each group of so many rooms – just in order to be assured that he was *grippé* enough for anything. What his visitor, making light of his attack, perversely told him was that he was, much rather, 'blue' enough, and from causes doubtless known to himself – which didn't come to the same thing; but he 'gave him something', prescribed him warmth and quiet and broth and courage, and came back the next day to readminister this last dose. He then pronounced him better, and on Saturday pronounced him well – all the more that the storm had abated and the snow had been dealt with as New York, at a push, knew how to deal with things. Oh, how New York knew how to deal – to deal, that is, with, other accumulations lying passive to its hand – was exactly what Mark now ached with his impression of; so that, still threshing about in this consciousness, he had on the Saturday come near to breaking out as to what was the matter with him. The doctor brought in somehow the air of the hotel – which, cheerfully and conscientiously, by his simple philosophy, the good man wished to diffuse; breathing forth all the echoes of other woes and worries and pointing the honest moral that, especially with such a thermometer, there were enough of these to go round. Our sufferer, by that time, would have liked to tell someone; extracting, to the last acid strain of it, the full strength of his sorrow, taking it all in as he could only do by himself, and with the conditions favourable at least to this, had been his natural first need. But now, he supposed, he *must* be better; there was something of his heart's heaviness he wanted so to give out.

He had rummaged forth on the Thursday night half a dozen old photographs stuck into a leather frame, a small show-case that formed part of his usual equipage of travel – he mostly set it up on a table when he stayed anywhere long enough; and in one of the neat gilt-edged squares of this convenient portable array, as familiar as his shaving-glass or the hair-brushes, of backs and monograms now so beautifully toned and wasted, long ago given him by his mother, Phil Bloodgood handsomely faced him. Not contemporaneous, and a little faded, but so saying what it said only the more dreadfully, the image seemed to sit there, at an immemorial window, like some long effective and only at last exposed 'decoy' of fate. It was *because* he was so beautifully good-looking, because he was so charming and clever and frank – besides being one's third cousin, or whatever it was, one's early school-fellow and one's later college class-mate – that one had abjectly trusted him. To live thus with his unremoved, undestroyed, engaging, treacherous face, had been, as our traveller desired, to live with all of the felt pang; had been to consume it in such a single hot, sore mouthful as would so far as possible dispose of it and leave but cold dregs. Thus, if the doctor, casting about for pleasantness, had happened to notice him there, salient since he was, and possibly by the same stroke even to know him, as New York – and more or less to its cost now, mightn't one say? – so abundantly and agreeably had, the cup would have overflowed and Monteith, for all he could be sure of the contrary, would have relieved himself positively in tears.

'Oh, *he's* what's the matter with me – that, looking after some of my poor dividends, as he for the ten years of my absence had served me by doing, he has simply jockeyed me out of the whole little collection, such as it was, and taken the opportunity of my return, inevitably at last bewildered and uneasy, to "sail", ten days ago, for parts unknown and as yet unguessable. It isn't the beastly values themselves, however; that's only awkward and I can still live, though I don't quite know how I shall turn round; it's the horror of *his* having done it, and done it to *me* – without a mitigation or, so to speak, a warning or an excuse.' That, at a hint or a jog, is what he would have brought out – only to feel afterward, no doubt, that he had wasted his impulse and profaned even a little his sincerity. The doctor didn't in the event so much as glance at his cluster of portraits – which fact quite put before our friend the essentially more vivid range of imagery that a pair of eyes transferred from room to room and from one queer case to another, in such a place as that, would mainly be adjusted to. It wasn't for *him* to relieve himself touchingly, strikingly or whatever, to such a man: such a man might much more pertinently – save for professional discretion – have emptied out there his own bag of wonders; prodigies of observation, flowers of oddity, flowers of misery, flowers of the monstrous, gathered in current hotel practice. Countless possibilities, making doctors perfunctory, Mark felt, swarmed and seethed at their doors; it showed for an incalculable world, and at last, on Sunday, he decided to leave his room.

## II

EVERYTHING as he passed through the place went on – all the offices of life, the whole bustle of the market, and withal surprisingly scarce less that of the nursery and the playground, the whole sprawl in especial of the great gregarious fireside; it was a complete social scene in itself, on which types might figure and passions rage and plots thicken and dramas develop, without reference to any other sphere, or perhaps even to anything at all outside. The signs of this met him at every turn as he threaded the labyrinth, passing from one extraordinary masquerade of expensive objects, one portentous 'period' of decoration, one violent phase of publicity, to another: the heavy heat, the luxuriance, the extravagance, the quantity, the colour, gave the impression of some wondrous tropical forest, where vociferous, bright-eyed, and feathered creatures, of every variety of size and hue, were half smothered between undergrowths of velvet and tapestry and ramifications of marble and bronze. The fauna and the flora startled him alike, and among them his bruised spirit drew in and folded its wings. But he roamed and rested, exploring and in a manner enjoying the vast rankness

— in the depth of which he suddenly encountered Mrs Folliott, whom he had last seen, six months before, in London, and who had spoken to him then, precisely, of Phil Bloodgood, for several years previous her confidential American agent and factotum too, as she might say, but at that time so little in her good books, for the extraordinary things he seemed to be doing, that she was just hurrying home, she had made no scruple of mentioning, to take everything out of his hands.

Mark remembered how uneasy she had made him — how that very talk with her had wound him up to fear, as so acute and intent a little person she affected him; though he had affirmed with all emphasis and flourish his own confidence and defended, to iteration, his old friend. This passage had remained with him for a certain pleasant heat of intimacy, his partner, of the charming appearance, being what she was; he liked to think how they had fraternized over their difference and called each other idiots, or almost, without offence. It was always a link to have scuffled, failing a real scratch, with such a character; and he had at present the flutter of feeling that something of this would abide. *He* hadn't been hurrying home, at the London time, in any case; he was doing nothing then, and had continued to do it; he would want, before showing suspicion — that had been his attitude — to have more, after all, to go upon. Mrs Folliott also, and with a great actual profession of it, remembered and rejoiced; and, also staying in the house as she was, sat with him, under a spreading palm, in a wondrous rococo *salon*, surrounded by the pinkest, that is the fleshiest imitation Boucher panels, and wanted to know if he *now* stood up for his swindler. She would herself have tumbled on a cloud, very passably, in a fleshy Boucher manner, hadn't she been over-dressed for such an exercise; but she was quite realistically aware of what had so naturally happened – she was prompt about Bloodgood's 'flight'.

She had acted with energy, on getting back – she had saved what she could; which hadn't, however, prevented her losing all disgustedly some ten thousand dollars. She was lovely, lively, friendly, interested, she connected Monteith perfectly with their discussion that day during the water-party on the Thames; but, sitting here with him half an hour, she talked only of her peculiar, her cruel sacrifice – since she should never get a penny back. He had felt himself, on their meeting, quite yearningly reach out to her – so decidedly, by the morning's end, and that of his scattered sombre stations, had he been sated with meaningless contacts, with the sense of people all about him intensely, though harmlessly animated, yet at the same time raspingly indifferent. *They* would have, he and she at least, their common pang – through which fact, somehow, he should feel less stranded. It wasn't that he wished to be pitied – he fairly didn't pity himself; he winced, rather, and even to vicarious anguish, as it rose again, for poor shamed Bloodgood's doom-ridden figure. But he wanted, as with a desperate charity, to give some easier turn to the mere ugliness of the main facts; to work off his obsession from them by mixing with it some other blame, some other pity, it scarce mattered what – if it might be some other experience; as an effect of which larger ventilation it would have, after a fashion and for a man of free sensibility, a diluted and less poisonous taste.

By the end of five minutes of Mrs Folliott, however, he felt his dry lips seal themselves to a makeshift simper. She could *take* nothing – no better, no broader perception of anything than fitted her own small faculty; so that though she must have recalled or imagined that he had still, up to lately, had interests at stake, the rapid result of her egotistical little chatter was to make him wish he might rather have conversed with the French waiter dangling in the long vista that showed the oriental *café* as a climax, or with the policeman, outside, the top of whose helmet peeped above the ledge of a window. She bewailed her wretched money to excess – she who, he was sure, had quantities more; she pawed and tossed her bare bone, with her little extraordinarily gemmed and manicured hands, till it acted on his nerves; she rang all the changes on the story, the dire fatality, of her having wavered and muddled, thought of this and but done that, of her stupid failure to have pounced, when she had first meant to, in season. She abused the author of their wrongs – recognizing thus too Monteith's right to loathe him – for the desperado he assuredly had proved, but with a vulgarity of analysis and an incapacity for the higher criticism, as her listener felt it to be, which made him determine resentfully, almost grimly, that she shouldn't have the benefit of a grain of *his* vision or *his* version of what had befallen them, and of how, in particular, it had come; and should never dream thereby (though much would she suffer from that!) of how interesting he might have been. She had, in a finer sense, no manners, and to be concerned with her in any retrospect was – since their discourse was of losses – to feel the dignity of history incur the very gravest. It was true that such fantasies, or that any shade of inward irony, would be Greek to Mrs Folliott.

It was also true, however, and not much more strange, when she had presently the comparatively happy thought of 'Lunch with *us*, you poor dear!' and mentioned three or four of her 'crowd' – a new crowd, rather, for her, all great Sunday lunchers there and immense fun, who would in a moment be turning up – that this seemed to him as easy as anything else; so that after a little, deeper in the jungle and while, under the temperature as of high noon, with the crowd complete and 'ordering', he wiped the perspiration from his brow, he felt he was letting himself go. He did that certainly to the extent of leaving far behind any question of Mrs Folliott's manners. They didn't matter there – nobody's did; and if she ceased to lament her ten thousand it was only because, among higher voices, she couldn't make herself heard. Poor Bloodgood didn't have a show, as they might have said, didn't get through at any point; the crowd was so new that – there either having been no hue and cry for him, or having been too many others, for other absconders, in the interval – they had never so much as heard of him and would have no more of Mrs Folliott's true inwardness, on that subject at least, than she had lately cared to have of Monteith's.

There was nothing like a crowd, this unfortunate knew, for making one feel lonely, and he felt so increasingly during the meal; but he got thus at least in a measure away from the terrible little lady; after which, and before the end of the hour, he wanted still more to get away from everyone else. He was in fact about to perform this manoeuvre when he was checked by the jolly young woman he had been having on his left and who had more to say about the hotels, up and down the town, than he had ever known a young woman to have to say on any subject at all; she expressed herself in hotel terms exclusively, the names of those establishments playing through her speech as the *leit-motif* might have recurrently flashed and romped through a piece of profane modern music. She wanted to present him to the pretty girl she had brought with her, and who had apparently signified to her that she must do so.

'I think you know my brother-in-law, Mr Newton Winch,' the pretty girl had immediately said; she moved her head and shoulders together, as by a common spring, the effect of a stiff neck or of something loosened in her back hair; but becoming, queerly enough, all the prettier for doing so. He had seen in the papers, her brother-in-law, Mr Monteith's arrival – Mr Mark P. Monteith, wasn't it? – and where he was, and she had been with him, three days before, at the time; whereupon he had said, 'Hullo, what can have brought old Mark back?' He seemed to have believed – Newton had seemed – that that shirker, as he called him, never *would* come; and she guessed that if she had known she was going to meet such a former friend ('Which he claims you are, sir,' said the pretty girl) he would have asked her to find out what the trouble could be. But the real satisfaction would just be, she went on, if his former friend would himself go and see him and tell him; he had appeared of late so down.

'Oh, I remember him' – Mark didn't repudiate the friendship, placing him easily; only then he wasn't married and the pretty girl's sister must have come in later; which showed, his not knowing such things, how they had lost touch. The pretty girl was sorry to have to say in return to this that her sister wasn't living – had died two years after marrying; so that Newton was up there in Fiftieth Street alone; where (in explanation of his being 'down') he had been shut up for days with bad *grippe*; though now on the mend, or she wouldn't have gone to him, not she, who had had it nineteen times and didn't want to have it again. But the horrid poison just seemed to have entered into poor Newton's soul.

'That's the way it *can* take you, don't you know?' And then as, with her single twist, she just charmingly hunched her eyes at our friend, 'Don't you want to go to see him?'

Mark bethought himself: 'Well, I'm going to see a lady—'

She took the words from his mouth. 'Of course you're going to see a lady – every man in New York is. But Newton isn't a lady, unfortunately for him, today; and Sunday afternoon in this place, in this weather, alone—!'

'Yes, isn't it awful?' – he was quite drawn to her.

'Oh, *you've* got your lady!'

'Yes, I've got my lady, thank goodness!' The fervour of which was his sincere tribute to the note he had had on Friday morning from Mrs Ash, the only thing that had a little tempered his gloom.

'Well then, feel for others. Fit him in. Tell him why!'

'Why I've come back? I'm glad I *have* — since it was to see *you*!' Monteith made brave enough answer, promising to do what he could. He liked the pretty girl, with her straight attack and her free awkwardness — also with her difference from the others through something of a sense and a distinction given her by so clearly having Newton on her mind. Yet it was odd to him, and it showed the lapse of the years, that Winch — as he had known him of old — could *be* to that degree on anyone's mind.

## III

OUTSIDE IN THE intensity of the cold — it was a jump from the Tropics to the Pole — he felt afresh the force of what he had just been saying; that if it weren't for the fact of Mrs Ash's good letter of welcome, despatched, characteristically, as soon as she had, like the faithful sufferer in Fiftieth Street, observed his name, in a newspaper, on one of the hotel-lists, he should verily, for want of a connection and an abutment, have scarce dared to face the void and the chill together, but have sneaked back into the jungle and there tried to lose himself. He made, as it was, the opposite effort, resolute to walk, though hovering now and then at vague crossways, radiations of roads to nothing, or taking cold counsel of the long but still sketchy vista, as it struck him, of the northward Avenue, bright and bleak, fresh and harsh, rich and evident somehow, a perspective like a page of florid modern platitudes. He didn't quite know what he had expected for his return – not certainly serenades and deputations; but without Mrs Ash his wail would have quite lacked geniality, and it was as if Phil Bloodgood had gone off not only with so large a slice of his small *peculium*, but with all the broken bits of the past, the loose ends of old relationships, that he had supposed he might pick up again. Well, perhaps he should still pick up a few – by the sweat of his brow; no motion of their own at least, he by this time judged, would send them fluttering into his hand.

Which reflections but quickened his forecast of this charm of the old Paris inveteracy renewed – the so prized custom of nine years before, when he still believed in results from his fond frequentation of the Beaux Arts; that of walking over the river to the Rue de Marignan, precisely, every Sunday without exception, and sitting at her fireside, and often all offensively, no doubt, outstaying everyone. How he had used to want those hours then, and how again, after a little, at present, the Rue de Marignan might have been before him! He had gone to her there at that time with his troubles, such as they were, and they had always worked for her amusement – which had been her happy, her clever way of taking them: she couldn't have done anything better for them in that phase, poor innocent things compared with what they might have been, than be amused by them. Perhaps that was what she would still be – with those of his present hour; now too they might inspire her with the touch she best applied and was most instinctive mistress of: this didn't at all events strike him as what he should most resent. It wasn't as if Mrs Folliott, to make up for boring him with her own plaint, for example, had had so much as a gleam of conscious diversion over his.

'I'm *so* delighted to see you, I've such immensities to tell you!' – it began with the highest animation twenty minutes later, the very moment he stood there, the sense of the Rue de Marignan in the charming room and in the things about all reconstituted, regrouped, wonderfully preserved, down to the very sitting-places in the same relations, and down to the faint sweet mustiness of generations of cigarettes; but everything else different, and even vaguely alien, and by a measure still other than that of their own stretched interval and of the dear delightful woman's just a little pathetic alteration of face. He had allowed for the nine years, and so, it was to be hoped, had she; but the last thing, otherwise, that would have been touched, he immediately felt, was the quality, the intensity, of her care to see him. She cared, oh, so visibly and touchingly and almost radiantly – save for her being, yes, distinctly, a little *more* battered than from even a good nine years' worth; nothing could in fact have perched with so crowning an impatience on the heap of what she had to 'tell' as that special shade of revived consciousness of having him in particular to tell it to. It wasn't perhaps much to matter how soon she brought out and caused to ring, as it were, on the little recognized marqueterie table between them (such an anciently envied treasure), the heaviest gold-piece of current history she was to pay him with for having just so felicitously come back: he knew already, without the telling, that intimate domestic tension must lately, within those walls, have reached a climax and that he could serve supremely – oh, how he was going to serve! – as the most sympathetic of all pairs of ears.

The whole thing was upon him, in any case, with the minimum of delay: Bob had had it from her, definitely, the first of the week, and it was absolutely final now, that they must set up avowedly separate lives – without horrible 'proceedings' of any sort, but with her own situation, her independence, secured to her once for all. She had been coming to it, taking her time, and she had gone through – well, so old a friend would guess enough what; but she was at the point, oh, blessedly now, where she meant to stay, he'd see if she didn't; with which, in this wonderful way, he himself had arrived for the cream of it and she was just selfishly glad. Bob had gone to Washington – ostensibly on business, but really to recover breath; she had, speaking vulgarly, knocked the wind out of him and was allowing him time to turn round. Mrs Folliott, moreover, she was sure, would have gone – was certainly believed to have been seen there five days ago; and of course his first necessity, for public use, would be to patch up something with Mrs Folliott. Mark knew about Mrs Folliott? – who was only, for that matter, one of a regular 'bevy'. Not that it signified, however, if he didn't: she would tell him about *her* later.

He took occasion from the first fraction of a break not quite to know what he knew about Mrs Folliott – though perhaps he could imagine a little; and it was probably at this minute that, having definitely settled to a position, and precisely in his very own tapestry *bergère*, the one with the delicious little spectral 'subjects' on the back and seat, he partly exhaled, and yet managed partly to keep to himself, the deep resigned sigh of a general comprehension. He knew what he was 'in' for, he heard her go on – she said it again and again, seemed constantly to be saying it while she smiled at him with her peculiar fine charm, her positive gaiety of sensibility, scarce dimmed: 'I'm just selfishly glad, just selfishly glad!' Well, she was going to have reason to be; she was going to put the whole case to him, all her troubles and plans, and each act of the tragi-comedy of her recent existence, as to the dearest and safest sympathizer in all the world. There would be no chance for *his* case, though it was so much for his case he had come; yet there took place within him but a mild, dumb convulsion, the momentary strain of his substituting, by the turn of a hand, one prospect of interest for another.

Squaring himself in his old *bergère*, and with his lips, during the effort, compressed to the same passive grimace that had an hour or two before operated for the encouragement of Mrs Folliott – just as it was to clear the stage completely for the present more prolonged performance – he shut straight down, as he even in the act called it to himself, on any personal claim for social consideration and rendered a perfect little agony of justice to the grounds of his friend's vividness. For it was all the justice that could be expected of him that, though, secretly, he wasn't going to be interested in her being interesting, she was yet going to be so, all the same, by the very force of her lovely material (Bob Ash *was* such a pure pearl of a donkey!) and he was going to keep on knowing she was – yes, to the very end. When after the lapse of an hour he rose to go, the rich fact that she *had* been was there between them, and with an effect of the frankly, fearlessly, harmlessly intimate fireside passage for it that went beyond even the best memories of the pleasant past. He hadn't 'amused' her, no, in quite the same way as in the Rue de Marignan time – it had then been he who for the most part took frequent turns, emphatic, explosive, elocutionary, over that wonderful waxed parquet while she laughed as for the young perversity of him from the depths of the second, the matching *bergère*. Today she herself held and swept the floor, putting him merely to the trouble of his perpetual 'Brava!' But that was all through the change of basis – the amusement, another name only for the thrilled absorption, having been inevitably for *him*: as how could it have failed to be with such a regular 'treat' to his curiosity? With the tea-hour now other callers were turning up, and he got away on the plea of his wanting so to think it all over. He hoped again he hadn't too queer a grin with his assurance to her, as if she would quite know what he meant, that he had been thrilled to the core. But she returned, quite radiantly, that he had carried *her* completely away; and her sincerity was proved by the final frankness of their temporary parting. 'My pleasure of you is selfish, horribly, I admit; so that if *that* doesn't suit you—!' Her faded beauty flushed again as she said it.

## IV

IN THE STREET again, as he resumed his walk, he saw how perfectly it would *have* to suit him and how he probably for a long time wouldn't be suited otherwise. Between them and that time, however, what mightn't for him, poor devil, on his new basis, have happened? She wasn't at any rate within any calculable period going to care so much for anything as for the so quaintly droll terms in which her rearrangement with her husband – thanks to that gentleman's inimitable fatuity – would have to be made. This was what it was to own, exactly, her special grace – the brightest gaiety in the finest sensibility; *such* a display of which combination, Mark felt as he went (if he could but have done it still more justice) she must have regaled him with! That exquisite last flush of her fadedness could only remain with him; yet while he presently stopped at a street-corner in a district redeemed from desolation but by a passage just then of a choked trolley-car that howled, as he paused for it, beneath the weight of its human accretions, he seemed to know the inward 'sinking' that has been determined in a hungry man by some extravagant sight of the preparation of somebody else's dinner. Florence Ash was dining, so to speak, off the feast of appreciation, appreciation of what she had to 'tell' him, that he had left her seated at; and she was welcome, assuredly – welcome, welcome, welcome, he musingly, he wistfully, and yet at the same time a trifle mechanically, repeated, stayed as he was a moment longer by the suffering shriek of another public vehicle and a sudden odd automatic return of his mind to the pretty girl, the flower of Mrs Folliott's crowd, who had spoken to him of Newton Winch. It was extraordinarily as if, on the instant, she reminded him, from across the town, that *she* had offered him dinner: it was really quite strangely, while he stood there, as if she had told him where he could go and get it. With which, none the less, it was apparently where he wouldn't find her – and what was there, after all, of nutritive in the image of Newton Winch? He made up his mind in a moment that it owed that property, which the pretty girl had somehow made imputable, to the fact of its simply being just then the one image of anything known to him that the terrible place had to offer. Nothing, he a minute later reflected, could have been so 'rum' as that, sick and sore, of a bleak New York eventide, he should have had nowhere to turn if not to the said Fiftieth Street.

That was the direction he accordingly took, for when he found the number given him by the same remarkable agent of fate also present to his memory he recognized the direct intervention of Providence and how it absolutely required a miracle to explain his so precipitately taking up this loosest of connections. The miracle indeed soon grew clearer: Providence had, on some obscure system, chosen this very ridiculous hour to save him from cultivation of the sin of selfishness, the obsession of egotism, and was breaking him to its will by constantly directing his attention to the claims of others. Who could say what at that critical moment mightn't have become of Mrs Folliott (otherwise too then so sadly embroiled!) if she hadn't been enabled to air to him her grievance and her rage? – just as who could deny that it must have done Florence Ash a world of good to have put her thoughts about Bob in order by the aid of a person to whom the vision of Bob in the light of those thoughts (or in other words to whom *her* vision of Bob and nothing else) would mean so delightfully much? It was on the same general lines that poor Newton Winch, bereft, alone, ill, perhaps dying, and with the drawback of a not very sympathetic personality – as Mark remembered it at least – to contend against in almost any conceivable appeal to human furtherance, it was on these lines, very much, that the luckless case in Fiftieth Street was offered him as a source of salutary discipline. The moment for such a lesson might strike him as strange, in view of the quite special and independent opportunity for exercise that his spirit had during the last three days enjoyed there in his hotel bedroom; but evidently his languor of charity needed some admonition finer than any it might trust to chance for, and by the time he at last, Winch's residence recognized, was duly elevated to his level and had pressed the electric button at his door, he felt himself acting indeed as under stimulus of a sharp poke in the side.

## V

WITHIN the apartment to which he had been admitted, moreover, the fine intelligence we have imputed to him was in the course of three minutes confirmed; since it took him no longer than that to say to himself, facing his old acquaintance, that he had never seen anyone so improved. The place, which had the semblance of a high studio light as well as a general air of other profusions and amplitudes, might have put him off a little by its several rather glaringly false accents, those of contemporary domestic 'art' striking a little wild. The scene was smaller, but the rich confused complexion of The Pocahontas, showing through Du Barry paint and patches, might have set the example – which had been followed with the costliest candour – so that, clearly, Winch was in these days rich, as most people in New York seemed rich; as, in spite of Bob's depredations, Florence Ash was, as even Mrs Folliott was in spite of Phil Bloodgood's, as even Phil Bloodgood himself must have been for reasons too obvious; as in fine everyone had a secret for being, or for feeling, or for looking, everyone at least but Mark Monteith.

These facts were as nothing, however, in presence of his quick and strong impression that his pale, nervous, smiling, clean-shaven host had undergone since their last meeting some extraordinary process of refinement. He had been ill, unmistakably, and the effects of a plunge into plain clean living, where any fineness had remained, were often startling, sometimes almost charming. But independently of this, and for a much longer time, some principle of intelligence, some art of life, would discernibly have worked in him. Remembered from college years and from those two or three luckless and faithless ones of the Law School as constitutionally common, as consistently and thereby doubtless even rather powerfully coarse, clever only for uncouth and questionable things, he yet presented himself now as if he had suddenly and mysteriously been educated. There was a charm in his wide, 'drawn', convalescent smile, in the way his fine fingers – had he anything like fine fingers of old? – played, and just fidgeted, over the prompt and perhaps a trifle incoherent offer of cigars, cordials, ash-trays, over the question of his visitor's hat, stick, fur coat, general best accommodation and ease; and how the deuce, accordingly, had charm, for coming out so on top, Mark wondered, 'squared' the other old elements? For the short interval so to have dealt with him what force had it turned on, what patented process, of the portentous New York order in which there were so many, had it skilfully applied? Were these the things New York did when you just gave her *all* her head, and that he himself then had perhaps too complacently missed? Strange almost to the point of putting him positively off at first – quite as an exhibition of the uncanny – this sense of Newton's having all the while neither missed nor muffed anything, and having, as with an eye to the *coup de théâtre* to come, lowered one's expectations, at the start, to that abject pitch. It might have affected one verily as an act of bad faith – really as such a rare stroke of subtlety as could scarce have been achieved by a straight or natural aim.

So much as this at least came and went in Monteith's agitated mind; the oddest intensity of apprehension, admiration, mystification, which the high north-light of the March afternoon and the quite splendidly vulgar appeal of fifty overdone decorative effects somehow fostered and sharpened. Everything had already gone, however, the next moment, for wasn't the man he had come so quite over-intelligently himself to patronize absolutely bowling him over with the extraordinary speech: 'See here, you know – you must be ill, or have had a bad shock, or some beastly upset: are you very sure you ought to have come out?' Yes, he after an instant believed his ears; coarse common Newton Winch, whom he had called on because he could, as a gentleman, after all afford to, coarse common Newton Winch, who had had troubles and been epidemically poisoned, lamentably sick, who bore in his face and in the very tension, quite exactly the 'charm', of his manner, the traces of his late ordeal, and, for that matter, of scarce completed gallant emergence – this astonishing ex-comrade was simply writing himself at a stroke (into our friend's excited imagination at all events) the most distinguished of men. Oh, *he* was going to be interesting, if Florence Ash had been going to be; but Mark felt how, under the law of a lively present difference, that would be an effect of one's having one's self thoroughly rallied. He knew within the minute that the tears stood in his eyes; he stared through them at his friend with a sharp 'Why, how do you know? How *can* accordingly that amount of connection; only it became further remarkable that from the moment his companion had sounded him, and sounded him, he knew, down to the last truth of things, his disposition, his necessity to talk, the desire that had in the morning broken the spell of his confinement, the impulse that had thrown him so defeatedly into Mrs Folliott's arms and into Florence Ash's, these forces seemed to feel their impatience ebb and their discretion suddenly grow. His companion was talking again, but just then, incongruously, made his need to communicate lose itself. It was as if his personal case had already been touched by some tender hand — and that, after all, was the modest limit of its greed. 'I know now why you came back — did Lottie mention how I had wondered? But sit down, sit down — only let me, nervous beast as I am, take it standing! — and believe me when I tell you that I've now ceased to wonder. My dear chap, I *have* it! It can't but have been for poor Phil Bloodgood. He sticks out of you, the brute — as how, with what he has done to you, shouldn't he? There was a man to see me yesterday — Tim Slater, whom I don't think you know, but who's "on" everything within about two minutes of its happening (I never saw such a fellow!) and who confirmed my supposition, all my own, however, mind you at first, that you're one of the sufferers. So how the devil can you *not* feel knocked? Why *should* you look as if you were having the time of your life? What a hog to have played it on *you*, on *you*, of all his friends!' So Newton Winch continued, and so the air between the two men might have been, for a momentary watcher — which is indeed what I

you?' To which he added before Winch could speak: 'I met your charming sister-in-law a couple of hours since — at luncheon, at The Pocahontas; and heard from her that you were badly laid up and had spoken of me. So I came to minister to you.'

The object of this design hovered there again, considerably restless, shifting from foot to foot, changing his place, beginning and giving up motions, striking matches for a fresh cigarette, offering them again, redundantly, to his guest and then not lighting himself — but all the while with the smile of another creature than the creature known to Mark; all the while with the history of something that had happened to him ever so handsomely shining out. Mark was conscious within himself from this time on of two quite distinct processes of notation — that of his practically instant surrender to the consequences of the act of perception in his host of which the two women trained supposably in the art of pleasing had been altogether incapable; and that of some other condition on Newton's part that left his own poor power of divination nothing less than shamed. This last was signally the case on the former's saying, ever so responsively, almost radiantly, in answer to his account of how he happened to come: 'Oh, then it's very interesting!' *That* was the astonishing note, after what he had been through: neither Mrs Folliott nor Florence Ash had so much as hinted or breathed to him that *he* might have incurred that praise. No wonder therefore he was now taken — with this fresh party's instant suspicion and imputation of it; though it was indeed for some minutes next as if each tried to see which could accuse the other of the greater miracle of penetration. Mark was so struck, in a word, with the extraordinarily straight guess Winch had had there in reserve for him that, other quick impressions helping, there was nothing for him but to bring out, himself: 'There must be, my dear man, something rather wonderful the matter with you!' The quite more intensely and more irresistibly drawn grin, the quite unmistakably deeper consciousness in the dark, wide eye, that accompanied the not quite immediate answer to which remark he was afterward to remember.

'How do you know that – or why do you think it?'

'Because there *must* be – for you to see! I shouldn't have expected it.'

'Then you take me for a damned fool?' laughed wonderful Newton Winch.

## VI

HE COULD SAY nothing that, whether as to the sense of it or as to the way of it, didn't so enrich Mark's vision of him that our friend, after a little, as this effect proceeded, caught himself in the act of almost too curiously gaping. Everything, from moment to moment, fed his curiosity; such a question, for instance, as whether the quite ordinary peepers of the Newton Winch of their earlier youth could have looked under any provocation, either dark or wide; such a question, above all, as how

*this* incalculable apparition came by the whole startling power of play of its extravagantly sensitive labial connections – exposed, so to its advantage (he now jumped at one explanation) by the removal of what had probably been one of the vulgarest of moustaches. With this, at the same time, the oddity of that particular consequence was vivid to him; the glare of his curiosity fairly lasting while he remembered how he had once noted the very opposite turn of the experiment for Phil Bloodgood. He would have said in advance that poor Winch couldn't have afforded to risk showing his 'real' mouth; just as he would have said that in spite of the fine ornament that so considerably muffled it Phil could only have gained by showing his. But to have seen Phil shorn – as he once had done – was earnestly to pray that he might promptly again bristle; beneath Phil's moustache lurked nothing to 'make up' for it in case of removal. While he thought of which things the line of grimace, as he could only have called it, the mobile, interesting, ironic line the great double curve of which connected, in the face before him, the strong nostril with the lower cheek, became the very key to his first idea of Newton's capture of refinement. He had shaved and was happily transfigured. Phil Bloodgood had shaved and been well-nigh lost; though why should one just now too precipitately drag the reminiscence in?

That question too, at the queer touch of association, played up for Mark even under so much proof that the state of his own soul was being with the lapse of every instant registered. Phil Bloodgood had brought about the state of his soul – there was can but invite the reader to become – that of a nervously displayed, but all-considerate, as well as most acute, curiosity on the one side, and that on the other, after a little, of an eventually fascinated acceptance of so much free and in especial of so much right attention. 'Do you *mind* my asking you? Because if you do I won't press; but as a man whose own responsibilities, some of 'em at least, don't differ much, I gather, from some of his, one would like to know how he was ever allowed to get to the point—! But I *do* plough you up?'

Mark sat back in his chair, moved but holding himself, his elbows squared on each arm, his hands a bit convulsively interlocked across him – very much in fact as he had appeared an hour ago in the old tapestry *bergère*; but as his rigour was all then that of the grinding effort to profess and to give, so it was considerably now for the fear of too hysterically gushing. Somehow too – since his wound was to that extent open – he winced at hearing the author of it branded. He hadn't so much minded the epithets Mrs Folliott had applied, for they were to the appropriator of *her* securities. As the appropriator of his own he didn't so much want to brand him as – just more 'amusingly' even, if one would! – to make out, perhaps, with intelligent help, how such a man, in such a relation, *could* come to tread such a path: which was exactly the interesting light that Winch's curiosity and sympathy were there to assist him to. He pleaded at any rate immediately his advertising no grievance. 'I feel sore, I admit, and it's a horrid sort of thing to have had happen; but when you call him a brute and a hog I rather squirm, for brutes and hogs never live, I guess, in the sort of hell in which he now must be.'

Newton Winch, before the fireplace, his hands deep in his pockets, where his guest could see his long fingers beat a tattoo on his thighs, Newton Winch dangled and swung himself, and threw back his head and laughed. 'Well, I must say you take it amazingly! – all the more that to see you again this way is to feel that if, all along, there was a man whose delicacy and confidence and general attitude might have marked him for a particular consideration, you'd have been the man.' And they were more directly face to face again; with Newton smiling and smiling *so* appreciatively; making our friend in fact almost ask himself when before a man had ever grinned from ear to ear to the effect of its so becoming him. What he replied, however, was that Newton described in those flattering terms a client temptingly fatuous; after which, and the exchange of another protest or two in the interest of justice and decency, and another plea or two in that of the still finer contention that even the basest misdeeds had always somewhere or other, could one get at it, their propitiatory side, our hero found himself on his feet again, under the influence of a sudden failure of everything but horror – a horror determined by some turn of their talk and indeed by the very fact of the freedom of it. It was as if a far-borne sound of the hue and cry, a vision of his old friend hunted and at bay, had suddenly broken in – this other friend's, this irresistibly intelligent other companion's, practically vivid projection of that making the worst ugliness real. 'Oh, it's just making my wry face to somebody, and your letting me and caring and wanting to know: that,' Mark said, 'is what does me good; not any other hideous question. I mean I don't take any interest in *my* case — what one wonders about, you see, is what can be done for him. I mean, that is—' for he floundered a little, not knowing at last quite what he did mean, a great rush of mere memories, a great humming sound as of thick, thick echoes, rising now to an assault that he met with his face indeed contorted. If he didn't take care he should howl; so he more or less successfully took care — yet with his host vividly watching him while he shook the danger temporarily off. 'I don't mind — though it's rather *that*; my having felt this morning, after three dismal dumb bad days, that one's friends perhaps would be thinking of one. All I'm conscious of now — I give you my word — is that I'd like to see him.'

'You'd like to see him?'

'Oh, I don't say,' Mark ruefully smiled, 'that I should like him to see *me*—!'

Newton Winch, from where he stood — and they were together now, on the great hearth-rug that was a triumph of modern orientalism — put out one of the noted fine hands and, with an expressive head-shake, laid it on his shoulder. 'Don't wish him that, Monteith — don't wish him that!'

'Well, but —' and Mark raised his eyebrows still higher — 'he'd see I bear up pretty well!'

'God forbid he should see, my dear fellow!' Newton cried as for the pang of it.

Mark had for his idea, at any rate, the oddest sense of an exaltation that grew by this use of frankness. 'I'd go to him. Hanged if I wouldn't – anywhere!'

His companion's hand still rested on him. 'You'd go to him?'

Mark stood up to it – though trying to sink solemnity as pretentious. 'I'd go like a shot.' And then he added: 'And it's probably what – when we've turned round – I *shall* do.'

'When "we" have turned round?'

'Well –' he was a trifle disconcerted at the tone – 'I say that because you'll have helped me.'

'Oh, I do nothing but want to help you!' Winch replied – which made it right again; especially as our friend still felt himself reassuringly and sustainingly grasped. But Winch went on: 'You *would* go to him – in kindness?'

'Well – to understand.'

'To understand how he could swindle you?'

'Well,' Mark kept on, 'to try and make out with him how, after such things——!' But he stopped; he couldn't name them.

It was as if his companion knew. 'Such things as you've done for him, of course – such services as you've rendered him.'

'Ah, from far back. If I could tell you,' our friend vainly wailed – 'if I could tell you!'

Newton Winch patted his shoulder. 'Tell me – tell me!'

'The sort of relation, I mean; ever so many things of a kind——!' Again, however, he pulled up; he felt the tremor of his voice.

'Tell me, tell me,' Winch repeated with the same movement.

you?' To which he added before Winch could speak: 'I met your charming sister-in-law a couple of hours since – at luncheon, at The Pocahontas; and heard from her that you were badly laid up and had spoken of me. So I came to minister to you.'

The object of this design hovered there again, considerably restless, shifting from foot to foot, changing his place, beginning and giving up motions, striking matches for a fresh cigarette, offering them again, redundantly, to his guest and then not lighting himself – but all the while with the smile of another creature than the creature known to Mark; all the while with the history of something that had happened to him ever so handsomely shining out. Mark was conscious within himself from this time on of two quite distinct processes of notation – that of his practically instant surrender to the consequences of the act of perception in his host of which the two women trained supposably in the art of pleasing had been altogether incapable; and that of some other condition on Newton's part that left his own poor power of divination nothing less than shamed. This last was signally the case on the former's saying, ever so responsively, almost radiantly, in answer to his account of how he happened to come: 'Oh, then it's very interesting!' *That* was the astonishing note, after what he had been through: neither Mrs Folliott nor Florence Ash had so much as hinted or breathed to him that *he* might have incurred that praise. No wonder therefore he was now taken – with this fresh party's instant suspicion and imputation of it; though it was indeed for some minutes next as if each tried to see which could accuse the other of the greater miracle of penetration. Mark was so struck, in a word, with the extraordinarily straight guess Winch had had there in reserve for him that, other quick impressions helping, there was nothing for him but to bring out, himself: 'There must be, my dear man, something rather wonderful the matter with you!' The quite more intensely and more irresistibly drawn grin, the quite unmistakably deeper consciousness in the dark, wide eye, that accompanied the not quite immediate answer to which remark he was afterward to remember.

'How do you know that – or why do you think it?'

'Because there *must* be – for you to see! I shouldn't have expected it.'

'Then you take me for a damned fool?' laughed wonderful Newton Winch.

# VI

HE COULD SAY nothing that, whether as to the sense of it or as to the way of it, didn't so enrich Mark's vision of him that our friend, after a little, as this effect proceeded, caught himself in the act of almost too curiously gaping. Everything, from moment to moment, fed his curiosity; such a question, for instance, as whether the quite ordinary peepers of the Newton Winch of their earlier youth could have looked under any provocation, either dark or wide; such a question, above all, as how squirm, for brutes and hogs never live, I guess, in the sort of hell in which he now must be.'

Newton Winch, before the fireplace, his hands deep in his pockets, where his guest could see his long fingers beat a tattoo on his thighs, Newton Winch dangled and swung himself, and threw back his head and laughed. 'Well, I must say you take it amazingly! – all the more that to see you again this way is to feel that if, all along, there was a man whose delicacy and confidence and general attitude might have marked him for a particular consideration, you'd have been the man.' And they were more directly face to face again; with Newton smiling and smiling *so* appreciatively; making our friend in fact almost ask himself when before a man had ever grinned from ear to ear to the effect of its so becoming him. What he replied, however, was that Newton described in those flattering terms a client temptingly fatuous; after which, and the exchange of another protest or two in the interest of justice and decency, and another plea or two in that of the still finer contention that even the basest misdeeds had always somewhere or other, could one get at it, their propitiatory side, our hero found himself on his feet again, under the influence of a sudden failure of everything but horror – a horror determined by some turn of their talk and indeed by the very fact of the freedom of it. It was as if a far-borne sound of the hue and cry, a vision of his old friend hunted and at bay, had suddenly broken in – this other friend's, this irresistibly intelligent other companion's, practically vivid projection of that making the worst ugliness real. 'Oh, it's just making my wry face to can but invite the reader to become — that of a nervously displayed, but all-considerate, as well as most acute, curiosity on the one side, and that on the other, after a little, of an eventually fascinated acceptance of so much free and in especial of so much right attention. 'Do you *mind* my asking you? Because if you do I won't press; but as a man whose own responsibilities, some of 'em at least, don't differ much, I gather, from some of his, one would like to know how he was ever allowed to get to the point—! But I *do* plough you up?'

Mark sat back in his chair, moved but holding himself, his elbows squared on each arm, his hands a bit convulsively interlocked across him — very much in fact as he had appeared an hour ago in the old tapestry *bergère*; but as his rigour was all then that of the grinding effort to profess and to give, so it was considerably now for the fear of too hysterically gushing. Somehow too — since his wound was to that extent open — he winced at hearing the author of it branded. He hadn't so much minded the epithets Mrs Folliott had applied, for they were to the appropriator of *her* securities. As the appropriator of his own he didn't so much want to brand him as — just more 'amusingly' even, if one would! — to make out, perhaps, with intelligent help, how such a man, in such a relation, *could* come to tread such a path: which was exactly the interesting light that Winch's curiosity and sympathy were there to assist him to. He pleaded at any rate immediately his advertising no grievance. 'I feel sore, I admit, and it's a horrid sort of thing to have had happen; but when you call him a brute and a hog I rather *this* incalculable apparition came by the whole startling power of play of its extravagantly sensitive labial connections – exposed, so to its advantage (he now jumped at one explanation) by the removal of what had probably been one of the vulgarest of moustaches. With this, at the same time, the oddity of that particular consequence was vivid to him; the glare of his curiosity fairly lasting while he remembered how he had once noted the very opposite turn of the experiment for Phil Bloodgood. He would have said in advance that poor Winch couldn't have afforded to risk showing his 'real' mouth; just as he would have said that in spite of the fine ornament that so considerably muffled it Phil could only have gained by showing his. But to have seen Phil shorn – as he once had done – was earnestly to pray that he might promptly again bristle; beneath Phil's moustache lurked nothing to 'make up' for it in case of removal. While he thought of which things the line of grimace, as he could only have called it, the mobile, interesting, ironic line the great double curve of which connected, in the face before him, the strong nostril with the lower cheek, became the very key to his first idea of Newton's capture of refinement. He had shaved and was happily transfigured. Phil Bloodgood had shaved and been well-nigh lost; though why should one just now too precipitately drag the reminiscence in?

That question too, at the queer touch of association, played up for Mark even under so much proof that the state of his own soul was being with the lapse of every instant registered. Phil Bloodgood had brought about the state of his soul – there was accordingly that amount of connection; only it became further remarkable that from the moment his companion had sounded him, and sounded him, he knew, down to the last truth of things, his disposition, his necessity to talk, the desire that had in the morning broken the spell of his confinement, the impulse that had thrown him so defeatedly into Mrs Folliott's arms and into Florence Ash's, these forces seemed to feel their impatience ebb and their discretion suddenly grow. His companion was talking again, but just then, incongruously, made his need to communicate lose itself. It was as if his personal case had already been touched by some tender hand – and that, after all, was the modest limit of its greed. 'I know now why you came back – did Lottie mention how I had wondered? But sit down, sit down – only let me, nervous beast as I am, take it standing! – and believe me when I tell you that I've now ceased to wonder. My dear chap, I *have* it! It can't but have been for poor Phil Bloodgood. He sticks out of you, the brute – as how, with what he has done to you, shouldn't he? There was a man to see me yesterday – Tim Slater, whom I don't think you know, but who's "on" everything within about two minutes of its happening (I never saw such a fellow!) and who confirmed my supposition, all my own, however, mind you at first, that you're one of the sufferers. So how the devil can you *not* feel knocked? Why *should* you look as if you were having the time of your life? What a hog to have played it on *you*, on *you*, of all his friends!' So Newton Winch continued, and so the air between the two men might have been, for a momentary watcher – which is indeed what I

The tone in it now made their eyes meet again, and with this presentation of the altered face Mark measured as not before, for some reason, the extent of the recent ravage. 'You must have been ill indeed.'

'Pretty bad. But I'm better. And you do me good' – with which the light of convalescence came back.

'I don't awfully bore you?'

Winch shook his head. 'You keep me up – and you see how no one else comes near me.'

Mark's eyes made out that he *was* better – though it wasn't yet that nothing was the matter with him. If there was ever a man with whom there was still something the matter—! Yet one couldn't insist on that, and meanwhile he clearly did want company. 'Then there we are. I myself had no one to go to.'

'You save my life,' Newton renewedly grinned.

# VII

'WELL, IT'S YOUR own fault,' Mark replied to that, 'if you make me take advantage of you.' Winch had withdrawn his hand, which was back, violently shaking keys or money, in his trousers pocket; and in this position he had abruptly a pause, a sensible absence, that might have represented either some odd drop of attention, some turn-off to another thought, or just simply the sudden act of listening. His guest had indeed himself – under suggestion – the impression of a sound. 'Mayn't you perhaps – if you hear something – have a call?'

Mark had said it so lightly, however, that he was the more struck with his host's appearing to turn just paler; and, with it the latter now *was* listening. 'You hear something?'

'I thought *you* did.' Winch himself, on Mark's own pressure of the outside bell, had opened the door of the apartment – an indication then, it sufficiently appeared, that Sunday afternoons were servants', or attendants', or even trained nurses' holidays. It had also marked the stage of his convalescence, and to that extent – after his first flush of surprise – had but smoothed Monteith's way. At present he barely gave further attention; detaching himself as under some odd cross-impulse, he had quitted the spot and then taken, in the wide room, a restless turn – only, however, to revert in a moment to his friend's just-uttered deprecation of the danger boring him. 'If I make you take advantage of me – that is blessedly talk to me – it's exactly what I want to do. Talk to me – talk to me!' He positively waved it on; pulling up again, however, in his own talk, to say with a certain urgency: 'Hadn't you better sit down?'

Mark, who stayed before the fire, couldn't but excuse himself. 'Thanks – I'm very well so. I think of things and I fidget.'

Winch stood a moment with his eyes on the ground. 'Are you very sure?'

'Quite – I'm all right if you don't mind.'

'Then as you like!' With which, shaking to extravagance again his long legs, Newton had swung off – only with a movement that, now his back was turned, affected his visitor as the most whimsical of all the forms of his rather unnatural manner. He was curiously different with his back shown, as Mark now for the first time saw it – dangling and somewhat wavering, as from an excess of uncertainty of gait; and this impression was so strange, it created in our friend, uneasily and on the spot, such a need of explanation, that his speech was stayed long enough to give Winch time to turn round again. The latter had indeed by this moment reached one of the limits of the place, the wide studio bay, where he paused, his back to the light and his face afresh presented, to let his just passingly depressed and quickened eyes take in as much as possible of the large floor, range over it with such brief freedom of search as the disposition of the furniture permitted. He was looking for something, though the betrayed reach of vision was but of an instant. Mark caught it, however, and with his own sensibility all in vibration, found himself feeling at once that it meant something and that what it meant was connected with his entertainer's slightly marked appeal to him, the appeal of a moment before, not to remain standing. Winch knew by this time quite easily enough that he was hanging fire; which meant that they were suddenly facing each other across the wide space with a new consciousness.

Everything had changed – changed extraordinarily with the mere turning of that gentleman's back, the treacherous aspect of which its owner couldn't surely have suspected. If the question was of the pitch of their sensibility, at all events, it wouldn't be

Mark's that should vibrate to least purpose. Visibly it had come to his host that something had within the few instants remarkably happened, but there glimmered on him an induction that still made him keep his own manner. Newton himself might now resort to any manner he liked. His eyes had raked the floor to recover the position of something dropped or misplaced, and something, above all, awkward or compromising; and he had wanted his companion not to command this scene from the hearth-rug, the hearth-rug where he had been just before holding him, hypnotizing him to blindness, *because* the object in question would there be most exposed to sight. Mark embraced this with a further drop – while the apprehension penetrated – of his power to go on, and with an immense desire at the same time that his eyes should seem only to look at his friend; who broke out now, for that matter, with a fresh appeal. 'Aren't you going to take advantage of me, man – aren't you going to *take* it?'

Everything had changed, we have noted, and nothing could more have proved it than the fact that, by the same turn, sincerity of desire had dropped out of Winch's chords, while irritation, sharp and almost imperious, had come in. 'That's because he sees I see something!' Mark said to himself; but he had no need to add that it shouldn't prevent his seeing more – for the simple reason that, in a miraculous fashion, this was exactly what he did do in glaring out the harder. It was beyond explanation, but the very act of blinking thus in an attempt at showy steadiness became one and the same thing with an optical excursion lasting the millionth of a minute and making him aware that the edge of a rug, at the point where an arm-chair, pushed a little out of position, over-straddled it, happened just not wholly to have covered in something small and queer, neat and bright, crooked and compact, in spite of the strong toe-tip surreptitiously applied to giving it the right lift. Our gentleman, from where he hovered, and while looking straight at the master of the scene, yet saw, as by the tiny flash of a reflection from fine metal, *under* the chair. What he recognized, or at least guessed at, as sinister, made him for a moment turn cold, and that chill was on him while Winch again addressed him – as differently as possible from any manner yet used. 'I beg of you in God's name to talk to me – to *talk* to me!'

It had the ring of pure alarm and anguish, but was by this turn at least more human than the dazzling glitter of intelligence to which the poor man had up to now been treating him. 'It's you, my good friend, who are in deep trouble,' Mark was accordingly quick to reply, 'and I ask your pardon for being so taken up with my own sorry business.'

'Of course I'm in deep trouble' – with which Winch came nearer again; 'but turning you on was exactly what I wanted.'

Mark Monteith, at this, couldn't, for all his rising dismay, but laugh out; his sense of the ridiculous so swallowed up, for that brief convulsion, his sense of the sinister. Of such convenience in pain, it seemed, was the fact of another's pain, and of so much worth again disinterested sympathy! 'Your interest was then—?'

'My interest was in your being interesting. For you *are*! And my nerves—!' said Newton Winch with a face from which the mystifying smile had vanished, yet in which distinction, as Mark so persistently appreciated it, still sat in the midst of ravage.

Mark wondered and wondered – he made strange things out. 'Your nerves have needed company.' He could lay his hand on him now, even as shortly before he had felt Winch's own pressure of possession and detention. 'As good for you yourself, that – or still better,' he went on – 'than I and my grievance were to have found you. Talk to *me*, talk to *me*, Newton Winch!' he added with an immense inspiration of charity.

'That's a different matter – that others but too much can do! But I'll say this. If you want to go to Phil Bloodgood—!'

'Well?' said Mark as he stopped. He stopped and Mark had now a hand on each of his shoulders and held him at arm's-length, held him with a fine idea that was not disconnected from the sight of the small neat weapon he had been fingering in the low, luxurious morocco chair – it was of the finest orange colour – and then had laid beside him on the carpet; where, after he had admitted his visitor, his presence of mind coming back to it and suggesting that he couldn't pick it up without making it more conspicuous, he had thought, by some swing of the foot or other casual manoeuvre, to dissimulate its visibility.

They were at close quarters now as not before and Winch perfectly passive, with eyes that somehow had no shadow of a secret left and with the betrayal to the sentient hands that grasped him of an intense, an extraordinary general tremor. To

Mark's challenge he opposed afresh a brief silence, but the very quality of it, with his face speaking, was that of a gaping wound. 'Well, you needn't take *that* trouble. You see I'm such another.'

'Such another as Phil——?'

He didn't blink. 'I don't know for sure, but I guess I'm worse.'

'Do you mean you're guilty——?'

'I mean I shall be wanted. Only I've stayed to take it.'

Mark threw back his head, but only tightened his hands. He inexpressibly understood, and nothing in life had ever been so strange and dreadful to him as his thus helping himself by a longer and straighter stretch, as it were, to the monstrous sense of his friend's 'education'. It had been, in its immeasurable action, the education of business, of which the fruits were all around them. Yet prodigious was the interest, for prodigious truly – it seemed to loom before Mark – must have been the system. 'To "take" it?' he echoed; and then, though faltering a little, 'To take what?'

He had scarce spoken when a long sharp sound shrilled in from the outer door, seeming of so high and peremptory a pitch that with the start it gave him his grasp of his host's shoulders relaxed an instant, though to the effect of no movement in *them* but what came from just a sensibly intenser vibration of the whole man. 'For *that*!' said Newton Winch.

'Then you've known——?'

'I've expected. You've helped me to wait.' And then as Mark gave an ironic wail: 'You've tided me over. My condition has *wanted* somebody or something. Therefore, to complete this service, will you be so good as to open the door?'

Deep in the eyes Mark looked him, and still to the detection of no glimmer of the earlier man in the depths. The earlier man had been what he invidiously remembered – yet would *he* had been the whole simpler story! Then he moved his own eyes straight to the chair under which the revolver lay and which was but a couple of yards away. He felt his companion take this consciousness in, and it determined in them another long, mute exchange. 'What do you mean to do?'

'Nothing.'

'On your honour?'

'*My* "honour"?' his host returned with an accent that he felt even as it sounded he should never forget.

It brought to his own face a crimson flush – he dropped his guarding hands. Then as for a last look at him: 'You're wonderful!'

'We *are* wonderful,' said Newton Winch, while, simultaneously with the words, the pressed electric bell again and for a longer time pierced the warm cigaretted air.

Mark turned, threw up his arms, and it was only when he had passed through the vestibule and laid his hand on the door-knob that the horrible noise dropped. The next moment he was face to face with two visitors, a nondescript personage in a high hat and an astrakhan collar and cuffs, and a great belted constable, a splendid massive New York 'officer' of the type he had had occasion to wonder at much again in the course of his walk, the type so by itself – his wide observation quite suggested – among those of the peacemakers of the earth. The pair stepped straight in – no word was said; but as he closed the door behind them Mark heard the infallible crack of a discharged pistol and, so nearly with it as to make all one violence, the sound of a great fall; things the effect of which was to lift him, as it were, with his company, across the threshold of the room in a shorter time than that taken by this record of the fact. But their rush availed little; Newton was stretched on his back before the fire; he had held the weapon horribly to his temple, and his upturned face was disfigured. The emissaries of the law, looking down at him, exhaled simultaneously a gruff imprecation, and then while the worthy in the high hat bent over the subject of their visit the one in the helmet raised a severe pair of eyes to Mark. 'Don't you think, sir, you might have prevented it?'

Mark took a hundred things in, it seemed to him – things of the scene, of the moment, and of all the strange moments before; but one appearance more vividly even than the others stared out at him. 'I really think I must practically have caused it.'

# *A Note on the Texts*

The texts of the tales in this selection are taken from their original magazine publications (or in the case of 'The Beast in the Jungle' and 'The Papers' their publication in James's 1903 collection *The Better Sort*), and not from the amended versions James prepared for the New York edition of his works:

'The Figure in the Carpet' (*Cosmopolis*, January/February 1896); 'The Real Right Thing' (*Collier's Weekly*, December 1899); 'The Great Good Place' (*Scribner's Magazine*, January 1900); 'Maud-Evelyn' (*The Atlantic*, April 1900); 'The Two Faces' (*Harper's Bazaar*, December 1900); 'The Beldonald Holbein' (*Harper's Monthly Magazine*, October 1901); 'The Story in It' (*The Anglo-American Magazine*, January 1902); 'Flickerbridge' (*Scribner's Magazine*, February 1902); 'The Beast in the Jungle' (*The Better Sort*, 1903); 'The Papers' (*The Better Sort*, 1903); 'The Jolly Corner' (*The English Review*, December 1908); 'A Round of Visits' (*The English Review*, April–May 1910).